PRAISE FOR THE #1 *NEW YORK TIMES* BESTSELLING AUTHOR SIDNEY SHELDON

"A master storyteller."
USA Today

....

"When it comes to concocting plots full of twists,
Sheldon has no peers."
Associated Press

....

"The master of the storytelling game."
People

....

"When you want a novel you simply cannot put down,
go to Sheldon."
New York Daily News

....

"The master of the plot twister."
Baltimore Sun

....

By Sidney Sheldon

CHASING TOMORROW
THE TIDES OF MEMORY
ANGELS OF THE DARK
AFTER THE DARKNESS
MISTRESS OF THE GAME
ARE YOU AFRAID OF THE DARK?
THE SKY IS FALLING
TELL ME YOUR DREAMS
THE BEST LAID PLANS
MORNING, NOON, & NIGHT
NOTHING LASTS FOREVER
THE STARS SHINE DOWN
THE DOOMSDAY CONSPIRACY
MEMORIES OF MIDNIGHT
THE SANDS OF TIME
WINDMILLS OF THE GODS
IF TOMORROW COMES
MASTER OF THE GAME
RAGE OF ANGELS
BLOODLINE
A STRANGER IN THE MIRROR
THE OTHER SIDE OF MIDNIGHT
THE NAKED FACE

Coming Soon in Hardcover

RECKLESS

SIDNEY SHELDON'S

Chasing Tomorrow

TILLY BAGSHAWE

𝓦𝓜
WILLIAM MORROW
An Imprint of *HarperCollins*Publishers

This is a work of fiction. Names, characters, places, and incidents are products of the author's imagination or are used fictitiously and are not to be construed as real. Any resemblance to actual events, locales, organizations, or persons, living or dead, is entirely coincidental.

WILLIAM MORROW
An Imprint of HarperCollins*Publishers*
195 Broadway
New York, New York 10007

Copyright © 2014 by Sheldon Family Limited Partnership, successor to the rights and interests of Sidney Sheldon
ISBN 978-0-06-230403-2
www.harpercollins.com

First William Morrow mass market printing: September 2015
First William Morrow paperback printing: October 2014
First William Morrow mass market international printing: October 2014
First William Morrow hardcover printing: October 2014

William Morrow® and HarperCollins ® are registered trademarks of HarperCollins Publishers.

Printed in the United States of America

10 9 8 7 6 5 4 3 2 1

For Katrina,
with love

PART ONE

PROLOGUE

RIO DE JANEIRO, BRAZIL

*H*E TURNED AROUND AND looked back down the empty church, a sinking feeling in the pit of his stomach.

"She's not coming, is she? She's changed her mind."

"Of course she's coming, Jeff. Relax."

Gunther Hartog looked at Jeff Stevens with genuine pity. *How terrible it must be to be so in love.*

Jeff Stevens was the second-most-talented con artist in the world. Sophisticated, urbane, rich and charming, Jeff was wildly attractive to the opposite sex. With his athletic build, thick dark hair and intensely masculine aura, Jeff Stevens could have had any woman he wanted. The problem was, he didn't want *any* woman. He wanted Tracy Whitney. And with Tracy Whitney, one could never *quite* be sure . . .

Tracy Whitney was *the* most talented con artist in the

world. It had taken Jeff Stevens a long time to realize that he couldn't live without her. But he knew it now. The sinking feeling in his stomach got worse. Thank God there were no guests in the church. No one to witness his humiliation, apart from Gunther and the crotchety old priest, Father Alfonso.

Where is she?

"She's fifteen minutes late, Gunther."

"That's a bride's prerogative."

"No. It's more than that. Something's wrong."

"Nothing's wrong."

The old man smiled indulgently. He'd been honored when Jeff asked him to be best man at his and Tracy's wedding. In his late sixties, with no children of his own, Gunther Hartog loved Jeff Stevens and Tracy Whitney like family. Their union meant everything to him, particularly after the blow of their joint decision to go straight. A tragedy, in Gunther Hartog's opinion. Like Beethoven retiring after his fourth symphony.

Still, it was wonderful being back in Brazil. The warm, wet air. The scent of *bolinhos de bacalhau,* the delicious codfish fritters cooked on every street corner. The riot of color that existed everywhere, from the jungle flowers, to the women's stunning dresses, to the frescoes and stained glass windows of the tiny, baroque Chapel of St. Rita, where they now stood. All of it made Gunther Hartog feel young again. Young and alive.

"What if Pierpont got wise?" The worry lines deepened on Jeff Stevens's face. "What if . . . ?"

He stopped, midsentence. There, silhouetted in the church doorway, stood Tracy Whitney. The sunlight blazing behind her looked almost like a halo, as if Tracy were an angel sent from heaven. *My angel.* Jeff Stevens's heart soared.

Tracy's slender figure was shown off to perfection in

a simple, cream silk dress, and her shining chestnut hair cascaded around her shoulders like poured molasses. Jeff Stevens had seen her in countless guises over the years—Tracy's was a fluid, changeable beauty, which accounted for part of her success as a con artist—but he had never seen her look more lovely than she did today. Tracy's mother used to tell her that she had "all the colors of the wind" in her. Jeff Stevens understood exactly what Doris Whitney had meant. Today Tracy's eyes, incredible eyes that could change from moss green to dark jade according to her mood, sparkled with happiness, and with something else besides. Triumph, perhaps? Or excitement? Jeff Stevens felt his heart rate quicken.

"Hello, Gunther, darling." Tracy walked purposefully toward the altar, kissing her mentor on both cheeks. "How wonderful of you to come."

Tracy Whitney loved Gunther Hartog like a father. Tracy missed her father. She hoped he would have been proud of her today.

Turning to Jeff Stevens, she said, "Sorry I'm late."

"Never apologize," said Jeff. "You're far too beautiful for that."

He noticed that her cheeks were very flushed, and a fine mist of sweat had begun to form on her brow. Almost as if she'd been running.

Tracy smiled.

"I have a good excuse. I was picking up your wedding present."

"I see." Jeff smiled back. "Well, I do like presents."

"I know you do, darling."

"Especially when they're from you."

The priest interrupted grumpily, looking at his watch. "Perhaps we could begin?"

Father Alfonso had a baptism to perform in an hour. He

wished these tiresome Americans would get a move on. The explosive sexual chemistry between Jeff Stevens and Tracy Whitney made Father Alfonso deeply uncomfortable. As if he were committing a sin just by standing next to them. On the other hand, they had tipped him very handsomely for the use of the chapel at such short notice.

"So did you get it?" Jeff asked, not taking his gray eyes from Tracy's.

"Get what?"

"My present, of course."

"Oh yes." Tracy grinned. "I got it all right."

Jeff Stevens kissed her passionately on the mouth.

Father Alfonso coughed loudly. "Please, Mr. Stevens. Restrain yourself! *Estão na casa de Deus.* This is a place of worship. You are not yet married."

"Sorry." Jeff grinned, looking anything but.

She did it. Tracy did it. She outwitted the great Maximilian Pierpont. After all these years.

Jeff Stevens gazed at his wife-to-be adoringly.

He had never loved her more.

CHAPTER I

*T*RACY WHITNEY LEANED BACK in her first-class seat, number 4B, and sighed with contentment. In a few hours she would be reunited with Jeff. They would be married, in Brazil. *No more capers,* Tracy thought, *but I won't miss them. Life will be thrilling enough just being Mrs. Jeff Stevens.*

Their last con, stealing the priceless Lucullan Diamond from the Netherlands diamond-cutting factory in Amsterdam, had been a fitting swan song. Together, Tracy and Jeff had outwitted both the Dutch police and Daniel Cooper, the dogged insurance agent who had tracked them all across Europe, in a daring and dramatic heist. *We'll never top that,*

thought Tracy. *And we certainly don't need any more money.*
It was the perfect time to retire.

"Excuse me."

A puffy, dissipated-looking middle-aged man was standing over her. He indicated the window seat. "That's my seat, honey. Great day for a flight, huh?" There was a leer in his voice as he squeezed past her.

Tracy turned away. She had no interest in making conversation, especially with this creep.

Sitting down, her companion nudged her. "Since we're going to be seatmates on this flight, little lady, why don't you and I get acquainted? My name is Maximilian Pierpont."

Tracy's mental Rolodex whirred into action, but she displayed no visible sign of emotion.

Maximilian Pierpont. Legendary corporate raider. Buys up companies and strips them. Ruthless. Three times divorced. Owner of the most valuable Fabergé egg collection outside the Hermitage in St. Petersburg.

"Countess Valentina Di Sorrenti." She offered him her hand.

"A countess, eh? Charmed." Maximilian Pierpont pressed his lips to Tracy's wrist. They were wet and slimy, like a toad. She forced herself to smile.

Tracy had first heard the name "Maximilian Pierpont" on board the *QE2,* many years before, when she and Jeff Stevens found themselves passengers on the same voyage bound for London. Jeff had been planning to rob the famously unscrupulous Pierpont, but had ended up pulling an ingenious betting scam with Tracy instead, tricking two chess grand masters into playing each other in a rigged game.

Later, Gunther Hartog had commissioned Tracy to rob Pierpont on the Orient Express train to Venice, but he never turned up.

Tracy's beloved mother, Doris Whitney, had killed herself after a local mafioso in her native New Orleans, Joe Romano, tricked her out of her family business. Tracy's father had spent his life building up the Whitney Automotive Parts Company. After his death, Romano raided the company, firing everybody and leaving Doris penniless.

Tracy had long since taken her revenge on Joe Romano. But her hatred of corporate raiders never left her. As far as she was concerned, there was a special corner of hell reserved for the Maximilian Pierponts of this world.

You won't get away this time, you bastard.

THE FLIGHT WAS LONG. Tracy chatted amiably with Pierpont for almost two hours before he fell asleep, snoring loudly like a beached walrus. It was enough time for her to embellish her alter ego a little. Tracy had played the Countess Valentina Di Sorrenti before and knew her history well. (She'd written the countess's Wikipedia page, after all.) Valentina was a widow *(Poor Marco! He died so young and so needlessly. A Jet Ski accident in Sardinia. Valentina witnessed it all from the upper deck of their yacht,* El Paradiso) and came from an ancient, aristocratic family. She had recently lost her father and hinted at a large inheritance, without being drawn into details. Details were best avoided, in Tracy's experience, especially while a con was still being formulated. She also made sure to display a charmingly feminine lack of understanding about financial matters and the ways of the world that made Maximilian Pierpont's greedy eyes shine almost as much as they did when he looked at her breasts, something he did frequently and with no hint of embarrassment. By the end of the conversation, Countess Valentina had agreed to meet him for dinner the following evening at one of Rio's finest restaurants.

Relieved that the odious Pierpont was finally asleep,

Tracy picked up an in-flight magazine. The first article she read was about the soaring value of beachside property in Brazil. One featured estate boasted an Olympic-size infinity pool and formal gardens that could have rivaled those at the palace of Versailles. Tracy ran a finger over the pictures in awe. *Jeff and I could be happy in a place like that. Our children could swim in the pool. They'll all be amazing swimmers. And one day our daughter could get married in the gardens, with a line of flower girls in front of her, carpeting the lawn with rose petals . . .*

She laughed at herself. Perhaps they should get married themselves first. One fantasy at a time.

The second article was about the environment, and the devastating effects of erosion on communities south of Rio. Tracy read about farmers who'd lost everything, of entire villages that had been abandoned, reclaimed by the sea. She read about terrible accidents, in which slum dwellers by the coast had drowned, and those inland had been buried alive under rivers of wet mud. *What a terrible way to die,* thought Tracy. In Brazil, more than anywhere else in the world, there was one country for the rich and another for the poor.

It wasn't until the seat-belt signs were switched back on and the plane began its descent into Rio that it came to her. As the images rolled through her consciousness one by one—of her and Jeff at an altar, getting married; of infinity pools and mansions and slums and mudslides; of Maximilian Pierpont pressing his revolting wet lips to her skin; of her mother, eyes shut tight, holding the revolver up to her temple—she suddenly murmured the word "Yes!"

"You all right, little lady?"

Pierpont, awake again now, leaned in closer. His breath smelled of stale onions.

"Oh, sorry. Yes, I'm fine." The Countess Valentina collected herself. "I love to visit Brazil. I always get excited when I'm going down."

"So do I, baby." Maximilian Pierpont squeezed her thigh and winked suggestively. "So do I."

MAXIMILIAN PIERPONT TOOK TRACY to Quadrifoglio, a Michelin three-star restaurant in the quaint, backstreet neighborhood of the Jardim Botânico.

"This is really too generous of you, Mr. Pierpont."

"Please, call me Max."

"Max." Countess Valentina Di Sorrenti smiled.

She was looking particularly ravishing tonight, in a white lace Chanel blouse and floor-length black skirt from Ralph Lauren that emphasized her tiny waist. The diamonds at her ears and neck were flawlessly cut, perfect enough to convey serious wealth, yet small enough to mark her out as "old money." Max Pierpont was a vulgar man, but he despised vulgarity in others, especially women. No danger of that with this lady. Max had Googled the Countess Di Sorrenti as soon as they landed. Her family was one of the oldest and grandest in South America.

Max wondered how long it would take him to get her out of her couture clothes and into his bed.

"So, Valentina. What brings you to Rio?" He filled Tracy's glass to the brim with red wine from the bottle of vintage Quinta de la Rosa he'd just ordered.

The Countess Di Sorrenti's beautiful face fell. "Business." She looked up at Pierpont with sad, soulful eyes. "And tragedy. My father recently passed away, as I told you."

Maximilian Pierpont reached across the table and closed his clammy hand over hers.

"He left me a beautiful property. Almost a mile of land

along the coast. I thought of building a home there. It could be an exquisite estate. I have all the permissions to build and the views . . . Well, you have to see it to believe it. But"—she sighed heavily—"it was not to be."

"Why not?" Like a hound picking up the scent of a fox, Maximilian Pierpont's business instincts stirred to life. Coastal property in Brazil was going through the roof.

"It would make you too sad. Always to be thinking of Papa." The Countess Di Sorrenti gave a heartfelt sigh.

"That's a shame. So what will you do with the land?"

Maximilian Pierpont framed the question casually. But Tracy could see the naked greed flickering in his piggy little eyes. She sipped at her wine.

"I thought about keeping it as is. But in the end I decided it was too much of a waste to let it just sit there. *Someone* should enjoy the beauty of that spot, even if I can't."

"That's a very generous way of looking at it. I can see you're a real giving person, Valentina."

"Thank you, Max."

Their food arrived. With typical arrogance, Max had ordered for both of them, although Tracy had to admit that the food was delicious. The *gema caipiri*—polenta caviar with egg yolk—was a highlight. Tracy could see why the likes of Bill Clinton and Fidel Castro had chosen to dine here, along with all of Rio's business elite.

"Perhaps we could help each other out, Countess." Maximilian Pierpont shoveled food into his mouth as if he were eating at a McDonald's.

"Valentina," Tracy purred.

"Well, Valentina, it just so happens that real estate is one of my passions. I could take the land off your hands and build something beautiful there. If I sell it for a good price, we could split the profits. How does that sound? That way the land wouldn't be wasted, and everybody would gain."

"It's a lovely idea." Tracy sighed again, leaning back in her chair. "If only I'd met you sooner, Max. But I'm afraid it's too late."

"What do you mean?"

"I already agreed to sell the land to the Church. It's six acres, the perfect site for a small monastic community. Monsignor Cunardi showed me his plans for the chapel he wants to erect there. Very simple and elegant. I think Papa would have approved."

Maximilian Pierpont experienced a stabbing pain in his chest. *Forget Papa. Who builds a church on prime beachfront land in Rio?*

"May I ask how much the monsignor has offered you?"

"Five million Brazilian reals. He's been very generous."

Maximilian Pierpont almost choked on his Quinta de la Rosa. Five million reals was a little more than $2 million. Six acres of land on the coast, *with* planning permission, was worth ten times that amount at least! The stupid bitch clearly hadn't even had the property appraised.

"It's a good price, Valentina." He looked at Tracy with a straight face. "But what if I could do better? Say I offered you six million. As a friend. I could build your dream estate exactly as you imagined it."

"Well, that would be wonderful, Max!"

"Great." Pierpont grinned triumphantly. What a stroke of luck, meeting this rich, sexy airhead on the flight. Now he would get to screw her *and* screw her over. And all for the price of one measly dinner! "When can I see the property?"

Tracy gave him a pained expression. "I'm afraid it's too late."

"What do you mean?"

"My deal with Monsignor Cunardi closes tomorrow."

"Tomorrow!"

"Yes. That's why I'm here, to oversee the transfer of the

funds. If only we'd met sooner. Anyway, enough about business. I must be boring you stiff! I hear the desserts here are to die for."

She began to peruse the dessert menu. Maximilian Pierpont wore the expression of a man who could feel millions of dollars slipping through his fingers.

"Look. I don't need to physically *see* the land. You say you have the necessary planning permissions?"

Tracy nodded gravely.

"If you could get me copies of those tomorrow morning, along with the deeds to the property, that'd be enough. Do you think that's possible, Valentina?"

"Well, yes!" The Countess Di Sorrenti's eyes lit up. "Of course. But surely you wouldn't want to pay such a huge amount of money without even *seeing* the land? I mean, one has to walk there to understand the true magic of the place. Papa always said—"

"I'm sure." Maximilian Pierpont cut her off, unable to listen to another minute of her vacuous rambling. As if he gave a damn about the "magic" or her stupid dead father. He *did* still want to maneuver the countess into bed. But he'd better wait until the deal was done first.

"Well . . ." Tracy smiled broadly. "I'll send over the paperwork in the morning, then. I must say, this really is incredibly kind of you, Max."

"Not at all, Valentina. I'd hate to see your dream for that land slip away. Waiter!" Maximilian Pierpont clicked his fingers imperiously. "Bring us some champagne. The best in the house! Countess Di Sorrenti and I are celebrating."

THAT NIGHT JEFF CALLED Tracy's cell.

"I'm trying to reach the future Mrs. Stevens."

Just hearing his voice again made Tracy's heart leap.

"I'm afraid you have the wrong number. This is the Countess Valentina Di Sorrenti."

No man had ever gotten to Tracy the way that Jeff did. Not even Charles Stanhope III, the first man she'd thought she wanted to marry, back in Philadelphia, in another life. Charles had betrayed her. When Tracy was sent to prison for a crime she didn't commit, Charles Stanhope III hadn't lifted one powerful finger to help her.

Jeff Stevens was different. Tracy trusted him with her life. And he had saved her life once. That was when Tracy first realized that he loved her. Every day with Jeff was an adventure. A challenge. A thrill. But the irony wasn't lost on her:

The one person on this earth that I trust completely is a con man.

Jeff said, "I thought you said we were done with capers?"

"We are. Just as soon as I'm done with this. It's Maximilian Pierpont, for God's sake!"

"How long will it take?" Tracy could hear the pout in his voice.

He misses me. Good.

"A week. Maximum."

"I can't wait that long, Tracy."

"Valentina," Tracy teased. "Although you can call me 'Countess.'"

"I want you in my bed, not on the end of a telephone line."

Jeff's voice was hoarse with desire. Tracy gripped the phone, feeling weak with longing. She wanted him too, desperately. It had been only a week since they had been together in Amsterdam, but her body was already crying out for him.

"We can't be seen together in Rio. Not until I've nailed Pierpont."

"Why not? I can be the Count Di Sorrenti."

"He died."

"Bummer. How?"

"Jet Ski accident in Sardinia."

"What a phony. He deserved it."

"I watched it happen from our yacht."

"Of course you did, Countess." Jeff chuckled. "How about I come back as his ghost?"

"I'll see you in church next Saturday, darling. I'll be the hot girl in the white dress."

"At least tell me where you're staying."

"Good night, Mr. Stevens."

THE LAWYER'S OFFICE WAS small and airless, tucked away in a small street off the Avenida Rio Branco in Rio's Centro business district.

"You're sure these permissions are genuine?"

"Yes, Countess Di Sorrenti."

"And complete? There's nothing else I would need, legally, apart from the deeds here"—Tracy held up a sheaf of papers—"to begin work on this site?"

"No, Countess." The lawyer's frown deepened. He'd explained the situation to the beautiful young lady multiple times now, but she still seemed unable to grasp it. The Countess Di Sorrenti might be rich and beautiful, but she was also clearly profoundly dim. He tried one last time. "You do understand, there is still the issue of—"

"Yes, yes. Thank you." Tracy waved an imperious hand before reaching into her vintage Louis Vuitton handbag for a gold Montblanc pen. "How much do I owe you?"

Suit yourself, thought the lawyer. He'd done his best.

FIVE DAYS AFTER HIS dinner with the Countess Di Sorrenti at Quadrifoglio, Maximilian Pierpont drove south of

Rio, along the breathtaking Green Coast road, toward his latest acquisition. As good as her word, the countess had couriered over copies of the deeds to her property along with building permits the very next morning. Pierpont had wired the six million reals to her Swiss account within an hour, and the land was his. *Go to hell, Monsignor Cheapskate!* But he hadn't had a chance to drive out and see it until today.

Six acres of prime cliff-side property—six acres!—with its own private beach, easily accessible from both the city and from Paraty, Rio's answer to East Hampton. Maximilian Pierpont could hardly believe his luck. Better still, he fully intended to nail the lovely Countess Valentina tonight, once he returned to the city. She'd invited him over to her apartment for dinner, always a good sign. The address was on one of the finest streets in Leblon, the most exclusive neighborhood in the whole of South America. Clearly neither "Papa" nor "poor Marco" had left the lady short of funds. The prospect of swindling the sexy young heiress out of still more millions, while availing himself of her smoking-hot body in bed, was giving Maximilian Pierpont the biggest hard-on he'd had in a decade.

He reached the property just before noon. There were a few houses along this stretch of road, but no real standouts. Pierpont's plot stood in splendid isolation at the very top of the bluffs. Valentina wasn't kidding about the views. They were spectacular. On one side the ocean blurred into the cloudless sky, a symphony in limitless blue. On the other, mountains smothered by vivid green rain forest sparkled like vast heaps of newly polished emeralds. *It's even prettier than I imagined.* Maximilian Pierpont congratulated himself again that he hadn't lost out on this deal by listening to his dumb-ass lawyer.

"It's the first rule of real estate, Max," Ari Steinberg had warned him. "Don't buy a pig in a poke. You taught me that, remember?"

"The problem is, some stupid monsignor's already poking my pig. He's got this chick wrapped around his little finger, Ari. I need to make a move before he does."

The lawyer was insistent. "You haven't seen the land. You gotta see the land."

"I've seen the deeds. I've seen the building permits. And I know where it is. Prime coast, Ari, the best. We're talking a Brazilian Malibu."

"But, Max . . ."

"If we were talking about a ten percent profit, or twenty, or even fifty, I'd agree with you. But I can get this for peanuts! A fraction of what it's worth. Wire her the money."

"I strongly urge you to reconsider."

"And I strongly urge you to do what the hell I tell you, Ari."

Maximilian Pierpont hung up.

Stepping out of his Bentley, he ducked under the orange construction tape that marked the entry to the Di Sorrenti property. *Make that the Pierpont property,* he thought gleefully. A team of surveyors were already on-site. Pierpont walked up to the chief surveyor, smiling broadly.

"Whaddaya think? Quite a view, huh?" He couldn't help boasting.

The chief surveyor looked at him steadily. "You can't build a house here."

Maximilian Pierpont laughed. "What do you mean I can't build a house here? I can do whatever I want. It's my land."

"That's not the point."

"Sure it's the point." Pierpont stopped laughing. This dweeb was starting to annoy him. "I got legal permits, set in stone."

"I'm afraid that's all that's set in stone," said the surveyor.

"The ground you're standing on?" He tapped at the grass beneath their feet with a stick. "This time next year it won't be here."

A chill ran down Maximilian Pierpont's spine. "What?"

"This is some of the worst erosion I've seen. Ever. It's an ecological tragedy. Anything you build here will be down there before the walls are dry." The surveyor pointed at the beach below. Reached by a charming set of winding wooden steps, its soft white sand looked mockingly perfect.

"But this area, this stretch of the coast . . . prices are sky-high," Pierpont spluttered.

"Halfway up the mountain, sure," said the surveyor. "You got this knockout view. But here?" He shrugged. "Here you *are* the view. Didn't anyone say anything to you when you applied for these permits?"

"I didn't apply for them. The previous owner did."

The surveyor frowned, confused. "Really? That's odd. Because they're only a week old."

Behind Maximilian Pierpont, the leaves of the rain forest rustling softly in the breeze sounded uncannily like Ari Steinberg's laughter.

THE APARTMENT IN LEBLON took up the entire top floor of a grand Victorian mansion. The door was opened by a British butler in full uniform.

"I want to see the Countess Di Sorrenti." Maximilian Pierpont's jowly face looked uglier than ever, like a bulldog chewing a wasp. *That bitch is giving me my money back if I have to beat it out of her with a crowbar.* Hopefully it wouldn't come to that. Valentina was so stupid, she probably didn't realize herself that the land was worthless. It should be a simple enough thing to convince her to go back to the monsignor.

"I'm sorry, sir. Who?"

Maximilian Pierpont glared at the butler.

"Now listen to me, Jeeves. I've had a bad day as it is. I don't need any more aggravation. You go and tell Valentina that Maximilian Pierpont is here."

"Sir, this apartment is owned by Mr. and Mrs. Miguel Rodriguez. The Rodriguezes have lived here for more than twenty years. I can assure you, there is no 'Valentina' at this address."

Maximilian Pierpont opened his mouth to speak, then closed it again, like a toad gaping uselessly at a fly.

There is no Valentina at this address.

There is no Valentina . . .

Racing back to his car, he called his accountant. "The money we wired on Tuesday, to that Swiss account? Make some calls. Find out who opened the account and where the funds are now."

"Mr. Pierpont, no Swiss bank is going to reveal that sort of information. It's proprietary, and—"

"DO IT!"

A vein began to throb in Maximilian Pierpont's temple. It was still throbbing forty minutes later when the accountant called back.

"I don't have a name, sir. I'm sorry. But I can tell you the account was closed down yesterday and all funds were withdrawn. That money is gone."

GUNTHER HARTOG DROVE THE wedding car, a vintage 1957 Daimler Conquest, with Tracy and Jeff cuddled up in the back.

"So, Mr. and Mrs. Stevens. Where to?"

"The Marina da Glória," said Tracy. "We have a small

yacht waiting there to take us to Barra da Tijuca. I packed us some clothes," she added to Jeff.

Jeff squeezed his wife's thigh. "I can't think why. You won't be needing any for the next week at least."

Tracy giggled. "Tomorrow morning we're on a private plane to São Paulo, then on to Tunisia for the honeymoon. It's too dangerous to fly direct from Rio. Pierpont or his goons might be waiting at the airport."

Jeff looked at her lovingly. "You've thought of everything, haven't you, darling?"

"I try."

Tracy leaned into him. She tried to remember if she had ever felt quite this happy before but nothing came to mind. *I'm Mrs. Stevens. Mrs. Jeff Stevens!* she told herself, over and over. The scam she'd run on Pierpont had gone perfectly. Now she and Jeff really would go straight and leave this crazy life behind them. Jeff could follow his dream of becoming an archaeologist, something he'd always been passionate about. And Tracy could fulfill her dreams too.

A baby. A baby of my own. Mine and Jeff's.

They would settle down to a normal, domestic life together and live happily ever after.

Tracy closed her eyes and imagined it.

"I must say, I was pleased you went for such a traditional wedding," observed Gunther, from the driver's seat. "Something old, something new, something borrowed and something blue."

"We did?" Tracy and Jeff exchanged puzzled glances.

"Why yes." Gunther smiled. "Tracy used the 'barred winner' scam on Pierpont. Where she had the winning ticket—in this case the land ripe for development—but couldn't claim the prize herself. That's as old as the hills."

Jeff grinned. "Okay, I get it. So go on, then, Gunther. What was new?"

"The money!" Tracy laughed.

"Quite so. The money is new. New to you, at least," said Gunther.

"Tracy's identity was borrowed," said Jeff. "I'm getting good at this game. But what's blue?"

Gunther Hartog arched an elegant eyebrow. "I imagine," he said, "that Mr. Maximilian Pierpont is blue. At this precise moment, in fact, I should say that our old friend Mr. Pierpont is feeling very blue indeed."

CHAPTER 2

LONDON, ENGLAND
ONE YEAR LATER

*T*RACY TORE OPEN THE plastic wrapper of the pregnancy test and sat down on the toilet.

She was in the downstairs bathroom at 45 Eaton Square, the beautiful Georgian house she'd bought with the proceeds from her first two jewel heists in the early days of her career. Gunther Hartog had helped her pick out the house and decorate it, and Gunther's impeccable, if slightly masculine, taste was still in evidence everywhere. The red damask wallpaper and eighteenth-century gilt mirror in the bathroom made the tiny room feel like a luxurious boudoir. It reminded her of a time gone by. Before Jeff. Before marriage. Before trying, and failing, to have a baby had become the sole obsession of her life.

After peeing on the test stick, Tracy replaced the plastic cap and laid the stick flat on the tiles around the basin, waiting for the requisite five minutes to pass. In the beginning she'd watched the tiny square window the whole time, as if she could make that longed-for second pink line appear simply by willing it to do so. Now she looked away, forcing herself to think about other things.

She thought about Jeff, on day three of his new job at the British Museum, and how happy he'd been when he bounded out of bed this morning, like a puppy chasing a shiny new ball.

"Can you believe it?" he'd asked Tracy two weeks ago, when he heard he'd gotten the job. "Me! Officially employed as a curator of antiquities at the British Museum. Isn't that a trip?"

"Of course I can believe it," said Tracy loyally. "You know as much about those treasures as anyone else on earth. More than most professional academics. You deserved that job."

The truth, as they both knew, was that Professor Trenchard had pulled some serious strings to get Jeff the position. Tracy and Jeff had met Nick Trenchard, a world-renowned archaeologist, on their honeymoon in Tunisia. Jeff had signed up for a dig at a Roman hill fort that Professor Trenchard was heading and the two men hit it off immediately. Strangely perhaps, as on the surface they had little in common. The professor was in his early sixties, cerebral, shy and utterly obsessed with the late Roman Empire. Jeff Stevens was an ex–con man with no formal education, who could have written what he knew about the Emperor Constantine II on the back of a postage stamp. But his enthusiasm and passion for learning were quite astonishing, as were his natural intelligence and capacity for hard work.

"I wish all my students were like your husband," Professor Trenchard told Tracy over dinner one evening at Jeff and Tracy's hotel. "I've never seen such commitment from an amateur. Is he this driven about everything?"

"When he wants something badly enough," said Tracy.

"I do feel guilty, monopolizing so much of his time when you're on your honeymoon."

"Don't." Tracy smiled. "We picked Tunisia because of its rich history. Jeff's dreamed of going on a dig here his whole life. I'm just happy to see him so happy."

She meant it. She *was* happy, watching Jeff thrive as they began their new life. She was happy when they returned to London and Jeff enrolled in class after class on everything from Byzantine sculpture to Celtic artwork to ancient Roman coins to Chinese ceremonial armor. Without effort it seemed, without sacrifice, he had traded the thrill of their old life as thieves and con artists, robbing only the bad guys and making a fortune for themselves in the process, for the thrill of acquiring new knowledge. And Tracy was happy. For him.

For herself, unfortunately, things were a little more complicated.

The truth was, she'd simply assumed she would get pregnant right away. She and Jeff made love every night of their honeymoon and often during the day as well, when Jeff would sneak away from Professor Trenchard's dig for "lunch" at the hotel. She took a test as soon as they got back to London and was so astonished when it was negative that she went to see her doctor.

"You've only been off the pill for a month, Mrs. Stevens," he reassured her. "There's no reason to think that anything's wrong. However, if you do decide to have your fertility tested, I can recommend Dr. Alan McBride at Seventy-seven Harley Street. He's the best in the business and a thoroughly nice man."

Tracy tried for six more months. She made sure she knew when she was ovulating, and that she and Jeff were having sex at the right time. Not that that was difficult. They were still having sex *all* the time. The happier Jeff felt, the more his libido went through the roof. Tracy still enjoyed their lovemaking. *I've married the most handsome, charming, clever, wonderful man in the world,* she reminded herself. *I should be dancing in the streets.* But for her, the transition from their old life had not been so easy, and she wasn't always in the mood the way she used to be. Part of it was stress about the baby, or rather the lack of a baby. But another, huge part of Tracy mourned the loss of her old identity. She missed the adrenaline rush of the daring heists she and Jeff used to pull off together; the thrill of outsmarting some of the most brilliant, devious, corrupt minds in the world, of beating them at their own game. It wasn't about the money. Ironically, Tracy had never been particularly materialistic. It was about the rush. Sometimes she would watch Jeff while he slept after sex, a look of pure contentment on his face, and feel almost aggrieved.

How can you not miss it? What's wrong with you?
What's wrong with me?

By the time she put that same question to Dr. Alan McBride, she felt wretched and desperate.

"I suspect that nothing is wrong with you, Mrs. Stevens. But let's run some tests, shall we? To put your mind at rest."

Tracy liked Dr. Alan McBride immediately. A handsome Scot with white-blond hair and a naughty twinkle in his intelligent, light blue eyes, he was not much older than her, and didn't take himself too seriously the way that so many senior doctors seemed to do. He also didn't beat around the bush when it came to medical matters.

"Right," he said, when Tracy's test results came back.

"The good news is, you're not infertile. You're ovulating every month, your tubes are all fine, no cysts."

"And the bad news?"

"Your eggs are a bit crap."

Tracy's eyes widened. This was not the sort of terminology she was used to hearing from eminent Harley Street doctors. *"A bit crap,"* she repeated. "I see. *How* crap exactly?"

"If Ocado delivered you a dozen of them in a box and you opened it, you'd probably send it back," said Dr. McBride.

"Riiiight," said Tracy. And then, to her own surprise, she burst into laughter. "So what happens now?" she asked, once she'd regained her composure.

"You take these." Dr. McBride pushed a packet of pills across the desk.

"Clomid," read Tracy.

"They're magic." Dr. McBride positively glowed with confidence. "Basically they're like those practice machines on tennis courts that fire off balls. *Bam bam bam bam bam.*"

"What's all the bamming?"

"That's your ovaries, shooting out eggs."

"Crap eggs."

"They're not all crap. Try it. No side effects and it will triple your chances of getting pregnant."

"Okay," said Tracy, feeling hopeful for the first time in nearly a year.

"If you're not up the duff within three months, we'll go nuclear on the problem with IVF. Sound good?"

That conversation had happened three months ago. Tracy had just finished her last round of Clomid. If today's test was negative, she would begin the brutal, invasive process of in vitro. She knew that millions of women did it, and told herself that it was no big deal. But deep down, IVF felt like failure. *I'm a useless wife,* thought Tracy. *A faulty model.*

Damaged goods. Jeff should return me and trade me in for one that works. One with eggs that aren't crap.

She looked at her watch. One minute to go.

Sixty seconds.

She closed her eyes.

She remembered the last time she'd been pregnant, with Charles Stanhope's baby. Charles's parents were rich Philadelphia snobs. They'd been furious when Tracy got pregnant, but Charles had assured her he wanted both her and the baby. But then Tracy had been sent to prison, framed for a crime she didn't commit, and Charles had turned his back on her. She could still hear his voice now, as if it were yesterday.

"Obviously I never really knew you . . . you'll have to do whatever you think best with your baby . . ."

Savagely beaten by her cell mates, Tracy lost her baby. She hadn't told that to Dr. McBride. Perhaps she ought to? Perhaps it made a difference, even now?

Thirty seconds.

Warden Brannigan and his wife, Sue Ellen, had taken pity on Tracy and hired her as a nanny for their daughter, Amy. Tracy had saved Amy's life, risking her own in the process, and had been granted parole as a result. She'd loved that little girl dearly. Too dearly, perhaps, for Amy wasn't hers. Would never be hers. How old must she be now?

Ten seconds.

Tracy opened her eyes. Nine seconds. Eight. Seven . . . three, two, one.

Heart pounding, she grabbed the test stick and turned it over.

JEFF STEVENS TURNED THE coin over in his hand and felt a shiver of excitement thinking about all the hands that had held it before him. *This is history. Living history. And I'm touching it.*

It was incredible how *new* the thing looked, as if it had been minted yesterday. In fact the small silver disk had been forged in the old English kingdom of Mercia in around the year 760. It bore the name and image of Queen Cynethryth, wife of the fabled King Offa, often considered the first, true king of all England. Jeff Stevens liked the sound of King Offa. The guy had clearly had an ego bigger than his kingdom and the balls to match. He'd had this particular coin fashioned in the style of the late Roman emperors, who often issued currency in the names of their wives. On one side of the disk was the name of the silversmith who'd made it. The other side bore the inscription: *CENETHRETH; REGINA (Cynethryth, Queen)* with a perfect *M* in the middle for Mercia.

The coin was a statement. "If it was good enough for the Roman emperors, it's good enough for me." Not bad for a Saxon warlord/thug who'd fought his way to the top with his bare, bloody hands.

Jeff Stevens loved working at the British Museum. People often talked about their "dream jobs." But for Jeff, this truly was a dream, a fantasy he'd nurtured since he was a small boy.

Jeff's mother had been killed in a car crash when he was fourteen. Two months later his father, an aluminum-siding salesman, married a nineteen-year-old cocktail waitress. One night when his dad was on the road, Jeff's stepmother had made a crude attempt to seduce him. The teenage Jeff made a run for it and headed for Cimarron, Kansas, where his uncle Willie ran a carnival. From that day on, Uncle Willie effectively became Jeff's father, and the carnival became his school. It was there that Jeff learned about human nature. About greed, and how blind and foolish it could make even the most intelligent of men. All the confidence tricks that he would later go on to use to devastating effect against some of the richest, nastiest individuals in the world, Jeff learned from Uncle Willie and the carneys.

But it was also one of the carneys who first instilled in Jeff a love of antiquity and a profound respect for the past. This man had been a professor of archaeology, just like Professor Nick Trenchard, before he was thrown out of the university where he taught for stealing and selling valuable relics.

"Think of it, son," he used to tell Jeff. "Thousands of years ago there were people just like you and me dreaming dreams, spinning tales, living out their lives, giving birth to our ancestors." His eyes took on a faraway look. "Carthage. That's where I'd like to go on a dig. Those people had games and baths and chariot racing. The Circus Maximus was as large as five football fields."

The young Jeff listened, entranced.

"Do you know how Cato the Elder used to end his speeches to the Roman senate? He'd say, *'Delenda est Carthago.'* Carthage must be destroyed. His wish finally came true. The Romans reduced the place to rubble and built a new city on its ashes. But boy, think of the treasures that must be under there!"

Jeff had never stopped thinking about them. He felt as much excitement, holding the ancient Saxon coin in his hand now, as he had ever felt stuffing a bag with priceless jewels, or walking brazenly out of a major art gallery with an Old Master tucked under his arm. Best of all, this job was legit. There were no Interpol or FBI or Mafia goons on his tail. He actually got *paid* to do this.

"Hey, boss. The volunteers from the Women's Institute just arrived. Where would you like them to start?"

Rebecca Mortimer, a Ph.D. student and intern, was the one member of the museum staff who was even newer than

Jeff. A striking twenty-two-year-old with brown eyes like gleaming horse chestnuts and almost waist-length auburn hair, she had started work just two days ago, but already Jeff had a good feeling about their working together. Rebecca was as passionate about the ancient world as Jeff was, and there was an earnestness about her that he found endearing and that brought out his paternal side. Like the small army of elderly volunteers that the British Museum used to help out with special exhibitions and keep costs down, Rebecca was unpaid, but Jeff got the sense she would happily have sold everything she owned for the joy of working here. He knew how she felt.

"Show them into the Special Exhibitions Reading Room," said Jeff, replacing the Mercian coin in its glass case and locking the display. "It's the little room right next to the Great Russell Street entrance. I'll give them a run-through of their duties next week and you can help me take questions."

"Really?" Rebecca's eyes lit up.

"Sure, why not? You already know more about Saxon burial sites than I do."

"Thanks, Jeff!"

She skipped delightedly out of the room, her long ponytail swishing behind her, but a few seconds later she was back. "Oh. I forgot to mention. Your wife is here to see you."

"Tracy's here?" Now it was Jeff's turn to light up.

"Yes. I heard her asking for you at the desk in the Great Court. I said you'd be right down."

TRACY GAZED UP AT the vast, modern, glass-domed ceiling of Lord Foster's Great Court with a combination of awe and surprise. Shamefully after all her years in London, she'd never been to the British Museum and had always pictured it as a grand, Victorian building, similar to the three South Kensington landmarks: the Natural History Museum, the Science Museum and the Victoria and Albert Museum.

In fact, as the leaflet she was now reading explained, the British Museum was actually pre-Victorian, although much of its present-day architecture was aggressively modern. At two acres, the Great Court in which Tracy now stood was the largest covered public space in Europe. But it led into numerous older wings within a vast Bloomsbury complex. Founded in 1753, the British Museum was the first national public museum in the world. Sir Hans Sloane, the famous naturalist and collector, bequeathed more than seventy-one thousand objects, including books, manuscripts and antiquities such as coins, medals and prints, to King George II for the nation, providing the basis of the museum's collection. Today it housed eclectic collections of treasures from around the globe, from Chinese ceramics to ancient Egyptian tomb relics to medieval manuscripts and Anglo-Saxon jewelry. Tracy thought, *No wonder Jeff fell in love with this place. Talk about a kid in a candy store.*

"Baby! What a wonderful surprise."

Jeff snuck up on her from behind. Tracy closed her eyes as his arms encircled her waist, pulling her into her body. He smelled of Penhaligon's cologne, his signature scent and one that Tracy had always adored. *I'm so lucky, so very lucky to have him.*

"What brings you here?"

"Nothing, really," Tracy lied. "I guess I was just curious to see the place."

"Impressive, isn't it?" Jeff sounded as proud as if he'd built the museum himself.

"It is. It's beautiful," said Tracy. "So's that girl you work with," she added archly.

"Rebecca? Is she? I hadn't really noticed."

Tracy laughed loudly. "This is me you're talking to, honey. We've met before, remember?"

"I'm serious," said Jeff. "You know I only have eyes for you. Although I must say I'm touched that you're jealous."

"I am *not* jealous!"

"Come with me." Jeff took her hand. "I wanna show you what we're working on." His fingers felt warm and strong around Tracy's. *Maybe I am a bit jealous.*

He led her into a small anteroom. The girl Tracy had met earlier, Rebecca, was inside, along with a group of about twelve women and a smattering of men, all in their sixties and seventies. Three rows of chairs had been arranged in front of an old-fashioned slide projector, which was beaming images of what looked like gold weaponry and utensils onto the screen at the far end of the room.

"We're about to open a brand-new exhibition of Saxon burial treasure," Jeff whispered in Tracy's ear. "This stuff was all found under a parking lot somewhere in Norfolk. It's the most complete royal gravesite from the period that's ever been found. Absolutely unique."

"Is that vase solid gold?" Tracy stared at the latest image on the screen, a gleaming, two-handled vase almost a foot tall.

Jeff nodded.

"Jesus Christ. How much must that be worth?"

"It's priceless," said Jeff.

Tracy frowned. "Nothing's priceless. I mean it, I'm curious. How much would a private collector pay for something like that?"

"I don't know. A helluva lot. There's more than a million pounds' worth of gold there, even if you melted the thing down. But as an irreplaceable piece of history?" He shrugged. "Two or three million? I'm guessing."

Tracy whistled. "Wow." She glanced around as the old

biddies finished their plastic cups of tea and began to sit down. "Who are the granny brigade?" she whispered in Jeff's ear.

"They're the volunteers. They're going to run the exhibition. They help catalog the treasures, man the admissions desk and give guided tours. I'm about to give them an introductory lecture."

"Are you kidding me?" Tracy looked shocked. "You leave amateurs in charge of millions of dollars' worth of gold?"

"They're well-informed amateurs," said Jeff. "Hell, *I'm* an amateur."

"Yeah, but if someone grabs that vase and makes a run for it, at least you can run after them. What are this bunch gonna do? Throw their walkers?"

Jeff laughed. "No one's gonna steal anything."

Rebecca Mortimer wandered over. "Sorry to interrupt," she said. Tracy noticed that her accent was cut-glass Oxbridge, and that she didn't look particularly sorry. "But we really ought to get started in a minute. Jeff?"

She touched his arm, only for a second. It was a tiny gesture, almost unnoticeable, but it implied a certain intimacy between her and Jeff that Tracy didn't like. At all.

"He'll be with you in a moment," she said coldly.

Rebecca took the hint and walked away.

"My, my," murmured Jeff, sotto voce, an amused look on his face. "You really *are* jealous."

"It must be my hormones." Tracy beamed back at him. "We pregnant women can get terribly overemotional, you know."

It took a few seconds for the impact of her words to sink in. When they did, Jeff swept her up into his arms with a whoop of delight and kissed her on the lips for a very long time. The assembled volunteers all turned to gawk at them.

"Really?" said Jeff, finally coming up for air. "You're sure?"

"I'm sure," said Tracy. "Four tests can't all be wrong."

"That's wonderful. The most wonderful news ever. I'll take you out to dinner tonight to celebrate."

Tracy felt a warm wave of elation flow over her.

Jeff walked over to begin his lecture and she turned to go.

Out of the corner of her eye, she could have sworn she saw the young intern, Rebecca, shoot her a resentful look.

DINNER WAS WONDERFUL. Jeff took her to Como Lario in Belgravia, one of their favorites. Tracy ate the *carciofi e radicchio* followed by a perfectly tender *scaloppine al limone*. Jeff wolfed down his filet steak, despite barely being able to chew thanks to the smile plastered across his face. Tracy wasn't drinking, but Jeff insisted on two flutes of champagne for a toast.

"To our future. Our family. To Jeff Stevens Junior!"

Tracy laughed. "Sexist pig. Who says it's a boy?"

"It's a boy."

"Well, if it is, over my dead body are we calling him Jeff Junior. No offense, darling, but I'm not sure the world could cope with two Jeff Stevenses."

Later, in bed, Tracy slipped into her sexiest Rigby & Peller negligee, a tiny silk slip in buttermilk with white lace trim. "Enjoy it while you can." She snuggled up to Jeff, running her fingers languidly through the tangle of hair on his chest. "Soon I'll be the size of a house. You'll need to use a forklift to move me."

"Nonsense. You'll be the most beautiful pregnant woman on earth," said Jeff, kissing her gently on the mouth.

"Do you ever miss the old days?" Tracy asked him suddenly. "The adrenaline? The challenge? You, me and Gunther against the world?"

"Never."

He said it with such sincerity and finality that Tracy felt silly for asking.

"Besides, as I remember it, half of 'the old days' was you against me, or me against you. As for dearest Gunther, he was always out for himself, playing each of us off against the other."

"That's true," Tracy admitted, smiling to herself at the memory. "But it *was* only playing, wasn't it? It was a game, between the three of us. A wonderful game."

"It was." Jeff stroked her face tenderly. "And you, my love, were the world champion. But we went out on a high, didn't we? And the life we have now . . . well, it's perfect." He ran a hand over Tracy's still-flat belly in wonder. Was there really a new life in there? A person who they had created?

"I love you."

"How much?" Tracy murmured in his ear. She reached down to touch his erection but Jeff stopped her hand.

"Very much. But I don't think we should be fooling around. It might hurt the baby."

And with that, to Tracy's astonishment, he turned out the light, rolled over and fell into a deep and instant sleep.

For a split second she felt irritated, but she soon snuffed out the feeling. Today was too special, too perfect to be spoiled with petty resentments. *He's only being careful because he loves me. When we go to see Dr. McBride together, he can explain to Jeff that it's perfectly safe to make love.*

Too excited to sleep, Tracy's mind began to wander. Oddly, it wasn't the baby she was thinking about, but the things she'd seen at the museum today. She thought about the young girl Jeff worked with. Was she being paranoid? Or *had* the girl given her a dirty look right after Jeff kissed her?

It doesn't matter anyway, Tracy told herself. *I trust Jeff.*

Her mind quickly shifted to the exhibition of Saxon gold Jeff had told her about, and the images she'd seen on the screen. Tracy still couldn't quite believe that an important institution like the British Museum would allow elderly volunteers to handle an event of such importance. These untrained, older people had effectively unfettered access to millions of pounds' worth of artifacts. And yet even Jeff seemed to think nothing of it. Tracy thought back to the complex security systems at the Prado, and at other famous galleries and jewelers that she and Jeff had stolen from back in their heyday. *Imagine if the only person guarding Goya's* Puerto *in Madrid had been a shortsighted old biddy. How easy our lives would have been!*

Jeff had told her tonight about a specific coin, rarer even than the museum's prized Mercian specimens, that would be one of the highlights of the new exhibition.

"Tomorrow I'm gonna get to hold it in my hand. It's Merovingian gold, minted for a Frankish king back in the sixth century. I swear to God, Tracy, it's not much bigger than a quarter, but the workmanship! It's the most beautiful thing I've ever seen."

Instinctively, without even thinking about it, Tracy's quick mind began to work out the best way to steal it. The awful thing was, there were so many options! *Maybe I should offer my services to the museum's trustees as a security consultant?* she thought idly. *God knows they could use the help.*

Then she realized she was about to become far too busy to hold down a job.

She was about to become a mother, at last. It was the one role she had dreamed of and longed for her entire life. Everything else had been a dress rehearsal.

For Tracy Whitney, tomorrow had finally come.

She slept.

CHAPTER 3

AGNES FOTHERINGTON OBSERVED THE gathering crowd outside the exhibition room and felt a warm glow of pride. *Merovingian Treasures* was the biggest event for Anglo-Saxon history enthusiasts in a generation. Not since the famous ship burial at Sutton Hoo was unearthed in the late 1930s had such an impressive array of treasures from the period been found in one place, and so perfectly preserved. And once again, Agnes Fotherington was part of it.

A keen amateur archaeologist, Agnes had assisted on some of the later digs at Sutton Hoo back in the 1980s. She'd been in her midforties then, teaching history at a local grammar school in Kent. Her husband, Billy, had gone with her, and together they'd had a whale of a time.

"Imagine!" Billy used to say, over a steak-and-kidney pie at the Coach & Horses in Woodbridge after a long day on-site. "A couple of nobodies like us, Ag, becoming footnotes to history!"

That was his expression. *Footnotes to history.*

Agnes missed Billy.

He'd been dead ten years now, but he'd have loved to see all the fanfare today. Jeff Stevens, the lovely American antiquities director, rushing about like a blue-arsed fly, anxious for everything to go well, but somehow always with a smile for everyone, despite his nerves. Billy would have liked Jeff.

He'd have liked Rebecca too, Jeff's young assistant. So many young people were getting interested in the period now; that was the really marvelous thing. Anglo-Saxon history used to be considered distinctly unsexy. It had never had the pizzazz of Egyptology, say, or the popular appeal of Ancient Rome. But perhaps *Merovingian Treasures* would change all that. How wonderful if the golden wonders unearthed beneath a Norwich parking lot should one day become as famous as Tutankhamen's tomb.

"It's a great turnout, isn't it?"

Tracy Stevens, Jeff's young wife, put an affectionate arm around Agnes Fotherington's shoulder. Agnes liked Tracy. They'd met a few times in the run-up to the exhibition when Tracy had popped in to say hello to Jeff or to help out with the cataloging. Of course all the volunteers knew that Mrs. Stevens was pregnant, and that she and Jeff were over the moon. The pair of them were obviously madly in love. Agnes Fotherington was sure they'd make wonderful parents.

"Phenomenal turnout," Agnes agreed. "And do look how *young* some of them are. I mean, take that chap over there with the tattoos. You'd never peg him as a seventh-century history buff, now, would you?"

"No," said Tracy, who'd been thinking exactly the same thing, although for very different reasons. "You wouldn't."

She'd already spotted at least four potential thieves in the crowd. The tattooed young man looked more like your smash-and-grab type. But there were others. A pregnant woman who seemed overly interested in the CCTV cameras in the lobby. A pair of Eastern European men in jeans and T-shirts who appeared nervous and kept making eye contact with each other without speaking. One dark-suited man in particular, quiet, unobtrusive and here alone, had caught Tracy's attention. It was nothing she could explain rationally. More of a sixth sense. But something told her he wasn't just an interested tourist.

Part of Tracy wouldn't have blamed them for trying to make off with the gold. With security this lax, the British Museum was almost asking to be robbed. She said as much to Jeff, but he didn't seem worried.

"I guess we'll just have to take our chances. A robbery attempt might even give the exhibition some spice! After all, there's nothing more authentically Anglo-Saxon than a bit of looting."

Tracy had loved him for that comment. It was the old Jeff to a tee.

At eleven o'clock exactly the red rope was unhooked from its silver clip and the visitors began streaming into the first of four display spaces. Their handbags and backpacks had already been spot-searched at the main entrance, but they were not examined again now, Tracy noticed. Instead the visitors were offered a chance to leave their coats in a cloakroom and encouraged to buy programs and take advantage of the audio tours being handed out by two of Mrs. Fotherington's friends.

After that they were ushered in a slow-moving figure eight past the various displays—weaponry, coinage, ceremonial objects and daily life—before being funneled into a temporary *Merovingian Treasures* gift shop, selling replicas of all the above, along with the usual key rings and "I Love the British Museum" T-shirts.

Jeff and Rebecca mingled with the visitors, moving from

room to room. Tracy left them to it, limiting her support for Jeff to an encouraging wave as she returned from the ladies' room to the front desk.

"Tracy, thank goodness. We're almost out of brochures!" Agnes Fotherington grabbed her arm in a panic. "I had a hundred copies here but they've gone in about six minutes."

"I can go and grab some more from the gift shop if you like," Tracy offered.

"Would you?" The old woman was visibly relieved. "You're an angel."

Weaving her way through the exhibition, already packed with people, Tracy hurried toward the shop. As she moved through the coin room she noticed the man who'd caught her attention earlier in the lobby. He was leaning over the display case housing the rare Frankish coins, looking at them with a controlled intensity that made her distinctly uneasy.

I must mention him to Jeff.

At the gift shop, Tracy had just collected a stack of brochures and asked Maurice Bentley, the volunteer in charge, to call down to the stockroom for more when it happened. An earsplitting alarm rang out, a combination of sirens and bells and a grating, electronic vibration that made the cheap Merovingian coins rattle and jump in their plastic display cases.

"What on earth . . . ?" Maurice Bentley covered his ears.

"What is that?" Tracy shouted through the din at a passing staff member. "Has something been stolen?"

"No. It's the fire alarm. Probably just kids messing about."

Or not.

Tracy's heart rate began to quicken.

"Don't look so panicked," Rebecca shouted in Jeff's ear. "It's probably just kids messing about."

Jeff wasn't listening. He was in Amsterdam, at the diamond-cutting factory. The lights went out and an alarm sounded, just like this one. An alarm that he and Tracy had triggered. In Amsterdam, steel shutters had slammed down over doors and windows, sealing the exits. But Jeff and Tracy had still made off with the Lucullan Diamond.

Tracy had posed as a pregnant tourist for that job, Jeff as a technician. *Wasn't there a pregnant woman in the crowd outside today?*

Jeff's mind raced. What would be the easiest thing to steal?

He sprinted into the coin room.

Everything seemed in order. The priceless sixth-century gold coin, the centerpiece of the exhibition, was still in its locked glass case. Nothing appeared to have been moved, or broken or disturbed. Visitors covered their ears and filed toward the exit, but there was no panic, no screaming or drama. It was all terribly British and reserved. A man in a suit was the last to leave, and he stopped and held the door politely for Jeff.

"False alarm, I expect." He gave Jeff a patient smile.

"I expect so."

ABOUT HALF AN HOUR later Jeff found Tracy, outside. The whole museum had been evacuated onto Great Russell Street, but no one seemed especially put out. People were chatting and laughing about the unexpected drama as they waited to be readmitted.

"Everything all right?" Tracy asked Jeff.

"I think so. Some idiot left a lit cigarette in the bathroom."

"Nothing was taken, then?"

Jeff shook his head. "I thought the same thing, but Re-becca and I went through everything three times. It's all there. None of the other departments have reported any problems."

"Good." Tracy hugged him. She felt hugely relieved.

"We're getting too cynical in our old age, you and I," said Jeff, only half joking. "We're gonna have to work on that before Jeff Junior arrives."

FOR THE NEXT FEW weeks, Tracy saw very little of Jeff. There were no further dramas at the museum, and *Merovingian Treasures* proved to be a huge hit as an exhibition, taking up all of Jeff's time.

Professor Trenchard called him.

"Everybody's raving about you in Bloomsbury. I can't tell you how much kudos I'm getting for having brought you in."

"I couldn't be happier," said Jeff. "I really don't know how to thank you, Nick."

"Just keep doing what you're doing. I'm quite happy enough to bask in your reflected glory."

THE NIGHT THE EXHIBITION closed, Jeff came home disconsolate.

"I can't believe it's all over."

"Poor baby."

Tracy wrapped her arms around him from behind, pressing her tiny baby bump against the small of his back. She'd been feeling exhausted recently, a side effect of the pregnancy according to Alan—Dr. McBride—but so far had avoided morning sickness and the smell of food didn't bother her. Tonight she'd prepared Jeff a special dinner of spaghetti carbonara. A delicious scent of bacon, cheese and cream wafted through from the kitchen.

"I've got something for you. To cheer you up."

She led Jeff into the drawing room, a beautifully proportioned Georgian living room with high ceilings, wide oak floorboards and original sash windows overlooking the richly planted "Queen Anne," British slang for a front garden.

"You already cheered me up," said Jeff, sinking into the sofa. "How are you feeling today, beautiful?"

"I'm fine." Tracy handed him a gin and tonic with ice and lemon. "But this is gonna cheer you up more. At least I hope it will."

She pulled a small, black leather box out of her pocket and handed it to him, a little nervously. She knew there was a chance Jeff might take the gift the wrong way, and she desperately wanted to please him, to bring a touch of their old life back with all its fun and excitement.

"Let's just say I went to *a lot* of trouble to get ahold of it."

Jeff opened the box. Tracy watched, delighted, as his eyes widened.

"Where did you get this?"

She grinned. "Where do you think?"

"My God." Jeff gasped. "It's the real thing, isn't it? I thought for a second it might be a really good copy."

"A copy? Please." Tracy sounded offended. "Copies are for the hoi polloi, darling. Only the best for you."

Jeff stood up. Tracy thought he was coming over to kiss her, but when he looked up she saw that his eyes were alight with anger.

"Are you out of your mind?" He held the coin up to her face accusingly. In his hand was the silver coin of Cynethryth of Mercia, one of the British Museum's rarest treasures. "You *stole* this."

"Yes. For you." Tracy looked confused. "I know how much it meant to you. Besides, you said it yourself. Nothing could be more Anglo-Saxon than a bit of looting."

She smiled. Jeff didn't smile back.

"That was a joke!" He looked at her aghast. "How did you . . . when . . . ?"

"The day your exhibition opened. I knew the other Saxon rooms would be totally empty. All anyone was interested in was *Merovingian Treasures*. So I set off the fire alarm, slipped into the south wing, and, well . . . I just took it. Those cases aren't even alarmed," she added, a note of disdain in her voice. "It's like if it isn't the Elgin Marbles or the Rosetta Stone, no one cares."

"Everybody cares!" said Jeff furiously. "*I* care. In any case, those cases are locked. Where did you get the key?"

Tracy looked at him as if he were mad.

"I copied yours, of course. Really, darling, it's not exactly rocket science. I Googled the coin, after you said you liked it so much, and I got a copy made at a little jeweler in the East End. Then I swapped it out for the original. Easy."

Jeff was speechless.

Upset by his reaction, Tracy added defiantly, "And you know what? *No one noticed the difference!* No one except you even looks at that thing. Why shouldn't you have it?"

"Because it's not mine!" Jeff said, exasperated. "It belongs to the nation. I've been trusted to protect it, Tracy. And now my wife, my own *wife,* goes and steals it!"

"I thought you'd be pleased." Tears welled up in Tracy's eyes.

"Well, I'm not."

She couldn't understand Jeff's reaction. Especially after she'd gone to so much trouble. *He used to be proud of me when I pulled off jobs like that.* No one had been hurt, after all. The old Jeff would have been pleased, amused, delighted. Tracy wanted the old Jeff back.

Jeff was staring down at the coin in his hand, shaking his head in disbelief. "Rebecca *said* she thought you seemed distracted on opening day," he murmured. "I remember she asked me if there was anything up with you."

"Oh, Rebecca said something, did she?" Tracy shot back angrily. "Well, bully for Rebecca! I'll bet perfect little Rebecca would never sink so low as to steal a *national treasure,* now, would she?"

"No, she wouldn't," said Jeff.

"Because she's not a dishonest con artist like me, right?"

Jeff shrugged as if to say, *If the shoe fits.*

Tears of anger and humiliation streamed down Tracy's cheeks. "Your little girlfriend may be better than me—"

"Don't be stupid," Jeff snapped. "Rebecca isn't my girlfriend."

"But if she's better than me, she's better than you too, Jeff. Have you forgotten who you are? You're a con artist, Jeff Stevens. You may have retired, but you've got a twenty-year life of crime behind you, my friend! So don't you come playing the high-handed saint with . . ."

Tracy stopped abruptly, like a child freezing in a game of musical statues.

"What?" said Jeff.

Tracy stared at him, her eyes wide and desperate, like a rabbit about to be shot. Then she looked down. Droplets of blood, dark and heavy, fell slowly from between her legs onto the floorboards.

She started to sob.

"All right, sweetheart. Don't panic." Jeff dropped the coin and put his arms around her. This was Tracy, *his* Tracy. What was he thinking, getting so angry with her in her condition. "It'll be okay. Just lie down."

Jeff ran for the phone. "I need an ambulance. Yes, Forty-five Eaton Square. As fast as you can, please."

CHAPTER 4

*B*ELGRAVIA WAS PARTICULARLY BEAUTIFUL in the springtime, Jeff Stevens thought as he set out from Eaton Square in the direction of Hyde Park. The cherry trees lining the Georgian streets were all in bloom, an eruption of white that mirrored the white stucco facades and laid a snowy carpet over the uneven paving stones. Frequent rain had left the grass in Chester and Belgrave Square a glowing, vibrant green. And everywhere people seemed cheerful and renewed, grateful to have emerged from another long, gray, relentless London winter.

For Jeff and Tracy Stevens, the winter had been longer than most. Tracy's miscarriage had hit both of them hard, but Jeff carried an extra burden of guilt, afraid that it was the fight they'd had over that stupid Mercian coin that had triggered it. He had discreetly returned the coin months ago, and no one at the British Museum had been any the wiser.

But the damage that had been done to his relationship with Tracy was not so easy to fix.

They still loved each other. Of that there was no doubt. But the coin incident had forced them both to realize that they'd been papering over some pretty seismic cracks within the marriage. Perhaps it was Tracy's struggle to conceive that had obscured them? Or Jeff's total immersion in his new job? Or both? Whatever the cause, the bottom line was that Jeff had changed since they gave up their old life of heists and capers. And Tracy, fundamentally, had not.

It wasn't that she wasn't prepared to give up the actual *act* of committing crimes. That she could do. The stealing of the Saxon coin had been a one-shot deal, which she had no intention of repeating. It was more that there was a part of her identity, an important part, that she didn't want to let go of. Jeff, at long last, was starting to understand this.

He still hoped that a child would eventually fill the void for Tracy, the way that his passion for antiquities had filled the void for him. They began IVF with high hopes. But as one cycle failed, and then a second, Jeff could only stand by and watch helplessly as the dark sadness inside his wife grew bigger and bigger, like a tumor nothing seemed able to stop.

Jeff tried to make Tracy whole with his love. He started coming home early from work, took her on romantic vacations and surprised her with all sorts of thoughtful gifts: a vintage oil painting of the quarter of New Orleans where Tracy had grown up; a beautiful leather-bound book on the history of flamenco, the dance to which Jeff and Tracy had first fallen in love; a pair of jet earrings from the Whitby coast, where the two of them had once spent a memorably awful weekend in a dreadful hotel, but where Tracy had become intoxicated with the wild, moorland landscape.

Tracy was touched by all of them. But the sadness remained.

"It sounds like depression," Rebecca suggested tentatively, listening to Jeff pour his heart out over tea in the museum café. "Has she seen anybody?"

"Like a shrink, you mean? No. Tracy doesn't believe in all that stuff."

"Yeah, well. Unfortunately mental illness happens, whether you believe in it or not," said Rebecca. "Having someone to talk to might help."

"She has me to talk to," said Jeff. Rebecca could hear the despair in his voice.

"Maybe there are things she *can't* talk to you about." Reaching across the table, she squeezed Jeff's hand.

Rebecca Mortimer had tried not to feel attracted to Jeff Stevens. It was unprofessional. But after months of working in close proximity to his gorgeous gray eyes and jet-black curls, his easy manner and his warm, infectious laugh, she'd given up the effort. How awful it must be to be married to a withdrawn, depressed wife who resented your work and shut you out emotionally. If she, Rebecca, had a husband like Jeff, she'd treat him like a king.

Jeff glanced up, as if something had suddenly occurred to him. "You know what? Maybe she *is* seeing someone. Maybe she has a shrink and is embarrassed to tell me. That would explain a lot."

"Explain a lot of what?" Rebecca asked.

"She's been . . . I don't know. Cagey, recently. Like she has these mysterious meetings and won't tell me where she is. Or she comes home late and she seems kind of happier. Less stressed."

Rebecca nodded silently. Inside she thought, *Well, well, well. I wonder if the perfect Mrs. Stevens has a boyfriend on the side?* It was typical of Jeff that such a thought had clearly never even crossed his mind. Jeff Stevens worshipped his wife. But perhaps the goddess Tracy was about to come crashing down off her pedestal.

Jeff had reached the park now. When the weather was fine he often walked all the way to work, but he was already late this morning, so he hopped on the number nineteen bus.

Rebecca greeted him when he came in. She and Jeff shared an office on the second floor of the museum. If you could call it an office. It was really more of a broom closet, with room for only one desk and two chairs wedged side by side.

"Hey." Rebecca handed him a cup of coffee, strong and black the way he liked it.

"Hey."

In a pair of tight black jeans and a bottle-green sleeveless top that contrasted strikingly with her titian hair, Jeff noticed she was looking particularly beautiful this morning. He also noticed that she seemed unhappy about something. She was biting her lower lip nervously and avoiding meeting his eye.

"What's up?"

"Nothing. I set up meetings with two different restorers for those Celtic manuscripts. I thought we could—"

"Celtic schmeltic," said Jeff. "Don't bullshit me. What's on your mind?"

Rebecca closed the office door and leaned back against it. "I'm scared if I tell you, you'll hate me."

The surprise registered on Jeff's face. "I won't hate you. Why would I hate you?"

"I don't know. People have been known to shoot the messenger. I don't want you to think I'm a gossip. But I . . . I'm worried about you. I don't like to see you being lied to."

Jeff frowned and sat down. "Okay. So now you have to

tell me. What's this about?" Had someone in the museum been bad-mouthing him? Was someone after his job? It wouldn't be unheard of. He *was* an amateur, after all, in a senior position. Perhaps one of his colleagues was—

"It's Tracy."

Jeff flinched as if he'd been stung.

"What about Tracy?"

"Last week, you told me she'd gone away to Yorkshire for the night. Some walking tour."

"That's right," said Jeff.

"No. It isn't." Rebecca blushed scarlet. "I saw her."

"What do you mean you saw her? Where?"

"In London. In Piccadilly, actually. It was the evening I left early to meet my mother, remember? I saw Tracy coming out of a restaurant. She was with a man and they were laughing and joking and—"

Jeff held up a hand. "You must be mistaken. It was probably someone who looked like her from a distance."

"I wasn't *at* a distance." Rebecca spoke quietly, clearly terrified of provoking him. "I was right there. It was her, Jeff. She didn't see me because she was too wrapped up in this guy she was with."

Jeff stood up. "I appreciate you telling me," he said with a stiff smile. "And I'm not angry because I know you meant well. But I assure you you're mistaken. Tracy was in Yorkshire last week. Now, I'd better get down to the manuscript room. I'm twenty minutes late as it is."

Rebecca stepped aside and he walked out, closing the door firmly behind him.

Damn it, thought Rebecca.

THE NEXT THREE WEEKS were torture for Jeff. He knew he ought to go home and confront Tracy after what Rebecca had told him. Not because he believed Rebecca. It was a mistake, it had to be. But so that Tracy could reassure him. Jeff needed that reassurance desperately, like a flower needs sunlight and water. And yet he couldn't bring himself to ask for it. Whenever he tried, all he could think about was Louise.

Louise Hollander, a stunning heiress whose father had owned half of Central America, had been Jeff Stevens's first wife. She had taken the lead in their courtship, chasing him relentlessly until he had given in. Jeff had genuinely loved her, despite her money rather than because of it. When he first overheard gossip about Louise's affairs, he'd dismissed it. Louise's friends were spiteful snobs, who wanted their marriage to fail. But soon the rumors grew from whispers to a deafening roar and Jeff had no option but to face the truth.

Louise Hollander broke Jeff's heart. He vowed never, ever to become emotionally vulnerable to a woman again. And then he met Tracy Whitney and realized he'd never really loved Louise after all. Tracy was Jeff's world, the mother he lost, the lover he dreamed of, the sparring partner he'd never been able to find.

Tracy wouldn't deceive me. She couldn't.

Tracy loves me.

Rebecca must be wrong.

And yet, something *was* up with Tracy. Jeff had felt it before Rebecca even said anything. He'd felt it for months. The missed dinners, the trips, the unexplained meetings, the total and utter lack of interest in sex.

Two weeks after Rebecca's bombshell Jeff finally found the courage to make an oblique reference to Tracy's Yorkshire trip. They were in bed, reading, when he blurted it out.

"When you went away a couple of weeks ago by yourself, didn't you feel lonely?"

"Lonely?" Tracy raised an eyebrow. "No. Why would I?"

"I don't know." Jeff moved in closer, wrapping his arms around her. "Maybe you missed me."

"It was only one night, darling."

"I missed you." He ran a hand down her bare back before slipping it beneath the elastic of her Elle Macpherson panties. "I *still* miss you, Tracy."

"What do you mean?" Tracy laughed, wriggling away from his hand. "You have me. I'm right here."

Are you? thought Jeff.

Tracy turned out the light.

Whereas before, work had been a welcome respite from the emotional tension at home, now Jeff felt almost as ill at ease with Rebecca as he did with Tracy. He'd promised not to shoot the messenger. And yet on some, unconscious level, he realized he *was* angry with the beautiful young intern. Rebecca was wrong about Tracy. Wrong, wrong, wrong. And yet she'd sown a seed of doubt in Jeff's heart that refused to die. Well meaning or not, in one fell swoop Rebecca had shattered his equilibrium, leaving him feeling awkward and out of place at the British Museum as well as at Eaton Square.

One rainy morning, Jeff arrived at their joint office dripping wet—he'd forgotten his umbrella and couldn't face going back home to retrieve it—to find Rebecca packing up her things.

"What's going on?"

Stuffing the last of her books into a cardboard box, Rebecca handed him a stiff white envelope. She forced herself to smile.

"No hard feelings, boss. I've had an incredible time working with you. But we both know we can't go on like this."

"Go on like what?" said Jeff. Irrationally, he found he felt even angrier than usual. "You're resigning?"

"I'm leaving," said Rebecca. "I believe it's only called resigning if you get paid."

"Because of me?" For the first time, Jeff felt a stab of guilt.

"I think you're amazing," said Rebecca. To Jeff's astonishment, she put her arms around his neck and kissed him, just once, on the lips. The kiss wasn't long but it was heartfelt. Jeff was embarrassed by how instantly aroused it made him.

"Look . . ." he began.

Rebecca shook her head. "Don't. Please." She handed him an unmarked disk. "Watch this, after I'm gone. If you ever want to talk, you have my numbers."

Jeff took the disk and the letter, staring at them both dumbly. It was a lot to take in at nine o'clock in the morning. Before he'd recovered enough to say anything, Rebecca was gone.

Depressed and exhausted suddenly, he sank down into his chair. Outside, the rain was still beating down relentlessly. The splatter of droplets on the tiny single window above his desk sounded like a hail of bullets.

What's happened to my life? Jeff thought miserably. *I feel like I'm under attack.*

Switching on his computer, he slipped the disk inside.

Within ten minutes, he'd watched the footage five times. Then he read Rebecca's letter.

He stood up, his feet unsteady beneath him, and opened the office door. He started walking down the corridor. After a few seconds he broke into a jog, then a run. The elevators took forever, so he bounded down the south stairs, two at a time.

"Did you see Rebecca Mortimer?"

The girl at the front desk looked startled.

"Hello, Mr. Stevens. Is everything all right? You look—"

"Rebecca!" Jeff panted. "Did you see her leave the building?"

"Yes. She was saying good-bye to some of the staff in the

café, but she just left. I think she was heading toward the tube on . . ."

Jeff was already sprinting out of the double doors.

TRACY WALKED DOWN Marylebone High Street with only a flimsy umbrella to protect her from the torrential rain, but nothing could dampen her spirits. It had been a long day but a wonderful one. She looked around for a cab.

It had been so long since she'd felt this happy, so long since she'd felt happy at all, that she almost didn't know what to do with herself. There was a part of her that felt guilty about Jeff. *Poor Jeff.* He'd tried so hard to understand her grief over losing their baby. Tracy could see the effort he was making, but somehow that made everything twenty times worse. None of this was Jeff's fault.

But it isn't my fault either. I can't help who I am. And I can't stop needing what I need.

Alan understood. Alan got it, got *her,* in ways that Jeff never could.

Tracy had seen him again today. It had reached the point where simply being in the room with him had the capacity to make her happy, and hopeful for the future. Perhaps that was the key. Hope. Tracy had tried, she really had, but she'd felt so trapped in her married life with Jeff since they got back to London, so hopeless. Forty-five Eaton Square, the home that used to be her sanctuary, had become a prison.

No more.

Tracy was on her way home now to talk to Jeff. She was nervous, but at the same time she wanted to tell him. Needed to tell him, to unburden herself at last. Just the thought of peeling off her wet clothes, climbing into the shower and washing away the pain of the past year filled her with a profound sense of relief.

No more secrets.

It was time for the next chapter to begin.

THE LIGHTS WERE OFF when she got back to the house. Jeff didn't usually get home till seven or eight and would probably be later tonight since he wasn't expecting her back. Tracy hadn't known what time she would leave Alan's, so had made up a story about dinner with a girlfriend.

That will be the last lie I tell him, she resolved, climbing the stairs. From now on it would be honesty all the way.

She pushed open the door to the master bedroom and froze. For a moment, quite a long moment actually, time stood completely still. Tracy's eyes were sending one message to her brain, but something—her heart, perhaps—kept intercepting the signal and sending it back. *This is what I am seeing,* her brain seemed to be telling her, *but it cannot be true.*

She was so silent and still, barely even breathing, that it took Jeff a few moments to realize she was standing there. When he did, and their eyes finally met, he was standing by the window, locked in a passionate embrace with an utterly oblivious Rebecca Mortimer.

They were both still dressed, but Rebecca's shirt was half unbuttoned, and Jeff's hands were on her back as they kissed passionately. When Jeff saw Tracy and tried to pull away, Rebecca grabbed him like a drowning woman clinging to a life raft.

Stupidly, Tracy's first thought was *She has an amazing figure.* Rebecca was wearing spray-on jeans that she was clearly itching for Jeff to help her out of. It was as if the whole thing was a scene in an erotic play. Some sort of fiction, from which Tracy could detach herself. It wasn't real. It couldn't be.

The real Jeff, my Jeff, would never do that to me.

It was only when Rebecca turned, saw Tracy and screamed that the illusion shattered.

"How could you?" Tracy looked witheringly at Jeff.

"How could I? How could *you*?"

Straightening his hair, Jeff walked toward his wife looking as aggrieved as it was possible for someone to look with lipstick smeared all over his face and neck.

"You started it!"

"I-I . . . what?" Tracy stammered. "You're in our bedroom with another woman!"

"Only because *you've* been having an affair with your fertility doctor!"

Tracy looked at him first with bafflement, then with disgust.

"Don't try to deny it!" Jeff shouted at her.

"You make me sick," said Tracy. As if seducing his intern wasn't bad enough, now Jeff was trying to turn this around onto *her*? "How long has this been going on?"

"Nothing's going on."

Tracy laughed, a loud, brittle, ugly laugh with no joy in it. *This can't be happening.* She couldn't bring herself to look directly at Rebecca. But out of the corner of her eye she could have sworn she saw a distinct gleam of triumph in the younger woman's eyes. Wrapping her anger around her like a cloak, Tracy turned on her heel and fled.

"Tracy! Wait!"

Pulling on a pair of shoes, Jeff ran after her. He heard the front door slam as he raced downstairs and chased her out into the street. It was still raining, and the pavement felt slippery and slick beneath his bare feet.

"For God's sake, Tracy!" He grabbed her arm. Tracy struggled but couldn't break his grip. "Why can't you admit it? I know I was wrong to kiss Rebecca—"

"Kiss her? You were about to do a lot more than kiss her, Jeff! You were in our bedroom, all over that girl like a rash! If I hadn't walked in . . ."

"What? If you hadn't walked in, what? I'd have slept with her? Like you did with Dr. Alan McBride?"

"You're ridiculous."

"And you're a liar!" There were tears in Jeff's eyes. "I saw the footage, Tracy. Saw it with my own eyes."

"What footage? What are you talking about?"

"YOU, coming out of the Berkeley Hotel with that man. That *bastard*! The two of you, kissing in the street at two in the morning. The same day you claimed to be in Yorkshire. You lied to me. And then you have the gall to accuse *me* of having an affair!"

Tracy closed her eyes. She felt as if she were going mad. But then she remembered that this was Jeff's signature, the way he always used to work, back in the old days. Baffling and bamboozling his victims till they couldn't tell up from down or right from wrong.

I'm no victim, Tracy thought. *I'm not one of your dumb "marks." This is about you, not me. You and that damn girl.*

"I don't know what you think you saw," she said. "But the only man I've slept with in the last four years is you, Jeff."

"That's a lie, Tracy, and you know it. You and McBride . . ."

Tracy lost her temper. "Don't say his name! Don't you dare. Alan's a decent man. An honest man. Unlike you. Go back to your girlfriend, Jeff."

With a sharp tug, she pulled her arm free and ran.

HOURS PASSED AND THE rain kept falling. Tracy had no idea where she was going, or why. Soon it was completely dark.

Eventually she found herself on Gunther Hartog's street, staring up at his splendid, redbrick house. Just around the corner from his Mount Street antiques shop, Gunther Hartog's Mayfair home was one of Tracy's safe places, her happy places. She and Jeff had spent many long, drunken, convivial evenings there, discussing jobs they'd done or planning new capers.

Me and Jeff.

The ground-floor lights were all on. Gunther would be in his study, no doubt, reading books on politics and art late into the night. Jeff used to call him the best-educated crook in London.

Jeff. Damn old Jeff. He's everywhere.

For the first time all evening, Tracy gave way to tears. The image of Jeff with that awful girl in his arms would never leave her. *They were in our bedroom. He was about to make love to her, I know he was. For all I know he's done it hundreds of times before.* Her natural instinct was to want to claw Rebecca's eyes out, but she checked herself. *I refuse to be one of those women who blame the other woman. Why should a young girl like that respect Jeff's wedding vows if he doesn't? No, Jeff's the bad guy here. He's the liar.*

A small voice inside her dared to remind her that she'd been lying too. But Tracy snuffed it out.

Hold on to the anger, she told herself. *Don't let go.*

She couldn't barge into Gunther's house and seek comfort there. She couldn't go home. Some wild, irrational part of her wanted to knock on Alan McBride's door. He always made her feel so safe. But Dr. McBride had his own family, his own life. She knew she shouldn't intrude.

I'm on my own, thought Tracy. Then, reaching down to stroke her barely swelling belly, she edited the thought.

"Sorry, sweetheart," she said aloud. "I meant *we're* on our own. But you mustn't worry. Mommy will take care of you. Mommy will always take care of you."

JEFF WOKE THE NEXT morning feeling like he'd been hit by a truck.

Rebecca had left right after Tracy.

"I can stay if you want," she'd offered hopefully.

"No. Go back to your apartment," Jeff told her. "And go back to work tomorrow. If anyone's leaving the museum, it's me, not you."

She'd done as she was asked, for now. Jeff knew he would have to deal with the situation eventually. But one crisis at a time.

He tried Tracy's cell phone. Turned off, of course. Then he tried her friends, acquaintances, contacts from the old days. After twelve hours he had made no progress. No one had seen or heard from her, not even Gunther.

"I'm worried." Jeff poured himself a third tumbler of Laphroaig from Gunther's decanter. He couldn't face the thought of sleeping at Eaton Square—Tracy wouldn't be back anytime soon, and their bedroom had become the scene of the crime—and Gunther had offered him a bed. Secretly Jeff hoped that eventually Tracy might also turn up on Gunther's doorstep and Gunther could act as referee while they worked things out. Because they *would* work things out. The alternative was unthinkable.

"What if something's happened to her?"

"Tracy can take care of herself," said Gunther. "Besides, something *has* happened to her. She's walked in on her hubby in bed with another woman."

"We weren't in bed."

"Near enough. Who is this ghastly strumpet anyway?"

"She's not ghastly and she's not a strumpet," said Jeff. "Her name's Rebecca, but she's not important here."

Gunther arched a dubious eyebrow. "Apparently that isn't Tracy's take on things."

"Jesus, Gunther, not you too? I told you, Tracy's the one who's been having an affair, okay? Not me."

"Hmm." Gunther frowned. "Yes. You did say that."

He found it terribly hard to believe that Tracy would cheat on Jeff. On the other hand, perhaps this was only because he deeply, desperately didn't *want* to believe it. Gunther Hartog was old and wise enough to know that every human being is capable of infidelity. Rationally, one must assume that professional con artists like Tracy and Jeff were more capable than most. And Tracy had been depressed lately, not at all herself.

"She's been lying to me for months," said Jeff. "Yesterday I saw hard evidence with my own eyes. It's all on video, Gunther. CCTV. I'm not making this up. It was only after I saw the truth in black and white that I . . . I slipped, with Rebecca."

"You've never slept with her before?"

"Never! I might have been tempted," Jeff admitted. "But I never touched her."

"*Would* you have slept with her," Gunther asked, ". . . if Tracy hadn't walked in?"

"Probably," said Jeff. "Yes. I would. Tracy broke my heart, for God's sake! Not that any of that matters now anyway, because Tracy's taken off into the night." He ran a hand despairingly through his thick, dark hair. "It's a mess."

"You really think she's been sleeping with this doctor chappie?"

"I know she has," Jeff said grimly.

"But you still want her back?"

"Of course I do. She's my wife and I love her. I'm pretty

sure she loves me too, despite everything. This baby stuff has thrown us both for a loop."

"Well . . ." The old man smiled. "That being the case, you will find her. Try not to panic, old boy. Tracy will turn up."

TRACY DIDN'T TURN UP.

Not that day, not that week, not the next week.

Jeff took a leave of absence from the museum. He knocked on every door of every contact of Tracy's, however tenuous. Fences and appraisers and restorers whom they'd worked with in the past. Staff at the various prisoners' charities to which Tracy gave money. Even her personal trainer got a call from a distraught and red-eyed Jeff.

"If I'd seen her, I'd tell you, honest." Karen, a bubbly bottle blonde from Essex, couldn't imagine what would possess any woman to run out on a bloke as fit as Jeff Stevens. Even a beauty like Tracy couldn't hope to do better than that, surely? "But she ain't been 'ere. Not for weeks."

Finally Jeff stormed into 77 Harley Street.

"I want to see Dr. Alan McBride. The bastard's been screwing my wife."

All the women in the waiting room put down their copies of *Country Life* and stared at him, shocked. At least Jeff assumed they were shocked. Most of them were in their forties, hence the trip to the fertility clinic, and had had far too much Botox injected around their eyes to be able to register more than mild surprise.

"They've been having an affair and now my wife's gone missing," Jeff ranted at the hapless receptionist. "I want to know what McBride knows."

"I can see you're upset, sir."

"That's very observant of you."

"But I'm afraid Dr. McBride's—"

"Busy? Yes, I'll bet he is." Ignoring the receptionist's protests, he barged his way into the doctor's office.

The room was empty. Or so Jeff thought, until he heard voices, a man and a woman's. They were coming from behind a green curtain that had been drawn around an examination table at the back of the room. Marching over, Jeff ripped back the curtain.

He saw three things in quick succession.

The first was a woman's vagina.

The second was the same woman's face, propped up on a pillow, her expression slowly transitioning from surprise to embarrassment to outrage.

And the third was a doctor.

The doctor was about sixty-five, heavyset and, Jeff guessed, Persian. He did not look happy. More importantly, he was not Dr. Alan McBride.

"I'm so sorry," he said smoothly. "Wrong room."

Back in the waiting room, the receptionist glared at him. "As I was saying, I'm afraid Dr. McBride's *on holiday.*"

"Where?"

"I don't think that's any of your business."

"WHERE?" Jeff bellowed.

The girl crumbled. "Morocco. With his family."

So he has a family, does he? Bastard.

"When will he be back?"

The receptionist regained her composure. "I must ask you to leave now, sir. This is a doctor's office, and you're upsetting our patients."

"Tell McBride I'll be back," said Jeff. "This isn't over."

Outside, he walked along Harley Street in a daze. *Where are you, Tracy? Where in God's name are you?* He took a cab to Eaton Square as he did every day, just in case Tracy had decided to return to the house. His heart soared when he saw a woman standing in the front garden, bending low over the rosebushes, but as he approached he saw that it wasn't Tracy.

"Can I help you?"

The woman turned around. She was in her early forties, blond and had the sort of hard, overly made-up face and heavily lacquered hair that Jeff usually associated with newscasters.

"Who are you?" she asked him rudely.

"I'm Jeff Stevens. This is my house. Who are *you*?"

Newscaster lady handed him a business card. It read: *Helen Flint. Partner, Foxtons.*

"You're a real estate agent?"

"That's right. A Mrs. Tracy Stevens has instructed me to put this property on the market. My understanding was that she is the sole legal owner. Is that not correct?"

"No. It's correct," said Jeff, his heart beating faster. "The house is in Tracy's name. When did she instruct you to sell it, if you don't mind my asking?"

"This morning," Helen Flint replied briskly. Pulling out a house key from her Anya Hindmarch handbag, she began unlocking the front door. Now that Jeff had confirmed the fact that he wasn't a co-owner, he'd become an irritation.

"Did you see her?" Jeff asked. "In person?"

Ignoring him, the agent punched in a code to turn off the alarm and walked into the kitchen, taking notes. Jeff followed.

"I asked you a question," he said, grabbing her by the elbow. "Did my wife come to your offices this morning?"

Helen Flint looked at him as if he were something unpleasant that was stuck to the bottom of her shoe. "Let go of me or I'll call the police."

Jeff did as she asked. "I'm sorry. It's just that my wife's

been missing for more than two weeks. I've been terribly worried about her."

"Yes, well. Your personal problems are none of my business. But in answer to your question, your wife instructed me by telephone. We haven't met."

"Did she say where she was calling from?" asked Jeff.

"No."

"Well, did she leave a number, at least?"

"She did not. I have an e-mail address. She said that would be the best way to contact her." On the back of another card, the agent scribbled something down. "Now, if you don't mind, Mr. Stevens, I really must get on."

Jeff looked at the card. His heart plunged for a second time. It was a Hotmail address, generic and untraceable.

"If she contacts you again, Miss Flint, please ask her to get in touch with me. It's really very important."

The real estate agent gave Jeff a look that clearly translated as *Not to me it isn't.*

Jeff went back to Gunther's.

"At least you know she's alive and well." Gunther tried to get Jeff to look on the bright side at dinner.

"Alive and well and selling our house," said Jeff. "She's dismantling our life together, Gunther. Without even talking to me. That's not fair. That's not the Tracy I know."

"I suspect she's still very hurt."

"So am I!"

It pained Gunther to see Jeff fighting back tears.

"I have to find her," he said eventually. "I have to. There must be something I've missed."

REBECCA MORTIMER WAS GETTING ready for bed when the doorbell to her apartment rang.

"Who is it?"

"It's me." Jeff Stevens's gruff, gravelly voice on the other side of the door made her heart skip a beat. "Sorry to come by so late. It's important."

Rebecca opened the door.

"Jeff! What a lovely surprise."

"Can I come in?"

"Of course."

He followed her into a living room littered with half-drunk cups of coffee and books on Celtic manuscripts. Rebecca's hair was wet from the shower and the nightshirt she was wearing clung in places to her still-damp skin. Jeff tried not to notice the way it rode up when she sat down on the sofa, exposing the smooth, supple skin of her upper thighs.

"The disk you gave me," said Jeff. "The footage of Tracy with McBride. Where did you get it?"

For a moment Rebecca looked nonplussed. Then she said, "Does it matter?"

"It does to me."

She hesitated. "I can't tell you, I'm afraid."

"Why not?"

"I'd be betraying a friend. It's complicated but . . . you'll just have to trust me."

Now it was Jeff's turn to hesitate. "Do you have another copy?"

Rebecca looked surprised. "Yes. Why?"

"I destroyed the original you gave me. I was angry and I wasn't thinking straight. But I'd like to look at it again. I'm hoping there might be some clue in there, something I missed the first time that might help me find Tracy. Can I have it?"

Rebecca pouted. "All right." She'd hoped, assumed, that Jeff had come here tonight to see her. Doing her best to mask her disappointment, she walked over to her desk drawer. Pulling out a disk, she handed it to him.

"She doesn't love you, you know."

Jeff winced.

"Not like I do."

He looked at Rebecca, genuinely surprised.

"You don't love me. You barely even know me."

"That's not true."

"Yes it is. Believe me. Besides, I'm far too old for you."

"Says who?" Rebecca coiled herself around him like a cobra, kissing him with a passion that caught Jeff completely off guard. She was a gorgeous girl, but he wasn't ready for this. Gently but firmly, he pushed her away.

"I'm married," he said. "What happened between us the other day—"

"*Almost* happened," Rebecca corrected him.

"Almost happened," Jeff agreed. "Well, it shouldn't have. I was hurt and angry, and you're a beautiful girl. But I love my wife."

"Your wife's a whore!" Rebecca's sweet, innocent features twisted suddenly into an ugly mask of jealousy and rage. Jeff stepped away from her, shocked. He had never seen this side of her before.

A horrible thought struck him. As if someone had cut the cable of an elevator he was taking, he felt his stomach lurch and the hairs on the back of his neck stand on end.

"How did you get the footage?" he asked again. "Tell me!"

"I won't!" snapped Rebecca. "Can't you see you're missing the point here? Tracy's been screwing around behind your back. *That's* the headline. Who cares how I caught her. The point is I did. I did it because I care about you, Jeff. I love you!"

But Jeff was already gone, the disk clutched tightly in his hand.

AT SEVEN O'CLOCK THE next morning, Jeff sat in Victor Litchenko's basement office in Pimlico, staring at a screen.

Victor was an old friend and one of the top audiovisual experts in the London underworld. A master at doctoring footage, both images and sound, Victor Litchenko described himself as a "digital artist." Few who'd worked with him disagreed.

"It's actually not a bad piece of work," the Russian said at last, sipping at the double espresso Jeff had brought him. "The most common mistake amateurs make is to go for something too complex. But here she simply doctored the time line and changed the lighting. Very easy. Very effective."

"So it *is* Tracy?"

"It *is* Tracy. The footage itself is genuine, nothing's been superimposed or patched together. All she did was to change the time clock in the bottom right-hand corner. You think this was shot at two A.M. because there's a set of numbers there telling you so. If you strip those out, like *so*"—he tapped a few keys—"and remove the superimposed shadowing she used like . . . *so* . . ." Some more tapping. "Voilà! Now, what do you see?"

Jeff frowned. "I see the same exact thing but in the daytime. There's Tracy, coming out of the hotel. And there's her lover."

"Ah, ah, ah." Victor interrupted him. "Look again. What makes you think that's her lover?"

"Well, they're . . . She kisses him. Right there," said Jeff.

"On the cheek," said Victor. "How many women do you kiss on the cheek every day? And then what happens?" He fast-forwarded the footage in slow motion. "They embrace. A friendly hug. They part ways. Shall I tell you what that looks like to me?"

"What?" Jeff's mouth felt dry.

"It looks like two friends having lunch."

Jeff watched the footage again, slowly.

"It's the oldest trick in the book, and one of the best," said Victor. "I've used it in countless divorce cases. A man and a woman coming out of a hotel at two A.M. and embracing, after the woman's told her husband she's spending the night three hundred miles away? *That's* an affair. But edit the circumstances just a little, and what have you got?"

Jeff's voice was a whisper. "Nothing."

Victor Litchenko nodded. "Exactly. Nothing at all."

THE DESK CLERK AT the British Museum smiled warmly.

"Mr. Stevens! Welcome back."

Jeff hurried past her up to his office and pulled open the door.

His desk had been dusted but otherwise was exactly as he'd left it the day he stormed out. The day he last saw Tracy.

Rebecca's desk was empty.

All her things were gone.

IT TOOK HIM TWENTY minutes to reach Rebecca's building. Ignoring the bell to her flat—no warnings, not this time— Jeff pulled a hairpin out of his jacket pocket and expertly picked the lock.

Once inside, he slipped upstairs, ready to break into the apartment itself and confront Rebecca. The bitch had deliberately deceived him, sabotaging his marriage and playing him for a fool. When he thought about how close he'd come to sleeping with her, he felt physically sick. But that was all in the past now. Now Jeff knew the truth. Now he was going to make her pay. He was going to find Tracy, and force Rebecca to tell her the whole truth. Tracy would still be angry, of course. She had every right to be. But when she saw how desperately sad and sorry he was for ever doubting her, when she realized what a Machiavellian, twisted young woman Rebecca Mortimer really was . . .

Jeff stopped outside Rebecca's flat. The door was wide open.

He stepped inside. The place looked like a bomb had hit it, clothes and books and trash strewn everywhere.

An elderly Indian man looked surprised to see him.

"If you're looking for the young lady, she's gone, sir. Took off last night and told the security guard she won't be back." He shook his head bitterly. "No scruples, these young people. She still owed me three months' rent."

CHAPTER 5

SHE OPENED THE BRIEFCASE and looked at the money.

"Two hundred and fifty thousand?"

"Of course. As agreed. Feel free to count it."

"Oh, I will. Later. Not that I think you'd cheat me."

"I should hope not."

"But people do make mistakes."

He smiled. "I don't."

He *had* made mistakes, of course, in the past. Mistakes that had cost him dearly. The worst mistake he'd ever made had involved taking Jeff Stevens and Tracy Whitney at their word. Those two repellent swindlers had destroyed his life, once. Now, in some small way, he had returned the favor. Destroying their marriage wasn't enough. But it was a start.

"I didn't enjoy this job," the girl was saying, emptying the contents of the briefcase into her own, tattered backpack. She'd cut her hair since he last saw her in London and now wore it short and black, in a sixties-style bob. He preferred it to the look she'd adopted for Rebecca Mortimer, all long tresses and freckles. Youthful innocence didn't suit her.

"Tracy Whitney may be a bitch, but Jeff Stevens is a nice man. I felt bad for him."

The man's upper lip curled. "How you felt is not relevant."

It is to me, she felt like saying, but she didn't bother. She'd learned long ago that arguments with this man were fruitless. Despite his brilliant intellect, or perhaps because of it, he had the emotional sensitivity of an amoeba. Come to think of it, the analogy was probably unkind to amoebas.

"Anyway." He smiled that creepy smile of his, the one that always made her shiver. "You got fucked, didn't you? Women all love getting fucked, especially by Stevens. Your little titties are probably tingling right now just thinking about it, aren't they?"

She ignored him, zipping up her backpack and locking it. She had not slept with Jeff Stevens, as it happened. Rather to her annoyance, Tracy Whitney had interrupted them right at the crucial moment. But this was not information she intended to share with *him.* She'd be happy when they got back to robbing art galleries and jewelry stores.

"I mean it," she said, standing up to leave. "Any more old scores you can settle yourself."

"I'll be in touch," said the man.

FOR A MONTH AFTER Tracy left him, Jeff went to ground. He rented a flat in Rosary Gardens in South Kensington, unplugged the phone and barely went out.

After more than ten unreturned voice mails, Professor Nick Trenchard tracked him down at the flat.

"Come back to the museum," he told Jeff. "You need to keep busy."

He tried not to show how shocked he was by Jeff's appearance. Jeff wore a full beard, which made him look decades older, and his crumpled clothes hung off his skinny frame like rags on a scarecrow. Empty beer cans and take-out boxes littered the apartment, and the TV was permanently on low in the background.

"I *am* busy. You wouldn't believe how many episodes of *Homeland* I missed since I got married," Jeff quipped. But there was no laughter behind his eyes anymore.

"I'm serious, Jeff. You need a job."

"I have a job."

"You do?"

"Sure. Drinking." Jeff collapsed onto the couch and opened another beer. "I'm pretty good at it, as it happens. I'm thinking of giving myself a promotion. Maybe something in the Jack Daniel's division."

Other friends tried and failed to intervene. In the end it was Gunther Hartog who refused to take no for an answer.

"Pack your bags," he told Jeff. "We're going to the country."

Gunther had turned up at the flat in Rosary Gardens with a small army of Brazilian women who set about picking up the mountains of trash that Jeff had accumulated during his self-imposed imprisonment. When he refused to move from the couch, four of the women lifted it off the ground with Jeff still on it, while a fifth swept the floor underneath.

"I hate the country."

"Nonsense. Hampshire's beautiful."

"Beauty's overrated."

"So's alcohol poisoning. Get your suitcase, Jeff."

"I'm not going, Gunther."

"You *are* going, old boy."

"Or what?" Jeff laughed. "You're gonna ground me?"

"Don't be silly," said Gunther. "That would be ridiculous."

Jeff felt a sharp stabbing pain in his left arm. "What the . . ."

He just had time to see the syringe, and Gunther's satisfied smile, before everything went black.

IT TOOK AN ENTIRE month to dry Jeff out. By the time he was sober, and sane enough to start eating and shaving again, summer was already upon them. Gunther had hoped that perhaps Tracy would have gotten in touch by now, but there was still no word.

"You must move on with life, old boy," Gunther told Jeff. "You can't spend the rest of your days waiting for the telephone to ring. That would drive anyone mad."

They were strolling in the grounds of Gunther's seventeenth-century manor house, a thirty-acre paradise of formal gardens, lake and woodland, with a small farm attached. Gunther had been a pioneer of self-sufficiency long before it became fashionable and prided himself on the fact that he lived almost entirely off the fat of his own land. The fact that the land had been bought with stolen antiques didn't dim his view of himself as an honest farmer.

"I agree that I need to move on," said Jeff, stopping to admire a cote full of homing pigeons. He and Tracy had used one of Gunther's birds on their last job together in Amsterdam. "But I can't face going back to the museum. Rebecca ruined that for me. Along with the rest of my life."

The bitterness in his voice was painful.

"Ah, about that," said Gunther. "I managed to unearth some information about the young lady. If you're interested."

"Of course," said Jeff. In some strange way, Rebecca felt like a link to Tracy, one of the few he had left.

"Her real name is Elizabeth Kennedy."

If Jeff was surprised that "Rebecca Mortimer" had been an alias, he didn't show it. He'd spent most of his life in a world where nothing was what it seemed.

"She grew up in Wolverhampton, poor thing, raised by adoptive parents who couldn't control her from the start. Very bright, evidently, but she did poorly at school. Two expulsions by the time she turned eleven."

"My heart bleeds," said Jeff.

"At sixteen, she'd had a string of minor run-ins with the law and got her first custodial sentence."

"For?"

"Credit-card fraud. She volunteered at a local charity and downloaded details of all the donors from their computer. Then she skimmed tiny amounts, a few pence here or there, off each contribution. She made off with over thirty thousand pounds in eighteen months before anyone caught on. Like I say, she's smart. She kept it simple."

Jeff thought about the amateurishly doctored video footage of Tracy and Alan McBride and felt sick.

"After she got out of prison, she never went home again. These days she's after bigger fish. Jewel thefts mostly. She's quite the expert. Works with a partner apparently, but nobody knows who."

"What was she after at the British Museum?" Jeff asked. "Apart from me."

"We don't know. But I suspect nothing. She used the internship as cover while she pulled off other jobs in London. Her name's been linked to that hit on Theo Fennell last Christmas."

Jeff's eyes widened. The theft of half a million pounds' worth of rubies from Theo Fennell's flagship store on Old Brompton Road had been the talk of the London underworld. The job had been perfectly executed, and the police had been left without a single clue.

"Any idea where she is now?"

"None," said Gunther. "Although if I knew, I'm not sure I'd tell you. I'd hate to see you spend the rest of your days banged up for murder, old boy. Such a waste."

They strolled on, along a gravel pathway lined with cottage garden plants: roses and hollyhocks and foxgloves and lupines. *He's right,* thought Jeff. *Hampshire is beautiful. At least Gunther's little corner of it is.* He wondered if he would ever be able to truly appreciate beauty again. Without Tracy, every sense seemed dull, every pleasure blunted. It was like looking at the world through glasses permanently shaded gray.

"I do need a job," he mused. "Maybe I could try a smaller museum. Or one of the university history departments. University College London is supposed to be looking."

Gunther stopped dead in his tracks. When he spoke, he was quite stern.

"Now look here. Enough of this nonsense. You're not cut out to be a bloody librarian, Jeff. If you want my opinion it was the nonsensical decision to give up your career that caused all the problems with you and Tracy in the first place."

Jeff smiled indulgently. "But, Gunther, my 'career,' as you call it, was breaking the law. I was a thief. I ripped people off."

"Only people who deserved it," said Gunther.

"Maybe. But it still meant I lived my life on the run, always looking over my shoulder."

The older man's eyes gleamed mischievously. "I know! Wasn't it fun?"

Jeff burst out laughing. It was the first time he could remember doing so in months. It felt good.

"Just think what a comeback you could have," Gunther said, waxing enthusiastic, "now that you're a bona fide specialist in antiquities. You have the contacts and the brains. You can talk the talk and walk the walk. Nobody else out there can do that, Jeff. You'd be unique! Have you any idea what some of these wealthy private collectors are willing to pay? These are people who are used to buying whatever they want: homes, planes, yachts, diamonds, lovers, influence. It *incenses* them when they covet objects that simply aren't for sale. Unique pieces of history. Objects that *only you* can track down and acquire."

Jeff allowed the appeal of the idea to wash over him for a moment.

"You could name your price," said Gunther. "What do you want, Jeff? What do you *really* want?"

The only thing I want is Tracy back, thought Jeff. *I'm just like Gunther's collectors. I can have it all. But the one thing I really want, no one can give me.*

Gunther watched Jeff's face begin to fall. Realizing he was losing him, that the moment was passing, he made his move.

"It just so happens I have exactly the job to get you started," he said, clapping his bony hands tightly onto Jeff's shoulders. "How would you like a lovely little jaunt to Rome?"

CHAPTER 6

ROBERTO KLIMT STEPPED OUT onto the balcony of his sumptuous apartment on the Via Veneto and watched the sun setting over his beautiful city.

Roberto Klimt considered himself a lover of beauty in all its forms. Tonight's wine-red sun, bleeding into the Rome skyline. The Basquiat portrait hanging above his bed, showing two simian faces in a riot of yellow and red and blue. The perfect curve of the rent boy's buttocks awaiting him in bed at his country house in Sabina, forty minutes outside the city. Roberto Klimt enjoyed and savored and delighted in them all.

I have them because I deserve them. Because I am a true artist.

Only true artists should be rewarded with true beauty.

Fifty years old and breathtakingly vain, with thick, dyed blond hair, a full-lipped, cruel, sensual mouth and the amber-yellow eyes of a snake, Roberto Klimt was an art dealer, businessman and pedophile, although not necessarily in that order. He made his first ten million in crooked real estate deals, cutting in the corrupt local police on a piece of the action from day one. The next ninety million came from art, a business for which Roberto Klimt had a uniquely brilliant commercial eye.

Roberto Klimt knew what beauty was, but he also knew how to sell it. As a result, he lived like a latter-day Roman emperor—rich beyond his wildest dreams, debauched, corrupt and answerable to no one.

A late-summer breeze chilled him slightly. Frowning, he withdrew from the balcony into his palatial drawing room, closing the tall sash windows behind him.

"Bring me a blanket!" he commanded, to no one in particular. Roberto Klimt kept a fleet of servants in all his homes. He was never quite sure what any one of them did, but he found that if one had enough milling around, one's desires were always promptly catered to. "And bring me the bowl. I want to look at the damned bowl."

Moments later, a pretty, dark-haired boy with long eyelashes and an adorably dimpled chin presented his master with a saffron-yellow cashmere throw from Loro Piana—with fall approaching, Roberto Klimt only tolerated an autumnal palette in his soft furnishings—and a locked, Plexiglas case containing a small, solid gold bowl.

Roberto Klimt unlocked the case with a key he kept on a platinum chain around his neck and cupped the bowl lovingly in his hands, the way a mother might cradle a newborn child.

No bigger than a modern-day dessert bowl, and entirely unadorned by any carving or decoration, the bowl was an object lesson in simplicity. Burnished and dazzling, its sides worn thin and smooth by two thousand years' worth of hands caressing it, it seemed to Roberto to glow with some sort of magical power.

"This belonged to the Emperor Nero, you know?" he purred to the boy who'd delivered it. "His lips would have touched it just here. Right where mine are now."

Roberto Klimt pressed his wet, fleshy mouth against the metal, leaving a glistening trail of saliva in its wake.

"Would you like to try?"

"No, thank you, sir. I wouldn't feel comfortable."

"TRY!" Roberto Klimt commanded.

Blushing, the boy did as he was asked.

"You see?" Klimt smiled, satisfied. "You've just touched greatness. How does it feel?"

The boy stammered helplessly.

"Never mind." Klimt dismissed him with a curt wave. "Philistine," he muttered under his breath. This was the cross that Roberto Klimt had to bear, to be surrounded constantly by lesser mortals, people incapable of grasping the true nature of beauty.

Still, he consoled himself, it was the cross borne by all great artists. *A noble suffering.*

Tomorrow, Roberto Klimt would leave Rome for his country house. Nero's bowl would follow a few days later. Klimt employed an elite private security team to protect his treasures. The head of this team had informed Roberto a few days ago about a rumored plot to rob the Via Veneto apartment.

"It's nothing concrete. Just rumors and whispers. Some hotshot foreign thief's in town apparently. He likes the sound of your collection."

"I'll bet he does!" Roberto Klimt laughed. A thief would have a better chance of infiltrating Fort Knox than of circumventing his state-of-the-art security. Even so, he'd been guided by his expert's advice and agreed to move Nero's bowl and a couple more of his rarest pieces to Sabina. The only private residence in Italy better protected than Roberto Klimt's Rome apartment was Roberto Klimt's country estate. He would be there himself to oversee the bowl's installation in his newly redesigned "Treasures Room," and would enjoy the rent boy's body while he awaited its arrival.

The boy was eighteen and had been paid handsomely in advance for his services. Roberto Klimt preferred them younger, and unwilling—feigned submission was a poor substitute for the real thing. But after the unfortunate incident with the two Roma Gypsy boys who'd gone and jumped off a building after an alleged encounter with the art dealer, Roberto Klimt had been forced to become more cautious.

Damned Gypsies. Human vermin, the lot of them.

There were those in Rome's high society who made apologies for them. Liberals, who excused their ugliness and filth and thievery on the grounds that they were poor. Roberto Klimt despised such people. Roberto had been poor himself once and considered it a grave stain on his reputation and good name.

He would rather die than go back to that life.

JEFF STEVENS CHECKED IN to the Hotel de Russie under the name Anthony Duval. Gunther gave him the brief.

"Anthony Duval, dual French/American citizenship, thirty-six years old. Lectures at the Sorbonne and acts as an art consultant to numerous wealthy collectors in Paris and New York. He's in Rome to make some acquisitions."

"I hope Anthony likes the good things in life?" asked Jeff.

"Naturally."

"How does he feel about the Hotel de Russie?"

"He only ever books the Nijinsky Suite."

"I like him already."

The girl at the check-in desk was a knockout, dark and voluptuous, like a 1950s Italian film star. "Your suite is ready for you, Mr. Duval. Would you like some help with your luggage? Or . . . anything else?"

For a split second Jeff considered the promising possibilities implied by "anything else." But he restrained himself. The job Gunther had sent him on was complicated and dangerous. He couldn't afford any distractions.

"No thank you. Just the key."

The Nijinsky Suite was spectacular. On the top floor of the hotel, it boasted an enormous king-size bed and flat-screen TV, a marble, mosaic-tiled bathroom with a sunken bathtub, a living room and office area stuffed with priceless antiques, and a terrace with breathtaking views of the Pincio and the rooftops of Rome. Jeff showered, changed into linen trousers and a duck-egg-blue shirt that perfectly complemented his gray eyes and headed for the Russie's famous "secret garden."

"Will you be dining with us tonight, Mr. Duval?"

"Not tonight."

Jeff ordered a double gin and tonic and strolled through the garden. The man he was waiting for sat quietly beneath the bougainvillea, reading *La Repubblica* newspaper. He wore a handlebar mustache and sideburns, and even sitting down, he was, Jeff could see, unusually tall. Not exactly the gray man in the crowd he'd been hoping for.

"Marco?"

"Mr. Duval. A pleasure."

Jeff sat down. "You're here alone? I was expecting two of you."

"Ah, yes. My partner experienced an unexpected delay. We will meet him tomorrow at the foot of the Spanish Steps at ten, if that's convenient?"

It wasn't convenient. It was irritating. Jeff disliked working with other people. With the exception of Tracy, he lived by the rule that you could never trust a con artist and preferred jobs that he could pull off alone. Unfortunately, robbing Roberto Klimt of the Emperor Nero's bowl, the centerpiece of one of the most closely guarded private collections in the world, did not fit into that category.

"Marco and Antonio are the best," Gunther Hartog had assured him. "They're both world class at what they do."

And what exactly do they do, Gunther? Jeff thought now. *Hang out in bars looking like the strongman from a traveling circus and blow off important meetings?* Worse than that, someone had obviously been bragging about the planned heist. Jeff had heard whispers almost the moment he got off the plane. He knew he hadn't said anything, and Gunther was far too discreet. Which only left one of these clowns.

Jeff waited for a woman to walk by before whispering in Marco's ear.

"Everything has to be ready by tomorrow night. You both need to know your roles inside out. Wednesday is our one shot to do this, you do realize that?"

"Of course."

"There can be no more delays."

"Don't worry, my friend." The mustachioed man smiled broadly. "We have completed many such jobs in Roma in the past. Very many."

"Not like this you haven't," said Jeff. "I'll see you both at ten. Don't be late."

LATER THAT NIGHT, IN bed, he turned on his laptop and reread the file Gunther had sent him on Roberto Klimt. Revulsion and anger swept through him again, hardening his resolve.

A notorious predator, Klimt had sexually abused and raped two young Gypsy boys two years ago. Posing as a wealthy mentor who could offer them an education and a better life, he had paid the boys' mother a thousand euros to have them accompany him on a tour of Europe. The older child reported Klimt to the authorities on their return to Rome, but thanks to the art dealer's connections and deep pockets, the case never made it to trial. A few weeks later, rejected by their own families thanks to some obscure Roma honor code, the boys leaped from the roof of a tenement building to their deaths. They were ten and twelve years old.

Jeff would never forget Wilbur Trawick, the disgusting old tarot-card reader at his uncle Willie's carnival. Wilbur had abused countless carnie kids before he made a pass at Jeff, who had ended the old man's career with a deftly placed knee to the groin. Wilbur Trawick had been grotesque, but he had never wielded the kind of power of a man like Roberto Klimt. Klimt knew that the law couldn't touch him.

But I can, thought Jeff. *I'm going to hit him where it hurts.*

He prayed Gunther was right about Marco and Antonio, that they wouldn't let him down. Jeff's plan was bold and daring, but it required absolute precision timing, and it could not be done alone.

Klimt's security team was SAS standard. Thanks to somebody's loose lips, they already knew that Nero's bowl was a target.

Jeff felt the adrenaline begin to pump through his veins.

It was on.

"HIS NAME IS JEFF STEVENS and he's posing as an art dealer."

Roberto Klimt was irritated. He was supposed to be at his country house by now, enjoying a professional blow job from his beautiful new boy. Instead he was still in Rome, locked in a meeting with the head of his security team, a fat, middle-aged man with sweat patches the size of dinner plates under each arm.

"He's checked in at the Russie under the name 'Duval.' "

"So? Have him arrested," Klimt snapped. "I don't have time for this nonsense."

"Unfortunately he has not yet committed a crime. The police have an irritating reluctance to arrest apparently innocent foreign citizens going about their business."

"Are you tailing him?"

The security expert looked affronted. "Of course. It appears he *is* planning to hit the apartment. He met with one of the top safe crackers in Southern Europe yesterday, Marco Rizzolio."

Roberto Klimt thought for a while.

"Should we move the bowl today? As an additional precaution?"

"I don't think that's necessary. I want to make sure the transit is totally secure. Angelo's sick, so I'm still vetting the new driver. But we can move it tomorrow. That's a day earlier than planned and should be enough to throw off our Mr. Stevens and his friend."

Roberto Klimt stretched and yawned, like a bored cat. "I'll stay another night too, in that case. I don't like to leave it here in the apartment without me. I'll also put in a call to my friends at the police department. See if we can't nudge them a little."

"That won't be necessary, Mr. Klimt. My team and I can handle this. To be frank, police involvement may do more harm than good."

"I don't doubt that you are taking the necessary precautions. But I want to see this Jeff Stevens character spend the rest of his life in an Italian jail. For that, we need the Polizia. It will all be off the record, don't worry."

He picked up the phone and began to dial.

JEFF CALLED GUNTHER.

"I have a bad feeling about this job. Something's wrong."

"My dear boy, you always have a bad feeling the night before. It's stage fright, nothing more."

"Your guys, Marco and Antonio. You trust them?"

"Completely. Why?"

Jeff told Gunther about the rumors that were sweeping through Rome's underworld. "Someone's leaking like a sieve. I've had to change the plan twice already. You should see that apartment! Dogs, laser tracking, armed guards. Klimt sleeps with the bowl at night like it's his teddy bear. They're waiting for us."

"Good," said Gunther.

"Easy for you to say."

"Do the police know anything?"

"No. All quiet on that front."

"Even better."

"Yeah, but we need to move quickly. Even the Italians will wake up and smell the espresso eventually."

"So when . . . ?"

"Tomorrow. I just hope Antonio's up to it. He seems so laissez-faire about the whole thing, but if anyone recognizes him in that car . . ."

"You'll be fine, Jeff."

Gunther hung up. Jeff wished he felt reassured.

You can still pull out, he told himself. *It's not too late.*

Then he thought about the two little Roma boys. It was too late for them.

Go to hell, Roberto Klimt. Tomorrow's the day.

"TOMORROW'S THE DAY."

"You're sure?"

"I'm sure."

Police chief Luigi Valaperti tapped his desk nervously. His source had better be right. Roberto Klimt was not a man Chief Valaperti wished to disappoint, under any circumstances. His predecessor had retired three years ago to a palatial apartment in Venice, bought and paid for by the art dealer. Chief Valaperti already had his eye on a villa outside Pisa. Or more accurately, his wife did. He and his mistress preferred the two-bedroom love nest overlooking the Colosseum, a deal at under two million euros. *Klimt probably has bigger dry-cleaning bills.* But Luigi Valaperti wasn't greedy.

"His henchmen are doing the legwork," the source went on. "You can catch them in the act, make yourself a hero, then pick up Stevens at the airport later. He'll be trying to board the eight P.M. BA flight to London."

"Without the bowl?"

"He'll have the bowl. Or what he thinks is the bowl. We know the drop-off location, so you can plant a decoy."

Chief Valaperti frowned. "And exactly *how* did you come by this information? How do I know we can trust . . ."

The line went dead.

ROBERTO KLIMT GAZED OUT of the tinted window of his armored town car as they left the city behind. The hills around Rome, dotted with poplar trees and firs and ancient villas whose terra-cotta-tiled roofs balanced precariously atop crumbling stone walls, had barely changed since the Emperor Nero's day. Cupping the gold bowl lovingly in his hands, Klimt imagined that legendary, insane, all-powerful man making this very same journey, leaving the stresses of Rome behind for the peace and pleasures of the countryside. Roberto Klimt felt a sublime kinship with Nero in this moment. The priceless gold artifact in his lap belonged to him for a reason. It was *meant* to be his. The pleasure and pride that that one bowl brought him was immense.

He wondered when, exactly, "Anthony Duval" and his accomplices would make their move on his apartment. Roberto Klimt imagined the scene. The alarms ringing out across the Via Veneto, the metal grilles slamming shut, the police, already waiting in force in the surrounding streets and alleyways, moving in for the kill. He smiled.

Chief Valaperti was a stupid man, but he knew on which side his bread was buttered. He had wisely diverted considerable resources to catching these vicious thieves, even though he knew that the bowl itself was safe. Roberto Klimt was looking forward to meeting the audacious Mr. Jeff Stevens in person. Perhaps at his trial? Or later, in the privacy of Jeff's prison cell. Apparently Stevens had outwitted some of the finest galleries, jewelers and museums in the world during his long criminal career, along with a prestigious smattering of private collectors.

He met his match with me, Roberto Klimt thought smugly.

"Not long to go now, sir." The driver's voice rang out through the intercom. Irritatingly. Klimt's usual driver, Angelo, would never have been so impertinent as to interrupt his master's thoughts with an unsolicited comment. Roberto Klimt wondered where his security chief had dug up this specimen. "We've been lucky with the traffic."

At exactly that moment, two police cars, their sirens wailing, drew up behind them.

"What on earth . . . ?"

Klimt gripped the car door for dear life as his driver accelerated, so suddenly that the bowl almost flew onto the floor.

"Are you out of your mind?" he roared. "Pull over! It's the police."

Ignoring him, the driver weaved insanely across two lanes of traffic, setting off a cacophony of beeping.

"I said pull over, you imbecile!"

Klimt caught the panicked expression on the driver's face as he turned sharply right off the autoroute. They were going so fast that for one awful moment Roberto Klimt thought that the car was about to flip over, killing them both. Instead, one of the police cars shot past them and pulled directly in front, forcing the driver to brake. They skidded to a halt on the side of the road.

"The bowl!" yelled the driver. He'd opened the partition to the backseat and was leaning through it menacingly. "Give me the bowl."

"Never!" Klimt cowered on the backseat, covering the bowl with his body like Gollum protecting his precious ring.

"For heaven's sake. Give it to me! We don't have much time."

A huge policeman yanked open the driver's door. After a brief struggle, the driver was knocked out by a sharp blow to the back of the head. Roberto Klimt let out a frightened squeal as the unconscious man slumped down on top of him.

"Are you all right, Mr. Klimt?"

Two other policemen had appeared at the window. There were three of them in all.

Klimt nodded.

"Sorry to panic you like that," said the giant. "But we learned at the last minute that Jeff Stevens had changed his plan. Your driver's real name is Antonio Maldini. He's a con artist, quite brilliant. Interpol has been after him for a decade."

"But my security people are the best in Italy . . ." Klimt spluttered. "This man was thoroughly vetted."

The policeman shrugged. "Like I say, Maldini's a pro. Faking a background check's nothing for this dude. Nor is hard-core violence. Antonio Maldini's a known sadist. He'd have beaten you to a pulp and left you for dead before he took that bowl."

Roberto Klimt shivered.

"We picked up his accomplice, Marco Rizzolio at dawn this morning," said the giant policeman.

"And Jeff Stevens?"

The big man glanced at his partners and frowned.

"We don't have him yet, sir. We raided his hotel this morning, but it appears he was one step ahead of us."

"He won't get far, Mr. Klimt," one of the other cops added, watching the art dealer's expression darken. "Chief Valaperti has set up roadblocks around the city. We have an alert out at the airport."

Antonio Maldini made a low, groaning sound. He was clearly beginning to come around. One of the cops handcuffed him and, with his colleagues' help, bundled him into the back of one of the police cars.

"Chief Valaperti's asked us to escort you back to the city," said the giant. "We'll need you to make a statement. And I'm afraid the artifact the gang was after will have to be impounded as evidence."

"I don't care about that," muttered Klimt. "Just catch that bastard Stevens."

"Oh, we will, sir. Don't worry. His entire plan's just blown up in his face, Mr. Klimt. He won't get away now."

THE DRIVE BACK TO Rome took less than forty minutes. Antonio Maldini, still handcuffed to the door, slipped in and out of consciousness beside Roberto Klimt as they pulled up in convoy outside the police headquarters building on the Piazza di Spagna.

"Wait here please, sir." One of the policemen carefully

took the gold bowl with a gloved hand, slipping it into a clear plastic evidence bag. "Chief Valaperti would like to escort you inside himself. He's arranged a private interview room."

"What about him?" Roberto Klimt gestured nervously toward Maldini.

"He can't hurt you now, Mr. Klimt." The policeman glanced smugly at the handcuffed man. "Although if you'd prefer to have one of my men wait with you . . ."

"No, no." Roberto Klimt was too vain to admit to feeling threatened, especially in front of such a good-looking young cop. "That won't be necessary. Just hurry up, would you? I'd like to get this over with."

"Of course."

The three policemen hurried into the building, locking the car behind them. Roberto Klimt heard the doors click. He looked uneasily at the man slumped beside him. A few hours ago, Antonio Maldini had planned to beat and rob him, leaving him for dead by the roadside. The big policeman's words came back to him. *He's a con artist. Quite brilliant. A sadist too.*

Roberto Klimt's nerves returned. Antonio Maldini had already outwitted his security team. Was it really beyond him to get himself out of a pair of handcuffs? *He might wake up and overpower me. He might take me hostage! He's a desperate man after all.*

Five minutes passed. Then ten.

No sign of the policemen, or Chief Valaperti. It was getting hot in the car. Maldini was groaning, muttering about the bowl. Soon he would be fully awake.

This is ridiculous.

Roberto Klimt tried to open the door, only to find it was locked from the inside as well as the outside. He flipped the unlock button. Nothing happened.

Feeling his panic build, he attempted to scramble into the front seat. With his blond hair flapping and his tie askew, he knew he looked ridiculous with his backside wedged between the back and front of the car, but he didn't care. Collapsing at last into the driver's seat, he discovered that that door didn't open either.

"Let me out!" He hammered on the windows, to the amused astonishment of passersby. "I'm trapped! For God's sake, let me out!"

THE THREE POLICEMEN WALKED casually out of the side door of the headquarters building. They walked a few blocks together before shaking hands, parting ways and evaporating into the city.

All three of them were smiling.

CHIEF VALAPERTI WAS STILL in his car outside Roberto Klimt's Via Veneto apartment when he got the call.

"He's *what*?" The color drained from Valaperti's face. "I don't understand. In one of *our* cars? That's not possible."

"It was definitely Klimt, sir. He was in there for more than an hour. Right outside headquarters, yes. Hundreds of people saw him, but they assumed he was some madman we'd picked up. By the time it was reported to us, he was delirious with heatstroke. He kept saying something about a bowl . . ."

GUNTHER HARTOG DABBED AWAY tears of laughter with a monogrammed linen handkerchief.

"So you just sauntered off into the street, with Nero's bowl tucked under your arm? How marvelous."

"Marco and Antonio were faultless on the day," said Jeff.

He was sitting on the red Knoll sofa at Gunther's country house, enjoying a well-earned glass of claret.

"I told you they were good."

"I felt bad for the poor driver, though. What a pro! He knew what was happening right away. Never slowed down for a second when we tried to pull him over. Even when we ran him off the road, he was trying to get Klimt to give him the bowl so he could get it to safety. But the old fool wouldn't let go of it."

"I do love that you left him outside the Polizia di Stato building. A wonderful theatrical flourish, if I may say so."

"Thanks." Jeff grinned. "I thought so. Tracy would have loved it."

Her name had come to his lips unbidden. It hung in the air now like a ghost, sucking all the celebration and bonhomie out of the atmosphere in an instant.

"I don't suppose you've heard anything?"

Gunther Hartog shook his head sadly. For a few moments a heavy silence fell.

"Well," Gunther said at last. "My client, the Hungarian collector, couldn't be more delighted with his acquisition. I wired our Italian friends their cut last night. And here, my dear boy, is yours."

He handed Jeff a check. It was from Coutts, the private investment bank, in his name, and it had an obscenely large number written on it.

"No thanks." Jeff handed it back.

Gunther looked perplexed. "What do you mean 'no thanks.' It's yours. You've earned it."

"I don't need it," said Jeff.

"I'm not sure I see what 'need' has to do with it."

"All right, then. I don't want it." Jeff sounded more angry than he'd intended to. "Sorry, Gunther. But money doesn't help me. It doesn't mean anything. Not anymore."

Gunther gave a nod of understanding. "You must give it away, then," he said. "If it can't help you, I'm sure it can help someone else. But that's your decision, Jeff. I can't keep it."

TWO WEEKS LATER, AN article appeared in *Leggo*'s Rome edition under the headline TINY CHARITY RECEIVES RE-MARKABLE GIFT.

> Roma Relief, an almost unknown nonprofit or-
> ganization devoted to helping Gypsy families
> in some of Rome's worst slums, received an
> anonymous donation of more than half a mil-
> lion euros.
>
> The mystery donor asked that the money be
> used to set up a fund in memory of Nico and
> Fabio Trattini, two Roma brothers who died in
> an accidental fall from a condemned building
> two years ago.
>
> "We're incredibly grateful," Nicola Gianotti,
> Roma Relief's founder told us in an emotional
> interview. "Overwhelmed, really. Thank God
> for the kindness of strangers."

CHAPTER 7

THREE MONTHS LATER
STEAMBOAT SPRINGS, COLORADO

*T*RACY STOOD ON THE deck of her new home and gazed out at the mountains. She'd chosen the place for its privacy, set back off a private road in the hills above the quaint town of Steamboat Springs, and for the views, which were breathtaking. The snowcapped Rockies loomed like protective giants against a vast sky, cloudless and blue even on this cold October morning. Tracy could smell wood smoke and pine, and hear the distant whinnying of the horses in the fields.

It's a far cry from my childhood in New Orleans, she thought, stroking her swollen belly protectively. Tracy's father had been a mechanic and her mother a housewife, and although Tracy had been very happy, the Whitneys had never had much money. As a little girl growing up in the city, Tracy had always dreamed of wide-open spaces and ponies. Or somewhere just like Steamboat Springs. *You're a lucky girl, Amy. You're going to grow up here and it's going to be perfect.*

It had not been an easy decision, returning to the States. Tracy hadn't been back since the day she set sail on the *QE2* from New York, to start a new life in Europe. Released from prison early, having spent years in the Southern Louisiana Penitentiary for Women for a crime she didn't commit, Tracy had tried hard to go straight. But she quickly learned that very few people were prepared to give an ex-con a second chance. Her old employer, the Philadelphia Trust and Fidelity Bank, had laughed in her face when she attempted to get her old job back. Tracy was a brilliant computer expert with a first-class education. But she found even menial cleaning jobs hard to come by, and even harder to keep. As soon as anything was stolen or damaged, Tracy would get the blame and find herself fired. Without a means to support herself, she grew bitter and desperate. It was desperation that drove her to her first job as a jewel thief, robbing a thoroughly unpleasant woman by the name of Lois Bellamy.

That was the job during which she had first met Jeff Stevens. He conned her out of Lois Bellamy's stolen jewels. Furious, Tracy had stolen them back. So began a rivalry that became an attraction that became love. *The love of my life.* Jeff Stevens had made Tracy Whitney's life an adventure, a wild roller-coaster ride of adrenaline, excitement and fun.

But all rides must come to an end. Tracy had trusted Jeff utterly, but he had betrayed her utterly, shattering that trust and, with it, Tracy's heart. The image of Jeff in the bedroom with Rebecca was seared permanently in Tracy's brain, like a cattle brand.

She still loved him. She would always love him. But she knew she could never go back. Not to Jeff, not to London, not to any of it. From now on it would just be her and the baby. *My baby. My Amy.*

Right on cue, Tracy's daughter gave a whopping kick. Tracy laughed out loud. *You're trying to break out of prison, aren't you, my darling? Just like Mommy did.*

Tracy had learned at her twenty-week scan that her unborn child was a girl, and she amazed herself by bursting into sobs of relief. A boy would have reminded her too much of Jeff. She decided at once to name her daughter Amy, after Amy Brannigan, the warden's daughter at the penitentiary whom Tracy had come to love like her own.

Amy Doris Schmidt.

It was a good name, a fitting blend of the past and the future. Doris was the name of Tracy's beloved mother. Doris Whitney would never know her granddaughter, but her memory would live on in Amy. Schmidt was the family name Tracy had chosen for her new identity, a tribute to dear old Otto Schmidt, her father's business partner back in New Orleans. Tracy had adopted countless alter egos over the last ten years, but this one was different. The name she chose now would be hers and Amy's for life. Tracy Whitney no longer existed. Nor did Tracy Stevens.

My name is Tracy Schmidt. My husband, Karl, a wealthy German industrialist, was killed in a freak skiing accident in February, shortly after Amy was conceived. I came to America to start a new life with our daughter. Karl always loved the mountains. I just know he would have adored Steamboat.

With Tracy's computer background and long experience as a con artist, forging a new identity had been easy. Passports, credit history, medical records and Social Security cards—all could be created and altered at the click of a mouse. Telling Amy the truth, as she would have to one day—that would be the hard part. But Tracy would simply have to cross that bridge when she came to it. For now, Mrs. Tracy Schmidt had enough on her plate, decorating the nursery—Tracy had gone for a whimsical, Flower Fairies theme—and attending pregnancy yoga classes and doctor's appointments down in town. Between that and managing the ranch—Tracy's luxurious log-cabin home came with over a hundred acres of private land—she had little time to dwell on the future. Or the past.

"Knock knock. Don't suppose you've got any coffee perkin', ma'am?"

Tracy spun around. Blake Carter, her ranch manager, was in his early fifties but looked older, thanks to countless hard winters and hot summers spent outdoors in the mountains. Blake was a widower and handsome in a craggy, rugged sort of way. He was also shy, hardworking and relentlessly old school. Tracy had been trying for months, but nothing would stop Blake from addressing her as "ma'am."

"Morning, Blake." She smiled. Tracy liked Blake Carter. He was quiet and strong and he reminded her of her father. She knew she could trust him not to ask questions about her background, or to gossip about her in the village. She knew she could trust him, period. "There's plenty in the pot. Help yourself."

She walked back into the kitchen. "Waddled" might be a more accurate word. At over eight months pregnant, Tracy's belly was enormous and in the last two weeks her ankles had started to swell terribly. Come to think of it, everything had started to swell. Her fingers looked like five sausages sewn together and her face was as puffy and round as a Dutch cheese. The effect was made worse by the ultrashort haircut she'd adopted for her new persona as Mrs. Schmidt. Tracy had thought it looked so chic in the salon, when she was still slim and barely showing. Now it made her feel like a lesbian prison warden.

"Are you all right, ma'am?"

Blake Carter watched anxiously as Tracy slowed down, grabbing her belly.

"Yes, I think so. Amy's been trying to break out of there all morning. She's got quite a kick on her now. I . . . *ow!*"

Doubling over, Tracy grabbed the kitchen counter. Moments later, to her intense embarrassment, her water broke all over the newly tiled floor.

"Oh my God!"

"I'll drive you to the hospital," said Blake. He had no children of his own but had delivered countless calves, and unlike Tracy, he wasn't remotely embarrassed.

"No, no," said Tracy. "I'm having a home birth. If you wouldn't mind just calling my doula and asking her to get up here? Her number's on the refrigerator."

Blake Carter frowned disapprovingly. "With all due respect, ma'am, your water just broke. You should be in a hospital. With a doctor, not a Dolittle."

"Dou-*la*." Tracy grinned.

She was determined to have a drug-free birth and to do it herself. Being a mother was the one role she had waited for her whole life. She needed to be good at it. Capable. In control. She needed to prove to herself that she could manage alone.

"I'd really feel better taking you to the hospital, ma'am. As your husband . . . you know . . . ain't with you."

"It's all right, Blake, truly." Tracy was touched by his concern and grateful for his calm, strong presence. But she'd planned for this. She was ready. "Just call Mary. She'll know what to do."

THE SCREAMS WERE GETTING LOUDER.

Blake Carter stood outside Tracy's bedroom feeling increasingly alarmed. He knew a woman's first delivery could take awhile. But he also knew that once the water has gone, the baby needs to get on out. Mrs. Schmidt had been in there for hours. And the noises she was making weren't normal. Blake Carter had only known Tracy Schmidt a short while, but it was long enough to see that she was a tough cookie, physically and emotionally. It simply wasn't like her to holler like that.

As for the do-lally, Mary, the girl looked like she was barely out of high school.

Another scream. This time there was fear in it. *Enough's enough.*

Blake Carter burst into the room. Tracy was lying on the bed. The entire sheet and mattress were soaked with blood. The girl, Mary, hovered beside her, white-faced and panicked.

"Jesus Christ," said Blake.

"I'm sorry!" The doula had tears in her eyes. "I . . . I didn't know what to do. I know some bleeding can be normal but I . . ."

Blake Carter pushed the girl aside. Scooping Tracy up into his arms, he staggered toward the door. "If she dies, or the baby dies, it's on your head."

TRACY WAS LYING ON the floor of the plane. It was a 747 from the Air France fleet headed for Amsterdam and it was bumping around like crazy. *Must be a storm.* She was supposed to do something. *Steal some diamonds? Tape up a pallet?* She couldn't remember. Sweat was pouring off her. Then the pain came again. Not pain, agony, like somebody cutting out her internal organs with a serrated kitchen knife. She screamed wildly.

In the front seat of the truck, Blake Carter fought back tears.

"It's all right honey," he told her. "We're almost there."

TRACY WAS IN A white room. She heard voices.

The prison doctor in Louisiana. *"The cuts and bruises are bad but they'll heal . . . she's lost the baby."*

Her mother, on the telephone, the night that she died. *"I love you very, very much, Tracy."*

Jeff, in the safe house in Amsterdam, screaming at her. *"For Christ's sake, Tracy, open your eyes! How long have you been like this?"*

"HOW LONG HAS SHE been like this?" the young doctor barked at Blake Carter.

"Waters broke about four hours ago."

"Four *hours*?" For a moment Blake thought the doctor was about to hit him. "Why the hell did you wait so long?"

"I didn't realize what was happening. I wasn't . . ." The words caught in the old cowboy's throat. Tracy was already being wheeled into the operating room. She was still screaming and delirious. She kept calling for someone named Jeff. "Will she be okay?"

The doctor looked him square in the eye. "I don't know. She's lost a huge amount of blood. There are some signs of eclampsia."

Blake Carter's eyes widened. "But, she'll live, right? And the baby . . . ?"

"The baby should live," said the doctor. "Excuse me."

THE PAIN WAS THERE, and then it was gone.

Tracy wasn't afraid. She was ready to die, ready to see her mother again. She felt suffused with an immense sense of peace.

She had heard the doctor. Her baby would live.

That was all that mattered in the end.

Amy.

Tracy's last thought was of Jeff Stevens and how much she loved him. Would he find out about his daughter eventually? Would he come looking for her?

It's out of my hands now.

Time to let go.

BLAKE CARTER COLLAPSED IN sobs in the young doctor's arms.

"I shouldn't have been so rough on you earlier," the doctor said. "This wasn't your fault."

"It *was* my fault. I should have insisted. I should have driven her here right away."

"Hindsight is twenty-twenty, Mr. Carter. The point is, you brought her here. You saved her life."

Blake Carter turned to look at Tracy. Heavily sedated after her emergency cesarean—she'd needed a blood transfusion while they stitched her back together—she was only now starting to come around. Her baby had been taken to the ICU for tests, but the doctor had assured Blake that everything looked good.

"My baby . . . ," Tracy called out weakly, her eyes still closed.

"Your baby's just fine, Mrs. Schmidt," said the doctor. "Try to rest a little longer."

"Where is she?" Tracy insisted. "I want to see my daughter."

The doctor smiled at Blake Carter. "Will you tell her or should I?"

"Tell me what?" Tracy sat up, wide-awake now and panicked. "What's happened? Is she okay? Where's Amy?"

"You might want to rethink that name." Blake Carter chuckled softly.

Just then a nurse walked in, holding the swaddled infant in her arms. Beaming, she handed the bundle to Tracy.

"Congratulations, Mrs. Schmidt. It's a boy!"

PART TWO

CHAPTER 8

INSPECTOR JEAN RIZZO OF Interpol stared down at the dead girl's face.

It was black and bloated, from the strangulation and from the drugs. Heroin. A huge amount of it. Track marks ran up both her arms, an advancing army of red pinpricks, harbingers of death. Her skirt was pushed up around her hips, her underwear had been removed, and her legs were splayed grotesquely.

"He positioned her after death?"

It wasn't really a question. Inspector Jean Rizzo knew how this killer operated. But the pathologist nodded anyway.

"Raped?"

"Hard to say. Plenty of vaginal lesions, but in her line of work . . ."

The girl was a prostitute, like all the others. *I must stop calling her "the girl."* Jean Rizzo chided himself. He checked his notes. *Alissa. Her name was Alissa.*

"No semen traces?"

The pathologist shook her head. "No, nothing. No prints, no saliva, no hair. Her nails have been cut. We'll keep looking, but . . ."

But we won't find anything. I know.

This was another of the killer's signatures. He cut the girls' nails after death, presumably to remove any traces of his DNA if they'd fought back. But there was more to it than that. The guy was a neat freak. He arranged his victims in degrading sexual positions, but he always brushed their hair, cut their nails, and left the crime scenes spotless. He'd been known to make beds and bag up trash. And he always left a Bible next to the corpse.

Today he'd chosen a verse from Romans:

> *For the wrath of God is revealed from heaven against all ungodliness and unrighteousness of men, who hold the truth in unrighteousness.*

Eleven murders, in ten different cities, over nine years. Police forces in six different countries had spent millions of dollars and thousands of man-hours trying to catch this bastard. And where had it gotten them? Nowhere.

Somewhere out there, a fastidious Christian with a grudge against hookers was laughing his sick ass off.

Jean Rizzo stared out of the window. It was a rainy April morning and the view from Alissa Armand's dingy studio apartment was relentlessly depressing. Alissa lived in an HLM, France's version of a housing project, in the rough northern Parisian suburb of Corbeil-Essonnes. Unemployment in this neighborhood ran at well over 50 percent, and the wreckage of addiction was everywhere. Beneath Alissa's window was a litter-strewn courtyard, its gray concrete walls covered in graffiti. A group of bored, angry-looking young men cowered in a doorway out of the rain, smoking weed. In a few hours they'd be onto something stronger, if they could afford it. Or down in the *métro,* armed with knives, terrorizing their affluent white neighbors to feed their habits.

Jean hummed under his breath. *"I love Paris in the springtime . . ."*

The pathologist finished her work. Two uniformed gendarmes began moving the corpse.

"Can you believe there are guys who would pay to sleep with that?" one of them said to his buddy as they zipped up the body bag.

"I know. Talk about rough. I'd rather stick my dick in a meat grinder."

Inspector Jean Rizzo turned on them furiously. "How dare you! Show some respect. She's a human being. She was a human being. That's somebody's sister you're looking at. Somebody's daughter."

"Sir."

The two men returned to their work. They would save the raised eyebrows for later, once the Interpol busybody had gone. Since when was a little black humor not allowed at a crime scene? And who the hell was Inspector Jean Rizzo anyway?

INTERPOL'S PARIS HEADQUARTERS WERE small and simply furnished but the view was spectacular. From Jean Rizzo's temporary office, he could see the Eiffel Tower looming in the distance and the white dome of the Sacré-Coeur in Montmartre in the foreground. It was all a far cry from Alissa Armand's squalid, lonely flat.

Jean Rizzo ran his hands through his hair and tried not to let the sadness overwhelm him. A short but handsome man in his early forties, with wavy dark hair, a stocky, boxer's build and pale gray eyes that glowed like moonstones when he was angry or otherwise emotional, Jean was well liked at Interpol. A workaholic, he was driven not by ambition—few people in the agency were less interested in climbing the greasy pole than Jean Rizzo—but by a genuine zeal for justice, for righting the wrongs of this cruel world.

Addiction had ravaged the Rizzo family. Both Jean's parents were alcoholics and his mother had died from the disease. Jean passionately believed that addiction *was* a disease, although growing up in Kerrisdale, an affluent suburb of Vancouver, he encountered few people who shared that view. Jean remembered neighboring families shunning his mother. Céleste Rizzo came from an old French-Canadian family and had been a great beauty in her youth. But drink destroyed her looks as it destroyed everything. When the end came, there was nobody there to help her.

Jean's father had recovered, but he too died young, of a heart attack at fifty. Jean's one consolation was that Dennis Rizzo had not lived to see his daughter's descent into crack-cocaine addiction. Like today's murdered girl, Jean's sister, Helene, had turned to prostitution in the last, desperate years of her life. How Jean hated that word: "prostitute." As if it contained the sum total of a woman's life: her worth, her personality, her struggles, hopes and fears. Helene had been a warm and wonderful person. Jean Rizzo chose to believe that Alissa Armand, and all this killer's victims, were warm and wonderful people too.

Jean's superiors back in Lyon were reluctant to assign him to the Bible Killer case.

"It's too personal." Henri Marceau, Jean's longtime boss and friend, cut to the chase. "You'll end up torturing yourself and you won't do a good job. Not without objectivity."

"I have objectivity," Jean insisted. "And I can hardly do a worse job than the last guy. Eleven dead girls, Henri. Ten girls! And we've got nothing."

Henri Marceau looked at his friend long and hard. "What's this really about, Jean? This case is colder than a ten-day-old corpse in the permafrost and you know it. You won't solve it. And even if you did, no one would care. It's not exactly a brilliant career move."

Jean shifted uncomfortably in his seat. "I want a challenge. I need something that will take up all my time. Distract me."

"From Sylvie, you mean?"

Jean nodded. His French wife Sylvie had divorced him a year ago, quietly and without acrimony, after ten years of marriage. They had two children together and still loved each other, but Jean worked ceaselessly, seven days a week, and in the end the loneliness proved too much for Sylvie.

Jean hated being divorced. He missed Sylvie and his children dreadfully, although he couldn't deny that he hardly saw them, even when he was married. As Sylvie pointed out to him when he complained of loneliness after dropping the kids back to her one weekend, "But, Jean, darling, it took you four months to realize we *were* divorced. The decree absolute came through in January, and you called me in May to ask me what it meant."

Jean shrugged. "It was a busy spring. I had a lot going on at work."

Sylvie kissed him on the cheek. "I know, *chéri.*"

"Can't we just get remarried? You'll hardly know I'm there."

"Good night, Jean."

The Bible Killer case was Jean Rizzo's therapy and punishment and atonement, all in one. If he could catch this bastard; if he could find justice for those poor girls; if he could stop another life being taken; somehow he believed it would make everything right. His divorce, Helene's death . . . it would all mean something. It would all be *for* something.

Ugh. He opened his eyes and leaned back in his chair, exhausted.

The problem is, I haven't caught him.

I didn't save Alissa.

Just like I didn't save Helene.

Outside, the rain had stopped and Paris was once again beautiful, glistening like a wet jewel in the spring sunshine.

Jean Rizzo vowed, *I can't leave here until I've got something. I can't go back to Lyon empty-handed.*

FOUR DAYS LATER, HE broke his vow.

His daughter, Clémence, had been rushed to the hospital with stomach cramps and given an emergency appendectomy.

"She's fine," Sylvie assured him. "But she's been asking for you."

Jean drove like the wind and was at Lyon's Clinique Jeanne d'Arc in three hours flat. Sylvie was at their daughter's bedside looking tired. "She just woke up," she whispered to Jean.

"Daddy!"

At six years old, Clémence was a carbon copy of her mother, all soft golden curls and saucerlike blue eyes. Clémence's younger brother, Luc, also took after Sylvie's family, much to Jean's annoyance. "It's totally unfair. I'm a genetic zero!" he would complain to Sylvie, who would laugh and ask him what he expected her to do about it.

"Maman said you were in Paris."

"That's right, *chéri.*"

"Did you catch the bad guy?" his daughter asked.

Jean avoided Sylvie's eye.

"Not yet."

"But you came back to see me?"

"Of course I did. Well, more to see your appendix really," Jean joked. "Did they give it to you in a jar?"

"Eeeew. No!" Clémence giggled, then winced.

"Don't make her laugh, you idiot," said Sylvie.

"Sorry. When I was a kid they used to give it to you in a jar to take home."

"In Canada?"

"Uh-huh."

"In the olden days?"

Sylvie grinned. "As you can see, she's making a quick recovery."

After a few minutes a nurse came in and ordered rest. Jean and Sylvie slipped outside into the corridor.

"Thank you for coming."

"Of course," said Jean. "You don't have to thank me. She's my daughter, I love her to death."

"I know you do, darling. I didn't mean that. How's the case going?"

Jean groaned. "It isn't. Paris was awful. This girl, the way she lived. You should have seen it."

His gray eyes were alight with emotion. Sylvie put a hand on his arm.

"You can't save them all, you know," she said kindly.

"Apparently I can't save any of them," Jean said bitterly. "Call me when you take her home."

BACK IN HIS SERVICED apartment a stone's throw from Interpol's General Secretariat at Quai Charles de Gaulle, Jean Rizzo switched on his computer. He typed in his user name, password and encryption code and watched as a cascade of windows opened relating to the Bible Killer murders.

Each of the victims had a serial number, under which local police had filed evidence. Or rather, where they'd bemoaned their lack of evidence before closing the cases, one after another. Internally, Interpol listed the girls simply as BK1, BK2 and so on. When Jean left for Paris, the file had ended with BK10, a Spanish redhead named Izia Moreno. Tomorrow, Jean Rizzo would add Alissa Armand's name and image. *BK11. That's all she is now.*

In addition to the official files, Jean had created his own, a much more visual affair that he thought of as a computerized whiteboard, like an online incident room. Pictures of the victims made up a montage in the center. To Jean Rizzo, these women would never be numbers. From this hub of faces, ideas fanned out like the spokes of a wheel: lines of inquiry, witnesses, common factors, forensic data, anything that seemed significant, or interesting.

Clicking open this personal file, Jean stared at it for a long time.

Nothing. We've got nothing.

A line one of his college professors used to use came back to him:

"In police work, what you don't know is as valuable as what you do."

If only that were true, Jean thought wryly.

The truth was, he didn't know an awful lot. But the clues must be there. They must. No one was that smart, all of the time. He had to start looking at things differently.

The crime scenes were all clean as a whistle. Barring a miracle, they weren't going to nail this guy on forensics. But there must be something else, some other link among the murders. *I'm missing the bigger picture. I need to zoom out.*

The concept of zooming out immediately made Jean think of Google Maps.

Maps. Geography.

He tapped the locations of the murders into the computer and brought them up on a map. Madrid, Lima, London, Chicago, Buenos Aires, Hong Kong, New York, Mumbai . . . For twenty minutes he played around, drawing lines between the map dots, rotating the shape, looking for a pattern. Nothing leaped out at him.

If not place, maybe time . . .

For the next two hours, Jean analyzed the dates, days and times of each murder. Was there a message in the numbers? He painstakingly cross-referenced every version of the figures with the biblical verses left at each crime scene. Did Genesis, chapter 2, verse 18, have anything to do with February 18, for example?

Of course it doesn't. He rubbed his temples wearily. *I'm losing my mind.*

He poured himself a whiskey and was about to call it a night when a final thought occurred to him. *Maybe our killer's not a mathematical genius. Maybe it's way simpler than that.*

Logging in to the central Interpol database, the unimaginatively named I–24/7 Network, he typed in the date of each murder, then pulled up a list of all the violent crimes committed in the *same* city on the *same* day.

Nothing obvious came up.

Jean widened the search criteria to a week before and a week after the murder dates.

A smattering of other unsolved homicides popped up, along with rapes and serious sexual assaults. But there was nothing that looked like a pattern as such. Nothing that linked the Bible Killer's work to any other crime.

On a whim, Jean deleted the word "violent" from the dialogue box. Now he was looking only for "serious crime" within a week either side of the BK murders, in the same locations.

One by one, they appeared on the screen.

Madrid: THEFT. $1m plus. Fine art. ANNTA Gallery.

Lima: THEFT. $2m plus. Fine art. Galería Municipal de Arte Pancho Fierro.

London: THEFT. $500,000 plus. Diamonds/ other. Private residence (Reiss).

New York: THEFT. Fine art. Pissarro. Private residence (McMenemy).

Chicago: THEFT. $1m plus. Jewelry. Commercial (Neil Lane).

Buenos Aires, Hong Kong, Mumbai.

THEFT. THEFT. THEFT.

Jean Rizzo felt his heart start to race. He picked up the telephone.

"Benjamin?"

"Rizzo?" Benjamin Jamet, Interpol's Paris Bureau chief, sounded distinctly groggy.

"I found something. Major thefts. Art, diamonds,

almost all of them seven figures. One or two days before *every single murder*. Has anything splashy gone down in Paris in the last two days?"

"Putain de merde," Benjamin Jamet growled. "Do you know what time it is?"

"This would have been big." Jean ignored him. "Did anyone hit Cartier or an embassy or . . . I don't know . . . the Louvre? Most likely art but could have been high-end jewels."

There was a long pause on the end of the line.

"As a matter of fact, there *was* something. The German ambassador's wife had a valuable collection of miniatures stolen from her safe."

"How valuable?"

"Over a million euros."

"When?"

"On Wednesday night." Benjamin Jamet sighed. "But look, Jean, this has nothing to do with your dead hooker. We're treating it as a domestic incident. All the embassy staff are being questioned. There were no signs of a break-in and . . . Jean? Jean, are you there?"

JEAN RIZZO STAGGERED INTO work at nine the next morning, looking like he hadn't slept in days. Ignoring colleagues' greetings and jokes about his haggard appearance, he went straight into his office and closed the door.

After five minutes, his secretary, Marie, braved the lion's den.

"Coffee?"

"Yes. Please. Lots."

"Your ex-wife called. She says your daughter's going home this afternoon."

"Good," said Jean. He didn't look up.

He had a lead. His first lead since he'd taken on this miserable case. Nothing else mattered.

Eleven murders, all bearing the hallmarks of the same killer.

Eleven audacious thefts, in the same cities, two days before the girls died.

None of the crimes solved.

There was a link. There had to be. It was simply too much of a coincidence.

But the link wasn't a simple one. On the surface, Jean could think of no plausible motive that connected the slayings of prostitutes with the pilfering of fine art. Moreover, in at least three of the robberies, the suspected perpetrator had been a woman. Although he didn't yet have the DNA to prove it, Jean Rizzo would have staked his children's lives on the fact that the Bible Killer was male. No woman could have inflicted those vile, sexual injuries on another woman.

The coffee arrived. Jean drank two strong cups. Without much hope of success, he ran an initial database trawl for suspected art and jewel thieves, operating internationally and at the very highest end of the market. The list ran to well over four hundred names.

Scrolling up to *sort by gender,* Jean checked the *female* box and hit search.

Five files appeared on his screen.

Five!

One was dead.

Three were in jail.

Jean Rizzo clicked open the fifth file. A young woman's face appeared on his computer screen. She was so beautiful, with her porcelain skin and chestnut hair and intelligent, moss-green eyes, that Jean found it impossible to look away.

"Tracy Whitney," he murmured to himself. "It's a pleasure to meet you."

CHAPTER 9

"TAKE A SEAT PLEASE, Mrs. Schmidt. Mrs. Carson."

Principal Barry Jones of Steamboat Springs Elementary School looked at the two mothers seated opposite him and their respective sons. Tracy Schmidt was a knockout. With her slender figure, shining chestnut hair and exquisite green eyes, she looked far younger than her thirty-seven years. Everybody knew that Mrs. Schmidt was a widow, and wealthy, but that was about all they knew. Living way up on that ranch with old Blake Carter, the lady kept to herself and had done so ever since she moved to the town almost a decade ago now. Of course, given her beauty, there were always rumors. Some said Tracy and Blake were an item. Principal Jones found that hard to believe. Others suggested she might be gay, but from where Principal Jones was sitting, she came across a lot more Ellen Barkin than Ellen DeGeneres.

Tracy's son, Nicholas, sat beside her. He had slightly

darker coloring but was equally good looking. Unfortunately he was also the scourge of third grade, in and out of hot water more often than a reusable tea bag.

On the other side of the principal's desk, their fat arms folded like giant, white sausages, sat Emmeline Carson and her boy, Ryan. Ryan Carson was a promising ice hockey player, popular in class, and a bully. He had a square head and close-set eyes that made him look dumber than he actually was. No mean feat. Ryan's nickname was "Rock" and it suited him on any number of levels. He also took after his mother. Emmeline Carson had one of those faces that looked oddly flattened, although her forehead bulged unappealingly above it. As if a steamroller had begun the job of running over her head, then thought better of it and reversed.

How Principal Jones wished he were here to reprimand Rock Carson and not Nicholas Schmidt! He certainly knew which mother he'd rather be pleasing.

"Are you gonna kick him out this time?" Mrs. Carson started things off with her usual charm. "My Ryan knows what he saw. The boy's a cheat."

"It's not true, Mom." Nicholas looked up at Tracy guilelessly. "I'm sure Rock—Ryan—genuinely thought he saw me do it. But he must be mistaken."

He's so handsome, Tracy thought adoringly. *And such a good liar.*

She turned her sweetest smile on Principal Jones. "Perhaps you'd tell me what happened?"

"I'm afraid a number of children witnessed the incident. Ryan was the one to come forward, but it happened during recess. Nicholas was caught at Mrs. Waklowski's desk, photographing the answers to tomorrow's math test on his cell. Apparently he was offering to sell the information to classmates, including Ryan here."

"That's right," Ryan piped up. "He wanted ten bucks.

Like I'm gonna give *him* ten bucks for some stupid math answers!"

"I mean, why would you need them?" said Nicholas. "You're so smart, Rock, you'd have aced the test anyway. Right?"

"Right." The bully's eyes narrowed. He suspected he was being mocked, but didn't fully understand how. "Anyway, the point is, he's a cheat."

"As I say, Mrs. Schmidt, it isn't a case of one kid's word against another's. Half the third grade has corroborated Ryan's story."

Tracy nodded understandingly. She looked at her son, not sure how, exactly, she was supposed to help him, when she saw a light go on in Nicholas's eyes.

"Check my phone."

"Excuse me?" said Principal Jones.

Nicholas reached into his pocket. A few moments later, he slid the offending cell phone across the principal's desk. "Check it. See if the pictures are on there."

"That seems sensible to me," said Tracy.

"Very well."

The principal switched on the device and fiddled about with it awkwardly. "How, er . . . where would I find pictures on here?"

"I'll show you," Nicholas said brightly.

"No. *I'll* show you." Mrs. Carson's huge white arm shot out across the desk and grabbed the phone. "He'll probably try and delete 'em."

Watching her fat fingers slide over the screen was like watching Lennie from *Of Mice and Men* stroke a mouse.

"Here ya go." She opened up the media files triumphantly, but her expression of smug satisfaction quickly faded. "Hey, what is this?"

"May I see the pictures?" Tracy asked sweetly. "Well,

now, as far as I can see, there's nothing that looks like a math paper here." She handed the phone back to Principal Jones.

"He's deleted 'em already. He's a liar!" Mrs. Carson was shouting. "Half the class saw those pictures."

"Any files deleted within the last hour would still be in the deleted items folder. I'm sure Mr. Farley would be happy to check that for you," Nicholas offered helpfully. Alisdair Farley was the head of the school's IT department. "But he won't find any pictures because I never took any. That's the truth. I was playing Angry Birds. I guess because I was near the teacher's desk, Rock kinda assumed . . ."

Look at those eyelashes fluttering! thought Tracy, rising from her chair.

"Is that all, Mr. Jones?"

Look at that figure! thought Principal Jones.

"I guess that's all, Mrs. Schmidt. It must have been a misunderstanding. Thanks for coming in."

OUTSIDE IN THE CORRIDOR, Nicholas kissed his mother good-bye.

"I'll see you after school. Glad we got that nonsense straightened out."

"Uh-huh," said Tracy. "See you after school. Oh, Nicky?"

"Yes?"

"Don't forget to bring that other chip in your backpack."

"What other chip?"

Tracy grinned. "The one with the pictures of the test on it, honey."

Nicholas Schmidt watched his mother walk toward the double doors. She was trying to hold it together, but he could see her shoulders shaking with laughter.

He loved her so much in that moment he could have burst.

DRIVING HOME THROUGH THE familiar Steamboat Springs streets, Tracy laughed for a long time.

Nicky might look like her, but his personality was all his father. Charming, handsome, funny and occasionally deceitful, at eight years old Nicholas Schmidt was a mini Jeff Stevens in every way. Some of the stunts he pulled were quite outrageous. Tracy did her best to disapprove. She was his mother, after all, and the whole reason she'd moved to Colorado was so that Nicholas could grow up to have a different life from the one that she and Jeff used to lead. A better, happier, more honest life. Nicholas must never know the truth about his past, or hers. And yet Tracy couldn't help but love her son's mischievous spirit.

I have to direct it, that's all. Make sure he uses his powers for good.

When Nicholas was three, he scammed a little girl at his preschool out of her lunch money for five days straight. By Friday, the girl's parents had gotten wise (she was coming home ravenous every afternoon) and the whole sorry story emerged.

"How did you get her to give you the money?" Tracy asked her son gently.

"I told her I would buy her a Beanie Baby. A special one. One that only I knew how to get."

"I see," said Tracy. "Why did you do that, honey?"

Nicholas gave his mother a look that seemed to say, *Is this a trick question?*

"Why did you tell Nora you would buy something for her, if that wasn't true?" Tracy pressed.

"So *I* could get the money," said Nicholas.

His mom really wasn't on top of her game today, it seemed to Nicholas. Maybe she needed more sleep?

"But that's dishonest sweetie," Tracy explained patiently. "You do see that, don't you? It's Nora's money."

"Not anymore it isn't!" Nicholas beamed. "Anyway, she's mean."

"She is?"

"Real mean. She called Jules 'fatty' and said his lunch smelled like poop. It *did* smell a bit like poop," he added contemplatively. "But Jules was crying because of her. I gave him half the money."

Well, thought Tracy. *That throws a different light on the matter.*

Sadly, the principal of Steamboat Springs' Sunshine Smile Preschool saw things differently. Nicholas spent the next year finger-painting at home.

Not all of his escapades were quite so altruistic.

There was the time in first grade when he removed the class mice, Vanilla and Chocolate, from their cage and dropped them into his teacher's purse "to see what would happen." (What happened was that poor Miss Roderick almost crashed her SUV on an icy stretch of I-90, and her screams could be heard all the way to Boulder.)

Or last year when he skipped school, aged only seven, to go to a hockey game by himself. Spotting a large family group with at least six kids at the stadium, Nicholas slotted himself in among the children and successfully slipped through the turnstiles. The game was almost over by the time a security guard noticed he was actually on his own and called the authorities.

"Do you know how worried everyone was?" a frantic Tracy chastised him afterward. "The school called the police. They thought you'd been abducted. So did I!"

"Because I went to a hockey game? That's a bit melodramatic, isn't it?"

"You were supposed to be at school!" Tracy yelled.

"Hockey's educational."

"How is hockey educational, Nick?"

"It's part of the curriculum."

"Playing it, not watching it. *You* were playing hooky, not hockey." Tracy sounded exasperated. "But that's not the point. The point is you were out in the city on your own. You're only seven years old!"

"I know." Nicholas smiled sweetly. "Do you know what our word of the week is? 'Initiative.' Don't you think I have a lot of initiative for my age?"

Raising Nicky was a full-time job. The older he got, the more damage control the job seemed to involve, and he was still only eight, God help her! But Tracy's son was her life now, and she wouldn't have traded that job for anything. Nicholas was her world, her center, her moon and stars and sun. And she knew she was the same for him.

Ironically, having a child had done all the things that Jeff had said it would do, all those years ago in London. It had filled the gap left by Tracy's old life. And it had helped her get over *him*. The scars from Tracy's marriage, and Jeff Stevens's betrayal, would never fully heal. But after nine years they had faded, like the other myriad scars in her life, from her mother's death, to the misery of jail, to the old friends she'd been forced to lose along the way.

Life is good now, she thought, turning up the winding mountain road that led to her ranch. It was April, and though there was still snow on the ground, it was melting fast. Soon "mud season," as spring was called in these parts, would be fully under way. Tracy didn't care. She loved the mountains in all their guises.

She was happy being Mrs. Tracy Schmidt. It wasn't a role to her anymore. It had become her reality.

It was Gunther Hartog who had taught her that, in order to succeed as a con artist, you had to utterly immerse yourself in the identity you adopted for each job.

"It's not enough to pretend to be the Countess of Nevermore, or whatever it is. You need to *believe* that you are that person. You need to become that person. Very few people can do that, Tracy. But you're one of them."

Dear Gunther. Tracy missed him.

Her mother used to pay her a similar compliment when she was a girl, although for very different reasons.

"Honestly, child," Doris Whitney would say, "sometimes I don't recognize you. You've got all the colors of the wind in you."

To be a chameleon was both a blessing and a curse. But Tracy felt thankful for it today. Without that ability, she would never have made it here, to Steamboat, to a life of safety and contentment with her beloved son.

At long last, Tracy was home.

TRACY WAS CLEARING AWAY the supper dishes late that night when Blake Carter knocked on the door.

"Blake. What are you still doing here? It's almost eleven."

"We had a lot of trees felled this afternoon. I've been walking the property, checking that the boys did a good job."

"By moonlight?"

"It wasn't moonlight when I started," said Blake. "Besides, I got a flashlight." He patted his pocket.

"Well, you should get home to bed," said Tracy, drying her hands on a dish towel. "Or did you want something?"

Blake looked suddenly awkward. "No, not really. I heard Nicholas was in some trouble again at school today, is all."

Tracy frowned. "News travels fast."

She wasn't angry with Blake Carter. Over the years Blake had developed a close bond with Nicholas. The boy needed a positive male role model and Tracy couldn't have asked for a better one than her ranch manager and friend. But one of the drawbacks of small-town life was small-town gossip.

"What happened?" Blake asked.

Tracy told him. "You should have seen the other mother's face!" She laughed. "It was priceless. She knew she'd been had but she didn't know how. They are *not* a nice family," she added, breaking off a square of chocolate from the bar on the counter and offering Blake a piece.

"So what consequence is Nicky facing?"

"Consequence?" Tracy looked confused.

"He tried to cheat on his test, and then he lied to you about it," Blake said sternly. "You don't think you should punish him for that?"

"I . . . well . . . I didn't really . . . we talked about it," Tracy blustered.

Blake Carter's raised eyebrow spoke a thousand words.

"Oh, come on," said Tracy. "No harm was done in the end. And this Rock Carson is such a vile boy."

"That's not the point," said Blake, "and you know it. You're too easy on him, Tracy. You keep this up, he's gonna be out of control at thirteen."

AFTER BLAKE LEFT, TRACY crept into Nicholas's bedroom.

Deep asleep, his dark curls spilling over the pillow and his arms flung wide across the bed, he looked positively angelic.

Tracy thought, *Blake's right. I am too easy on him. But how can I not be? He's so . . . perfect.*

She tried not to think about Jeff Stevens, but this was another impulse beyond her control. Was Jeff sleeping somewhere now too? Was he well and happy? Married to someone else? Was he even alive?

If she put her mind to it, Tracy could probably have found out the answers to all these questions. But over the years she'd trained herself not to. Jeff Stevens existed only in her heart and in her memory. She found her mind wandering back to the last job the two of them had done together. It was a diamond heist in Holland, before they were married. A mental picture came back to her of Daniel Cooper, the odd little insurance agent who had doggedly followed them across Europe, but had never been able to pin them to any crime. He'd been watching, the day that Tracy left Amsterdam. She'd actually seen him, seen the crushing disappointment on his face. She remembered feeling sorry for him.

Where was *he* now?

Where were any of the characters from those long-gone days?

For Tracy, and for Jeff, the scams and heists and capers had become a game. But to Daniel Cooper they'd clearly been more than that. *Did we hurt people back then, with the things we did?* Tracy wondered. She'd never regretted her old life, but perhaps she should have? As she gazed down lovingly at her sleeping son, it occurred to her that maybe her moral compass was off. Certainly Blake Carter represented goodness and decency and honesty in a way she aspired to, but didn't really recognize in herself. Or in Nicky.

I must do better.

I must be a better mother, for Nicky's sake.

Tracy kissed her son good night and went to bed.

CHAPTER 10

$\mathcal{L}$ISA LIM LOOKED AT the man zipping up his suit pants and fastening his cuff links beside the bed. As a high-class hooker, servicing Singapore's elite, she was used to all kinds of clients. Fat or skinny, old or young, straight or kinky, married or single, overbearing or shy. As long as they could pay the requisite $500 an hour and agreed to wear a condom, Lisa Lim was an equal-opportunity employee. She did this job for the money, nothing else. Still, it was a pleasant surprise to come across a client she not only found attractive, but actually liked. Thomas Bowers checked both boxes.

"Are you all right to get home?" he asked her, slipping her fee plus a hefty gratuity into a hotel envelope. He was staying at the Mandarin Oriental in the Oriental Suite and had picked Lisa up in the lobby. "Can I call you a cab?"

"I'm fine, thank you. I have my own transport." She took the money. "I enjoyed myself tonight."

"So did I."

Thomas Bowers pulled her close and kissed her. He smelled of expensive cologne and his stubble felt wonderfully masculine and rough against Lisa's soft skin. His kiss was like his lovemaking. Passionate. Tender. Confident. Thomas Bowers was that rarest of things, a john who actually liked women.

"If you'd like to see me again while you're in town, I could make myself available."

"I'd love to. But unfortunately I leave tomorrow." Bowers walked her to the door. "I'm taking the Orient Express to Bangkok. I'm rather looking forward to it."

"How lovely." Lisa smiled. "I've heard that's a stunning journey, through the Malaysian jungle. Is the trip for business or pleasure?"

Thomas Bowers thought about it, then grinned broadly.

"A little of both, I suppose. I'm meeting a friend. But let's just say I intend to enjoy myself."

THOMAS BOWERS, AKA JEFF Stevens, had jumped at the Singapore job for three reasons.

First, because he loved Asia. The food was delicious, the climate warm and the women wildly uninhibited in bed. Second, because he'd always wanted to try the E&O, the Singapore-to-Bangkok version of Europe's famous Orient Express. There was, in Jeff's opinion, a romance to old-fashioned train travel that not even the most luxurious private jet could match. Third, and most important, because the object he had come here to steal was one of the rarest and most exciting pieces he had ever gone after, an early Sumerian statue of King Entemena in perfect condition.

Gunther Hartog told Jeff, "The statue is currently in the possession of General Alan McPhee."

"The American war hero?"

"Exactly. The general will be on the Eastern and Oriental Express (E&O) leaving Singapore on April twenty-fourth at three o'clock. He plans to hand it over to his buyer in Bangkok on the twenty-eighth. Your job is to see to it that he doesn't."

Jeff had arrived in Singapore four days early, to give himself time to rest and to recover from jet lag. He'd enjoyed his time in the city, especially his last night with Lisa. These days, Jeff slept only with hookers. They were good at what they did, honest about their motivations and expected nothing from him other than money, of which he had plenty. He no longer missed Tracy with the raw, visceral pain he'd felt for the first year after she left him. But he knew that he would never love again. Not like that. Fleeting liaisons, such as the one with Lisa, fulfilled him sexually and protected him emotionally. These days Jeff reserved all deeper feelings for his work. He specialized in rare antiquities, and the only objects he ever stole were ones that genuinely fascinated him.

"I don't need the money," he told Gunther Hartog. "If I work, it will be for the love of it or not at all. Think of me as an artist."

"Oh, but I do, dear boy. I do."

"I need to be inspired."

Singapore had been fun, but sorely lacking in inspiration. Jeff had dined on oysters at Luke's on Club Street and indulged in some rocket-fueled cocktails served by gorgeous waitresses at the Tippling Club on Dempsey Hill. But overall the city reminded him of nothing so much as an Asian Geneva: clean, pleasant and, after a few days, really quite crushingly dull.

Thomas Bowers was ready to board that train.

Let the battle begin.

GENERAL ALAN MCPHEE'S VOICE carried through the intimate dining car like a stage actor booming out a soliloquy.

"Of course Iraq's a beautiful country. Bringing freedom to those folks is probably the thing I'm most proud of in my life. But I don't know if I'll ever go back. A lot of painful memories there . . ."

It was the second night aboard the Orient Express and the general was holding court, just as he had done the first night. Jeff Stevens, aka Thomas Bowers, observed the way the people around the man listened with rapt attention. The women, particularly, seemed impressed by him. There were four at his table tonight, along with two men. Two older Japanese ladies, sitting with their husbands, were part of a large group of Japanese tourists who had boarded the train at Woodlands Station in Singapore. They were joined by an elegant Frenchwoman, traveling alone, and an American goddess with waist-length red hair, a knockout figure and amber eyes, who rejoiced in the name of Tiffany Joy. Thomas Bowers had made Ms. Joy's acquaintance the previous night. A few discreet inquiries had confirmed his suspicions that she was the general's mistress, traveling as his secretary in an adjoining cabin.

"Amazing, isn't it, Mr. Bowers, to be sharing our journey with a true hero."

"Absolutely."

Jeff smiled at Mrs. Marjorie Graham, an English widow in her sixties traveling with her sister. The management of the E&O, and in particular Helmut Krantz, the train's hilariously uptight German chief steward, encouraged guests to "mingle" at mealtimes and share tables. Last night Jeff had endured his overcooked duck à l'orange in the company of a profoundly tedious Swedish couple from Malmö. Tonight he had the Miss Marple sisters. Complete with tweed skirts, twinsets and pearls, Marjorie Graham and her sister,

Audrey, both looked as if they'd walked directly right off the pages of an Agatha Christie novel.

"One hears about celebrities on these trips," Marjorie Graham went on. "I half expected some ghastly pop star. But General McPhee, well, that's quite a different matter."

"I couldn't agree more," said Jeff. "Believe me, no one's more excited than me to have the general on board."

"Being an American, you mean?"

"Sure." He nodded absently. Tiffany Joy had gotten up from the table, presumably to use the restroom in the next car down. As she passed, she smiled at Jeff, who smiled back, touching her lightly on the arm and exchanging some pleasantry or other. Out of the corner of his eye, he could see the general watching them, and observed the jealous souring of his expression.

At the end of the meal, another depressingly average offering—putting a German in charge of hospitality was bad enough, but Jeff strongly suspected that they'd hired one of Helmut's countrymen as head chef as well, which was unforgivable—Jeff headed toward the piano bar. As he passed the general's table, a sharp jolt from the train propelled him into the lovely Miss Joy once again.

"I'm terribly sorry." He grinned, looking anything but. "These narrow-gauge tracks are hellish, aren't they?"

"Oh, they're awful." The redhead giggled. "I was rattling around like a coin in a jar last night in my bunk. You should see my bruises."

"I'll show you mine if you'll show me yours," Jeff quipped.

"I don't believe we've met." General McPhee looked at Jeff with all the warmth of a nuclear winter.

"I don't believe we have. Thomas Bowers." Jeff extended a hand.

"Mr. Bowers is an expert in antiques," said Tiffany.

"Antiquities," Jeff corrected. "And I wouldn't say an expert, exactly. I'm a dealer."

"Is that so?" The general's expression shifted. "Well, Mr. Bowers, we should have a drink later. I have something in my cabin that I think may interest you greatly."

Jeff allowed his eyes to linger on Tiffany Joy's quite spectacular bosom. "I'm sure you do, General."

"It's not for sale," the general snapped. "Not that you could afford it even if it were. It's priceless."

"Oh, I believe you, sir." Jeff's eyes were still fixed on Tiffany's, and hers on him.

Thomas Bowers really was disconcertingly good-looking. Tiffany knew she shouldn't flirt. It upset Alan. Married or not, General Alan McPhee was a wonderful man, noble and brave and lionhearted. It was his strength and integrity that had attracted Tiffany to him in the first place. Well, that and the power, if she was honest. But she couldn't let him down, just because a handsome stranger paid her some attention. She blushed, ashamed of herself.

"I'll take you up on that drink tomorrow, General, if that's all right," Thomas Bowers was saying brightly. "Unfortunately I have some work I need to catch up on tonight. Sorry to have intruded, Miss Joy."

He nodded gallantly and took his leave.

Tiffany Joy's blush deepened. "Mr. Bowers."

Well, Jeff thought, grinning all the way back to his cabin. *That should put a fox in the henhouse. Step one completed.*

JEFF'S CABIN WAS CHARMING but minuscule. Tracy had once pulled off a spectacular jewel theft aboard the Venice Simplon-Orient-Express traveling from London to Venice and had compared her room to "the inside of a candy box."

This was similar, a riot of red velvet and brocade with

a single armchair, tiny table and foldout bunk bed that Jeff
suspected had been shipped in especially from Guantánamo
Bay, so torturous was it to attempt to sleep on. The decor
was certainly nostalgic, and had a certain Art Deco glamour
to it. But Jeff's enthusiasm for the romance of the Pullman
car was fading almost as fast as his appetite. Roll on, Bangkok.

Having attempted to shower in a stall so cramped Houdini
would have thought twice before entering it, Jeff lay on his
bunk rereading Gunther's encrypted file on General Alan
McPhee.

In 2007, the general was in command of U.S. forces in
the holy city of Nippur, about 160 kilometers southeast
of Baghdad between the Euphrates and Tigris rivers.
Since 2003, Coalition forces had been charged with
preventing looting at archaeological sites like Nippur,
a treasure trove of pre-Sargonic, Akkadian and old
Babylonian artifacts. A statue of King Entemena, a
Mesopotamian monarch from around 2400 BC, similar to the one looted from the National Museum of
Iraq in 2003 and of equivalent value, was discovered
in a tomb in Nippur by a French ground unit. It went
missing from a "secure" Coalition safe house six
weeks later, days before it was due to be transferred
to the Louvre. Extensive local searches produced no
result, although a wealth of circumstantial evidence
pointed to a local man, a petty thief named Aahil
Hafeez. Hafeez was arrested, but before he could be
tried, he was abducted and hanged by an angry mob.
He always protested his innocence. The statue was
never seen again.

Reliable sources now suggest that General McPhee
himself commissioned the theft. The much-decorated

general has in fact for years been running a profitable sideline in looted treasures and war spoils, although nothing quite as spectacular as this. Having paid off his local accomplices, the general wisely waited some years before searching for a suitable buyer for the Entemena statue. He has agreed to sell it for two million U.S. dollars to a Thai drug lord by the name of Chao-tak Chao. Chao is an exceptionally corrupt and ruthless individual, responsible for countless abductions, murders and incidents of torture. Illiterate and uneducated, he is nevertheless a collector of statuary in all its forms.

The general is traveling by boat and train to avoid the more intrusive customs searches prevalent throughout Asian airports. He is also clearly protected to a large degree by his status, both in the United States and abroad, as a military hero, much decorated for his valor and admired for his charitable endeavors.

Jeff thought, *Everybody loves this guy. Almost as much as he loves himself. But he's a fraud. Worse than that, he's a killer.*

Jeff closed his eyes and tried to imagine the terror of the young Iraqi man as he was dragged to some makeshift gallows by his own people. Strung up like an animal and choked to death for a crime of which he knew nothing. General McPhee could have stepped in and saved him. He didn't *need* a scapegoat. The crime could have remained unsolved, like so many others in the chaotic aftermath of the war. But in order to cover his own tracks twice over, that powerful, guilty man had allowed the powerless, innocent man to die a horrific death.

And that was when Jeff changed his mind.

Stealing the statue's not enough.
This bastard deserves a taste of his own medicine.

IT DIDN'T TAKE LONG for Thomas Bowers to engineer his next meeting with Miss Tiffany Joy.

He'd observed that the general always went to breakfast before his "secretary," and alone. Once he'd gone, Miss Joy would slip back into her own cabin, making sure it looked as if both berths had been slept in; there she showered and dressed, then joined her boss after a suitable interval. It was the easiest thing in the world to bump into her as she emerged into the corridor.

"Miss Joy. You look lovely this morning, as ever. How are the bruises?"

"Mr. Bowers!"

Tiffany blushed despite herself. She wished she didn't enjoy these encounters with the antiques dealer, or whatever he was, quite as much as she did. But Thomas Bowers was so *young,* and handsome, and Alan, bless him, was so *old.* Quite the antiquity himself, come to think of it!

"Is something funny? You know you're frighteningly pretty when you smile."

"And you're a terrible flirt."

"I'm crushed. Here was I thinking I was rather a good one."

Tiffany laughed. "I mean it. Alan . . . General McPhee . . . he wasn't too pleased last night. He said you bumped into me on purpose."

"He was quite right." Jeff moved closer. The train corridor was so narrow, his nose and Tiffany's were almost touching. "Not that I see what business it is of his. Isn't there a Mrs. McPhee somewhere? Keeping the home fires burning and all that."

"Well . . . yes," Tiffany admitted. "I'm just not sure she keeps the general's fires burning, though. Not anymore."

"What about *your* fires, Miss Joy?" Jeff's hands slid around her waist, then down over her deliciously pert bottom.

"Oh, Mr. Bowers!"

"Thomas."

"Thomas. I want to but I . . . we can't. He's my boss."

"You know what they say about all work and no play . . ."

The boring Swedish couple emerged from their cabin. Reluctantly Jeff released the general's secretary—*"under" secretary*—and let them pass.

"Your boss was boasting last night about having something priceless in his cabin," he said nonchalantly, once they were alone again. "He wasn't *only* talking about you, was he?"

"No. But I can't talk about it," Tiffany said primly.

"Why not?" Lunging forward, Jeff kissed her suddenly and passionately on the mouth.

"Thomas!"

"He obviously wanted me to know. Come on, I won't tell. What's he got stashed in there? The world's biggest bottle of Viagra?"

"Don't be mean."

"A toupee spun from threads of pure platinum?"

"Stop it!" Tiffany giggled. "If you must know, it's some sort of statue. Between you and me, it's quite hideous. It was a gift from a grateful Iraqi gentleman, after the liberation. Apparently it's very old and very rare."

"Just like Alan's erection," Jeff couldn't resist saying. "Look. It's the boat tour of the River Kwai this afternoon."

"I know." Tiffany sighed. "The general's an expert on World War Two history. I've been hearing all about it since Singapore. He really is an incredibly learned and eminent—"

"Get out of it. Say you're not feeling well."

"But he knows I'm—"

"Fake something. Come *on*, Miss Joy. Live a little! I'll make sure your boss and I are on different boats. Then I'll duck out early and come and take a look at the general's priceless treasure."

"I assume you're referring to the statue, Mr. Bowers?" Tiffany threw back her hair coquettishly.

"I'll show you what I'm referring to this afternoon, Miss Joy. Enjoy your breakfast."

IT WAS A HUNDRED degrees and a hundred percent humidity at the River Kwai. Dressed in khaki slacks and a linen shirt, and carrying a small rucksack, General Alan McPhee was sweating like a pig.

"You must be used to these sort of conditions, General. What's your secret?"

General McPhee scowled. He disliked Thomas Bowers. The man was too handsome by half, too smooth, too full of himself. Bowers looked immaculate as ever today in a white shirt and shorts, and if he was feeling the heat he didn't show it. *Bastard.*

"No secret, Mr. Bowers. Just perseverance."

"Very admirable. I notice your secretary isn't with us. Military history not her thing?"

"Miss Joy isn't feeling very well. I believe she's resting in her cabin."

The E&O passengers were divided into two groups and herded toward separate rafts. The Asians were directed toward the vessel with a Japanese-speaking guide, and the Europeans to one with an Australian ex-serviceman providing the commentary.

Jeff made his way toward the Japanese raft. He was immediately accosted by the train's chief steward, a look of panic on his face.

"No, no, Mr. Bowers. For a tour in English, you must join the other line."

"Thanks, Helmut. But I prefer this one."

Jeff pushed forward.

"Please, Mr. Bowers, it is most important. We ask all our European visitors to board the other raft."

"I'm sure you do." Jeff smiled. "But I'm taking this one."

Noticing the minidrama being played out behind him, General McPhee came over.

"What's the matter, Bowers?"

Jeff whispered in the general's ear. "I heard they give very different versions of the tour on the Japs' boat. Apparently they tell them about how brave and noble their soldiers were, and how their mistreatment of the Allied prisoners of war was exaggerated. I'm curious to hear it."

"That's outrageous! Who told you that?"

"A little bird." Jeff shrugged. "The narration's in Japanese but Minami here's agreed to translate for me." He nodded toward a Japanese woman a few feet ahead of them in line.

"I'm taking this raft too," the general announced loudly.

"Sir! I must protest." The poor chief steward looked as if he might spontaneously combust. "Really, we have a system . . ."

"I'll bet you do." The general followed Jeff onto the raft, leaving the little man helpless on the quayside.

THE GENERAL'S TEMPER WORSENED as they made their way down the river. Bowers was right. The crap they were feeding the Japanese tourists bore no resemblance to the truth. He was damn well going to complain to the management and in the strongest terms! He tried to concentrate on everything his Japanese translator was saying. But the woman was so short and spoke so softly, it was impossible to hear her at times over the noise of the engine. Between straining his ears, stooping uncomfortably and attempting to swat away mosquitoes the size of small bats, it was a thoroughly unpleasant trip. The humidity was also horrendous, like breathing hot soup. Removing his backpack and loosening the buttons on his shirt, the general was relieved to see that Bowers had been forced to do the same.

BACK ON THE TRAIN, General McPhee headed straight to his cabin. As soon as he'd peeled off his wet clothes, he intended to dictate a strongly worded letter of complaint to the relevant authorities. He was stopped in the corridor, however, by a borderline-hysterical Helmut.

"I'm terribly sorry, General. I really have no idea how this happened. But I'm afraid you can't return to your cabin."

"What do you mean I can't return to my cabin? I can do as I damn well please."

"It appears there has been a robbery." The German looked as if he might faint. "Both your cabin and Miss Joy's were targeted. The young lady appears to have been chloroformed. The police are on their way."

THE BREAK-INS AT GENERAL McPhee's cabin and that of his pretty young secretary were the talk of the train for the remainder of the journey. After a six-hour delay, the Malay police allowed them to continue across the border to Thailand. Other than a few inconsequential items of jewelry and some of the general's personal effects, nothing appeared to have been taken.

Tiffany accosted Jeff angrily on the outdoor viewing platform later that night.

"What the hell happened, Thomas? Where were you?"

"I'm sorry. I got stuck on the same raft as your boss. I couldn't get away."

"Well, someone got away. Whoever they were, they were obviously after that stupid statue."

"I imagine so. You poor thing. You must have been terrified." Jeff wrapped an arm around her shoulder. Despite herself, Tiffany leaned into him.

"Actually I didn't know a thing about it. The police think whoever it was must have gassed me through the keyhole. All I remember was waking up and the room looked like a bomb had hit it. Anyway, they didn't find what they were looking for."

"So I heard," said Jeff. "How did he manage to conceal it so well in such a tiny space? That's what I don't understand."

"I told you." Tiffany shrugged. "The general's a brilliant man. He's smarter than he looks."

"He must be," said Jeff.

AFTER THE CRAMPED CONFINES of the Eastern and Oriental Express, Bangkok's Peninsula Hotel was the last word in luxury. The food was exquisite, the service faultless and the beds so soft and capacious that General Alan McPhee could have wept with relief. Freed from the prying eyes of his fellow train passengers, the general had decided to dispense with the subterfuge and install Miss Tiffany Joy in his palatial suite. After all, it wasn't as if his wife was about to drop in and discover them. With only a few days left in his trip to Asia, the general was looking forward to spending some quality time with his young secretary's delicious body, away from the distractions of the infuriating Mr. Thomas Bowers.

Sprawled out by the Peninsula's spectacular swimming pool overlooking the harbor, in a minuscule gold bikini that left little to the imagination, Miss Joy looked particularly ravishing this morning.

It's a pity to have to leave her, the general thought. *On the other hand, by dinner tonight I'll be two million dollars richer. We can celebrate together.*

"I have some business to take care of." Leaning over her sun lounger, he kissed her on the top of the head. "I'll be back before tonight."

"Good luck." Tiffany sighed, rolling over onto her stomach.

Watching the general walk away, with that distinctive stiff, military gait of his, she was glad she hadn't slept with Thomas Bowers in the end. He was charming, of course, and sexy. But men like him were a dime a dozen. Alan was different. He was a war hero, a man of true intellect and gravitas. A little pompous perhaps, but a good man at heart.

I made the right choice.

HOW THE HELL DO people live here?

General Alan McPhee's lip curled in distaste as the crowds of sweaty Thais surged around him like vermin.

He'd taken the Skytrain to Bang Chak, preferring the anonymity of Bangkok's famous monorail to a cab, where he ran the risk of the driver remembering him. From there he made his way by foot through the market, holding tightly to his precious backpack as he weaved through stalls selling everything from textiles and electronics to cheap religious icons and revolting herbal charms made from chicken's feet and the like.

In every corner, junkies sat slumped like the corpses they would soon become. *Chao-tak's customers.* General McPhee felt no compassion for them. Their misery was self-inflicted.

The general had heard the horror stories about Chao-tak's torture chambers, and the toe-curling punishments he apparently inflicted on perceived rivals, enemies or delinquent debtors. He wasn't impressed. These drug lords and gang leaders thought of themselves as warriors. *Pathetic! Put them in a real war zone and they wouldn't last a day.* Most of them were illiterate thugs who'd risen to the top like scum in a jar full of pond water. It pained the general in a way, to be handing over the beautiful Entemena statue to such a philistine. But business was business. Two million dollars would pay for the luxurious retirement that General Alan McPhee deserved.

A minion emerged from an alleyway and scuttled alongside the general like a rat.

"McPhee?"

The general nodded.

"This way."

Chao-tak's office was a sparsely furnished room in a nondescript apartment building. Not quite a tenement, it was nevertheless extremely run-down, with patchy air-conditioning, peeling paint and carpets that looked as if they hadn't been cleaned since the day they were laid. In Mexico, the drug barons lived like emperors. Clearly Chao-tak had other uses for his money.

"You got the statue?"

General McPhee laid his backpack gently down on the desk.

"You got the money?"

A different minion handed him a briefcase.

"Do you mind if I count it?"

Chao-tak wasn't listening. Like a greedy child on Christmas morning, he was attacking the general's backpack, clawing at the Bubble Wrap protecting Entemena.

"Be careful with that!" The general couldn't stop himself. "There's over two thousand years of history in that bag."

The squat little Thai turned the statue over in his hands, like a monkey examining a troublesome nut. *Ignorant peasant.*

Suddenly something happened. Chao-tak's face darkened. He shook the statue hard, like a baby with a rattle, then started shouting something in Thai. Two of his men rushed forward. Each examined the base of the statue. Then all three glared at General McPhee.

"You try to cheat me!" Chao-tak spat.

"Don't be ridiculous."

"Ridiculous? *You* ridiculous. Two-thousand-year-old statue, you think I'm stupid?" Snatching the Entemena back from his henchmen, Chao-tak threw it at the general, who only just caught it in time.

"For Christ's sake! What are you doing?"

"Look at bottom. Look at base!" Chao-tak commanded.

The general's face drained of color.

"They have serial number two thousand year ago? They have bar code?"

"I . . . I don't understand," the general stammered. "This is a mistake. Someone must have switched the statues somehow." He thought about the robbery on the train, but that made no sense. *It couldn't be. I had the statue with me on the Kwai. It was never in the room.*

"Look, I'll straighten this out. You can keep your money." He closed the briefcase and pushed it back across the desk. "I don't know how this happened but—"

Four hands gripped his arms from behind. Before he could react, someone brought a metal crowbar slamming into the back of his knees. He screamed and slumped to the floor.

"You try to cheat me."

The Harvard-educated American war hero looked into the eyes of the illiterate Thai drug dealer and saw his own black, compassionless heart staring back at him.

Tears welled up in his eyes.

He knew there would be no way out.

TIFFANY JOY HAD BEEN waiting at the table for over forty minutes when the champagne and note arrived.

She smiled. *About time.*

She waited until the waiter had opened the bottle, poured her a glass and left before she opened the note. When she read it, the smile dissolved on her lips.

The General is dead. I paid your check. Get out of Bangkok now or they will kill you too. Don't pack. Your friend. T.B.

T.B.

Thomas Bowers.

Tiffany Joy got up from the table and started running.

JEFF STEVENS WAS AT the boarding gate, about to board Qantas flight 22 8419 to London via Dubai, when a Thai police officer pulled him roughly to one side.

"Is there a problem?"

The officer said nothing. Snatching Jeff's carry-on out of his hand, he unzipped it and pulled out a Bubble Wrapped package.

Jeff's palms began to sweat.

"What's this?"

"It's a statue," said Jeff. "A gift for a friend of mine."

"Really?" The guard made a gesture. Three of his colleagues approached. In addition to their handguns, each one had a vicious Alsatian dog straining at the end of a leather leash. The dogs went nuts as they approached Jeff, barking wildly and baring their teeth.

"Passport!" the first officer barked.

Jeff handed it over. *What the hell was happening?*

"Are you familiar with the drug laws in this country, Mr. Bowers?"

"Of course I am," said Jeff. He could barely hear himself over the dogs. He'd heard the stories of innocent travelers having bags of heroin planted on them, of course, but he'd been so careful. For obvious reasons, his bag had never left his sight for a second. Unless someone at security . . .

The policeman tore off the Bubble Wrap and held the statue of Entemena high above his head. "Maybe the gift for your friend is *inside,* hmm?"

Jeff's heart stopped. *He's going to smash it! He's going to shatter two thousand years of history.* "NO!"

Without thinking, he lunged for the statue.

Three pistols were instantly raised and pointed at his head. Jeff closed his eyes and waited for the sound of shattering stone. Instead he heard a man shriek in agony. Opening his eyes, he saw that one of the dogs had leaped onto the man standing next to him and sunk its formidable jaws into the poor guy's crotch. A melee ensued, with much barking and screaming and waving of firearms. Eventually a plastic bag containing a small amount of white powder was produced from somewhere inside the man's pants.

The first policeman calmly handed the statue back to Jeff.

"Sorry, sir. Our mistake. We hope you enjoyed your stay in Thailand."

TWENTY MINUTES LATER, JEFF finally exhaled as the Airbus A380 soared and juddered its way into the sky.

Reaching down, he stuck his hand into the bag at his feet and touched the statue lovingly.

That was close. Too close.

He thought about Francine, the Frenchwoman on the E&O. It was she who'd tried to steal the Entemena while both Jeff and the general were at the Kwai. Jeff recognized her from a job he and Tracy had tried to pull years ago in Paris. He was sure she was on the train with the same intention as he had. She'd beaten them to the punch in France—a lovely Dutch still life, if Jeff remembered rightly. But not this time. Once the general was distracted by dear, sweet little Minami on the Japanese raft, his outrage had gotten the better of him. It had been preposterously easy to switch his backpack for the one Jeff had brought with him, packed with a worthless fake statue, as sold in museum gift shops all over Europe.

He thought about Tiffany Joy and wondered whether she'd taken his advice. He did hope so. Chao-tak was not in the habit of leaving loose ends, and Miss Joy didn't deserve the fate of her heartless lover.

He thought about General Alan McPhee, and about Aahil Hafeez, and about the collector in Switzerland who was eagerly awaiting the arrival of his treasure.

He thought about Tracy, and how nothing was quite as much fun without her.

Then he fell into a deep and dreamless sleep.

CHAPTER 11

"OH MY GOD! THAT'S Zayn Malik!"

Nicholas's eyes were on stalks. He'd never been to Los Angeles before, or to any big city other than Denver, and that was only for a day-trip. His mother had brought him to Cecconi's on Melrose for lunch, a celebrity watcher's heaven.

"Who's Zayn Malik?" Tracy asked.

"Zayn Malik? One Direction?"

Tracy looked blank. Nicholas gave her a look that was half pity, half disdain.

"Oh, never mind. Can I have another sundae?"

It was July and ninety degrees outside. While the Angelenos wisely headed to the beach, or locked themselves inside their air-conditioned cars and offices, Tracy and Nicholas had spent the morning pounding the streets, rushing from one tourist attraction to the next. In prior years, Tracy had sent her son to a local summer camp in Colorado called

Beaver Creek. Nick spent his vacations swimming and fishing and kayaking and camping, and always had a great time. But this year she decided it was time he saw a bit more of the world.

Blake Carter was against the idea.

"I don't see what Los Angeles has to offer that Steamboat doesn't."

Tracy raised an eyebrow. "Variety?"

"Them freaks on Venice Beach, you mean?"

"Come on, Blake. I know you're not a city person. But there's Hollywood, all that movie history. There's museums and theme parks. I'll take him to Universal Studios and maybe a Lakers game. He's so sheltered here."

"Kids are supposed to be sheltered," grumbled Blake. "Maybe if he were a teenager. But he's too young, Tracy. You mark my words. He won't enjoy it."

Nicholas loved it.

Everything about L.A. excited him, from the food and the blazing heat to the streets full of Lamborghinis and Ferraris and Bugattis and Teslas and the Venice Beach freaks that Blake Carter so despised: silver-sprayed mimes and snake charmers and transvestite stilt walkers and fortune-tellers with their faces covered in exotic tattoos.

"This place is awesome!" he told Tracy, night after night in their suite at the Hotel Bel-Air. "Can we move here, Mom? Please?"

A sundae arrived, Nicholas's second. He attacked the mountain of whipped cream and fudge with the same enthusiasm he'd shown its predecessor. Tracy was sipping her coffee, content simply to watch him, when a party walked in and caught her attention.

The first thing Tracy saw was the necklace. *Once a jewel thief, always a jewel thief.* Although in all honesty, this one was hard to miss: a string of rubies, each one the size of a baby's fist, hung around the scrawny neck of an otherwise unattractive, middle-aged woman. It was the most dazzling, over-the-top piece of jewelry that Tracy had ever seen. And she'd seen quite a few.

The woman was with her husband, a squat, toad of a man with bulging eyes whom Tracy was sure she recognized but couldn't quite place. Another, younger woman completed the group. From behind, Tracy could see that this second woman was tall, slender and elegant. Then she turned around.

Tracy choked, scalding jets of coffee burning the back of her throat and making her eyes water.

"Are you okay, Mom?"

"I'm fine, honey." Tracy dabbed her eyes with the napkin, simultaneously using it to hide her face. "Finish your dessert."

It couldn't be.

It *couldn't be.*

But it was.

Rebecca Mortimer! The girl from the British Museum. The girl Tracy had caught in her bedroom with Jeff, all those years ago. The girl who'd singlehandedly destroyed Tracy's married life was here, not only in Los Angeles but in this very restaurant, sitting less than ten feet away from her!

Of course, she looked different. It had been almost a decade, after all. Her long red hair was now platinum blond and short, almost boyish. But there was nothing remotely masculine about her figure, especially when it was shrink-wrapped in an Hervé Léger minidress as it was today. Or in the coquettish toss of her head as she laughed at the fat man's jokes.

I know who he is now, Tracy thought. *Of course. That's Alan Brookstein, the director. Which means those must be the famous Iranian rubies.*

She couldn't remember the whole story. But it involved a mistress of the former shah of Iran being tortured and strangled for her necklace, or something equally awful. *Vanity Fair* did a piece on it, and nobody came out well. Liz Taylor had tried and failed to buy the necklace before her death, after which it went underground again. Brookstein had bought it for his wife last year in a secret, possibly illegal deal, for an undisclosed sum. And here it was in the flesh, swinging around the woman's neck at a casual lunch, like a mayoral chain!

Tracy summoned the maître d'.

"That's Alan Brookstein and his wife, isn't it?" she asked discreetly.

"Yes, ma'am. They're regulars here."

"I wonder, do you know the young woman dining with them?"

The maître d' didn't usually stoop to gossip with patrons. But the very beautiful Mrs. Schmidt was clearly far from one's average tourist. She positively radiated class.

"I believe her name is Liza Cunningham. I've seen her in here before with Sheila . . . Mrs. Brookstein. She's British. An actress."

That's about right, thought Tracy bitterly. *A damn good actress.*

Tracy watched the way "Liza" divided her attention between the director and his wife, expertly flattering them both. In her prior incarnation as "Rebecca," an innocent archaeology student, she'd played the doe-eyed, butter-wouldn't-melt role equally well.

That's when it hit Tracy like a thunderbolt between the eyes.

She's not an actress, or a student. She's a con artist, like Jeff and me!

She's one of us.

It was so obvious now, Tracy couldn't imagine why she

hadn't realized it before. Back in London. Back when it mattered.

She's a con artist and she's here to steal that ruby necklace.

"Mom? You look weird. Are you sure you're feeling okay?"

"I'm fine, honey." Tracy had almost forgotten Nicholas was there. Her cheeks were flushed, her eyes glazed and her heart rate had started to rise, beating to a familiar but long-neglected beat.

I'm going to play her at her own game.
And this time I'm going to win.

By the time Tracy paid the check, the decision had already been made.

Tracy was going to steal Sheila Brookstein's rubies.

IT WAS HARD TO say who enjoyed the next week more—Tracy or Nicholas. In between playing mommy and taking her son to all the L.A. sights, Tracy prepared for the job. Stealing the most famous ruby necklace in the world from a powerful Hollywood director's wife was not exactly "easing oneself back in gently." Long days running around town with her son were followed by equally long nights researching everything there was to know about Alan and Sheila Brookstein and the fabled Iranian rubies.

In two days she had a plan.

It was difficult, audacious and wildly risky. Worse, she had only ten days to pull it together.

TRACY AND NICHOLAS WERE at the Hollywood sign. Tracy's phone rang.

"Hello?"

"So it really is you!" The man on the other end of the line gave a raspy chuckle. "I'll be damned. I thought you were dead."

"Thanks, Billy. Good to know." Tracy grinned. "Are you still in the jewelry business?"

"Are priests still screwing little boys? Whaddaya got for me, sweetheart?"

"Nothing, yet. Can you meet me at the Bel-Air later?"

TRACY HATED ROLLER COASTERS. Somehow Nicholas had badgered her into taking the Apocalypse Ride at Six Flags Magic Mountain. They had just strapped themselves in and Tracy was focusing on keeping her lunch down when an e-mail popped up on her iPhone.

Is this who I think it is?

Tracy typed back, *Absolutely not.*

Shame. The person I was thinking of used to have amazing breasts. I wonder if she still does?

I need a contact at a Beverly Hills insurance agency. Do you have one?

Possibly. Do you have a recent photograph of your breasts you can send me?

Tracy laughed loudly.

"See?" Nicholas grinned over his shoulder as they lurched forward. "I *told* you. The Apocalypse is fun."

ALAN AND SHEILA BROOKSTEIN lived in a very large, very ugly home set behind very large, very ugly gates, just north of Sunset Boulevard in Beverly Hills. The mock-Tudor manor was surrounded by garish flowers in a variety of clashing colors, and the driveway was lined with hundreds of truly hideous ceramic gnomes.

"You liked the gnomes, huh? My wife collects them. Has 'em shipped in from all over the world. Japan, France, Russia, even Iraq. You'd never guess the Iraqis were into garden statuary, would you? But I tell you, Miss Lane—"

"Please, call me Theresa."

"Theresa." Alan Brookstein smiled broadly. "It's a funny old world we live in."

The gorgeous young insurance agent smiled and nodded in agreement. Alan Brookstein rarely took meetings like this in person. "Home Insurance" fell squarely under the job description of his PA, Helen. But he'd happened to run into the beautiful Miss Theresa Lane yesterday, the first time she'd come around. One look at that slim figure, topped by the pretty, intelligent face and the cascade of chestnut hair, offset by those exquisite, dancing green eyes, and Alan Brookstein's schedule opened up faster than a Kardashian's legs in an NBA player's hotel room.

"Your wife has great taste. That necklace is the most stunning piece I've ever seen."

"Ah, well, that was *my* taste," Alan Brookstein boasted. "I'm the one who picked it for her. You wanna see the safe?"

Tracy smiled warmly. "That's why I'm here."

Nicholas was in surf camp for the day out in Malibu. Tracy didn't have to pick him up for hours, but she was still eager to get this done and get out of here sooner rather than later. She had nightmares of a genuine agent from Christie's bespoke insurers telephoning or stopping by out of the blue and spectacularly blowing her cover. *It's not going to happen,* Tracy told herself firmly. But her adrenal glands didn't seem to be listening. The stakes were very high.

"This way, Theresa. Watch your step, now."

Alan Brookstein led her through a baffling series of hallways, each one smothered in thick, beige carpet like marzipan frosting. Saccharine impressionist paintings in a riot of pinks and blues and greens hung on walls papered with busy floral prints that would have made Liberace wince. Two maids in full uniform flattened themselves against the wall as Tracy and the director passed. Tracy clocked the fear in their faces. Evidently the rumors she'd heard of both the Brooksteins' bullying and unpleasantness toward their staff were true.

The safe—or rather safes—were in the master suite, behind a panel in Sheila's dressing room.

"You have three?"

"Four." Alan Brookstein's chest puffed out with pride, making him look more like a toad than ever. "These three are all decoys. I put a few, less valuable pieces in each one, just enough to make a thief think he's hit pay dirt. The third one has a perfect replica of the Iran piece. Real rubies, artificially produced. You can't tell the difference with the naked eye. Wanna see?"

Unlocking the safe, he pulled out the necklace Tracy had seen at Cecconi's and draped it over her hands. The stones were heavy and glowed like coal embers between her fingers.

"This is a fake?"

"That's a fake."

"Impressive."

"Thank you, Theresa." Alan Brookstein's eyes seemed to have developed a magnetic attraction to Tracy's nipples.

"Does your wife wear this out?"

"Sometimes." Brookstein replaced the necklace. "She wears both. The fake and the real one. If it's something really big, like the gala at LACMA on Saturday night, she'll wear the real deal. I'm being honored with a Lifetime Achievement Award," he couldn't resist adding.

"Congratulations! Your wife must be thrilled for you."

Alan Brookstein frowned. "I don't know. She's thrilled to

have a chance to flash those rubies, make all her girlfriends feel like crap, you know what I mean?" He laughed mirthlessly. "The truth is, Sheila can't tell the difference any more than the rest of 'em. If it's big and red and sparkly, she likes it. Kind of like the gnomes."

Tracy followed the director through to his dressing room. A false panel at the back of a closet pulled aside to reveal a fourth safe.

"The code is changed every day."

"For all the safes, or just this one?"

"For all of them."

"Who changes the codes?"

"Me. Only me. Nobody knows what I come up with each day, not even Sheila. I appreciate your company's concern, Theresa, but between this and our guards and the alarm system, I truly don't think we could be better protected."

Tracy nodded. "Mind if I look around a little?"

"Be my guest."

Removing her shoes, Tracy flitted from room to room. She stepped inside closets and began climbing shelves, rifling through the Brooksteins' suits and shirts and dresses and shoes. From her capacious Prada purse, she pulled out a variety of equipment, much of which looked like electronic monitors of some sort, which made an ominous, static-y, crackling sound when run along the edges of mirrors.

"Okay." From her position at the top of a wooden stepladder, where she'd been examining the safety of a ceiling panel, Tracy suddenly spun around.

Standing at the foot of the ladder, Alan Brookstein, who'd been within inches of getting a clear view of her underwear, jumped a mile.

"What? Is there a problem?"

"Happily, no." Tracy smiled. "No cameras or devices of any kind. I agree, you're sufficiently protected. Although I *would* be careful which staff members you allow access to this room. We have had cases of maids installing pinhole cameras close to known safes, capturing the lock and unlock codes, and passing them on to boyfriends who then raid the houses in question."

"Not our maids," Alan Brookstein joked. "Trust me, those cholas don't have a whole brain cell between them. You'd get more ingenuity out of an ape."

Still, he thought, *it was a good observation. The last schmuck from the insurance agency never gave me any practical advice like that.*

"You're a smart girl, Theresa. Thorough, too. I like that. You got any other tips for me?"

Tracy paused for a beat, then smiled slowly.

"As a matter of fact, Alan, I do."

ELIZABETH KENNEDY HAD NO time for stupid, rich women. Unfortunately, in her line of work, she dealt with a great many of them. Although few were quite *as* stupid as Sheila Brookstein.

"I honestly don't think I can stand it much longer," Elizabeth told her partner. "The woman's a card-carrying moron."

"Focus on the money," Elizabeth's partner reminded her curtly.

"I'm trying."

Elizabeth Kennedy usually had no problem keeping her mind on the silver lining—or in this case, ruby lining—of being forced to spend so much time with rich, stupid women like Sheila Brookstein. Elizabeth had grown up poor and had no intention of ever, ever going back there. But playing the role of British actress Liza Cunningham, Sheila's new best friend, was really beginning to grate. It was like making small talk to a lobotomized cabbage. On a really off day.

"WHICH ONE, LIZA? THE Alaïa or the Balenciaga?"

"Liza" was in Sheila Brookstein's dressing room, helping her friend get dressed for tonight's ceremony at LACMA. Alan Brookstein, Sheila's fat, self-important husband, was being given some award.

"Try the Balenciaga first," she called into the bedroom.

While Sheila swathed her bony frame in complicated layers of black silk, Elizabeth pulled the fake necklace that her partner had commissioned out of her purse. It was the work of a moment to exchange it for the real one, which Alan had removed from the safe in his dressing room earlier and laid out helpfully on his wife's dresser.

"Should I bring the necklace through?"

"Would you? You're an angel, Liza," Sheila gushed.

Elizabeth fastened the fake rubies around Sheila Brookstein's scraggy throat. She felt a moment's anxiety as the older woman frowned into the mirror. *Surely she can't tell the difference?* But the frown soon vanished, replaced by Sheila's usual vacuous, smug, self-satisfied smile.

"How do I look?"

Like a wrinkled old turkey with a string of worthless red rocks around its neck.

"Ravishing. Alan's going to die of pride."

"And all the other directors' wives are going to choke with envy. Bitches." Sheila cackled nastily.

IT WAS ALMOST ANOTHER hour before Sheila finally left in the back of her chauffeur-driven Bentley Continental. In that time "Liza" had styled and sprayed her thinning hair three different ways and helped the makeup artist apply the thick layers of foundation that Sheila felt made her seem younger, but that actually gave her skin the look of hardened clay. And all the while Sheila had talked and talked and talked.

"Whatever did I do before I met you, Liza?

"You're like a sister to me.

"Isn't it incredible how we have so much in common? Like we're both such incredible *listeners*. Alan never listens to me. He thinks I'm stupid. I swear to God, that bastard . . ."

Never again, Elizabeth thought, speeding toward the Century City condo for the rendezvous with her partner, the priceless ruby necklace tucked safely in her purse. *This time tomorrow I'll be on a yacht in the Caribbean.*

Good-bye, Sheila! Good-bye, Liza Cunningham!

And good riddance.

"YOU'RE AN IDIOT. YOU'VE been duped."

Elizabeth Kennedy felt the color rise in her cheeks. Not out of embarrassment. Out of anger. How dare her partner berate her like this? After the months she'd spent getting close to the Brooksteins! The endless, mind-numbing hours in Sheila's company. Flirting with the repellent Alan.

"My job was to swap out the necklaces. That's what I did. What the hell was *your* contribution?"

"Your job was to acquire the Iranian rubies. These are not the Iranian rubies." Elizabeth's partner looked up from the magnifying loupe. "You swapped a fake for a fake."

Elizabeth's mind began whirring. It was impossible that Sheila had deliberately deceived her. For one thing, she had no reason to. For another, she wasn't smart enough. Alan Brookstein must have switched the necklaces and laid out the fake tonight without telling his wife. But why would he . . . ?

An unpleasant thought suddenly occurred to her.

"What if he never bought the real rubies in the first place? What if *he* was duped?"

"Don't be stupid," her partner said rudely.

"It's possible."

"No, it isn't. Don't you think I checked that out months ago? Unlike you, when I do a job I do it thoroughly. And accurately. Brookstein has the necklace. It must still be in the safe. You'll have to go back and get it."

Elizabeth hesitated. She longed to tell her partner to stick it. That she wasn't in the business of taking orders. But then she thought about all the time and effort she'd put into this job. And the Brooksteins' empty house . . .

"Give me the damn code."

ELIZABETH THOUGHT QUICKLY, HER agile mind skipping through all the possible risks and strategies. The gala itself would go on for another few hours at least, probably longer, so there was little danger of either of the Brooksteins returning home. Conchita, their housekeeper, would also have gone home by now, so the house would be empty but alarmed. That was no problem. Elizabeth had a key and had memorized the code.

More problematic were the two security guards, Eduardo and Nico, who patrolled the property at night. Both of them knew "Liza" by sight, which gave her the option of brazening it out, walking in through the front door and explaining that she'd forgotten some personal item. The downside to that was that it would definitely pin down Liza Cunningham as the guilty party once the theft was discovered, which might be as soon as later that same night. That meant cops and FBI out looking for her, E-FIT pictures, and all sorts of irritations and complications that Elizabeth would rather do without.

On balance, she decided it would be easier simply to burgle the house—cover her face and slip in through a window. She would have forty seconds to disable the alarm, more than enough time. And Eduardo and Nico were hardly the CIA. She'd simply wait until they were distracted, talking to each other on one side of the property, and quietly make her entrance somewhere else.

By the time Elizabeth pulled up in the alley behind the estate and switched off her engine and lights, her heart rate was barely elevated. Coming away with the wrong necklace had been an annoyance. But it was easily rectified, and would be well worth the effort.

Slipping her black silk balaclava over her face (it was terribly important to work in comfort; Elizabeth's trusty mask was like a second skin), she was about to open the door when she suddenly froze.

The master-bedroom window popped open. Elizabeth heard the familiar, soft slither of a rope being thrown out. Seconds later a diminutive black-clad figure emerged, abseiling down the rear wall of the property with the silent grace of a spider gliding down a line of its own silk. It was quite beautiful to watch, like ballet. The figure stopped on a small flat roof about twelve feet off the ground. From there he paused, seemed to judge the distance, then made a catlike leap onto the boundary wall of the property, about thirty feet from where Elizabeth was parked.

Belatedly, she began to feel angry. The burglar's exit had been such a virtuoso performance, Elizabeth had been momentarily blinded by admiration. But now she felt a different, more raw emotion.

I don't believe it. After all that effort, someone beat me to it. That bastard's got my necklace!

At that precise moment the figure on top of the wall turned and looked directly at Elizabeth's car. Reaching into his backpack, he pulled out the string of rubies and dangled them mockingly in Elizabeth's direction.

What the . . .

Elizabeth turned on her headlights. Even from this distance she could see the red glow of the stones, taunting her. Then the black-clad figure removed his balaclava. A cascade of chestnut hair burst forth. *A woman!* A face Elizabeth Kennedy thought she would never see again smiled down at her, with a look of the purest triumph in her green eyes.

Climbing into her own car, Tracy Whitney blew her rival a kiss before speeding off into the night.

ELIZABETH KENNEDY SAT IN her car for a full five minutes before she made the call.

"Did you get it?"

Her partner's voice was cold, curt, demanding. Elizabeth had come to hate it over the years.

"No." She responded in kind, without apology. "I was too late."

"What do you mean, 'too late'? The gala's only halfway through."

"By the time I got here, someone else had stolen the necklace. I saw them leaving, just now."

There was a long silence on the other end of the line.

Elizabeth said, "You'll never guess who it was."

More silence. Elizabeth's partner did not like guessing games. Or any games, for that matter.

"Tracy Whitney."

When her partner spoke again, Elizabeth could have sworn she detected a trace of emotion.

"That's impossible. Tracy Whitney's not active anymore. She's almost certainly dead. No one's seen her for—"

"—almost ten years. I know. I was there, remember? But I'm telling you, it was Tracy Whitney. I recognized her immediately. And I'm pretty sure she recognized me."

TRACY PAID THE BABYSITTER at the hotel and tipped her very generously.

"Wow, that's so nice of you. Thanks. How was the movie?"

"Exciting. I loved every minute of it."

The sitter left. Tracy walked into Nicholas's room and watched him sleeping. She'd taken a huge risk tonight, letting that girl—Rebecca, as Tracy would always think of her—see her face. But it had been worth it.

I wanted her to know it was me who outsmarted her.

Tomorrow Tracy would bring the ruby necklace to her dealer contact and leave Los Angeles seven figures richer than when she'd arrived. But it wasn't the money that was making the adrenaline course through her body or the pleasure chemicals flood her brain. It wasn't even outsmarting her nemesis—or not entirely. It was the joy of a virtuoso pianist reunited with her instrument after years in exile. It was the delight of an expert surgeon regaining the use of his hands after an accident. It was coming back to life, when you hadn't even realized you were dead.

Tracy Schmidt is who I am now, Tracy told herself firmly. *Tonight was a one-shot deal.*

She said it so many times, and with such conviction, that by the time she fell asleep she almost believed it.

BACK IN THE CENTURY City condo, Elizabeth Kennedy's partner hung up the phone and sat down on the bed, shaking.

Tracy Whitney's alive?

Was it really possible, after all these years?

Elizabeth seemed quite sure. For all her sloppiness, she was unlikely to make an error about something as important as that. Besides, logic dictated that Elizabeth's conclusions were correct. Unlike fickle human emotions, logic could be relied upon. Logic was never wrong. It was Tracy who'd stolen the necklace. Tracy who'd outsmarted them somehow, not the dim-witted Brooksteins. Tracy Whitney was brilliant, a virtuoso at her craft. In terms of pulling off the perfect con, she had taught Elizabeth Kennedy's partner everything he knew. He wouldn't even be in this business if it weren't for Tracy. How ironic life could be sometimes!

Elizabeth's partner no longer cared about the necklace. The necklace didn't matter. Nothing mattered anymore except for that one, simple, incredible, intoxicating fact:

Tracy Whitney was back.

CHAPTER 12

$\mathscr{S}$ANDRA WHITMORE STOOD ON the corner of Western and Florence in Hollywood, hitching up her skirt and looking hopefully at the traffic.

Things were slow tonight, which was good and bad. Mostly bad. Still, at least she wasn't desperate for a hit. Not like Monique.

Sandra felt bad for Monique. It was crack that had driven both of them onto the streets. Them and all the other girls who walked these blocks. But while Sandra had kicked the habit, clean for sixteen weeks now, Monique was still deep in her addiction. Sandra looked at her friend's sunken eyes and protruding bones with a mixture of pity and shame. The shame was for her own past, for what she'd put her son Tyler through.

Not for much longer though.

Sandra was working tonight to pay off the last of her drug debts. Soon she'd be off the streets for good. She felt bad for

Monique and the others, but she knew she would never look back.

A beat-up Mitsubishi Shogun slowed as it approached them.

"Can I take this one?" Monique hopped from foot to foot like a toddler needing to pee and ran her tongue back and forth over her gums when she spoke. Her jaw was thrust permanently forward so that her teeth looked bared, like a dog's. Her whole body vibrated with desperation. "I know it's your turn . . ."

"Sure. No problem."

Sandra watched her friend climb up into the car. The man inside was heavyset and rough. He looked mean. Sandra noticed that he didn't help Monique when she struggled to close the passenger door. Her arms were so frail, she needed both just to move it. It would have been the easiest thing in the world for the guy to reach over and do it for her. But he just sat there as if she were invisible. As if she were nothing.

A shiver of fear ran through Sandra's body as she watched the car drive off.

I hope she'll be okay.

A few minutes later, a silver Lincoln sedan drew up.

"Looking for a ride?"

He was clean, attractive even, and wore a suit and a smile. When Sandra nodded he leaned over and opened the door for her. The car smelled of leather and air freshener. This was more like it. Sandra moved a book off her seat so she could sit down. She read the spine. *New Interpretations of the Gospel.*

"You're a Christian?"

"Sometimes." He put a manicured hand on her leg. "I'm working on it."

Sandra thought, *If more johns were like this, I might not retire after all.*

She pictured poor Monique, in the truck with the fat ass-hole, and felt a second stab of guilt. But she pushed it aside.

Maybe there was a reason that girls like Monique always got the short end of the stick?

Good things come to you when you start putting good things out there, Sandra. It starts here, in this fancy car. But it's gonna end somewhere much, much better.

Sandra Whitmore and her son were headed to a better life.

CHAPTER 13

A CONFERENCE WAS UNDER WAY at 11000 Wilshire Boulevard, Suite 1700, the FBI's Los Angeles headquarters. It was taking place in the office of Assistant Director John Marsden, but the man in charge was Agent Milton Buck. Agent Buck was in his early thirties and boyishly handsome. He would have been attractive had it not been for the twin handicaps of his pushy, arrogant personality and his height. At five foot seven, Milton Buck was easily the shortest man in the room.

The other people present were Assistant Director Marsden, FBI agents Susan Greene and Thomas Barton and Inspector Jean Rizzo of Interpol.

Agent Buck said, "There's no connection. I'm sorry, but there just isn't."

Jean Rizzo bit back his irritation. He'd met hundreds of Milton Bucks at Interpol, ambitious, cocky little megalomaniacs with no thought in their empty heads beyond further-

ing their own careers. Depressingly, they always seemed to
rise to the top. Like scum.

"You haven't even read the file."

"I don't need to. With respect, Mr. Rizzo—"

"Inspector Rizzo," said Jean. *Why was it that people
always began the most insulting sentences by saying "with
respect"?*

"My team and I are investigating a string of sophisticated, high-end thefts involving jewelry and fine art worth
multiple millions of dollars. What you have is a few dead
crack whores."

"Twelve. Twelve victims. If you'd read the files you'd—"

"I don't need to read your files to understand that there is
no possible connection between our respective cases."

"You're wrong." Jean pulled a sheaf of photographs out
of his briefcase and handed one to everyone in the room.
"There *is* a connection. You're looking at her. Her name is
Tracy Whitney."

"Tracy Whitney?" For the first time, Assistant Director
John Marsden's ears pricked up. Twenty years Milton Buck's
senior, Marsden was a far more impressive character in Jean
Rizzo's view. Measured. Thoughtful. Not a total dick. "Why
do I know that name?"

Jean Rizzo opened his mouth to speak but Agent Buck
cut him off.

"Cold case, sir. That's cold as in permafrost. Or cold as in
morgue. Whitney's almost certainly dead. She served time
in Louisiana for armed robbery."

"She never committed that crime," Jean interjected.
"Later evidence showed—"

"She got early release," Milton Buck talked over him.
"After that, her name was linked with a number of international swindles and burglaries. Interpol made a big deal out

of her for a while, but nothing was ever proved. Eight or nine years ago she dropped off the radar completely."

"And you know this how?" Assistant Director Marsden asked.

"We looked into her after the McMenemy Pissarro theft in New York, and again after the Neil Lane diamond heist in Chicago. No connection whatsoever." Buck looked pointedly at Jean Rizzo. "Tracy Whitney is old news."

Susan Greene, a plain young woman who was part of Buck's team, turned to Jean Rizzo.

"You obviously believe there's a connection between Ms. Whitney and this young woman's death. What was her name again?"

Agent Greene picked up the picture of the grotesquely mutilated corpse that Rizzo had shown them earlier.

"Her name was Sandra Whitmore."

"The crack whore," Milton Buck said nastily.

Jean gave him a look that could have melted stone.

"Sandra had been clean almost four months. She was a single mom with a day job at Costco."

"And we all know what her night job was." Buck sneered.

"She was murdered within forty-eight hours of Sheila Brookstein's Iranian ruby necklace being stolen. By the same individual who killed all the other girls. In every single one of these cases, the homicide takes place immediately following a 'sophisticated, high-end theft' in the same city." Rizzo emphasized each word, using Agent Buck's own phrase against him. "In many of those thefts, local police have reason to believe that the key suspect is female. As I'm sure you're all aware, there aren't many viable female suspects on file with a track record of this sort of flashy, audacious crime."

Assistant Director Marsden asked, "Was Tracy Whitney the one who conned the Prado? Didn't she steal a Goya?"

Jean Rizzo smiled. "The Puerto. That's right. You have an excellent memory."

"She had a partner. A guy."

"Jeff Stevens." Rizzo nodded.

Milton Buck was irritated. "Look. Nothing was ever proved against Tracy Whitney. Or Stevens, for that matter. And the Puerto wasn't stolen. The museum sold it in a private deal."

"After Whitney convinced them it was a fake She made a fortune out of that scam."

"The point is, whatever happened back then is ancient history. Tracy Whitney is not a suspect in the Brookstein job."

"Do you *have* a suspect?" Jean Rizzo asked bluntly.

"As a matter of fact we do."

"Is it a woman?"

Milton Buck hesitated. He badly wanted to tell the irritating Canadian from Interpol to stick his wild-goose chase theories where the monkey stuck his nuts, but for some reason the AD seemed to like the guy. Grudgingly, Buck sent one of his junior agents to fetch the Brookstein file.

A few minutes later he handed a photograph to Jean.

"Her name is Elizabeth Kennedy. That's one of her names anyway. She also goes by Liza Cunningham, Rebecca Mortimer and a string of other aliases. She's a con woman, a very good one. We have reason to believe she knew Sheila Brookstein. She's also a suspect in the Chicago job."

Jean looked closely at the beautiful young woman with the white-blond hair, wide sensual mouth and high cheekbones, like a doll's. It was hard to imagine what possible connection she might have to Sandra Whitmore, or any of the other murdered and mutilated girls. On the other hand, the same was true of Tracy Whitney.

The advantage Ms. Kennedy had over Ms. Whitney was

that she was definitively alive. As a rule, Jean preferred live suspects to dead ones. Even so, he wasn't prepared to let go of the Whitney connection just yet.

"Do you know where she is? This Kennedy woman."

For the first time, Buck looked uncomfortable. "Not at present, no. We're working on it. As I said, she uses a number of aliases."

"May I keep this picture?"

Milton Buck sighed heavily. "If you want to. But it's not going to help you. Look, Rizzo, you know as well as I do: hookers get killed in major cities all over the world, every day. There is no connection between your dead girl and the Brookstein rubies. You're clutching at straws, man. Now, if you'll excuse me, I have a job to do."

BACK IN HIS HOTEL room at the Standard in Hollywood, Jean tried to switch off. It was still only lunchtime, but the abortive meeting with the FBI had exhausted him, physically and emotionally. He hated L.A. More than any other city in the world, it made him feel homesick. There was something so lonely and desolate beneath its glitz and glamour. Everybody was trying too hard. The smell of burned hopes lingering in the air made it hard to breathe.

Jean telephoned his children in France, desperate suddenly to hear their voices. Clémence was out at a sleepover. Luc was watching *Winnie l'ourson* and refused to be torn away from the TV.

"Don't take it personally," Sylvie said kindly. "He's tired, that's all."

"I know. I miss him. I miss all of you."

There was a pause. "Let's not do this, Jean. I'm tired too."

Divorce sucked.

Hanging up, Jean took out the pictures of Sandra Whitmore's wrecked corpse and spread them out on the bed. Work was the best cure for heartbreak that Jean knew and he turned to it now, as he'd done so many times before.

The room Sandra was slaughtered in had been scrupulously cleaned, just like all the others. The Bible was there, with the highlighted text. Sandra's nails had been cut and her hair brushed. She'd been posed with her legs splayed wide. Jean closed his eyes and pictured the killer staging the scene, "fixing" his victim's body as if she were some sort of store mannequin. He felt a wave of hatred so strong it made him want to vomit.

Why wouldn't the FBI help him?

Why wouldn't Milton Buck even consider the possibility that either Tracy Whitney or his girl, Elizabeth Kennedy, might be involved? That there might be a connection between the con women and the prostitutes? Assistant Director Marsden had mentioned Whitney's partner in crime today, Jeff Stevens. Jean didn't know much about Stevens, beyond his name. Perhaps now was the time to do some more digging?

One step at a time. Let's check out Tracy Whitney first.

Jean had three days left in L.A. before he was due to fly home to Lyon. The LAPD was understaffed and the FBI clearly had no intention of helping him. Whatever investigative work he wanted to do, he would have to do on his own.

He picked up the phone.

SET BACK FROM THE Pacific Coast Highway, with spectacular views over the ocean, Nobu Malibu is a favorite Friday-night dinner venue for Hollywood's elite. Even a player like Alan Brookstein had had to call in a favor to get the coveted table nineteen out on the terrace. Wedged between Will and Jada Smith on one side and a billionaire Internet entrepreneur on the other, Alan Brookstein had hoped tonight's dinner might help break Sheila out of her funk. So far, no dice. Ever since her rubies had been stolen, Sheila had been about as much fun as root-canal surgery without anesthetic.

Looking at her now, scowling down at her sushi, her small, mean mouth pursed like a cat's anus, Alan Brookstein thought, *I don't love you. I don't even like you. I wish I'd never bought you that damned necklace in the first place.*

"Excuse me, Mr. Brookstein, Mrs. Brookstein? Do you mind if I sit down?"

The question was apparently rhetorical. The stocky little man with the Canadian accent had already pulled up a chair and positioned himself between the director and his wife.

"This won't take long. I'm investigating a homicide here in Los Angeles. A young woman was murdered in Hollywood last Sunday night, the evening after the robbery at your property." Jean Rizzo pulled out his Interpol ID card and laid it on the table.

"Murdered? How awful!" Sheila Brookstein said gleefully. The policeman was very handsome. A murder investigation would at least give her something to gossip about with her girlfriends. "Do we know the young woman?"

"I doubt it," said Jean. "She worked as a prostitute."

The gleeful look vanished from Sheila's face, replaced by an accusatory glare directed toward her husband.

"Jesus. Don't look at me. I don't know any hookers!"

"I wonder, sir, is this woman familiar to you?"

Jean took out Tracy Whitney's picture.

"Is *she* the prostitute?" Sheila Brookstein was still looking daggers at her husband, who was studying the image closely.

"No," said Jean. "But she may be connected to the case. Mr. Brookstein, do you recognize the woman in the picture?"

"I don't know. Maybe."

"What do you mean 'maybe'?" Sheila Brookstein's shrill voice was like nails on a chalkboard. "Either you know her or you don't."

"My God, Sheila, would you shut up for five seconds?" Alan Brookstein looked at the picture again. "Her hair's different now. And she's older than she is in this picture. But I think it might be the chick from the insurance company."

"You met this woman?" Jean tried to conceal his elation.

"Yeah."

"Recently?"

"She came to the house a week ago. Warned me about these pinhole cameras—turns out that's exactly what the thieves used to get the code to my safe. I guess I should have taken her more seriously."

"Thank you, Mr. Brookstein. Mrs. Brookstein. You've been a great help."

"Did this woman have anything to do with the robbery? What about my necklace?" Sheila Brookstein demanded.

Jean Rizzo was already out the door.

THE NEXT MORNING, JEAN Rizzo was in the car at six o'clock. Back in her heyday, Tracy Whitney had stayed in nothing but the best hotels. Armed with her picture, Jean started downtown and headed west, hitting L.A.'s most luxurious establishments. By ten, he had drawn a blank at five of the seven hotels on his list: the Ritz-Carlton, the Four Seasons, the Peninsula, the Roosevelt and the SLS. He began to doubt himself. *Maybe she rented a mansion? Maybe she stayed with a friend or a lover? Maybe she lost all her money somehow and is holed up in a motel? Maybe Alan Brookstein was mistaken and she was never here in L.A. at all?* Jean Rizzo wouldn't be the first person to end up chasing shadows where Tracy Whitney was concerned.

The manager at Shutters on the Beach in Santa Monica was polite but insistent.

"I recognize *all* our guests, Inspector. I am one hundred percent positive this young lady has not been staying with us."

That left only the Hotel Bel-Air. More in hope than with any expectation of a positive response, Jean showed the manager Tracy's picture.

"Ah, yes, Mrs. Schmidt. Bungalow six. She checked out four days ago."

"She did?" Jean was so delighted, he couldn't quite take in the information. "Did she leave a forwarding address?"

"Um . . ." The manager typed something into his computer. "No. I'm afraid not. But I have a billing address for the credit card. Would you like that?"

Jean nodded enthusiastically.

"Lovely lady," the manager said as he printed out the details. "If only all our guests were as kind and conscientious. She left a *very* generous tip and was politeness itself."

"Mm-hmm." Jean wasn't listening.

"Her son was delightful too."

The manager handed Jean the address.

"Her *son*?"

"Nicholas. Charming boy. Terribly good-looking too, although I suppose it's hardly surprising with genes like that." The manager smiled, then frowned suddenly as if something had just occurred to him. "She's not in any trouble, is she?"

"No no," said Jean. "Nothing like that."

Out in the car, he read the address the manager had given him.

Steamboat Springs, Colorado.

Jean Rizzo wasn't sure how he'd pictured Tracy Whitney's life, assuming that she was, indeed, still alive. But he found it hard to imagine the most successful con artist of all time living quietly as a small-town mom up in the mountains. He thought for a moment about calling Milton Buck and telling him what he'd discovered. It would be fun to wipe the smug smile off the arrogant FBI man's face. But he soon thought better of it. Buck's only interest was in solving the robbery cases and finding the missing jewelry and artworks. Jean Rizzo had a killer to catch. Besides, this was *his* information. *The FBI isn't scratching my back. Why should I scratch theirs?*

His flight home to France would have to wait.

It was time to pay a visit to Mrs. Tracy Schmidt.

CHAPTER 14

"CHECK."

"What? How is that check?" Tracy looked at the board, then at Nicholas. Her eyes narrowed. "Did you move my queen while I was putting the pizza in the oven?"

"You're so suspicious, Mom! Why is that?"

"Did you?"

Nicholas put on his best, wide-eyed innocent expression.

"You know the first rule of chess is never take your eyes off the board. You shouldn't have to ask me that question."

"Have you ever thought of going into politics?" Tracy asked, amused. "You'd be great at it."

"Thanks." Nicholas grinned. "Your move."

Tracy moved her last remaining bishop, which Nicholas promptly took with his pawn. Four moves later it was check-mate.

I really must call him on the cheating, she thought, after Nicholas disappeared outside to find Blake Carter. Blake would have hit the roof if he'd witnessed that little maneuver with the queen. But Nicky was so charming, at least in his mother's eyes, that Tracy didn't have the heart to play bad cop. Since their return from L.A., she'd felt even more protective of her son than usual. Stealing that necklace and showing her face to her rival had been a crazy risk to take. The guilt had hit Tracy belatedly, but it hit hard.

A knock on the door interrupted her thoughts just as she was pulling the pizza out of the oven. Blake Carter's ability to smell a thin-crust pepperoni from more than three fields away was quite unrivaled. Smiling, Tracy opened the door to find herself face-to-face with a good-looking stranger.

"Can I help you?"

Dark and stocky with gray eyes and a kind, oddly off-kilter face, the man was staring at her with a strange intensity. Then he said three words that felt like lead being poured into Tracy's heart.

"Hello, Ms. Whitney."

IT TOOK TRACY A few seconds to regain her breath, never mind her composure. Jean Rizzo watched the blood drain from her face, then rush back to her cheeks. She was prettier in the flesh than he'd expected. More youthful- and natural-looking.

"I'm sorry. You must have me mistaken for someone else."

Tracy started to close the door. Jean stuck out a hand to stop her. He briefly flashed his Interpol ID.

"I tell you what. Let's make a deal. You don't waste my time and I won't waste yours. I know you took the Brookstein rubies."

"Really, I have no idea what—"

"I couldn't care less about the necklace."

Tracy paused for a split second, then said, "What necklace?"

Jean Rizzo sighed.

"I don't want to arrest you, Ms. Whitney. But I will if I have to. I'm here because I need your help. Can I come in?"

Tracy's quick mind began working overtime. Her first thought was Nicholas. He was out at the stables with Blake, but he was sure to return soon.

"You've got ten minutes," she told Jean curtly.

He followed her into a large, country-style kitchen. It was warm and homey rather than grand. Chess pieces and kids' magazines littered the farmhouse table and childish artwork had been framed and hung everywhere, along with countless photographs of a cute, dark-haired boy in various stages of development. The boy looked vaguely familiar.

"Your son?"

"What do you want, Inspector Rizzo?" Tracy's tone was far from welcoming.

Jean responded in kind. "You can lose the attitude, Ms. Whitney. Like I said, I know you stole Sheila Brookstein's ruby necklace in Los Angeles last week. I could arrest you right now and we could do this interview down at the local police station if you prefer."

"Go ahead." Tracy held out her arms mockingly. "Arrest me."

When Jean hesitated, she laughed loudly. "You have no proof of anything, Inspector. If you *could* arrest me, you would. So I suggest *you* lose the attitude, or get the hell out of my house."

Jean took off his coat and sat down at the table. "You're very sure of yourself, Ms. Whitney. How do you know I have no proof?"

Tracy looked at him levelly. In *this* game of chess she had no intention of taking her eye off the board, not for a second.

"Because I haven't stolen any ruby necklace."

Now it was Jean's turn to laugh. This woman was a piece of work.

"And by the way, my name is Tracy Schmidt."

"Yeah? And mine's Rip Van Winkle."

"How unfortunate for you, Inspector Van Winkle." Tracy's green eyes danced.

"I blame my mother." Jean played along.

"Why's that? Surely it was your father's name?"

"That's true. But Mom didn't have to go with 'Rip.' " Tracy grinned.

Jean said, "I tell you what. How about I call you 'Tracy,' and you can call me 'Jean'?"

He extended his hand.

"Okay, Jean." Tracy liked him instinctively, but she kept her wits about her. This man was a cop. He was not her friend. "How can I help you?"

"I'm investigating a series of murders."

A look of surprise crossed her face. Jean gave her the details of the Bible Killer cases in broad brushstrokes. Tracy listened intently. She was horrified at the crimes Jean was describing, but she was also anxious to get him out of her house before Nicholas returned.

"The last girl was killed a week ago, in Hollywood. The day after you sto— The day after Sheila Brookstein's rubies were stolen. The victim's name was Sandra Whitmore. She had a son about the same age as yours."

"I'm sorry," said Tracy. "Truly I am. There are some sick bastards out there. But I'm afraid I can't help you. I know nothing about any Sandra Whitmore, or any of these women."

"It's more complicated than that," said Jean. "I have a theory . . . I need to go through each of the cases with you one by one, in detail. It's going to take time."

Tracy stood up. Nicholas and Blake would be back any minute.

"I'm sorry. I don't *have* time. You need to leave now."

"I'll leave when you've answered my questions," Jean said angrily.

He stood up and looked out of the window. A young boy was walking toward the house, arm in arm with an older man.

The manager of the Hotel Bel-Air was right. The boy was very good-looking. It suddenly struck Jean where he'd seen him before.

"That's a handsome kid you got there."

"Thank you."

"Is that his father with him?"

Tracy stiffened. "No."

She looked over Jean's shoulder. Nicholas and Blake were getting closer. She felt the fear rising up within her. If this man said anything in front of them, in front of Nicky . . .

"Please. You have to leave."

"Where *is* his father?"

"His father is dead."

"Interesting," Jean Rizzo said. "Because last I heard, Mr. Stevens was very much alive. According to the FBI, he has a very interesting sideline these days. In the historical-treasures business."

Tracy gripped the countertop. The floor seemed to be giving way beneath her.

She turned to Jean, unable either to speak or to hide the turmoil of emotions churning inside her. How did he know about Jeff? She did not want to hear about Jeff. Not now, not ever. And certainly not from this strange, aggressive little man who somehow knew who she was and was here talking about murders, and rapes and crimes that had nothing to do with her.

"Help me solve these killings," said Jean.

"I can't. You must believe me. Your theory is wrong. I have nothing to do with this!"

"Help me or I'll tell your boy the truth."

The kitchen door swung open.

Nicholas looked up curiously at the strange man with his mother.

"Hello."

"Hello." Jean smiled.

"Who are you?"

The boy seemed surprised but in no way unnerved to see an unknown male in his kitchen. Unlike the rugged cowboy who'd walked in with him, who was glowering at Jean with obvious distrust. The guy looked like a throwback to an old Clint Eastwood movie. *Boyfriend?* wondered Jean.

Tracy seemed to have lost the power of speech. All her earlier confidence had evaporated. She felt as if she might faint. Eventually she stammered, "Th-This is, er . . . this is . . ."

"My name is Jean. I'm an old friend of your mother's."

"From Europe?" asked Nicholas. "Before I was born?"

Jean Rizzo glanced at Tracy. She nodded imperceptibly.

"That's right. I was hoping your mother might be able to have dinner with me tonight. To catch up on old times. I'm staying down in town."

"She can't tonight. We have plans."

Blake Carter's voice rang out, as steady and solid and reassuring as the chiming of an old church bell.

"Right, Tracy?"

One look at Tracy had been enough to convince Blake that her "old friend" Jean was nothing of the sort. Blake thought, *She's frightened. Tracy's never frightened.*

"Tomorrow, then?" asked Jean.

The old cowboy had wrapped a protective arm around

Tracy's shoulder in a gesture that could have been paternal or romantic. Jean found himself wondering about their relationship, and what, if anything, the older man knew of Tracy's past. Or her present, come to think of it.

"Okay," said Tracy, to Blake Carter's evident distress. "Tomorrow."

She never wanted to see Jean Rizzo's face again. But what choice did she have?

The game of chess was on and it was Tracy's move.

GIANNI'S, A COZY ITALIAN in the mountain village area, right at the foot of the ski slopes, was popular with locals and tourists alike. The staff all knew Tracy by sight, although Mrs. Schmidt rarely ate out. Everyone wondered who the handsome man was, dining with Steamboat's wealthiest widow in the corner booth. But nobody asked.

Jean got straight to business. He handed Tracy a sheaf of pictures, mostly family snapshots of the twelve victims. Izia Moreno at her high school graduation in Madrid. Alissa Armand laughing with her sister at a campsite outside Paris. Sandra Whitmore cradling her baby son in her arms.

"The women were all prostitutes. They were killed over a nine-year period, in different cities all over the world."

"But you think it's the same killer?"

"It *is* the same killer. There aren't many certainties in this investigation but that's one of them."

Jean told her about the murderer's obsession with neatness and the Bible verses. "He's familiar with police procedures, or at least with the ways in which DNA evidence is collected. He cleans up the crime scenes to protect himself, but it goes beyond that. He's staging the bodies. It's like theater."

Tracy listened but said nothing. She ordered *linguine vongole* for both of them, a specialty of the house, but barely touched her plate when it arrived.

"I still don't see where I come in."

"Each murder took place between twenty-four and forty-eight hours after a major heist of some kind in the same city. None of those robberies were solved. All of them were complicated, meticulously planned and executed. More than half involved a woman. There aren't many women in your business, as you know."

"What business is that, Inspector?"

Jean raised an eyebrow. "Come on now, Miss Whitney."

"Let's stick with 'Tracy.' And lower your voice."

"Sorry. The point is there are very few females operating at this level. We're talking seven-figure jobs here. Highly sophisticated."

Tracy nodded. "Go on."

"I started researching the robberies and looking for female suspects. Your name popped up on the Interpol database. The first thing I noticed was that no one had seen hide nor hair of you in nine years, when you disappeared from London."

"So?"

"So the first victim, Karen Harle, was killed nine years ago. In London. Same time. Same city. You disappeared, and these murders began."

Jean sipped his wine and looked at Tracy expectantly.

Tracy stared back at him. If this man weren't threatening to expose her identity and destroy her and Nicholas's life, she might almost have laughed.

"That's it? That's your connection? The nine-year London thing?"

Jean bristled. "It's a link."

"It's nothing of the sort! It's a coincidence! And I didn't disappear. I left. I needed a new start and I got one."

"A coincidence?" said Jean. "Really? Let's fast-forward, shall we? New York City, three years later. A Pissarro is stolen from a private residence on Fifth Avenue in broad daylight by a woman posing as an employee of the Metropolitan Museum of Art. Does that not sound like one of your jobs to you?"

"It sounds audacious," Tracy conceded. "I like the broad-daylight part. But I was nowhere near New York at that time."

Jean went on.

"Okay. Chicago. A diamond bracelet and two pairs of matching earrings are stolen from a Neil Lane store. Not only were cameras and alarms disabled *and then reset,* but it was three weeks before anybody discovered that the gems were even missing. The fakes used to replace them were such expert reproductions."

"Again, impressive attention to detail."

"But not ringing any bells?"

Tracy sipped her wine. "None whatsoever."

"Mumbai, two years ago. An unscrupulous property developer is conned into buying a nonexistent title to a piece of land the size of a handkerchief by a beautiful young American woman whom he believes to be romantically interested in him."

"Was the man married?"

"He was, as it happens. Why do you ask?"

Tracy shrugged. "Serves him right, then, wouldn't you say?"

"I'll tell you what *I* would say." Jean Rizzo leaned across the table. "I would say that every one of these jobs has your name written all over it."

"Except for the one *tiny* issue . . . that I wasn't *in* New York or Chicago on the dates in question! As for Mumbai, I've never been to India in my life. And Hong Kong and Lima and . . . all of these . . ." She pushed the stack of files that Jean had placed on the table between them back in his direction. "I haven't left the United States in nine years, Inspector. Ask any mother at Nicky's school if you don't believe me. I've been right here, in Steamboat Springs. The whole town's my alibi."

A waitress came over and removed the *vongole*s, untouched. Jean Rizzo ordered coffees and a plate of *cantuccini*. All that wine on an empty stomach was starting to go to his head.

Tracy said, "I'd like to help you, Inspector. I would. I think what happened to these women is horrific and I hope you get the guy who did it. But you came here looking for Tracy Whitney, and the truth is that Tracy Whitney is dead. She died nine years ago."

"Hmm," said Jean.

"Even if she were alive, she was never in the business of hurting people."

"Hmm," said Jean again.

"What? What does 'hmm' mean?"

"I was just thinking that for a dead chick, she pulled off a pretty neat job in L.A. ten days ago. Tracy Whitney must have been quite a lady."

Tracy laughed. "I believe she was."

"Those rubies must be worth, what? Two, three million? Maybe more to a private collector."

"I'm afraid I have no idea what you're talking about." Tracy smiled sweetly. "Ah, lovely. The coffee's arrived."

Watching her sip the thick, black liquid, Jean Rizzo could see quite clearly why so many men had become obsessed with Tracy Whitney. She was beautiful, of course, but there was far more to it than that. She was clever and funny, and she clearly took delight in outwitting her adversaries on both sides of the law. He decided to change tack.

"So your son knows nothing. About your past, or about his father."

Tracy put down her cup slowly and fixed Jean with a steely glare. There was no more banter now. Battle lines had been drawn.

"No, he doesn't. And he never will."

"Does Jeff Stevens even know he has a child?"

"Jeff Stevens doesn't have a child!" Tracy shot back angrily. "At least, not with me. Nicky's mine. Only mine. I raised him. I'm all he needs."

Aware that she'd just raised her voice, Tracy shrank back into the shadows of the booth. Jean Rizzo thought about his own children and how desperately he missed them. He felt a stab of pity for Jeff Stevens.

Reading his mind, Tracy said, "You don't understand, Inspector."

"Jean."

"Jean," Tracy corrected herself. "You don't know Jeff like I do."

"I don't hate him like you do, you mean."

"Hate him?" Tracy looked genuinely shocked. "I don't hate Jeff. I just love Nicky. That's a very different thing. You're going to have to trust me when I tell you that Jeff would have made a lousy father. Oh, he's loving and charming and perfectly adorable. But you can't rely on him. Jeff would have broken Nicky's heart in the end. Just like he broke mine."

"What happened between you? If you don't mind my asking."

Did she mind? Jean Rizzo was a total stranger. Worse than that, he was a cop. But somehow, Tracy found herself

pouring out the whole story. She told him about losing her
first baby with Jeff. She told him about her struggles to
adjust to married life and domesticity. She told him about
walking in on Jeff and Rebecca Mortimer kissing in the
bedroom in Eaton Square, about the terrible, searing pain
of betrayal. Finally she told him about seeing Rebecca again
out of the blue in L.A. last month, having dinner with Sheila
Brookstein.

"I went to Los Angeles for a vacation with my son. That's
the truth. I had no intention of"—she searched around for
the right word—"coming out of retirement. But as soon as I
saw her, I knew she was after that necklace. I had a chance
to pay her back in some small way for what she did to me,
and I took it."

"I understand," said Jean.

Tracy's eyes narrowed. "You do?"

"Of course. You'll be pleased to know that your friend
'Rebecca' is the FBI's prime suspect in the Brookstein job.
Her real name is Elizabeth Kennedy, by the way." Jean re-
trieved the picture Milton Buck had given him from his
briefcase and handed it over.

Tracy stared at it intently.

Elizabeth.

It was too nice a name, too innocuous. It didn't feel right.

Tracy was silent for a long time, lost in thought. Eventually Jean Rizzo said, "They want her for the other two U.S.
jobs as well. The Pissarro theft in New York and the Chicago diamonds."

Tracy took this in.

"What about the other robberies?" she asked. "The ones
in Europe and Asia, where the girls were murdered afterward?"

"The feds don't believe there's a connection between any
of the robberies and the Bible Killer murders," Jean said bit-

terly. "Besides, you know how it works. The Bureau doesn't give a crap about things that happen outside their jurisdiction. They could pass the intel on to us, but they don't. They don't even share with the CIA. It's political and pathetic, and meanwhile these girls are out there getting butchered." He filled her in on his abortive meeting with Agent Milton Buck in Los Angeles.

"Okay. But now *you* know about 'Elizabeth,'" said Tracy. The name still felt odd to her. "Surely you can get the word out through Interpol? You don't need the FBI."

"Hmm," Jean said again.

Tracy waited patiently for his vocabulary to catch up with his brain. She was used to policemen who shot their mouths off first and thought later. Arrogant, impulsive, sloppy policemen had helped Tracy make her fortune. Jean Rizzo was different.

I like him, she thought. *I'll have to watch that.*

When Jean finally spoke, it was slowly, as if he were thinking aloud, piecing things together as he went along.

"The problem is, I didn't believe it *was* Elizabeth. I thought it was you."

"You thought *I* ran around the world killing prostitutes?"

"No no no. Of course not. Our killer's a man."

"Okay, good. Glad we got that straightened out."

"But I thought you were the link between the robberies and the murders."

"Because of the nine-year thing?"

"Because of the nine years. Because of London. Because you're a woman. Because these robberies were so close to your old MO—clever but simple, well planned, geographically spread out, always at a worthwhile price point."

Tracy smiled. "You're making me feel quite nostalgic."

"Because you *did* do the Brookstein job," he continued, counting the reasons off on his fingers. "Because I don't believe in coincidences. At least, not twelve in a row. And because there wasn't another viable suspect."

"Until now," said Tracy.

Jean nodded. "Until now. I guess."

"What do you mean, you guess? Now you have Elizabeth Kennedy. Right?"

"Hmm."

"Really? We're back to 'hmm'?"

Jean looked up at her. "I still think you're the link."

Tracy put her head in her hands.

"Think about it," said Jean. "These jobs are *exactly* like yours."

"There are some similarities, on the surface," Tracy conceded. "But I wasn't *there,* Jean."

"It's more than similarities. If you didn't do the robberies yourself—"

"No 'if.' I didn't. I can prove it."

"Then whoever did them is mimicking your techniques. That means they know you. Intimately. They know how you worked."

No one knows how I worked, Tracy thought. *No one except Jeff. And Gunther. But I hardly think Gunther's running around the world pulling off jewel heists.*

Aloud, she asked Jean, "Do you think someone's trying to frame me?"

"It's a possibility. Do you have any enemies that you know of?"

Tracy laughed loudly. "Hundreds!"

"I'm serious."

"So am I! Let me think. There's a man named Maximilian Pierpont who probably doesn't have me at the top of his Christmas-card list. Then there's Lois Bellamy, Gregory Halston, Alberto Fornati . . ." She listed some of her more prominent former victims. "Quite a number of people at the Prado museum in Madrid . . . Luckily most of them think I'm dead. Just like your friends at the FBI. If it's all the same to you, I'd like it to stay that way."

"Of course, we may not be looking for an enemy at all," said Jean. "There may be other motives in play. Possibly this person admired your work and wants to follow in your footsteps."

"Like a fan, you mean? Or a tribute band?" Tracy asked mockingly.

"Is that so unlikely?"

"Unlikely? From where I'm sitting, it's completely ridiculous. Look. Your only viable suspect for these robberies is Elizabeth Kennedy. She's a woman, she's active, and she operates at this level. I know for a fact that she'd been working Sheila Brookstein for months. But I can assure you that that woman is no fan of mine. She seduced my husband, Inspector. She destroyed my life. And not for money. For fun." Tracy's voice hardened. "I hate her. And I'm pretty sure the feeling's mutual."

"Yes, but don't you see?" said Jean. "That still makes you the link. Elizabeth Kennedy emerges as a new suspect, totally unknown to Interpol until now . . . and even *she's* connected to you."

"Meaning?"

Jean groaned. "I don't know. I don't know what it means."

He'd lost the thread, if he ever even had one in the first place. He was hungry and exhausted. Trying to hold on to a thought felt like swimming through molasses.

"Forget me for the moment," said Tracy. "Let's assume there is a link between the robberies and the murders. Let's also assume that Elizabeth *was* involved in all the robberies. Given that we know I wasn't."

Jean nodded. "Okay."

"Shouldn't your next move be to find Elizabeth? Whatever your doubts, Jean, the way I see it, she's all you've got."

"You could be right. But finding Elizabeth Kennedy may be easier said than done. The young lady's a pro. She's given the FBI the slip on at least three occasions that I know of. She evaporated out of L.A. after the Brookstein job even faster than you did."

"And more successfully, evidently," Tracy added ruefully. "So what *do* you know about her?"

"Not much." Jean gave her the bare bones of Elizabeth's history as provided by the FBI. Her upbringing in England, her juvenile record, the string of crimes in which she'd been identified as a "person of interest" and some of her known aliases. "The feds are convinced she works with a partner. A man. Just like you did with Jeff Stevens."

"I doubt that."

Jean looked surprised. "Why?"

"Why split the money if you don't have to? Jeff and I were different. A one-shot deal, if you like. Only a man would assume that a woman like Elizabeth needs a man behind her, pulling the strings."

Jean signaled for the check.

"Thanks for coming out tonight, Tracy."

"I didn't have much choice, did I?" she said.

"Look. I like you," said Jean. "I do. I can see you've built a good life here. I don't want to cause trouble for you and your son."

"Then don't." Despite herself, Tracy's eyes began to well up. "I've told you as much as I know. Truly. Please leave us alone now."

"I can't," said Jean. "Not yet."

"What do you mean, you can't? Of course you can!"

Jean shook his head. "I have a job to do, Tracy. I have to

catch this bastard before he kills again. If the FBI catches up with Elizabeth Kennedy before I do, they'll charge her with the thefts and send her to jail and we'll lose our only link to this psycho, whoever he is. What you said just now was right. We need to find Elizabeth."

"I didn't say 'we.' I said 'you,'" Tracy shot back angrily. "*You* need to find her, Jean."

"We need to find her and follow her until we find *him*."

"If there *is* a him."

"I need your help, Tracy."

"For God's sake, I don't *know* Elizabeth," Tracy pleaded. "How can I possibly help you? I told you, I ran into her in L.A. by chance. Before that I hadn't seen her in years. Almost a decade! I didn't even know her real name till tonight."

"The point is, she knows *you*," said Jean. "She thinks like you. She operates like you. You're inside her head, Tracy, whether you want to be or not. You have to help me find her before Milton Buck does."

"And if I refuse?" Tracy's eyes flashed defiantly.

"I'll expose you. I'll tell your son the truth. I'm sorry, Tracy"—Jean sighed—"but I don't have a choice."

There were a few moments of silence. Then Tracy said, "Once we find her, do you swear you will leave me alone? You will never, ever try to contact me again?"

"You have my word."

Jean offered her his hand. Tracy shook it. He had a firm handshake, and his palm was warm and dry against her own.

Tracy thought, *I trust him.*

God help me.

Jean signed the check and they walked outside. The crisp night air felt reviving to both of them as they walked to Jean's car.

"So," said Jean. "You're Elizabeth Kennedy. You've spent the last six months planning to steal the Brookstein rubies only to have your archrival beat you to the punch at the very last moment. What's your next move?"

Tracy thought for a moment.

"Regroup. When a job goes wrong, you need some time to recover. You analyze it, try to learn from your mistakes."

"Okay. Where? If it were you, where would you go to do that?"

"If it were me?" Tracy paused, then smiled. "Home. If it were me, I'd go home."

CHAPTER 15

*E*DWIN GREAVES WATCHED THE rain stream down his kitchen windowpane and wondered, *What did I come in here for again?* Edwin Greaves's large, comfortable flat looked over Cadogan Gardens. The communal tennis courts were drenched and deserted, overhung by trees stripped bare of their leaves by the driving rain and bitter autumn winds.

I used to play tennis. Charlie could always beat me, though. Even as a little boy.

Where is Charlie?

Charlie Greaves, Edwin's son, usually came on a Tuesday, to help Edwin with his mail and his grocery shopping at Harrods. Edwin Greaves always shopped at Harrods. One must maintain some standards after all, even in one's nineties.

Why wasn't Charlie here yet? Perhaps it wasn't Tuesday? Although Edwin could have sworn it was.

"Can I help you with the tea, Mr. Greaves?"

A young woman's voice drifted through from the drawing room.

Ah, that was it. Tea. I'm making tea for me and the nice young lady from Bonhams auction house.

"No, no, my dear. You make yourself comfortable. I'll be through in a moment."

The young woman smiled warmly when the old man finally shuffled back into the room. Setting down the tray with a rattle, he handed her a cup of tea in an antique Doulton china mug. It was stone cold.

"Thank you." She sipped it anyway, pretending not to notice. "I've signed the paperwork here and attached the check. But perhaps we should wait for your son?"

"Why? It's not his painting."

"Well, no. But . . ."

"I'm not dead yet, you know." Edwin Greaves laughed. His lungs made a ghastly, wheezing sound, like a broken accordion. "Although to hear Charlie's wife talk, you'd think everything I owned was already theirs. Bloody vultures." The old man's face darkened suddenly. The young woman dealt with a lot of rich, elderly people. She knew well how their moods could shift at the drop of a hat, like clouds in a stormy sky.

"Besides," Edwin went on, "it's not as if it's a genuine Turner. Everyone knows it's a fake."

"That's true," the young woman said amiably. "But it's still valuable. Gresham Knight was one of the most brilliant forgers of his generation. That's why my client is prepared to make such a generous offer."

"May I?" Edwin Greaves's gnarled fingers reached for the check. He held it up close to his face, scanning and rescanning the number with his rheumy old eyes. "Fifty thousand pounds?" He looked at the woman from Bonhams in astonishment. "That's far too much money! Good gracious, my dear, I can't possibly accept that."

She laughed. "Like I say, it's not a Turner, but that doesn't mean it's worthless. My advice is that you make the sale. But of course, if you prefer to wait for your son . . ."

"No, no, no," Edwin Greaves said tetchily. "Charlie's coming on Tuesday. It's not his painting anyway. We're going to go through my mail."

The young woman passed him a pen. Edwin Greaves signed the papers.

"We were going to play tennis, but then this beastly rain set in."

"That's a shame. May I take the painting now?"

"Charlie comes on Tuesdays."

She slipped the painting into the padded canvas bag she'd brought along for the purpose.

"There's the check, Mr. Greaves, on the coffee table. Would you like me to put it somewhere safe for you?"

"This dratted tea's gone cold." Edwin Greaves frowned down at his cup in confusion. "He's terribly good at tennis, Charlie. He always beats me."

The old man was still muttering as the young woman took her leave, closing the front door of the flat behind her.

ELIZABETH KENNEDY LAUGHED TO herself as the black cab splashed along the Embankment toward the City.

Stupid old fool.

Unzipping the canvas bag, Elizabeth looked lovingly at the painting, an exquisitely executed oil of a classic, Turner-esque pastoral scene. Everything she'd told Edwin Greaves was true. The painting wasn't a Turner. It was a forgery, one of Gresham Knight's best. And it was valuable. At least ten times more valuable than the £50,000 Elizabeth had just paid for it. The check she'd given Edwin was real enough, although the account was untraceable to her. Greaves would get something for his stupidity, which was more than he deserved. Perhaps he could buy his grasping, inheritance-hungry son a new tennis racket?

London looked gray and dreary in the rain. The Thames snaked beside the road, swollen and sluggish. Commuters scurried into the tube stations like rats down a drain, stooped and shivering beneath their umbrellas and mackintosh raincoats. But Elizabeth was pleased to be home. Warm and safe in the back of the cab, with her latest acquisition nestled triumphantly in her lap, she felt her confidence slowly returning.

L.A. had been a disaster. Months of work "grooming" the Brooksteins had ended in failure and humiliation at the hands of none other than Tracy bloody Whitney. Elizabeth loathed Tracy. Partly because people in the business still spoke of her in hushed tones, as if she were some sort of goddess whose record as a con artist could never be broken. By Elizabeth's count, she had already outperformed Tracy Whitney on every measurable scale. She'd pulled off more jobs, for more money than Whitney had ever earned, even in her heyday. But the root of Elizabeth's dislike was not professional envy, but sexual jealousy.

Jeff Stevens loved Tracy Whitney.

Elizabeth could not forgive Tracy for that.

Nor could she understand it.

I'm better looking than that bitch, and I'm infinitely better in bed. Why would Jeff choose her when he could have had me?

Elizabeth hadn't intended to fall for Jeff. Indeed, of all her countless scores of male conquests, Jeff Stevens was the *only* man with whom she'd ever felt something more than a straightforward desire to have sex. Perhaps it was the fact that she'd never had him sexually, apart from that one kiss. And yet there *had been* intimacy there, emotionally. Jeff brought out something deeper in Elizabeth, something no other man had, before or since.

He's like my mirror. My twin. He's part of me.

Over the years, Elizabeth had researched Jeff's life and background extensively. The more she discovered, the more similarities she found between his life and her own. They had both been abandoned by their parents when young, both effectively "adopted." They'd learned to live by their wits from their midteens, and to use their good looks and street smarts to outwit the greedy and make their way in the world. They both did what they did for the thrill as much as for the money. And because they were the best at it. The best of the best. Add to that their powerful sexual chemistry and it was clear to Elizabeth that she and Jeff Stevens were destined to be together.

There was only one fly in the ointment. Jeff Stevens hated Elizabeth Kennedy with a passion bordering on the psychotic. Their paths had crossed once or twice over the past decade—they were in the same business after all. Jeff never failed to cut her dead.

Jeff's last words to Elizabeth had been said in Hong Kong three years ago. Elizabeth was on a job at the time, a rather daring diamond heist at the airport—a high point of her career, as it turned out. Jeff was after some ancient Chinese stone tablets for a collector in Peru. He'd returned to his hotel room one night to find Elizabeth naked and waiting for him in his bed.

"Admit it," she purred, spreading her smooth, caramel-brown legs and arching her perfect dancer's back. "You want me. You want me as much as I want you. You always have."

The bulge in Jeff's pants seemed to confirm her suspicions. But the look of revulsion on his face spoke otherwise.

"I wouldn't sleep with you if you were the last woman on earth."

"Sure you would," said Elizabeth. "Remember how badly you wanted to in London? Before your wife walked in and ruined it all."

"Get out."

He picked up Elizabeth's clothes, threw them at her and opened the door.

"I lost the only woman I ever loved because of you."

The humiliation of Jeff's sexual rejection had faded, but the memory of his words still stung. *The only woman I ever loved . . .*

Tracy Whitney wasn't Jeff Stevens's soul mate.

Elizabeth Kennedy was.

Someday, somehow, she would force him to open his eyes.

"Here we are, love."

The cab had stopped. They'd reached Canary Wharf already. Elizabeth paid the fare and hurried into her building, a glass-and-steel monolith with panoramic views across London. Her apartment was stunning, a five-thousand-square-foot penthouse stuffed full of fine art and exquisite modern furniture. Having grown up in a poky, cramped council house in Wolverhampton, Elizabeth craved space and simplicity. Much of her decor had an Asian theme and the entire space was high-ceilinged and open plan. A bamboo screen separated Elizabeth's enormous, bespoke bed with its red silk sheets from a living room that looked more like an art gallery than a private home. Kicking off her shoes and setting the Gresham Knight oil painting gently down on the red lacquer dining table, she poured herself a glass of perfectly chilled Château d'Yquem and sank down onto the sofa.

Too pumped to watch television, she tapped a manicured finger on her iPad and closed her eyes, allowing the calming sounds of Verdi to flood her senses. As they did so often, her thoughts turned to Jeff Stevens.

Darling Jeff. Where are you now, I wonder?

Elizabeth had heard through the grapevine that Jeff was planning a big job in New York over Christmas. She didn't know what it was yet, although Jeff being Jeff, it was sure to involve some obscure medieval manuscript or piece of Etruscan pottery. Elizabeth did not share his fascination with old and dusty relics of civilizations past. Why limit your resale market if you didn't have to? Elizabeth almost never took jobs on commission, preferring to auction off her spoils on the black market to the highest bidder.

Running her fingers through her hair—she was growing out the severe cut she'd had in L.A., and now sported a midlength auburn bob—Elizabeth pondered a return to the States. She hadn't given up on Jeff Stevens. New York would be her best opportunity to seduce him since Hong Kong. This time, she would try a less direct approach. She would attempt to impress him professionally before turning on the big guns. If she pulled off something spectacular and ingenious, she might at least win his respect. That would be a start.

Various possibilities presented themselves. The rich and stupid flocked to New York at Christmastime. It was really just a question of picking off that one juicy, stray gazelle. That and convincing her business partner to let her go in the first place.

"It's far too soon," he snapped when Elizabeth suggested it over the phone. "We do nothing more in America for a year at least."

"That's ridiculous."

The debacle over the Iranian rubies had dented Elizabeth's confidence, but it seemed to have shattered her partner's equilibrium completely. Ever since the failed Brookstein job, he'd been jumpy and neurotic, perpetually looking over both their shoulders.

"The FBI is all over us."

"All over me, you mean," Elizabeth corrected. "Anyway, so what? Since when do we run scared from the federal bunch of idiots? I want to do New York."

"No."

"There's a charity gala on the—"

"I said no."

The line went dead.

Elizabeth Kennedy was beginning to grow increasingly weary of her partner. The longer they worked together, the more weird and controlling he became. In the beginning she'd been happy to play second fiddle, the young rookie to his seasoned mentor. Especially as he was prepared to split profits fifty-fifty. But now, with each succeeding job, she questioned whether or not she really needed him. They'd been a great team and made a phenomenal amount of money together. But all great partnerships came to an end eventually.

Who knows, perhaps when Jeff finally sees the light, he and I could start working together. New York could be the start of a new chapter.

Elizabeth Kennedy sipped her wine and allowed herself to dream.

Jean Rizzo yawned as the tube train rattled toward Paddington Station. He'd barely slept the previous night, and was dead on his feet, but there was no chance of getting a seat. The car was overcrowded and dirty. A horrible stench of bad breath and body odor mixed with commuters' competing perfumes and aftershaves made his stomach churn.

This time tomorrow I'll be on the Eurostar on my way home.

It couldn't come soon enough for Jean Rizzo. He missed his children, his apartment, his life. But he felt deflated. He'd arrived in London two weeks ago full of hope and excitement. Tracy's hunch about Elizabeth Kennedy had been the right one. Elizabeth *had* returned to London after her failed L.A. job, to regroup and plan her next move. After a lot of good old-fashioned detective work, Jean had tracked her down and begun a grueling, week-long surveillance. He'd watched Elizabeth set up to swindle Edwin Greaves, the multimillionaire philanthropist and art collector. Brilliant in his day, Greaves had been cruelly ravaged by Alzheimer's in old age, making him a vulnerable target. Like a shark smelling blood, Elizabeth Kennedy had exploited the old man's weakness, making off with a painting worth millions.

Jean Rizzo thought, *She has no scruples. She'd sell her own child if the price was right.*

But he wasn't here to catch Ms. Kennedy out in a con, or to recover stolen art. He was here to catch a killer. There had been no more murders since Sandra Whitmore, back in the summer. Since Elizabeth walked out of Cadogan Gardens with the oil painting, Jean Rizzo hadn't let her out of his sight. But she'd met with no accomplices, made no sudden or unusual moves of any kind. More importantly, no murder had followed the art theft. Four days had passed now. The Bible Killer always struck within two days. The trail was as cold as Jean's toes in his sodden, rain-drenched socks.

Tracy called from Colorado. "Maybe she works without a partner. It's perfectly possible, Jean."

"Maybe."

"Or maybe the murders only happen after bigger, more

high-profile jobs? It could be an adrenaline thing. If so, this con on Mr. Greaves might have been too low-key."

"Hmm."

Tracy had been true to her word and had helped Jean immensely with the investigation. Her insights into the workings of the con artist's mind had been invaluable. And yet Jean Rizzo couldn't shake the feeling that he was missing something, something crushingly obvious.

Maybe I'm barking up the wrong tree entirely. Maybe Milton Buck was right after all. Maybe there is no link. Jean had been able to trace Elizabeth Kennedy to some of the cities at the times of the murders, but not to all of them. Was he spinning something out of nothing? Had finding first Tracy and now Elizabeth made him complacent—a king admiring a fine, golden cloth that no one else could see? A cloth woven from the threads of his own desperation?

"This is Paddington Station. Paddington is the next station stop. Please alight here for trains to Oxford, Didcot, Birmingham New Street and Reading."

The tinny-sounding announcement jolted him back to reality. He'd decided to pay a visit to Gunther Hartog, Tracy Whitney's old mentor and partner in crime. Not really in the hope or expectation of a breakthrough, but because he couldn't think of anything else to do. According to Tracy, Hartog's country house was a treasure trove of fine art, albeit mostly stolen or at least dubiously sourced.

"It's the eighth wonder of the world," Tracy told Jean. "And Gunther's unique. You can't leave London without meeting him."

GUNTHER HARTOG LAY SPRAWLED out on a chaise longue, a cashmere blanket draped over his frail frame like a shroud. An oxygen tank hung next to him on an ugly metal frame that was utterly out of place in such a beautiful room. Tracy's hyperbole on that score had turned out to be an understatement. From the second Jean Rizzo's taxi pulled up outside the seventeenth-century manor house, he realized he was in for a treat. The gardens were as immaculately manicured as any park. If the exterior was a delight, the interior was a veritable Aladdin's cave of treasures. Oak-paneled walls dripped with fine art the way that an old Vegas drag queen might drip with diamonds. Every rug was antique Persian, every glass Venetian, every cornice original, every stick of furniture plundered from one of Europe's grand estates or Asia's great palaces. Gunther Hartog was a man of both immense wealth and impeccable taste. In Jean Rizzo's experience, the two very rarely went hand in hand.

Gunther Hartog was also dying. The gray patina of death hung over his sunken eyes and skeletal frame like an early morning mist. His limbs were like twigs and his skin was as dry and fragile as old parchment. He dismissed his nurse and invited Jean to sit beside him.

"Thank you for seeing me," said Jean.

"Not at all. I have a conflicted relationship with most members of your profession, Inspector, as I daresay you know. But when you mentioned dear Tracy's name, well . . . curiosity got the better of me." Gunther's voice was faint, but his mind was as sharp as ever. The devilish twinkle in his eye was also undiminished. "Have you seen her?"

"I have."

"Is she well?"

"She is," Jean answered cautiously. "She sends you all her love."

Gunther sighed. "I suppose you can't tell me where she is or what she's been doing all this time?"

Jean shook his head.

"Even though I'm dying and would take the secret to my grave?"

"Sorry," said Jean.

"Oh, don't apologize," wheezed Gunther. "I daresay you and she came to some arrangement. And I daresay she has her reasons for staying away. I do miss her, though."

His pale eyes misted over. Jean could see that he had slipped back into the past, back to the glory days when he, Tracy and Jeff used to outwit the authorities again and again, from one side of the globe to the other. They'd helped to make one another rich, but Jean could see that the bond between them ran far deeper than that.

"So Tracy is helping you with your inquiries, is she?" Gunther asked.

"She is."

"And what dastardly deed is it that you're investigating, Inspector?"

"Murder."

The playful smile on Gunther's lips disappeared.

"Twelve murders, to be more precise."

Jean Rizzo filled Gunther Hartog in on the Bible Killer's victims, and the link he'd discovered between the murders and the string of robberies. He explained how he'd tracked Tracy down, suspecting that she might be the missing link that would lead him to the killer. Tracy had helped him to find Elizabeth Kennedy, but that was where the trail had gone cold.

At the mention of Elizabeth's name, the old man became quite animated.

"Vile woman. So she's still working, is she? I suppose I'm not surprised, although I'd rather hoped she might be rotting in a Peruvian jail by now."

"You're not a fan?"

"Oh, don't get me wrong, Inspector. She's a class act, very good at what she does. But she's typical of the younger generation."

"In what way?"

"She's heartless and greedy. Utterly devoid of principles, never mind romance."

"Romance?" Jean frowned.

"Oh yes!" Gunther cried. "There was terrific romance to our business in the old days, Inspector. Tracy and Jeff weren't thieves, they were artists. Each job was a performance, a perfectly choreographed ballet, if you will."

Jean thought, *It's a game to him. To all of them. But no one told Sandra Whitmore or Alissa Armand or any of the other girls the rules. Somehow they got caught up in the dance and paid for it with their lives. There was no romance in their lives, or their deaths, God help them.*

Gunther was still talking. "Tracy and Jeff only ever took from the undeserving. They weren't in the business of mugging old ladies. Not like Miss Kennedy. Money's the only thing that motivates her and she'll stop at nothing to acquire it. She destroyed Jeff and Tracy's marriage, you know. From what I could learn at the time, she was paid to do it. Someone with a grudge against one or both of them hired Elizabeth to wreck things. Can you imagine such a thing? In my day such behavior was considered beyond the pale."

He slumped back on the chaise longue, exhausted by the effort of such a long diatribe.

Once Gunther had caught his breath, Jean asked, "Did you ever hear about Elizabeth working with a partner? A man?"

"Years ago, yes. But I haven't exactly followed the young lady's career. Why?"

Jean shrugged. "The Bible Killer's male. I'm looking for a man connected to Elizabeth Kennedy or Tracy Whitney. Or both. Of course, there is one person who fits that description perfectly."

Gunther frowned.

"You don't mean Jeff?"

"Jeff Stevens was intimate with both women. He's also still active, traveling all over the world looting antiquities."

"Whatever else Jeff's doing, it isn't *looting*," Gunther protested.

"The point is he's out there, using a string of aliases. He could have been in any of the cities in question at the right time."

Gunther shook his head. "Jeff had nothing to do with this. I'd bet my life on it."

"According to his FBI file, he regularly uses prostitutes. Did you know that?"

"No," Gunther said truthfully. "I didn't. What I do know is that Jeff wouldn't hurt a fly, still less a woman."

"People change," said Jean. "Maybe the split with Tracy pushed him over the edge. He could have had some sort of psychotic break. It happens." He added, seeing Gunther's skeptical expression, "When did you last see Jeff Stevens?"

"Some time ago," Gunther said carefully. "I don't remember exactly."

"Months? Years?" Jean prompted.

"Years. Unfortunately."

"Do you have any idea where he is now?"

"No," said Gunther. "Although if I knew, I wouldn't tell you."

He rang an old-fashioned brass bell to summon his nurse. His attitude toward Jean had clearly shifted for the worse.

"Is that why you came to see me, Inspector? To try to get me to betray one of my oldest friends?"

"Not at all. I came to see you because Tracy told me you're the best-connected man in England. And that if there were any rumors flying around, about Elizabeth Kennedy or her partner or anything else that might help me solve this case, you would have heard them."

"Hmm." Gunther was flattered but not mollified. "Does Tracy know you suspect Jeff of these murders?"

"I don't suspect him," said Jean. "I don't suspect anyone, yet. Mostly because I have no damn evidence. But I can't rule Jeff Stevens out to spare Tracy's feelings, or yours. He may know nothing about this or he may know something. I don't know. What I do know is that I would like to speak to him. My only obligation is to the women who were killed, and to those who may still be in danger. I have to catch this man, Mr. Hartog. That's all *I* care about."

The nurse came back in. A diminutive Filipina with limited English, she made up for what she lacked in stature with a fiercely protective manner. Immediately sensing her patient's hostility toward his visitor, she positioned herself between the two of them like a bulldog, folding her arms and glaring at Jean.

"Mister very tired now," she announced. "You leaving."

Jean looked at her, then at Gunther Hartog.

"If you know anything, *anything,* and you don't tell me . . . and another girl dies . . . it's on your head. This isn't a game anymore, Mr. Hartog."

He walked away. As he reached the door Gunther called out to him.

"I'm hearing a lot of buzz about New York. Wonderful city for thieves, New York. Fine art, fine jewelry, fine museums and galleries to inspire one. Especially at Christmas." He sighed. "Just thinking about it almost makes me feel young again."

"New York?" said Jean.

"New York. The Winter Ball at the Botanical Garden is supposed to be particularly magical, I believe. Everyone who's anyone will be there.

"You can see yourself out, Inspector."

CHAPTER 16

$\mathcal{S}$HE OPENED THE BOX slowly, savoring the smooth soft-
ness of the silk ribbon beneath her fingertips.

"I hope you like it."

Jeff Stevens watched her expression shift from anticipa-
tion to surprise to deranged delight as she lifted the white-
gold-and-diamond watch out of its case. With her high,
Slavic cheekbones, full lips and perfect, alabaster complex-
ion, Veronica had always looked more like a duchess than a
hooker. But her practiced hauteur deserted her now. Fling-
ing her arms around Jeff's neck, she burst into tears of joy.

"Oh my God! Oh my God oh my God oh my GOD! I
can't believe you did this! It must have cost a fortune."

"No more than you deserve." Jeff smiled, happy to have
pleased her. "Merry Christmas, V."

They were in Veronica's apartment in the West Village.
Although not flashy, the space was luxurious and elegant,
just like its owner. Veronica worked exclusively in the upper

echelons of her profession, with a small and elite client list that she chose carefully and without the assistance of a pimp. Before hooking, she'd been a model and occasional actress, but both jobs had come to bore her in the end. The truth was she enjoyed what she did. She liked sex, and the men who paid to sleep with her were all interesting, successful, intelligent people. Few of them were as generous as Jeff Stevens. But then Jeff truly was one of a kind.

He never spoke about his work, although Veronica knew he was in town for a job. He came to New York about twice a year and always looked her up. Perhaps it seemed odd to say so, but Veronica considered Jeff a friend.

"Listen," she said. "It's Christmas in a few days. You probably have plans, but if you're on your own, you'd be very welcome to join me. My sister's coming over with her boyfriend. I make a mean pecan pie."

"You're so sweet to offer." Jeff kissed her on the cheek. "But I have plans."

He picked up his watch from the bedside table and fastened his cuff links while Veronica fixed her makeup in the bathroom. Remembering he'd left his tie on the countertop, Jeff walked in to find her snorting a freshly cut line of coke on the side of the bathtub. He froze, frowning.

Veronica looked up. Misinterpreting his expression, she said, "Sorry, sweetie, did you want some? I should have asked."

Jeff shook his head. "I've gotta run. I'll call you, okay?"

"Okay," Veronica called after him. "And thank you so much for my present. I love it!"

OUTSIDE, THE CITY LOOKED like a fairy tale. Two feet of snow had fallen during the night, frosting Central Park like a wedding cake and casting a brilliant, white glow over every street and car and building. Christmas music was being piped out of every store, and the window displays shone and glittered with multicolored lights and toys and candies, making Jeff wish he was eight years old again.

Jeff buttoned his overcoat against the cold, and against his own anger.

Why would a beautiful girl like Veronica touch that stuff?

It didn't bother him that she sold herself for sex. In Jeff's worldview there was an honesty to prostitution, to the simple transaction between man and woman in the pursuit of pleasure. But drugs? That was something else. He had seen what drugs did to people. Seen how they reduced human beings to immoral beings, cringing slaves prepared to do anything and betray anyone for their master.

Disgusting.

Tracy had never done drugs. They were always around. The circles that she and Jeff used to move in were extremely decadent. But, like Jeff, Tracy had never been interested. If he closed his eyes, he could still hear her voice now.

"Why would I need ecstasy, my darling, when I've got you?"

"Why indeed."

Jeff always missed Tracy more at Christmastime.

Still, this was no time to be getting maudlin. Jeff loved visiting New York, especially when the trip combined business and pleasure. He was staying at the Gramercy Park under the name of Randall Bruckmeyer, an old-school Texas oilman and one of Jeff's favorite alter egos. Randy lived up to his name, and had helped Jeff out on a number of jobs that required the seducing of one or more women. In this case, the target was a gorgeous Russian socialite, Svetlana Drakhova, who was in New York to attend the famous Winter Ball at the Botanical Garden with her boyfriend. In addition to her busy career as a professional partier/slut, Svetlana also happened to be the latest, very young mistress of Oleg Grinski, a Russian oligarch with a penchant for anal sex, torture and Byzantine treasures, not necessarily in that order. Preposterously, Oleg had given the scheming Svetlana a priceless collection of coins minted during the reign of the Emperor Heraclius in 620 as a gift. Knowing Svetlana as he now did, Jeff, aka Randy Bruckmeyer, was convinced it was only a matter of time before she melted them down or turned them into a pair of novelty earrings. As much a stranger to taste as to basic human decency, Svetlana was as ugly inside as she was beautiful outside, and that was saying something. Jeff was not enjoying sleeping with her, hence today's trip to Veronica's place. He was, however, looking forward to robbing her, and to handing the coins over to the charming Spanish collector who'd commissioned him. They had agreed on a fee of $1 million, a fraction of what the coins were worth, but enough to make the job worth Jeff's while. The main thing was that the coins would be in safe hands once again, cherished and appreciated as they should be. These days, Jeff Stevens felt a closer connection to ancient objects than he did to people. Unlike people, they never let you down.

Jumping into a cab to Lexington, Jeff got out a block before his hotel. Randall Bruckmeyer III always stayed at the Gramercy Park. The Ritz might have grander rooms, but this was the only place in town with access to its own, private park and with genuine Warhols and Basquiats hanging on the walls. You got what you paid for at the Gramercy: glamour, luxury and exclusivity.

Slipping into character was second nature to Jeff, like putting on an old familiar sweater.

"Afternoon, ladies." He offered his arm to two overly made-up women in ankle-length minks as they approached the lobby doors. "Are y'all in town for the Winter Ball?"

"That's right." The first woman looked up coquettishly

at the handsome Texan, almost blinding him with the diamonds that were swinging around her neck like golf balls.
"How did you know?"

"Just a lucky guess. I'm invited myself, as it happens."

Randall Bruckmeyer *was* invited to the annual Botanical Garden event, but he wouldn't be going. He had a rather
more pressing engagement arranged for that evening. Svetlana Drakhova *would* be attending, along with her repulsive
sugar daddy, Oleg, hopefully for long enough to allow Jeff
to do what he needed to do. The ball provided the perfect
cover, not least because every cop, fed and private security
firm was going to be all over the event like bees around a
honey pot. After last year's spectacular thefts—not one, but
two multimillion-dollar jewel heists had gone down, one of
them involving a very high-profile Hollywood actress and a
sapphire bracelet that used to belong to Grace Kelly—no one
was taking any chances. Despite this, or perhaps because of
it, rumors abounded that another big job was being planned.
Every con artist in the Western world worth their salt was in
Manhattan right now, wondering whether to try their hand.

Except me, thought Jeff. He tightened his grip around
the fur-clad ladies' waists as they swept into the Gramercy's
grand, high-ceilinged Rose Bar.

"Name's Randy," he drawled. "Randy Bruckmeyer. Can
I buy y'all a drink?"

JEAN RIZZO IDLY PERUSED the belts in the Ermenegildo
Zegna concession in Barneys. He was just wondering who
would pay almost a thousand dollars for a simple strip of
leather, when he realized his target was on the move. Time
to go.

Jean was tailing Elizabeth Kennedy. Using the pseud-
onym Martha Langbourne, Elizabeth had flown to New

York from London three weeks ago and checked in to Morgans Hotel in Midtown. Jean Rizzo followed. After his meeting with Gunther Hartog, Jean had half expected to find Jeff Stevens in Manhattan too. He'd put some feelers out, but so far had found no sign of Tracy Whitney's elusive ex.

If that was disappointing, Elizabeth Kennedy was proving to be even more so. For the last twenty days, "Martha" had done a good impression of being a wealthy tourist like any other. Jean had patiently followed her to two Broadway plays, numerous dinners in expensive restaurants (always solo) and a string of deathly dull visits to museums, galleries and every conceivable tourist attraction, from the Rockefeller Center ice rink to the Empire State Building.

Back in Lyon, Jean's boss was not amused.

"We're not the CIA," Henri Marceau said grumpily. "We don't have the budget for this crap."

"Elizabeth Kennedy's my only live lead."

"She's not a lead. She's a hunch. You have nothing on her, Jean. Not as far as the Bible killings go."

"That's why I need to stay here. At least until next weekend. She's planning something for the Winter Ball at the Botanical Garden, I'm sure of it. Sooner or later she'll have to make contact with her partner. He's our guy, Henri. He's our guy."

Henri Marceau had known Jean Rizzo a long time. He was a good detective with sharp instincts, but his heart was ruling his head on this one. Running all over the world, chasing shadows on the spurious advice of Gunther Hartog, a dying con artist with an ax to grind. And for what? A string of dead hookers. There were live cases, human-trafficking operations and drug rings and pedophile networks that desperately needed resources.

"I can't justify it, Jean. I'm sorry. As of tomorrow, you're there on your own dime."

Sylvie, Jean's ex, was equally unimpressed.

"It's Christmas. You've been gone a month. What about the children?"

"I'll bring them back something amazing from FAO Schwarz."

"Something amazing? Really. Like what? A father who keeps his promises?"

Jean felt terrible about Clémence and Luc. But he couldn't go home, not until he'd made progress. If another girl got killed in New York and he'd done nothing to stop it, he'd never forgive himself.

Finally, yesterday, his tenacity had paid off. Elizabeth Kennedy still hadn't met up with her elusive partner. But she *had* begun tailing Bianca Berkeley.

TV actress, Scientologist and wife of the billionaire real estate mogul Butch Berkeley, Bianca Berkeley was beautiful, rich and *weird*. Gossip columnists loved her for her Howard Hughes–esque fits of hypochondria. Bianca had variously been reported as sleeping in an "oxygen helmet," drinking her own urine daily and employing an astrologer to determine her diet, all in hopes of strengthening her immunity to any number of imagined diseases. Butch stuck with her because she was beautiful and famous and because she didn't care if he slept with his assistant or his trainer as long as he kept her in jewels and jets.

The Berkeleys were confirmed attendees at this year's Winter Ball. Yesterday "Martha Langbourne" had left her hotel after an early breakfast and followed Bianca Berkeley, first to her Pilates class, then to her psychic's office and finally to Tiffany's, where Bianca had spent an hour locked in conference with the store's manager, Lucio Trivoli. Today Mrs. B was at Barneys buying Louboutin boots and "trinkets" for her staff, including (so far) a Patek Philippe watch with a seven-figure price tag and a crystal bracelet that claimed to "neutralize the ions" in the body.

Martha was right behind her. It was beyond question now. Bianca Berkeley was Elizabeth Kennedy's latest target.

Jean watched as the two women moved through furs and accessories, then back into haberdashery. Mrs. Berkeley bought nothing else, although "Martha Langbourne" treated herself to some three-hundred-dollar cashmere-lined gloves with a silk gold trim, paid for with an unlimited AmEx in the same name, just like her hotel room. Jean Rizzo had checked the statements a week ago. ML was obviously an identity Elizabeth had used before while in the United States, although the cards hadn't been used in more than a year. The abortive Los Angeles jaunt had been paid for with other monies. Ms. Kennedy and her partner were nothing if not careful.

Jean watched as Bianca Berkeley left the store by the main exit on Madison Avenue. He was about to follow when some sixth sense made him hold back. As expected, Elizabeth Kennedy followed her quarry. But this time Jean clocked the two young men walking behind her. They were dressed in jeans and sweaters. One carried a woolen overcoat over his arm. Jean couldn't see their faces, but something about the way they moved, the slight inclination of their heads toward each other, told him at once that they were working together.

Could Elizabeth have more than one accomplice? Did she work as part of a gang?

Unhurriedly, Jean raised his cell phone and began taking pictures, making sure to look as if he were focusing on Barneys' spectacular Christmas display and not on the two men. To his dismay, moments later a crowd of shoppers surged forward, sweeping the two men out of the store and onto Madison Avenue just yards behind Elizabeth.

Jean didn't know if he'd caught their faces or not. His mind raced. *There's too many people. By the time I make it onto the street, they could all be gone.* This might be the contact he'd been waiting for and he was seconds away from missing it!

Pushing rudely past a fat woman and her fatter son, he rushed to the nearest ground-floor window, behind a relatively sedate display selling Smythson diaries and notebooks. Pressing his face to the glass, he saw Bianca Berkeley step into her waiting town car and speed away. He couldn't see Elizabeth or the two men.

"Damn it!" he said aloud, earning himself more than one bemused glance from nearby shoppers. Just as he was about to make a belated run for the doors, one of the two men appeared in front of the window, literally inches from where Jean was standing. Instinctively, Jean shrank back. The man had his coat on now. He was short with dark hair, but he still had his back turned. *Turn around, damn you.* At one point he leaned back so that his woolen coat actually touched the glass. Then he edged forward, apparently waving to someone across the street. Jean couldn't see who it was. Seconds later the man's hand shot out. A yellow cab pulled up.

"No!" Jean was running like a madman, falling over himself as he careered toward the store exit.

"Watch it, asshole!"

Outside, the crisp December air hit him in the face like a punch. Christmas shoppers swarmed the sidewalks like ants. Along both sides of Madison Avenue, a line of yellow taxis stretched for block after block, like bricks on the road to Oz. Jean's heart sank. One man had gone. Jean doubted he would have recognized the other, even if he saw him. He was about to head back to Elizabeth's hotel, more in hope than expectation that the three might regroup there, when suddenly he saw her. She was on foot, headed toward the subway.

Jean Rizzo followed. Neither of the males was anywhere to be seen, but he was determined not to lose Elizabeth again. He followed her down into the tunnels and onto a train that was heading uptown. Keeping Elizabeth in sight, and staying close enough to the doors that he could follow her out at a second's notice, Jean scrolled through the pictures on his phone. The tech guys at Interpol could work wonders with images, but even Jean knew that these looked unpromising. Two distant figures in a sea of people. *Damn it. How did I screw this up?*

Elizabeth got off the train at Central Park West. She seemed in no hurry, back in tourist mode. Jean followed her through the park at a discreet distance. It was four o'clock. Light was fading and the earlier crowds had begun to thin. Snow began to fall again. Thick heavy flakes like goose down stuck to Jean's hair and coat. *Where is she going?*

Suddenly Elizabeth stopped. She looked around her briefly, perhaps to ascertain if she was being followed, then sat down on a bench, clearing off the newly fallen snow with a sweep of her arm. Jean kept walking. Once he reached the top of the hill, he slipped behind a small clump of trees. It was a perfect vantage point, close and completely hidden. Jean pulled out his phone and waited.

He didn't have to wait long. A tall gentleman in a cowboy hat began walking purposefully toward the bench. There was no hint of subterfuge, no attempt at discretion. As the man drew near, Elizabeth stood up and smiled broadly, holding out her arms. Then the man took off his hat and gave Jean a clear view of his face. It was the first time Jean Rizzo had seen those handsome features in the flesh but he would have known them anywhere.

Well, I'll be damned.

He lifted his phone and began taking pictures. *Click, click, click.*

TRACY WAS AT THE top of a ladder, fixing a dog-eared Christmas angel to the top of the tree when the phone rang.

"Would you get that, honey?" she called down to Nicholas.

They'd spent a lovely afternoon decorating the house to-gether, with Blake Carter helping to put up the enormous Norwegian pine. Tracy loved Christmas. This house had been made for it, with its high ceilings, roaring open fires and log-cabin charm. Blake rolled his eyes every year at Tracy's over-the-top decor, including tacky carol-singing dogs from CVS and a life-size plastic Santa with flashing boots and hat who said "Ho! Ho! Ho!" whenever you rubbed his belly. "It looks like an elf threw up in your living room." But Tracy suspected Blake secretly loved the display as much as she did. Especially when he saw the delight in Nicholas's eyes.

"Oh, hi, Jean." Nicholas's cheerful voice sent chills through Tracy's body. "How are you? Did you want to talk to Mama?"

Tracy descended the ladder, a fixed smile on her face. Nicholas handed her the phone. "It's your friend Jean," he said, heading back to the tree and the big cardboard box of decorations.

Tracy walked into the kitchen, out of earshot.

"I thought we agreed. No calls to the landline," she hissed. "Not until after he's asleep."

"This couldn't wait. I just saw Jeff Stevens in Central Park."

Tracy's stomach lurched.

"He was meeting Elizabeth Kennedy. They looked close, Tracy."

The elevator hit the ground. Tracy felt her knees start to give way. She leaned against the table for support.

"I sent you pictures. Check your phone. They talked for about half an hour and then went back to his hotel together.

Elizabeth's planning a hit on Bianca Berkeley. It looks like
Jeff's involved. Can you open the pictures?"

Silence.

"Tracy? Are you there?"

"Yes." Tracy's voice came out high-pitched and strangled. "I'm here. Go on."

Jean filled her in on the events of this afternoon. The two
men at Barneys. His certainty that Bianca Berkeley was the
target and that the heist would go down at the Winter Ball,
just like Gunther Hartog predicted. And his growing suspicion of Jeff Stevens.

"She was in his hotel for an hour. She left first, then he
did. I followed him."

"Where did he go?" Tracy asked calmly.

"He went to the Meatpacking District and picked up a
hooker."

Tracy's heart cracked. She felt as if she were having an
out-of-body experience. She looked at her son, hanging
glass reindeer figurines onto the Christmas tree. Carols
were playing in the next room. Jean Rizzo's voice didn't
belong in this picture. Nor did Jeff.

I came here to escape him, to escape that life.

Anger overwhelmed her. Wild, irrational anger.

*How dare Jeff work with Elizabeth! How dare he sleep
with prostitutes! How dare he still have the power to hurt
me, after all these years!*

And yet another part of her felt protective of Jeff and furious with Jean Rizzo.

*Why was Jean telling her these things? Why did he keep
pouring poison back into her life?*

"What do you want, Jean?" Her voice was cold. "Why
did you call me?"

"I want you to come to New York."

Tracy laughed bitterly. "Don't be ridiculous. It's Christmas."

"I need you. You know Jeff Stevens better than anyone."

"Not anymore I don't."

"Aren't you listening to me?" Jean's voice rose in frustration. "Something's going down here, Tracy! The Winter Ball is happening in less than a week. Elizabeth and Jeff are planning something together, something big. There may be others involved, a gang, I don't know. Jeff's already seeing hookers. He's getting excited, aroused. His adrenaline's up . . . This time next week, if we don't do something, another girl could be dead."

"Hold on a minute." Tracy dropped her voice to a whisper. "Am I hearing you right? You think *Jeff's* the Bible Killer?"

"I think it's a serious possibility."

Tracy shook her head. *Is this a nightmare? Is this conversation even real, or am I going to wake up in a minute and laugh?*

"You're out of your mind."

"Then come to New York and help me. Help Jeff. Prove me wrong."

"Are you deaf? I'm not coming to New York. That wasn't part of our deal."

"Tracy, you get on a plane!" Jean was yelling now. "Do you hear me? You get on a plane or I will tell your son the truth."

Tracy hung up. She unplugged the phone from the wall. On the counter, her cell phone was flashing red.

Jean's photos.

Jeff and Elizabeth.

Together.

Tracy picked it up and turned it off. Her hands trembled as if she were disarming a bomb.

"Mom?" Nicholas's voice drifted through from the living room. "Are you done? Come and help me."

Tears stung the back of Tracy's eyes. "I'm coming, honey."

IT WAS MIDNIGHT, BUT Jean Rizzo was too wired to sleep. He was wide-awake when his phone rang.

"Do you really believe Jeff's involved in these killings?" Tracy sounded as tired as he was.

"I don't know. Do you really believe he isn't?"

Tracy didn't answer. The truth was she didn't know what to believe anymore. She just wanted this nightmare to be over.

"There's a flight leaving Denver tomorrow at noon. You can pick up your ticket at the American Airlines desk."

"And you can kiss my ass. I already told you. I'm happy to help and advise you if I can. But I have a life here. I am not coming to New York."

"Mmm-hmm," said Jean.

"It's Christmas!"

"So everyone keeps telling me."

"I mean it, Rizzo. I'm calling your bluff. I am not coming to New York."

CHAPTER 17

"WELCOME TO NEW YORK!"

Jean Rizzo met Tracy at JFK with a beaming smile.

"I'm so glad you decided to come."

"I didn't 'decide to come.' You blackmailed me."

"Oh, now, now. Let's not squabble." Jean nudged her in the ribs jokingly. "It'll do you good to get out of Steamboat. Small-town life can get so boring, don't you think?"

"I guess you'd know all about boring. Being Canadian and all." Tracy smiled sarcastically.

They ordered coffee at an airport café.

"Let's talk about ground rules," said Tracy.

"Do we have to?"

Jean couldn't stop smiling. He still couldn't quite believe she was here.

"I'm not going to help you catch Jeff Stevens."

"What do you mean?"

"I mean what I say. You asked me last night if I was certain Jeff had nothing to do with these murders. Well, you know what? I am."

"But, Tracy—"

"No 'buts.' Let me finish. I looked at the pictures you sent me. I agree that Jeff is mixed up in this somehow."

"Thank you."

"But he's no killer, Jean. He just isn't."

Jean Rizzo paused for a moment. Then he said, "Okay. But somebody's killing these girls."

"Yes."

"Every time Elizabeth Kennedy pulls off a big job."

"Yes."

"Which she's about to do, with Jeff Stevens's help."

"Possibly."

"Unless we catch them red-handed."

"Catch *her* red-handed," corrected Tracy. "I'll help you nail Elizabeth. But I won't help you get Jeff. That's the deal, Jean, take it or leave it. It's not negotiable. Jeff walks away from this."

Jean Rizzo thought, *Good God. She still loves him.*

"All right," he said. "We'll focus on Elizabeth. Where do we start?"

"With the target." Tracy drained her coffee cup and stood up. "I'm going to my hotel now to freshen up and to call my son. Send me everything you have on Bianca Berkeley and this Winter Ball."

"Wouldn't it be easier if we talked? We can go through the files together, bounce some ideas around. I'd like you to—"

"No," Tracy said. "I work better alone. Meet me for dinner at Great Jones Café on Prince Street at eight. I'll have a plan for you by then."

JONES WAS A CHARMING, candlelit hole-in-the-wall tucked away between two more famous restaurants in the heart of SoHo. It served classic American fare, ribs and corn and mashed potatoes and cheeseburgers and turkey sandwiches. Everything was delicious.

Tracy had changed into a gray turtleneck sweater and woolen wide-leg pants. Her cheeks were flushed from the cold and her green eyes shone like two shards of kryptonite. She was still angry at Jean, but in the few hours since he left her at the airport, something had clearly lifted her spirits. When she spoke she sounded energized. It wasn't long before Jean realized why.

"I know what Elizabeth's going to steal."

"You do?"

Tracy nodded. "Bianca Berkeley's not wearing any of her own jewels to the Botanical Garden. She's borrowing an emerald choker from Tiffany's. It's worth two and a half million dollars but it's insured for three."

Jean's eyes widened. "How on earth do you know that?"

"I walked into the store and asked. I think the clerk liked me."

Jean thought, *I'll bet he did.*

"The choker's being delivered to the Berkeley residence at three P.M. on the day of the ball," Tracy went on. "It will be transported in an armored van, with two guards and a driver. An employee of the insurance company will be at the house to have someone sign the paperwork. It's due to be returned at ten o'clock the next morning. The same van will arrive to collect it."

Jean nodded mutely.

"Between three P.M. and six P.M., when the Berkeleys' driver will set off for Brooklyn, the chances are it will be mayhem in that house. There'll be a PA there, a stylist, a makeup artist, a hairdresser. Also Bianca's Scientology minders."

"Her what?"

"Her minders. Butch is a big donor to the church. You didn't know that?" Tracy frowned.

"It never came up," said Jean.

"It should have. Believe me, everything I am telling you now, Elizabeth Kennedy already knows. Inside and out. 'Martha Langbourne's' a Scientologist, by the way."

Jean looked astonished.

"It's on her passport, under religion." Tracy answered his unspoken question. "Anyway, the point is that the choker will likely be moved from room to room and will change hands several times. That's one clear window of opportunity. Especially if 'Martha' has worked the Scientology angle and has access to the property."

"So you're saying you think Elizabeth's going to try to steal the emeralds from the Berkeley house, between three and six P.M.?"

"No." Tracy waved down a waiter and ordered another glass of Cabernet. "I'm saying that's one window. There are others."

"Such as?"

"In the store. In transit. At the ball itself. The following morning. In transit again."

Jean groaned. "Okay," he said eventually. "How would you do it? If this were your job?"

"I'd take it in transit."

"Why?"

"Because it's simpler. Cleaner. Fewer witnesses, fewer prints. More anonymous. But you need inside help. A team of some sort."

"She has that," said Jean.

"Yes." Tracy sipped her wine contemplatively.

"I'm sensing there's a 'but.'"

Tracy smiled.

She's enjoying herself, thought Jean. *She doesn't want to admit it, but she is. She's enjoying the challenge.*

"You need one of two things to be a successful thief. Brains or balls."

"I'm not sure I follow."

Tracy explained. "The biggest jewel theft of all time— all modern time, anyway—happened a few years ago at the Cannes Film Festival. Eighty million dollars' worth of diamonds were taken in one night, by one man, at a crowded event full of celebrities and security."

"I vaguely remember reading about that," said Jean. "How did he do it again?"

"I'll tell you how." Tracy grinned. "This criminal mastermind climbed through an open window in broad daylight, stuffed as many gems as he could carry into a sports bag while waving a toy gun around, hopped back out of the window and escaped on foot. He dropped about twenty million dollars' worth as he ran. But eighty *million* dollars of diamonds were never recovered. Balls."

"And this related to Elizabeth Kennedy . . . how?"

"The question is not how *I* would do it. It's how *she* would do it," Tracy said. "Elizabeth's smart. But if she's behind all these other jobs you've told me about, the ones that took place before the murders, then I'd say her balls are at least as big as her brains." She sat back in her chair, a triumphant look on her face. "I think she's going to do it at the ball. I think she's going to steal that choker on the night, in front of a thousand guests and God knows how many cops. And I think she's going to walk right out of there."

Her certainty was contagious.

Jean Rizzo asked the obvious question. "And just how,

exactly, is she going to do that? Rip the thing off Bianca Berkeley's neck?"

Tracy laughed. "Of course not. I pulled off a similar job once at the Prado in Madrid, before Jeff bait-and-switched me. It's quite simple really."

Jean raised a questioning eyebrow.

"Bianca's going to give Elizabeth the choker."

THE WINTER WONDERLAND BALL in New York's famous Botanical Garden was considered *the* party of the year among Manhattan's elite. Glamorous enough to tempt the city's fashionistas and hedge-fund millionaires to travel all the way up to the Bronx, it also attracted an international crowd of superwealthy patrons. Those who would see and be seen flocked from around the globe to the iconic glass-and-steel building with its breathtaking palm dome, illuminated by thousands of simple white candles. Outside, the twin backdrops of pure white snow and a pitch-black winter sky, peppered with stars, provided the perfect setting for the dazzling couture gowns and decadent jewels of the female guests as they arrived.

Hollywood was out in force this year, both the old guard and the new. Sharon Stone wowed in a white Giambattista Valli and the Fanning sisters looked cute in matching Chanel minis with hot-pink ruffles. They mingled with Washington heavyweights—the vice president and his wife were here, as well as the new secretary of state and Harvey Golden, White House chief of staff. There were supermodels and designers, billionaires and generals, writers, artists and oil tycoons. The official purpose of the ball was to raise money for New York's underprivileged children. In reality, of course, it was yet another opportunity for the city's overprivileged children to gorge themselves on a cloying feast of excess. The air was scented with tropical blooms and expensive perfume, and the aroma of white truffles wafted in from the kitchen. But in the end, the one overpowering smell was money.

Jean Rizzo could hardly breathe. Weaving his way through the *Vogue* photographers and other press gathered outside, he grabbed a flute of champagne and slipped into the throng. Bianca Berkeley and her husband, Butch, were already here and surrounded by hangers-on. Butch Berkeley was having a loud conversation with Warren Gantz, a Wall Street titan, about the merits of various different private planes (Warren favored the Dassault Falcon 900, a bargain at $33 million, while Butch remained faithful to his Embraer Legacy 650). Jean Rizzo thought of the ancient Volvo 760 he'd driven since his twenties rusting outside his Lyon apartment and smiled. Guys like Gantz and Berkeley were so out of touch with reality.

Although perhaps Bianca Berkeley was even more so. Standing a few feet behind her husband, flanked by two Scientology staffers labeled as "publicist" and "assistant," she had the glazed, not-there look of a rabbit with myxomatosis. There was the famous emerald choker, wrapped around Bianca's elegant neck like a vise. *It doesn't suit her,* thought Jean. Amazing how a piece of jewelry could look at once wildly expensive and breathtakingly ugly.

In any event, she was wearing it, which meant that whatever Elizabeth Kennedy had planned had yet to take place. Score one for Tracy's theory.

Bianca's dark hair was pulled up in a severe-looking bun, and she wore a simple black column dress, both no doubt intended to showcase the Tiffany emeralds to better effect. Instead they merely served to make a beautiful woman look as stiff and uncomfortable as a store mannequin.

As for Elizabeth, so far she was nowhere to be seen. Jean had done three complete circuits of the Botanical Garden conservatory, moving from one gaggle of rich partygoers to the next. But neither "Martha Langbourne" nor "Randall Bruckmeyer," Jeff Stevens's brash Texan alter ego, had yet arrived, despite being confirmed attendees as of this morning.

For the first time since his dinner with Tracy, Jean Rizzo began to have doubts. What if Bianca Berkeley's emeralds *weren't* the target after all, but a red herring set up deliberately to throw him off the scent? Arrogantly he had assumed that Elizabeth Kennedy remained unaware of his surveillance. But Elizabeth was a professional after all, at the top of her game. What if she knew that Jean had been onto her all along? That was just the sort of dance these people enjoyed. Elizabeth, Jeff Stevens, even Tracy. Tracy claimed to have put her life of capers and con tricks behind her for her son's sake, but how well did Jean really know her? This was a woman who lied for a living, after all.

Unbidden, Jean's boss's words came back to him.

"Elizabeth's not a lead," Henri Marceau had told him. *"She's a hunch. You're running around on a wild-goose chase based on the 'advice' of two former con artists! You're wrong on this one, Jean. Come home."*

Jean finished his champagne and picked up another glass. His trained eye had already clocked a veritable army of undercover police, federal agents and private security men milling around among the invitees. Maybe Elizabeth had realized it was simply too risky to try something here and chickened out at the last moment? Perhaps the lady's balls weren't as big as Tracy imagined after all?

Jean Rizzo's uneasiness grew.

Where the hell is she?

THE FBI AGENT ADJUSTED the strap on her shimmering silver gown. In other circumstances, she'd have let her hair down at a glamorous party like this one. But not tonight. She was here to work.

Bianca Berkeley was the target, or, more specifically, the cluster of garish green rocks she wore around her neck. Wedged between her church minders like the meat in a cult sandwich, Butch Berkeley's actress wife had no idea what danger she was in. Did those goons actually make her feel safe? The FBI agent shook her head. *Funny how easy it is to trust the wrong people.*

The dark wig she was wearing was itchy and uncomfortable. She hadn't wanted to wear it, but there was an outside chance that one of tonight's guests might recognize her from another job. The world of the superrich and supercorrupt was smaller than one might think, a sort of vice village. She recognized a number of the other cops and agents milling about, trying to blend into the crowd. The funny little Canadian guy from Interpol had shown up too, the one nobody took seriously. The rumor was that even his own people back in France had cut ties with him.

She looked at her watch. Eight fifteen.

She had to make contact with Bianca soon or it would be too late.

SVETLANA DRAKHOVA THREW HER head back and laughed at one of Oleg Grinski's jokes.

Stupid oaf. Svetlana sipped her vintage Burgundy. *Fat, ugly pig. I'm not your wife. Go and bore someone else with your tedious stories.*

Svetlana was in a bad mood. She'd wasted the last six months of her life with the repellent Grinski, with very little to show for it. It had been her twenty-second birthday last month, and what had the pig given her? Some stupid old coins! She'd hoped that this trip to New York at least might involve some jaunts to Graaf or Cartier. But the tightfisted son of a bitch had kept his wallet manacled shut. Apart from a watch and a few paltry Balenciaga bags, he'd bought her nothing. Nothing!

The only silver lining to the entire trip had been hooking up with Randy. Randall Bruckmeyer was everything that Oleg Grinski wasn't. Handsome, good in bed and generous. Admittedly his net worth was a fraction of Grinski's. But Randall had already promised Svetlana the pair of diamond earrings she'd been hankering after from Neil Lane. Her only quandary now was how to jump ship without Oleg getting vengeful. The last mistress to jettison Grinski had wound up with a glass of acid thrown in her face.

Randy was supposed to be here tonight. Svetlana had worn her sexiest evening dress for his benefit, a skintight red Cavalli that left nothing to the imagination. But so far he hadn't shown up, further souring her mood.

"Oh my God! Watch what you're doing!"

A clumsy dark-haired woman bumped into Svetlana from behind, so hard she almost went flying. Her glass flew out of her hand, dousing the man in front of her in red wine.

The dark-haired woman moved forward. Pulling a handkerchief out of her purse, Svetlana began dabbing ineffectually at the huge purple stain on the man's dress shirt.

He brushed her away, irritated. "It's fine. I'll go clean up in the bathroom."

"What happened?" Bianca Berkeley turned around. The man with the stained shirt was her publicist.

He gestured toward Svetlana. "This chick just dumped a glass of red all over me!"

"How rude! It wasn't my fault."

Voices began to get raised. Butch Berkeley joined the discussion, quizzing the second Scientology minder while the first argued loudly with Svetlana. Jean Rizzo's antenna shot up. *This is it! Something's going down.* He walked toward the group, but Oleg Grinski stepped in front of him, wrapping an arm around his mistress and temporarily obstructing Jean's view.

By the time Jean got past the Russian, Bianca Berkeley was nowhere to be seen.

IT HAD HAPPENED SO quickly, at first Bianca thought she'd misheard. But the dark-haired woman repeated herself, leaning in close to Bianca's ear.

"FBI. You're in grave danger, Miss Berkeley. Please come with me."

A frisson of fear, tinged with excitement, ran through Bianca's body. Butch mocked her, called her a conspiracy theorist. But she'd always known there were dark forces out there, trying to harm her. Here, at last, was the proof.

She followed the woman into one of the powder rooms and locked the door.

JEAN RIZZO RAN OUT onto the fire stairs.

No sign.

His heart rate began to quicken. It was happening, now, somewhere in this building, and he was going to miss it. Somehow, Kennedy and Stevens had outsmarted him. But they weren't even here! It made no sense.

Back in the conservatory, he grabbed a waiter. "I'm looking for Bianca Berkeley. Do you know who that is?"

"No, sir. I'm afraid I don't."

"She's wearing a long black dress with her hair up."

"I'm sorry, sir. There are a lot of black dresses."

"She has a huge emerald necklace on."

"Oh! Yes." The man's face lit up. "I do know the lady. She came through here a few moments ago with her friend."

Jean's heart tightened.

"I think they were headed to the powder room. It's right over . . ."

Jean was already running.

"YOU UNDERSTAND, MISS BERKELEY?"

Bianca nodded, her eyes wide with fright. The excitement had all gone now. This was no made-for-TV drama. This was real.

"The ambulance is on its way? You're sure."

"My colleagues already called. You'll be fine, ma'am. You have time."

"Oh God!" Bianca started sobbing. "I can feel it already. My skin! It's burning!"

The FBI agent took her hand and squeezed it. "Help is on the way. Try to stay calm. You understand I need to leave now?"

"Of course. Go. GO!"

JEAN RIZZO HAMMERED ON the locked door.

"Mrs. Berkeley! Mrs. Berkeley, are you in there?"

A strangled voice came from inside. "Are they here yet?"

"Are who here yet?"

"The ambulance."

"Ma'am, this is the police. Please open the door."

"I can't! I have radiation sickness. You might be contaminated!"

Jean took a deep breath. He knew Bianca Berkeley was a kook but this took the cake. "Open the door, ma'am."

Slowly, the door opened. Bianca Berkeley flung herself into Jean's arms, crying hysterically. "Where are they?" she screamed. "She said they'd be here! I don't have much time left."

She was clutching her neck.

The emerald choker was gone.

ELIZABETH KENNEDY WALKED SLOWLY but purposefully out of the building. The dark wig still itched, but she no longer cared. Swinging her evening bag, she felt the weight of the Tiffany choker inside and grinned.

Jeff said it couldn't be done. But I did it.

Now he'll have to admit I'm the best.

She could see the Metro-North station, just a few yards away.

BIANCA BERKELEY WAS SO hysterical, it took Jean Rizzo some minutes to get the description he needed. *Silver dress, dark hair. A large green evening purse.*

"That's where she kept the device. The radiation scanner. It's Russian intelligence, you see. They've used this technique before, because it's untraceable."

Jean ran into the street.

THE METRO-NORTH STATION WAS CLOSED.

Elizabeth asked the cop outside, "What's going on?"

"Bomb threat. They think it's a hoax but no more trains'll be running tonight. You'd best get a cab."

IT WAS PURE CHANCE that he saw her. A flash of silver caught his eye from fifty yards away. She was crossing the street in front of the train station, apparently looking for a cab.

No getaway driver. No partner coming to meet her. She just wanders out into the city without a care in the world.

Tracy was right. The lady had balls.

Putting his head down, Jean quickened his pace. Elizabeth was forty yards away now.

Thirty.

Ten.

A yellow cab pulled up. She leaned in to talk to the driver. Jean ran forward. At the exact same moment another male figure darted toward the cab from the opposite side of the street. The man wore an overcoat and turtleneck sweater and Jean recognized him from the way he ran as one of the guys from Barneys. A split second later, the second man emerged from the shadows—also from Barneys. Also running.

This time, Jean Rizzo knew where he'd seen them before.

Elizabeth opened the door to the cab and had one leg inside when Jean grabbed her wrist.

"What are you doing? Let go of me!"

At the same time the other door to the cab opened.

For a split second Interpol Inspector Jean Rizzo and FBI Agent Milton Buck glared at each other.

Then both said simultaneously: "You're under arrest."

CHAPTER 18

"INTERVIEW RESUMED, DECEMBER twenty-first, four fifteen A.M. Miss Kennedy, Mrs. Berkeley has made a statement that you posed to her as an FBI agent. Is that the case?"

Elizabeth Kennedy gave Milton Buck a look of withering disdain but said nothing. Just as she had said nothing to all of Buck's questions for the last five hours.

"You told Mrs. Berkeley that the emeralds in the choker she was wearing had been irradiated. You further convinced her that her life was in danger from exposure to the irradiated gemstones, a deception you maintained with the use of a number of simple props, including these."

Milton Buck placed an oval-shaped piece of plastic on the table. Not unlike one of those monitors people used to listen in on their sleeping babies, it was battery-powered and flashed red with a crackling sound when you pressed a button at the back.

Elizabeth smirked.

"Is that what happened, Ms. Kennedy?"

Silence.

"The device was found in your possession, along with the emerald choker. Can you suggest any other explanation for those items being found in your purse, Ms. Kennedy?"

Elizabeth yawned and looked away.

Milton Buck finally lost his temper, banging his fist down on the table.

"You seem not to understand what a phenomenal amount of trouble you are in, Ms. Kennedy. Tonight's felony alone carries a jail sentence of over a decade. Did you know that?"

Silence.

"Then there's entering the U.S. on a fake passport. Illegal use of credit cards. Identity theft. Impersonation of a federal agent. That's twenty years, before we even begin to talk about the jobs you and your partner pulled in Chicago and Los Angeles and Atlanta." Buck's eyes bulged furiously. "You help me, Elizabeth, and I'll help you. But keep this up and I will personally see to it that you *rot* in jail for the rest of your natural life. Do you understand?"

Elizabeth cast a critical eye over her French manicure. Milton Buck counted to ten.

"We know you were involved in at least three other high-profile robberies on U.S. soil. We also know you work with a partner."

"You seem to know an awful lot, Agent Buck."

They were the first words she had spoken. Milton Buck looked suitably surprised.

"How clever you are! I'm surprised you need to ask me any questions at all."

Her tone was amused, mocking.

"I want the name of your partner, Ms. Kennedy."

"What partner, Agent Buck?"

"Is it Jeff Stevens?"

Elizabeth threw back her head and burst into gales of laughter. Milton Buck felt his anger returning.

"Oh dear." Elizabeth wiped away tears of mirth. "Is that the best you can do? I think I might re-exercise my right to remain silent. If it's all the same to you."

Milton Buck stood up, quivering with rage.

"Interview suspended."

He stormed out.

OUT IN THE CORRIDOR, Milton took a few moments to compose himself.

This was not going according to plan. What should have been a night of celebration, the greatest triumph of his career so far, was turning into a fiasco.

Milton Buck blamed Jean Rizzo.

The irritating, sanctimonious little Canadian had been a thorn in Milton's side ever since he showed up in L.A. this past summer, spewing out his preposterous theories about prostitutes and homicides and Tracy friggin' Whitney. Now, after months of work tracking Elizabeth Kennedy, Rizzo had popped up like the proverbial bad penny, making a mockery of Elizabeth's arrest and point-blank refusing to accept his lack of jurisdiction, or Milton Buck's authority. Embarrassingly, the two men had argued about it in the cab, in front of the suspect, with Rizzo insisting he had a right to interview Elizabeth and refusing to relinquish custody unless Buck allowed him access.

"Don't get comfortable," Milton Buck snapped as Jean helped himself to a coffee from the machine at the FBI's field office on the twenty-third floor of 26 Federal Plaza. "You can talk to her when I'm done. Not a minute before."

"And how long will that be?"

"As long as it takes. Days probably. You may as well go home and get some sleep."

"I'm not going anywhere."

Jean Rizzo had been as good as his word. Milton Buck peered through the glass into the waiting room and saw Jean sharing a Domino's pizza with a bunch of older agents. No one ordered pizza unless they were there for the duration.

"How's it going, Buck? You don't look too happy."

The head of the field office, Special Agent Barry Soltan materialized at Milton's side. Soltan was only a few years older than Milton Buck. Milton resented his superior rank intensely.

"She's not talking, sir."

"I see the fellow from Interpol's still here."

"Rizzo. Yes, sir. I've asked him to leave but—"

"Let's get the two of you into my office."

"There's really no need for that, sir. Interpol has no jurisdiction here. At no time have we invited them to—"

"Agent Buck," Barry Soltan interrupted. "You just told me your witness isn't talking. Now, I'd like to get some sleep tonight, even if you wouldn't. Let's hear what Inspector Rizzo has to say."

JEAN RIZZO HAD A lot to say, to Agent Buck's great irritation. Special Agent Barry Soltan listened, then allowed him twenty minutes to try to break Elizabeth.

"If I understand it correctly, you both want the same thing. For the young lady to give up the name of her accomplice. Right?"

Agent Buck nodded grudgingly.

"In which case, I don't see what harm it does to let Inspector Rizzo have a crack at her."

Jean Rizzo said, "If she doesn't talk, there's every chance

another young woman will end up being butchered by this maniac. He always kills within two days after Elizabeth completes a job."

"Except she didn't complete this job," Special Agent Soltan reminded him. "She got caught."

"For all we know, that may make him even more desperate."

"For all we know, there may be no connection between the two cases whatsoever!" Agent Buck failed to conceal his exasperation. "With respect, sir, Inspector Rizzo's wasting our time."

"Enough, Agent Buck." Special Agent Soltan raised a weary hand. "He's going in."

MILTON BUCK NEEDN'T HAVE WORRIED.

Jean Rizzo was no more successful in getting Elizabeth Kennedy to speak than he had been. After half an hour, Special Agent Soltan asked a few senior agents to join Buck, Rizzo and him in conference.

"I have an idea." Jean Rizzo addressed himself to the group. "Let's get Tracy Whitney in there. She may be able to get Elizabeth to open up."

Milton Buck threw his hands in the air in frustration. "My *God*. Tracy Whitney? Are you still on that?"

"Last time we spoke, Agent Buck, if you remember, you assured me Miss Whitney was either dead or untraceable. Well, guess what? Not only was she very much alive, but I found her within forty-eight hours of our conversation."

Milton Buck grunted gracelessly. "So? She's still not relevant to this case."

Jean longed to tell the arrogant Buck that it was Tracy who'd stolen the Brookstein rubies. Not only was she relevant to his case, she *was* his case. But he bit his tongue, for Tracy's sake as well as his own. *Let Buck keep chasing his own tail.*

Special Agent Soltan raised a hand.

"Hold up a second. We aren't talking about *the* Tracy Whitney? The lady who took down Joe Romano?"

"Allegedly," said Jean.

"The con artist?"

"She's been living quietly in Colorado for the last decade. She agreed to help me with my investigation, as long as I promised her immunity from prosecution."

Milton Buck exploded. "My God! The arrogance! In what alternate universe can an Interpol operative promise immunity to a U.S. citizen on U.S. soil?"

"Cool it, Buck. Has Ms. Whitney been helpful in your investigation, Inspector Rizzo?"

"As a consultant, she's been invaluable. She understands the mind-set of the professional jewel thief. Plus she has a personal connection with Elizabeth Kennedy going back years. They were both romantically involved with Jeff Stevens."

"Isn't he one of your suspects?" Soltan asked Milton Buck, whose face was now livid, from anger or embarrassment or both.

Jean Rizzo answered for him. "Stevens is a person of interest in my investigation and Agent Buck's. Tracy Whitney is convinced he has nothing to do with the murders. But he's here in New York right now and he's had contact with Elizabeth Kennedy within the last twenty-four hours."

An uneasy silence descended.

"Is she still insanely hot?" One of the older agents was talking to Jean Rizzo. "Tracy Whitney, I mean."

"She's attractive," Jean conceded.

"Is she single?"

Barry Soltan frowned. "Okay, Frank. This ain't a dating service." He turned to Jean. "Where is Miss Whitney right now?"

"She's here. In New York."

"Where exactly?" Milton Buck demanded.

"Somewhere safe."

Barry Soltan said, "Can you convince her to come down here?"

"I can try. You'd have to guarantee she won't be arrested."

"We're not guaranteeing anything!" Milton Buck snapped.

"Sure we are. For now." Special Agent Soltan overruled him. "The main thing is that we get Miss Kennedy to talk. Bring her in, Inspector Rizzo."

TRACY'S HEART RACED AS she approached the interview room. She'd dressed carefully when she left the hotel, in a black cashmere turtleneck and figure-hugging bottle-green corduroy pants tucked into flat boots. She hoped the look conveyed casual confidence, but the very obvious leers of the FBI agents when she walked into the building made her second-guess herself.

Why the hell am I feeling nervous? She's the one going to jail, not me. I hold all the cards here.

The last time Tracy had seen Elizabeth face-to-face had been in L.A., in the alleyway behind the Brooksteins' mansion. That had been a triumphant moment. This should have been too. So why were her palms sweating?

Of course, it could have had something to do with the venue. The FBI's New York headquarters did not exactly qualify as one of Tracy's "happy places."

"You're perfectly safe," Jean Rizzo told her. "I'm on the other side of the glass, along with Agents Buck, Soltan."

"Surrounded by the FBI. That's very reassuring," quipped Tracy. "Do I need my lawyer, Jean?"

"No. Nothing's off-limits."

Special Agent Soltan nodded his agreement. "We appreciate you being here, Miss Whitney. You say whatever you need to in there to get Kennedy to talk. You have complete immunity, so you won't incriminate yourself."

Tracy glanced at the short, good-looking agent next to Jean. He looked as if he'd just swallowed a handful of jalapeños.

Jean Rizzo patted her on the shoulder. "Good luck."

ELIZABETH LOOKED UP WHEN the door opened, an expression of profound boredom etched on her face. Then she saw who it was and smiled broadly.

"Tracy!" She leaned back in her chair. If she were nervous, she was doing an excellent job of hiding it. "Well, well, well. Playing for the other team now, are we? I must say I'm surprised. Especially after our last run-in. Out of curiosity, how much did you get for Sheila Brookstein's rubies?"

"One-point-seven million," Tracy said coolly. "You're so sweet to ask."

On the other side of the mirrored glass, Milton Buck's jaw hit the floor.

"Tracy Whitney pulled the Brookstein job?"

"Shhh." Jean Rizzo waved a hand dismissively, his eyes glued to the two women. Tracy was talking.

"I donated the money to charity."

"Of course you did." Elizabeth's upper lip curled slightly. "You always were quite the saint."

"Oh, I don't know about that." Tracy smiled. "Then again, it's all relative."

Milton Buck hissed in Jean Rizzo's ear.

"You knew about this! You knew Whitney did the Brookstein job! Why the hell didn't you say anything?"

"And compromise my source? Why should I?" said Jean. "Besides, you weren't exactly falling over yourself to help *me* with my investigation. Remember?"

"Be quiet, both of you," Special Agent Soltan snapped.

Tracy had sat down now, face-to-face with Elizabeth.

"It hasn't been your year, has it?" she said mockingly. "First you screw up the Brookstein job and now you manage to get arrested by not one but two law enforcement agencies on the same night. Not very impressive. Especially when you consider that a monkey could have outsmarted Bianca Berkeley."

"Bianca took the bait hook, line and sinker," Elizabeth shot back. "I executed the job perfectly."

"Hmm. That must be why you're here."

Tracy's confidence was returning now. She was starting to enjoy herself. Elizabeth radiated the same cold beauty Tracy remembered. Her features were perfect, but she was as dead inside as a marble statue. Running her eyes up and down her slender figure, Tracy said, "They're going to love you in prison. Trust me. I've been there."

Elizabeth looked at her curiously.

"Why do you take things so personally?"

"Probably because I'm a person. Not a machine, like you."

"A machine?" Elizabeth smiled, composed again now. "Come now, that's not fair. We're the same, Tracy, you and I."

Tracy's eyes narrowed. "The same? I don't think so."

"Why ever not? You're a thief. I'm a thief."

"I only robbed from the greedy, from people who deserved it."

"Deserved it according to whom? You?" Elizabeth snorted with derision. "Who made you judge and jury?"

Outside, Milton Buck muttered under his breath, "Exactly." He couldn't understand how Rizzo and the others could listen to this baloney.

"You prey on the old and the weak," said Tracy.

Elizabeth shrugged. "Sometimes. The old and weak can be greedy too, you know."

"All you care about is money."

"Again, not true. I care about Jeff. That's something else we have in common."

Tracy jumped in her seat as if she'd been shocked. The atmosphere inside the room was suddenly electric.

"Where's your sense of sisterhood, Tracy?" Elizabeth taunted. "I'll admit, in the beginning it was just business. I seduced Jeff as part of a job. But the sexual chemistry between us was so insane, it soon became more than a job. For both of us," she added, like a scorpion delivering its sting.

Beneath the table, Tracy dug her nails into her palms so hard they bled.

Don't cry. Don't show emotion. Not to her.

"So what was this job?" Her voice was calm and measured. "I'm curious."

"I was hired to split the two of you up."

"Why? Who hired you?"

Elizabeth smiled. "That would be telling. Let's just say that not everyone out there is as convinced of your saintly status as you seem to be. Some people just see you as a conniving, thieving little bitch who deserves to get her comeuppance. And did you ever get it, Tracy!" She laughed cruelly.

Tracy kept her cool. "How much were you paid?"

"Two hundred and fifty thousand," said Elizabeth. "Of course I wouldn't get out of bed for that today. But this *was* a decade ago. And all I had to do was get into bed, Jeff's bed. Which wasn't exactly a hardship."

Jean Rizzo winced. He knew how much this exchange

must be hurting Tracy, but he prayed she stayed on this track. Elizabeth was getting emotional, giving far more away than she intended to. If Tracy could just press the right button, surely, he told himself, she'd crack.

Tracy said, "They think Jeff's involved in this, you know."

"Oh, I know." Elizabeth laughed. "Agent Buck seems to believe Jeff masterminded my entire career and that odd little Canadian fellow thinks he's running around bumping off prostitutes. Or that I am, I wasn't quite sure. He showed me some horrible photographs. Not very gentlemanly of him."

"So you don't work with Jeff?" Tracy pressed her.

Attagirl, thought Jean Rizzo.

"No. I don't. And I don't know anything about any murders either. I wouldn't have the stomach for that sort of thing."

"If you don't work with Jeff, what were you doing at his hotel last week? You were seen meeting in the park, then returning to the Gramercy together."

"Was I now?" Elizabeth smirked.

"What were you doing?" Tracy repeated.

"What do you think we were doing? Playing Scrabble? Dear oh dear, poor Tracy. Has it really been that long?" Elizabeth laughed. "I'm not a nun and Jeff's certainly no monk. We were enjoying ourselves. You interrupted us in London all those years ago. So let's just say we made up for lost time. I'm not in business with Jeff. Our relationship is based purely on pleasure."

The pain seared through Tracy like a hot poker. It wasn't just Jeff, although God knew the thought of him with this cold, calculating, horrendous woman hurt like hell. It was the embarrassment. The shame. The truth was, it *had* been that long. After Jeff's betrayal, Nicholas had filled the void left in Tracy's heart. But the sexual side of her, the romantic, passionate life that had once meant so much to her? That had gone forever. Elizabeth Kennedy had taken it from her. *That* was what Tracy couldn't forgive. It was *that* that made today a victory for Elizabeth, not for her. Elizabeth might be going to jail. But it was Tracy who was serving a life sentence with no parole.

With a huge effort of will, she managed to control her emotions.

"You say you care about Jeff. If that's true, you should want to help clear his name."

Elizabeth frowned. "I don't follow."

"Everyone knows you work with a partner."

"Who's everyone?"

"This is me you're talking to," said Tracy. "At least three of the jobs you pulled off could not possibly have been done alone. I know that for a fact."

"And which three might those be? Hypothetically, of course. Your friends on the other side of that glass have nothing on me other than what they discovered tonight." Elizabeth waved mockingly at the mirror. "Let's not insult each other's intelligence by pretending otherwise."

Tracy said, deadpan, "Hong Kong, Chicago and Lima."

Elizabeth nodded but said nothing.

"What if Rizzo's right and your partner is the one killing these girls?"

"He isn't right."

"Are you sure? Because someone is killing them, Elizabeth. After each of your jobs. For all we know, he might be out there right now, looking for his next target."

Elizabeth looked thoughtful. There was a long pause. Jean Rizzo held his breath.

Then Elizabeth said, "Let's say I have a partner. And let's say I give you his name. What do I get in return?"

"You don't get anything," said Tracy. "Other than clearing Jeff of suspicion and potentially saving another woman's life."

Elizabeth shook her head. "No deal. I want my lawyer here and a plea deal in place. I'll serve no more than a year for tonight's robbery. Sorry. Attempted robbery." She bowed dramatically to the audience behind the mirror. "No other charges will be brought against me."

Tracy burst out laughing. "You're out of your mind! They'll never agree to that."

"Then they don't get their name."

The door opened. Jean Rizzo asked Tracy to step out.

In the anteroom, Tracy told the assembled agents, "You heard her. I tried, but without a deal she won't talk. Not yet, anyway."

Milton Buck looked at his boss. "I say give her the deal."

Tracy's eyes widened. "What? No! Are you insane? You'd let her walk away from this?"

"She's the monkey. I want the organ grinder."

"I agree." Jean Rizzo's voice was low but firm. "I'm sorry, Tracy, but Buck's right. Elizabeth Kennedy hasn't killed anyone. It's her partner we need."

In desperation, Tracy turned to Special Agent Soltan. "You can have both. She'll give you that name if you keep up the pressure. Maybe trade it for a shorter sentence . . . But a year? And dropping all charges? You're just rolling over. She's playing you! All we need is a little time."

"We don't have time," said Jean. "What if he's in New York right now? He could kill again in hours."

Special Agent Soltan said, "Call her lawyer."

AFTER THAT, EVERYTHING HAPPENED so quickly, Tracy felt as if she were in a dream. Elizabeth's attorney arrived within fifteen minutes. The deal was hammered out and signed in less time than it took one of the junior agents to brew a fresh pot of coffee.

"I want the name," Agent Buck said.

Buck sat opposite Elizabeth and her lawyer in the interview room, making much of being back in charge. Jean Rizzo stood at the back of the room, a few feet from Tracy. Tracy's face was set like flint. She couldn't bring herself to look at Jean.

He promised me Elizabeth would go to jail. He promised me, if I helped him find her, he would put her away. I trusted him and he lied to me.

Milton Buck went on. "I want every scrap of information you have about him. I want dates, I want times, I want details. On every job. And I want to know where he is right now."

"You can have the name and the details. But I don't know where he is right now."

Agent Buck stiffened. "Are you for real?"

"I haven't seen him face-to-face in almost three years."

"You're a liar!"

Elizabeth shrugged. "We're all liars when we need to be, Agent Buck. But this happens to be the truth. We communicate by e-mail and occasionally by phone. It's business. We aren't *friends*. If we were, I wouldn't be talking to you. I am capable of loyalty, you know, whatever the saintly Miss Whitney may think."

Tracy looked away.

"In any case, that's my offer. You can take it or leave it."

Jean Rizzo was getting antsy. "For Christ's sake, Buck. We don't have time for this."

"Fine," Milton Buck barked. "Give me the name."

Elizabeth glanced at her attorney, who nodded.

"My partner is actually an old acquaintance of Tracy's. Funny how closely our lives have become intertwined, isn't it?"

Despite herself, Tracy looked up.

"His name"—Elizabeth paused for effect—"is Daniel Cooper."

PART THREE

CHAPTER 19

 ANIEL COOPER WAITED PATIENTLY for the captain to turn off the seat-belt sign. Then he pushed his economy seat back as far as it would go and snapped off a single square of Lindt chocolate in celebration, closing his eyes and savoring the sweetness as it melted on his tongue.

All pleasure was sin, of course. Over the years, Daniel Cooper had learned to rein in most of his baser human desires. *I am a vessel of justice, a pure servant of the Lord.* And yet he knew he was still not worthy. Not yet. When he became worthy, when he'd fully atoned for his sins, the Lord would deliver Tracy Whitney to him. He felt sure that that day was moving ever closer. Tracy—*his* Tracy, his soul mate—was coming to him at last. All those years he'd thought she was dead! Or if not dead then disappeared, gone, lost to him forever. But he'd been wrong. The Lord had given him another chance. Daniel intended to grab that chance with both hands.

Beneath the cover of his airline blanket, Daniel Cooper started to touch himself.

God had called Daniel Cooper to hunt down lawbreakers and bring them to justice, but society had other ideas. When Daniel tried to join the New York City police force he had been rejected. Officially he was deemed too short, but in reality Daniel knew that his assessors simply didn't like him. They found him creepy. When the FBI also rejected him, but accepted far less qualified candidates in his class, Daniel hacked into his psychiatric evaluation. *Highly intelligent. Lacking empathy. Deceitful.* Someone had added a handwritten note: *borderline psychotic?*

With law enforcement closed to him, Daniel Cooper worked first as a private investigator and later as an employee of an insurance company, tracking down defrauders. It was in this latter capacity that he first crossed paths with Tracy Whitney.

Daniel Cooper believed he could save Tracy Whitney. God had told him so in dream after dream, even as the devil tempted him with unclean thoughts about Tracy's body. Daniel made it his personal mission to catch Tracy and bring her to justice. But throughout her long career as a con artist, she had eluded him time and time again. First by herself, and later with the appalling Jeff Stevens, she mocked all her would-be captors. In their arrogance, police forces across the globe underestimated Tracy Whitney. Daniel Cooper tried to warn them—in Madrid, in London, in New York, in Amsterdam. But like the Pharisees, they remained blinded with pride. And so the evildoers triumphed.

It was Amsterdam that changed everything.

Tracy and Jeff had stolen the Lucullan Diamond, smuggling it out of the city by homing pigeon. Weeks of surveillance and planning by Daniel Cooper had been for naught. This time it was the moronic Inspector van Duren who had let Whitney slip through Cooper's net. Daniel would never forget the way Tracy stopped at the boarding gate at Schiphol Airport, turned to him and waved. *Waved.* Tracy Whitney had looked right into his eyes and seen his secrets. It was in that moment that the bond between them had been cemented.

What God has joined together, let no man cast asunder.

Daniel Cooper had looked back at Tracy Whitney on that fateful day and seen something in her eyes that he could neither forgive, nor forget: pity. Tracy Whitney—thief, goddess, whore—had *dared* to feel sorry for *him.*

It was not to be borne.

God was sending him a message that day. Clearly, he had not atoned sufficiently for his sins. He had not paid a high enough price. Tracy was to be his salvation and he hers, but he did not yet deserve her. There was more work to be done.

Daniel Cooper resigned from the insurance company the next day. He would begin by humiliating the police and authorities who had allowed Tracy to escape so many times through their arrogance and pride. *And lo, the proud will be made humble and the humble raised high.* From his years spent chasing Tracy across Europe, Daniel Cooper knew better than anyone just how easy it was to outwit dummy local law enforcement. As for Interpol, the entire organization was a joke! Just like the Federal Bureau of Ineptitude. Daniel would enjoy outsmarting them, just as Tracy had done. Only Daniel's heists would be even bigger, even grander, even better executed than Tracy's.

Tracy Whitney and Jeff Stevens had taught him how useful a woman could be as a lure in scams, disabling weak, carnally corrupted men. Preferring to work in the shadows himself, Daniel Cooper began scouting around for a suitable female partner.

He found Elizabeth Kennedy by chance, through a contact in London. She was very young, perhaps nineteen, sexually alluring and utterly amoral. Perfect, on paper. When Daniel Cooper met her in person, in a café in Shoreditch, he found her devoid of human emotion or at least of feminine frailty. Fresh out of Youth Custody, where she'd been sent for credit-card fraud—rather an ingenious case in Daniel Cooper's opinion, in which she'd been unlucky to get caught—Elizabeth was mature, intelligent and focused. Of equal importance, she was willing to accept Daniel Cooper's authority in exchange for a steady stream of work and a fifty-fifty share of the profits.

For the first couple of years, the partnership worked flawlessly. Daniel and Elizabeth planned and executed a string of jewel and art thefts around the globe, closely following the successful Whitney-Stevens model. But they were better than Tracy and Jeff. They worked harder, aimed higher and made more money. It was astonishing how quickly they became rich.

Elizabeth bought herself diamonds and cars and vacations and invested in real estate. Daniel Cooper saved every penny in a string of safe, untraceable Swiss bank accounts. He had no need for material comforts, nor, he felt, did he deserve them, preferring to live simply. Besides, the money was for him and Tracy. One day, once the other part of the Lord's work had been completed and Daniel's soul had been washed clean of his mother's blood, he and Tracy would be married. Daniel Cooper would treat Tracy Whitney like a queen and she would worship and adore him, and live to please him, and tell him every day how much better a lover he was than that vacuous popinjay Jeff Stevens.

It was Daniel Cooper's hatred of Jeff Stevens that led him to make his first mistake: using Elizabeth as a "honey trap" to break up Jeff and Tracy's marriage. The plan had worked. All Daniel Cooper's plans worked. He was a genius. But success came at a cost. The first, tragic consequence was that Tracy Whitney went to ground, disappearing so effectively that not even Daniel Cooper could find her. For nine long years Daniel had believed she was dead. Just thinking about that time made him shiver.

The second consequence was the effect of the job on Elizabeth. Much to Daniel Cooper's surprise, it turned out that the aloof Miss Kennedy *did* have feelings after all. She had begun to care for Stevens and to fall under his spell, just as Tracy had done before her. Daniel and Elizabeth continued to pull off spectacular heists together across the globe. But after the honey-trap episode, and Tracy's disappearance, the dynamic between the two of them was never quite the same. Elizabeth began to grow restless, and to tire of her partner's demands. Inevitably, her standards began to slip.

Things came to a head last summer in L.A. when Elizabeth screwed up the Brookstein job. But, as Daniel now knew, it had all been part of God's plan. For it was in Los Angeles, miraculously, that the Lord had brought Tracy Whitney back to him. Back from the dead.

Once again, God had sent Daniel a message, and he had used Tracy Whitney as the messenger.

I am pleased with you, My son, God was saying. *Through your sacrifices, you have appeased My wrath and atoned for your sins. Now you shall win your bride, and achieve eternal redemption.*

Elizabeth Kennedy's arrest in New York had been a surprise to Daniel Cooper, but not a problem. Elizabeth had outlived her usefulness anyway. She was no longer Daniel Cooper's concern. God's plan for him had moved into a new, and a final, phase.

It was all about Tracy now.

Beneath the blanket, Daniel Cooper was about to reach climax. Reaching lower, he grabbed his scrotum and dug his fingernails into his own flesh so hard he drew blood. Tears of agony streamed down his face. He bit his tongue to stop himself from screaming as his erection collapsed in his hand.

"I'm sorry, Lord," he whimpered. "I'm so sorry!"

The plane soared upward into the night.

THE RESTAURANT WAS OFF Bleecker, and quaint and European in feel. There were gingham tablecloths and old wicker chairs with floral cushions and mismatched china. Christmas carols were playing on low in the background. Under different circumstances, it would have been romantic. As it was, Tracy and Jean Rizzo were both exhausted.

It had been three days since Elizabeth Kennedy's arrest and the breakthrough in Jean's case. Three days of relentless debriefing about Daniel Cooper, overshadowed by gnawing anxiety: the Bible Killer had *not* struck again, at least not in the expected time frame. If it *was* Cooper, he was changing his MO, perhaps in response to Elizabeth's arrest. Or perhaps, as Milton Buck repeatedly and smugly reminded both Jean and Tracy, Daniel Cooper had better things to do than waste his time bumping off hookers. Perhaps Jean Rizzo's theory of a connection between the murders and the thefts was no more than a fantasy, a castle in the sky.

Jean ordered a bottle of Bordeaux and poured a large glass for Tracy.

Tracy said, "I'm still angry with you. You do know that?"

"I know."

"You promised me Elizabeth would be put away."

"And she will be. Just not for as long as we would have liked."

"A year! That's a joke, Jean, and you know it. You realize

you may never find Cooper? You and Buck had Elizabeth, and you traded her for what? A name. A shadow."

Jean Rizzo took a big slug of wine. "We'll find him. We have to."

He didn't sound convincing, even to himself.

Tracy looked at his heavy-lidded gray eyes and the traces of salt and pepper in his once-dark hair and thought, *He looks tired. Defeated.* Though she wouldn't admit it, even to herself, she'd grown fond of Jean. She hoped for his sake, as much as for the murdered girls', that Daniel Cooper was the man they'd been looking for. Deep down she still found it hard to reconcile her own memories of Cooper with this image of a ruthless, sadistic killer.

"You knew him," said Jean, once their appetizers arrived, two Caesar salads with extra anchovies. He and Tracy had remarkably similar tastes. "I know we've been grilling Elizabeth for days. But what were *your* perceptions?"

Tracy rubbed her eyes. She was tired too. "I really *didn't* know him. He was a shadow to me. Always a step or two behind. Never really a threat. I guess I thought he was kind of . . ."

"What?"

She searched for the right word. "Pathetic? I don't know. He was smart. Jeff used to think he was in love with me," she added, laughing.

"And was he?"

"He never gave me any reason to think so. In fact he spent years of his life doing everything he could to send me back to jail, so I'm gonna say no! Jeff thought he was dangerous."

"But you didn't?"

"Not really. Which is weird because I had a lot more reason to hate him than Jeff ever had."

Rizzo raised an eyebrow. "How so?"

"Daniel Cooper knew I was innocent of the crime I went

down for. He actually came to see me in that hellhole in Louisiana and told me as much."

"Cooper came to the penitentiary?"

Tracy nodded, an involuntary shiver running through her. She never spoke of her time in prison. Never. Those were the darkest days of her life. It had taken her decades to stop dreaming about Big Bertha and Ernestine Littlechap and Lola and Paulita. The beatings. The terror. The hopelessness.

"The insurance company sent him. He sat there and told me he could prove I never took that Renoir. That Joe Romano framed me for the insurance money. But when I asked him for help, he refused. He left me in that filthy prison to rot."

Jean digested this information. "Why do you think he did that?"

Tracy considered. "I don't know. It was as if . . ." She struggled to put her impressions into words. "I got the sense it wasn't personal. He was like a machine. I guess he and Elizabeth have a lot in common in that regard. I honestly don't think it occurred to him that he *should* have gotten me out of there."

"That's very forgiving of you to say," Jean observed.

Tracy shrugged. "You asked me my impressions of Cooper. I'm telling you. When I got out of jail there were a long list of people I needed to get revenge on. Joe Romano, Anthony Orsatti, Perry Pope, that bastard judge, Lawrence. They were so corrupt, so wicked, and they thought they were untouchable." Tracy's green eyes flashed with anger at the memory. Not for the first time Jean Rizzo thought how beautiful she looked when her blood was up. "Daniel Cooper was many things but he wasn't corrupt. Quite the opposite in fact. There was something of the zealot about him."

"And yet he's spent the last decade as a world-class art and jewelry thief," said Jean. "Isn't that corruption?"

"It depends on how you look at it," said Tracy. "I doubt he sees it that way."

"So you're not surprised Cooper turned to crime?"

"To be frank with you, I haven't given Daniel Cooper a thought in the last ten years."

"Do you think he killed those girls?"

The question was so direct, Tracy was taken aback.

"I don't know."

She watched Jean's face crumple, like a paper bag with the air sucked out of it.

"I know that's not the answer you want. You want me to have a gut instinct on this, but the truth is I just don't know. Part of me always felt a little sorry for him. Now that I know all that stuff from the FBI files, about his mother being murdered when he was a kid and him finding her body . . ." She trailed off. "I don't know. He seems to have led a sad and lonely life, that's all."

"A lot of killers do," Jean Rizzo said darkly.

His phone rang. Tracy watched him answer it. Then she watched the blood drain from his face. She knew what had happened before Jean said a word.

"It's happened again, hasn't it? They found another girl."

Jean Rizzo nodded grimly. "Let's get out of here."

EIGHT HOURS LATER, TRACY was in her hotel room, packing, when Jean Rizzo knocked on the door.

He'd been at the crime scene all night and was still wearing the same shirt he'd had on at the restaurant. He looked close to tears.

"You need some sleep," Tracy told him.

"It's our man, no question." Jean collapsed into a chair. "The girl's name was Lori Hansen and she'd been dead at least thirty hours by the time anyone found her. Raped, tortured, strangled. The apartment was immaculate, the corpse too. And that damned Bible . . ."

Tracy put a hand on his shoulder. "There was nothing you could have done."

"Of course there was," Jean exploded. "I could have stopped him! I could have found him and stopped him in time. It *is* Daniel Cooper, it has to be. Elizabeth told Buck the guy was always spouting religion at her."

"I'll admit, it *is* starting to look more likely." Tracy closed her suitcase.

"She also told him Cooper was obsessed with you and Stevens. That he deliberately planned their jobs to copy your methods. It was Cooper who paid Elizabeth to seduce Jeff and break up your marriage."

Tracy had pulled a picture of Nicholas out of her wallet and was staring at it like it was a talisman, trying to block Rizzo out. Her son represented peace and goodness and sanity. She longed to return to him, to feel his small, strong body in her arms, to smell the clean, soft smell of his cheeks. She did not want to hear about Daniel Cooper anymore, or about Jeff friggin' Stevens. This morning at breakfast she'd seen a report in the newspaper about a stolen Byzantine coin collection—some Russian girl had been robbed while she was at the Winter Wonderland Ball. Tracy knew it was Jeff who'd been the thief, and the report had made her feel momentarily close to him again, and then angry and then bereft. She had to get out of here, out of this city, away from Jeff and all of the madness that she'd worked so hard, so very hard, to escape.

Jean Rizzo said, "I think Jeff Stevens was dead right. I think Daniel Cooper *was* in love with you."

Tracy lifted her case off the bed.

"I think he still is in love with you."

"That's ridiculous."

Tracy moved toward the door, but Jean put a hand out to stop her.

"No, it's not. It's not ridiculous. I knew you were at the heart of this, Tracy. I knew it and I was right. He's going to come for you, you know. Eventually."

"I have to go."

"Go? No. You can't go," Jean told her. "You have to stay, now more than ever. We're so close! Please, stay in New York, at least for a few more days. Cooper may still be in the vicinity."

"He may also be anywhere else on the planet."

"Tracy, please. With your help we have a chance of—"

"Jean." Tracy spoke kindly but firmly. "I'm not staying. Not another day, not another minute. You can threaten to tell Nicholas till you're blue in the face. Who knows, maybe you'll even carry out on your threat. But it's Christmas and I'm going home to my son." Pushing past him, she opened the door. "You have my number if you need it."

Jean Rizzo stood and watched her go. He felt bereft, and not just because of the case. With Tracy around, he felt hopeful, energized, empowered. Without her, all the despair and emptiness came rushing back. How the hell had Jeff Stevens let a woman like that slip through his fingers?

"Don't you have a home to go to?" Tracy stopped at the door. "You have kids, right?"

Jean thought about Luc and Clémence. He realized guiltily that he hadn't given them a thought in days.

"I'll call you," Tracy said.

She was gone.

BLAKE CARTER DRIED THE dishes slowly and carefully. It was the same way he did everything else, the way his father had taught him. Blake's father had a saying he was fond of.

"God made time, but man made haste." William Carter had been a good man, the best. Blake had often wondered what he would have made of Tracy Schmidt. Would he have understood Blake's love for her, with her warmth and kindness and beauty, her secrets and sadness and pain? *Probably not.* William Carter had lived in a world of moral absolutes, of right and wrong, black and white. There was much that Blake didn't know about his employer, the woman whom he'd loved silently and steadfastly these past ten years. But he did know that the world Tracy had come from before they met her was a world of gray. Nothing was black and white with Tracy. Nothing was what it seemed.

Jean Rizzo had come from that world. Ever since Tracy took Nicholas to L.A. in the summer, Blake had watched the gray world of her past come back to haunt her. But since the day Rizzo had shown up at the door, things had gotten exponentially worse. Blake had watched Tracy grow tense and fearful, jumping every time the telephone rang. She'd returned from her "Christmas shopping trip" to New York looking haggard and thin—and without any purchases. Blake knew he had to say something. He just didn't know what, or when, or how.

It was nine P.M. on Christmas Day, and Tracy was curled up on the couch in the family room with Nicholas watching *The Polar Express* for the nine hundred and eighty-eighth time. *That's another paradox about her,* Blake reflected. *She's practical and tough but she's wildly sentimental too.* Blake Carter's own mother had died when he was young. That was probably one of the reasons why he'd never married, and learned to rely only on himself. Tracy's maternal side exerted a huge pull over Blake. *Who am I kidding? Every hair on her head exerts a huge pull.* Blake Carter had never been in love before. He was not enjoying the experience.

Tracy caught him staring. "You okay in there?"

"I'm fine. Almost done."

Leaving Nicholas wrapped up in a faux-fur blanket, Tracy came over to join Blake in the kitchen. "You don't have to do all that, you know."

"Sure I do." Blake smiled. "You sure as hell ain't going to."

"True. But Linda'll be in tomorrow."

"Never put off till tomorrow what you could do today," said Blake. "Close that door, would you?"

He dried the last of the dishes. Tracy closed the door to the family room and opened a box of chocolates.

"Want one?"

"No thanks. Tracy, listen. There's been somethin' I've been meaning to say for a while now."

Tracy noticed that Blake's hands were shaking. He was always so calm. She began to feel nervous herself.

"You're not sick, are you?"

"Sick?" Blake frowned. "No. I'm not sick. I'm . . . well, fact of the matter is . . . I'm in love with you."

Tracy stared back at him with naked astonishment.

"I'd like you to consider becoming my wife."

For a long time, Tracy said nothing. Once she'd had time to think about it, she came back with the impressively articulate: "I . . . wow."

"Now, I know I'm older. Too old for you, really," Blake continued in his quiet, comforting, gentle manner. "But I reckon we get along pretty well up here. And I love the boy like he's my own."

"I know you do," Tracy said. "Nicky loves you too. And so do I."

Blake's heart soared.

"But I can't be your wife, Blake."

The old cowboy took two deep breaths. "Is there someone else, Tracy?"

She hesitated. "Not in the way you mean. But in my heart, yes. There is."

"Is it Nick's father?"

Tracy felt utterly miserable in that moment. Because the answer to Blake Carter's question, the answer she could never admit to, was yes.

She'd told Jean Rizzo that she needed to leave New York to get back to her son, and that was true as far as it went. But there was another need, equally strong, another force propelling her to take the first plane out of the city and never look back. Being in New York, talking to Elizabeth, reading about the theft of the Byzantine coins, Tracy was forced to face the truth. She was still in love with Jeff Stevens. She'd never stopped loving Jeff, and never would stop. She hated herself for it, and she cried and screamed and railed at the heavens. But the feelings were still there, as deep and true as they had been the day she married him in that tiny Brazilian chapel, years ago.

Blake saw the torment in her eyes. His compassion trumped his disappointment. He took Tracy's hand.

"Nick's father isn't dead, is he?"

"No."

"You can talk to me, you know. I know you aren't who you claim to be. I know you've got some kind of past. I'm not stupid, Tracy."

"I never thought you were," Tracy said vehemently.

"It's that Rizzo character, isn't it?" There was a bitterness to Blake's voice that Tracy had never heard before. "He's the one that's sucked you back in. To whatever it was you came here to forget."

"Jean Rizzo's a good man," Tracy said. "It may not seem that way. But he is. He's doing what he has to do."

"And what about you?" said Blake. "What do you have

to do? For God's sake, Tracy, what hold does that man have over you?"

Tracy said nothing. A heavy silence hung in the air between them.

When Blake next spoke he'd regained his composure. Looking Tracy steadily in the eye, he said, "I don't need to know who you were before, Tracy. Not if you don't want to tell me. I'm in love with who you are now. I'm in love with Tracy Schmidt. I want Tracy Schmidt back."

"So do I." Tracy started to cry. Hot tears rolled down her cheeks and splashed onto the chocolate box. "But it isn't that simple, Blake."

"Isn't it? Marry me, Tracy. Choose *this* life, *our* life, not your old one. You're happy here in the mountains with Nicholas and me."

Tracy thought, *He's right. I am happy here. At least I was. Will I ever be happy again?*

"Don't say no," said Blake. "Think on it awhile. Think about what you want the rest of your life to look like. Yours and the boy's."

Blake left. The movie finished and Nicholas went to bed.

Tracy followed suit, but she couldn't sleep.

She thought about Jeff Stevens and Daniel Cooper and Jean Rizzo and Blake Carter. The four of them weaved in and out of her consciousness like dancers around a maypole, their ribbons becoming tangled and entwined as the music played on and on and on.

CHAPTER 20

$\mathscr{P}$ROFESSOR DOMINGO MUÑOZ TURNED the Byzantine coin over in his hand. The gold gleamed as if it had been minted yesterday. The engraver's artistry was exquisite.

"Beautiful." Domingo smiled at Jeff Stevens. "Truly beautiful. I can't thank you enough."

"Please. It was a labor of love. Those coins are where they were always meant to be." Jeff raised a glass of vintage Tempranillo in salute to the elderly professor. "Not that the half a million dollars didn't come in handy," he added with a grin.

"Well, you earned it, my boy."

It was March, three full months since Jeff had left New York with the Heraclian Dynasty coins safely Bubble Wrapped in his luggage. He'd spent a month in England, organizing his affairs and spending time with Gunther Hartog, who was close to death. Gunther's physical deterioration was hard to watch, but it was the unraveling of his once-razor-sharp mind that Jeff found the most heartbreaking. He talked a lot about Tracy. In particular, he had one rambling fantasy about Tracy living in the mountains somewhere and working with the FBI. Jeff humored him, nodding and smiling in all the right places.

"You should find her, you know," Gunther would mumble during his bouts of lucidity. "She always loved you."

Each word was like a dagger in Jeff's heart. He changed the subject as often as he could. Gunther still loved hearing about his capers and exploits. He was delighted by Jeff's tales of New York, and stealing the Russian oligarch's priceless coin collection while the Winter Ball was in full swing.

"Do tell me more about bedding the vile Svetlana. How long did it take her to fall for Randy Bruckmeyer's charms? You know I've always been keen on the Texan. One of your better characters, if you don't mind my saying so."

Through Gunther's eyes, everything seemed like fun, like a great game that they were all caught up in. Jeff thought, *It used to be like that for me. Not anymore.*

He decided not to tell Gunther about his encounter with Elizabeth Kennedy. It would only get the old man back onto Tracy again, and Jeff couldn't stand that.

Bizarrely, Elizabeth had discovered Jeff was in town and had come to see him at his hotel, supposedly to bury the hatchet after all these years. In fact she had some splashy jewel theft planned that she wanted to cut him in on. It was odd meeting her again. Jeff had expected to feel all his old anger toward her, but in fact there was nothing, no feelings at all. Elizabeth was flirtatious, coquettish even, but Jeff felt nothing toward her. It was a disappointment and a relief at the same time, which made no sense, but there it was. They'd parted on cordial terms. Only after he left New York did Jeff learn of Elizabeth's arrest for her failed con on Bianca

Berkeley. *Thank God I didn't take her up on her offer to get involved.*

Jeff felt guilty admitting it, but it was a relief to leave Gunther and get away to Spain.

Professor Domingo Muñoz was Jeff's client. It was he who'd commissioned the theft of the Byzantine coins. But he was also a friend and fellow lover of the ancient world. Domingo had extended an open invitation for Jeff to stay at his "casa," an idyllic, sprawling farmhouse nestled in La Campina, the fertile valley surrounding the Rio Guadalquivir in the south of Spain. About twenty miles outside Seville, the farm boasted stunning views of the Sierra Morena countryside, with its gently rolling hills thickly clad with oak trees and its patchwork fields of wheat and olive groves. The combination of Domingo's hospitality, the idyllic surroundings and so much history and art and architecture on one's doorstep was too much for Jeff to resist.

A maid brought another enormous platter of paella to the table. They were dining outside, beneath a pergola overgrown with laurel, watching the bloodred sun bleed into the horizon.

Jeff said, "I have to get out of here soon. Leave you in peace."

"Nonsense. Stay as long as you like. Spain is good for the soul."

"Less good for the waistline, though." Jeff patted his groaning stomach. "A few more suppers like this and I'm gonna have to take up a new profession. Maybe opera singing. No one wants to hire a fat cat burglar."

"You're hardly a cat burglar," Domingo corrected him, refilling his glass. "You're an artist."

"And a thief."

"A gentleman thief. As you said, the coins are where

they're supposed to be. You could hardly leave them in the hands of that grasping, philistine young woman, could you?"

Jeff agreed that he could not.

"So what's next?" Domingo asked him, his bony fingers coiling around the stem of his wineglass like a snake choking its prey. "Not that I'm trying to get rid of you."

"I have no idea." Jeff sat back in his chair. "This is actually the first time in forever that I haven't had jobs lined up back to back. I might take a vacation. Travel through Europe, revisit some of my favorite museums."

"You've seen the Shroud in Seville, I assume?"

The Holy Shroud of Turin was on display in Seville's Antiquarium, a museum housed beneath the city in an ancient Roman crypt, for twelve weeks. It was the first time the relic had been allowed out of Italy in a generation, so the exhibition had attracted worldwide interest. Believed by many Catholics to be the actual cloth in which Jesus' body had been wrapped after crucifixion—and by most historians to be an elaborately worked medieval fake—the Holy Shroud was almost certainly the most celebrated and revered religious artifact in the world. For many, including Jeff Stevens, the beauty and serenity of the man's face so perfectly captured on the faded cloth meant more than all the wild conspiracy theories regarding its origin. Whether or not it was Jesus' face didn't matter to Jeff. The Shroud was a thing of sublime beauty, of magic, an image of human suffering and goodness that transcended religion and science and even time. The thought of going to see it, in the flesh, made his hair stand on end with excitement, like a small child about to enter Santa's workshop for the first time.

"Not yet," he told Domingo. "I've been saving it for last."

"Well, don't wait too long." The professor finished his rioja and poured himself another glass. "Rumor has it there's a sting in the offing. Someone's going to try and steal it."

Jeff laughed loudly. "That's ridiculous."

"Is it? Why?"

"Because it's impossible. And pointless. Trust me, I should know. Why would anybody want to steal the Shroud of Turin? It's not like you can sell it. It has to be the most recognizable artifact in the known world. It'd be like trying to fence the *Mona Lisa*!"

Domingo shrugged. "I'm only passing on information. But I've heard it from a number of sources. Besides, you used to tell me there was no such thing as impossible," he added, a wry smile playing on his thin lips.

"Yeah, well. I was talking out of my behind." Jeff laughed, but he didn't seem amused. "What sources?"

Domingo gave him a look that clearly said, *You know I can't answer that.*

"What have you heard, exactly?"

"Nothing 'exactly.' Just rumor, some of it conflicting. But the common thread is that there's a fundamentalist out there, Iranian, unimaginably wealthy. He wants the Shroud so he can destroy it. 'Burn the tokens of the heretics,' that sort of thing. I'm sure you know the type."

Jeff shuddered. He felt physically ill.

Domingo went on. "Anyway, supposedly this ayatollah wannabe has hired some brilliant American to come up with a plan to spirit the Shroud out of Seville. I gather he's been offered an insane amount of money."

"How much is insane?"

"The figure I heard was ten million euros. Why? Are you thinking of going into competition with him?" Domingo asked teasingly.

"I wouldn't steal the Shroud of Turin for a hundred million," Jeff said hotly. "Especially not for a guy who wants to burn it. That's disgusting! That's criminal and inhuman and anyone involved in something like that should be shot."

"Heavens above, calm down. I was only joking with you."

"Has anybody informed the authorities?"

"Called the police, you mean? Of course not. These are rumors, Jeff, nothing more. You know how people like to gossip in this underworld of ours. It's probably all hot air. After all, you said yourself that stealing the Shroud would be impossible."

"It would."

"Well then. Have another drink."

Jeff did. But he could no longer relax. The image of some bearded, robed, Iranian lunatic dousing the Holy Shroud in gasoline refused to dislodge itself from his brain. Eventually he asked Domingo, "Did you hear a name at all? Among all these sources of yours. Did anyone know who the 'brilliant American' was supposed to be?"

Domingo said, "As a matter of fact, I did. Not that it meant anything to me." He looked Jeff directly in the eye and asked innocently, "Have you ever heard of Daniel Cooper?"

"HAVE YOU EVER HEARD of Daniel Cooper?"

This time it was Jeff speaking. He was at another dinner table, also in Spain, fourteen years earlier. *Had it really been that long?*

Madrid. Jeff and Tracy were both in town to steal Goya's Puerto from the Prado, although neither would admit to the other. Jeff had booked a table at the Jockey, an elegant restaurant on Amador de los Ríos. Tracy had agreed to join him. He could see her now, sitting opposite him, radiant as always. Jeff couldn't remember what she was wearing, but he remembered the challenge blazing in her green eyes. They were competing with each other. The dance had begun.

Jeff thought, *I love her.*

I'm going to beat her to that painting.

And then I'm going to marry her.

"Who?" Tracy asked.

"Daniel Cooper. He's an insurance investigator, very bright."

"What about him?"

"Be careful. He's dangerous. I wouldn't want anything to happen to you."

"Don't worry."

Jeff had put his hand over Tracy's.

"But I have been. You're very special. Life is more interesting with you around, my love."

Madrid had been the start of everything. Jeff and Tracy had fallen in love there. And all the while Daniel Cooper had hovered like a shadow in the background. On the trip to Segovia, Cooper had tailed them in a Renault. That night, Jeff had taken Tracy to the bodega where they'd watched some flamenco dancers perform, their wild frantic rhythms mimicking Jeff and Tracy's own desire, undeniable now.

Cooper was there too. Brooding. Waiting.

Jeff *did* beat Tracy to the Puerto, stealing it out from under her nose after she'd done all the hard work, poor darling. It was years before she forgave him.

But Tracy wasn't the only one who'd been outsmarted. After Madrid, Daniel Cooper followed Tracy and Jeff across Europe, always just half a step behind. Jeff had grown increasingly fearful of him, but Tracy never took him seriously.

Jeff thought, *Cooper was the third person in our relationship from the start. He was Tracy's shadow.*

"JEFF?" DOMINGO MUÑOZ'S VOICE dragged Jeff back into the present. "Are you all right?"

"Hmm? Oh, yes. I'm fine."

"I lost you there for a moment. So I take it you *do* know Daniel Cooper?"

"In a way," said Jeff. "Although when I knew him he wasn't a criminal. Quite the opposite in fact. Is he here, in Seville?"

"That's what I heard."

Jeff frowned.

Domingo said, "You look worried. Do you think Cooper might really try something like this?"

"I don't know what he might try," Jeff said truthfully.

"Do you think he could succeed?"

Jeff thought for a moment.

"No. It's impossible. Daniel Cooper's very smart. But no one could steal the Shroud."

THAT NIGHT IN BED, Jeff made a decision.

I'll go to Seville tomorrow. Stay for a few days and check out the Antiquarium for myself. Just to make sure.

He didn't really believe Domingo's "rumors." It was all too far-fetched. But if the Shroud of Turin were stolen, and destroyed, and he'd done nothing to prevent it, Jeff Stevens would never forgive himself.

CHAPTER 21

$\mathscr{H}$OUSED BENEATH THE ULTRAMODERN Metropol Parasol project in Seville's famous Plaza de la Encarnación, the Antiquarium museum is a maze of Roman remains, dating from the first century AD. Jeff Stevens marveled at the mosaic of Bacchus and the perfectly preserved pillars of an ancient mansion as he lined up for his ticket to the "Sábana Santa" exhibition, the Spanish term for the Holy Shroud.

Jeff had expected lines around the block. After all, this was the first time in almost half a century that the icon had left its carefully temperature-controlled home in the royal chapel of the Cathedral of Saint John the Baptist in Turin, an industrial city in northern Italy. But perhaps because this was March, the off-season for tourists, as well as midweek, only a handful of people had turned out to see the linen cloth bearing the image of a man who may or may not have been Christ Himself.

"Would you like the audio tour?"

The girl smiled at Jeff, addressing him in perfect English.

"Thank you. Yes."

Jeff slipped the headphones on and proceeded into the first chamber of the exhibition. He already knew most of the history of the Shroud and the intense scientific and theological debate that accompanied it. But it never hurt to learn more, and the earphones gave him a chance to move slowly through the museum, carefully detailing all of the security arrangements, alarms, fire exits and so forth with an expert eye. He'd noticed that there was no additional security at the entrance to the museum, besides the usual, unarmed security guards. But there was a permanent police presence in the square throughout the exhibition's run. Plus the fact that the Antiquarium was basically a crypt meant that there were only two ways out to ground level—the front entrance and a single set of fire stairs leading up into the Metropol Parasol. As for the Shroud itself, it was housed at the end of the exhibition, in the center of a large spiral of "false" rooms, like the bull's-eye on a dartboard or the end of a Victorian maze. Anyone attempting to remove it would have no option but to retrace their steps to the outermost ring of the circle, and choose an exit from there. With each room along the way alarmed and monitored by a high-tech system of infrared beams, not to mention the ubiquitous cameras, Jeff felt reassured that any attempt at a straightforward smash and grab would certainly fail.

Moving from room to room, Jeff began to focus less on his surroundings and more on the audio tour. It was quite fascinating.

"The image on the cloth, thrown into sharp relief as a photographic negative, shows a man who has suffered physical trauma consistent with crucifixion and torture. Although radiocarbon dating places the cloth's origins in the

medieval period, between 1260 and 1390, later scientific studies have cast doubt on those findings. Chemical tests suggest that parts of the Shroud at least may be considerably older."

Jeff walked through room after room, with the audio explaining the science. Never-seen-before images of the Shroud captured by sophisticated NASA satellites were displayed next to early Christian artwork and sculptures relating to the cult of the Sábana. Despite apparently definitive carbon dating and other tests carried out in the 1970s and again in 1988, experts still remained baffled as to the nature of the image and *how,* exactly, it was fixed on the cloth. No paint had been used. Human blood had been found and DNA-tested, but the negative photographic image made no sense. One gruesome, and widely held theory was that some poor soul had been deliberately tortured and crucified in the Middle Ages in order to fake Jesus' Shroud. But that still didn't explain how such a perfect image was captured, eternally, on the cloth.

By the time Jeff entered the final room and stood in front of the Shroud itself, he was so engrossed in the mysteries of its origin that he'd almost forgotten why he had come. But then he found himself gazing into a face from the distant past and it came back to him in a rush of emotion, so violent he could hardly breathe.

That face! So full of human suffering, and yet so peaceful in death. The injuries to the body were horrific—from nails through the wrists to flagellation, bones shattered by beatings to stab wounds, scores of them, blow after blow after blow. *This isn't about God and man,* Jeff thought. *It's about cruelty and forgiveness, life and death. It's about humanity, in all its glory and all its filth, its beauty and its ugliness.*

In that moment, he realized, he would quite happily fight

to the death to protect this object: this relic, this scrap of cloth, this miracle, this fraud.

If Cooper *was* in Seville . . . if there *was* some madman out paying millions to have the Shroud stolen and destroyed . . . they must be stopped.

Jeff Stevens had to stop them.

THE PLAINCLOTHES POLICEMAN IN the green parka watched Jeff Stevens leave the museum. He had dark hair and a beakish, aquiline nose that gave him an almost Roman look. The girl at the front desk noticed it when he flashed his ID and thought, *He fits in here, down among the ruins.* She almost expected him to start speaking in Latin, or at least Italian.

Instead, he asked her in perfect Spanish: "The man who just left. Did he pay for his ticket by cash or credit card?"

"By cash."

"Did he do or say anything unusual when he came in?"

"No. Not that I noticed. He was smiling. He seemed relaxed."

The man in the green jacket turned and walked away.

THE ALFONSO HOTEL WAS the grandest in town, a 1929 landmark built in an Andalusian style and full of opulent, Moorish touches. The lobby and bars boasted marble pillars and mosaic floors, high, ornately carved ceilings and walls hung with exquisitely eclectic artwork and lit by thousands of gold lamps, like vast Aladdin's caves. There were one hundred and fifty-one guest rooms, accessed by old-fashioned, 1930s elevators with gold grille gates, or by a wonderfully grand and sweeping staircase that wound its way around a central courtyard filled with flowers.

Jeff's room boasted an antique walnut four-poster bed and a bath big enough for a family of five to live in. He figured if he were going to leave the comforts of Professor Domingo Muñoz's farm, it should be for somewhere spectacular. The Alfonso was certainly that.

The only downside was that it was full of American tourists, as Jeff discovered when he went downstairs to the bar.

"Couldn't we have met somewhere more private?" The contact Jeff was meeting glanced furtively around the wood-paneled room. They were seated at a corner table, sipping grappa. "I feel like a monkey in a zoo."

"I can't think why," Jeff observed drily. "Nobody's looking at us. They're all on vacation, getting drunk."

Right on cue, a group of American businessmen at the bar laughed loudly, patting one of their party on the back in some sort of private joke.

"What have you got for me?"

The man pulled some photographs out of his coat pocket and slid them across the table. The first two showed a man with a Roman nose and curly dark hair deep in conversation with a traditionally dressed Arab. They appeared to be in a hotel lobby. *Not here though,* thought Jeff. There were too many Arabs in the background for the photo to have been taken here in Seville. The hotel looked grand and opulent. *Maybe Dubai?*

Jeff's contact asked, "Do you know them?"

"No. I'm assuming the guy in the robes is this Iranian Domingo mentioned?"

"Sharif Ebrahim Rahbar. The world's sixth richest man. Reclusive. Ruthless. And not an enormous amount of fun. Drinking, sex, personal freedom of any kind, are all no-nos for this dude. He's not the biggest fan of women's rights either."

"A woman hater?" Jeff sounded curious.

"I wouldn't say that. He has at least eleven concubines in a harem in Qatar. Anyway it's the other guy you're interested in, right?"

"I was," Jeff said. "But I'm not sure it matters anymore." He studied the man in the picture. "That's not Daniel Cooper. Domingo's sources must have made a mistake."

"Could be. But I'll tell you this. Whoever he is, he's interested in the Sábana Santa. And he's interested in you, my friend."

Jeff flicked through the other pictures. They showed the same man, but this time in Seville. In some shots he was entering the museum housing the Shroud. In others he was walking in the vicinity, sometimes taking pictures or stopping to talk on the phone. Most of the time he wore a green parka.

"He's visited the Antiquarium fourteen times in the last five days. He claims to be Luís Colomar, a detective in the Cuerpo Nacional de Policía."

Jeff nodded. The CNP were Spain's national police.

"Problem is, no one's ever heard of him. Not in Seville, not in Madrid, not anywhere as far as I can tell. He could be secret service."

"CNI, Centro Nacional de Inteligencia?"

"It's possible. Or even CIA. His Spanish is flawless, but plenty of Americans speak good Spanish. *Or,* he could be here to steal the Shroud for Rahbar. Maybe he's working with this guy Cooper."

"I doubt it," said Jeff. "Cooper's not much of a team player. Then again, I don't see how he could even attempt a job like this without help. And he does like to hang back in the shadows. Maybe this Colomar is his front man?"

"Maybe. Anyway he was at the exhibition again today, following you. He asked a bunch of questions after you left. Maybe he thinks *you're* here to steal the Shroud."

Jeff shook his head. "Why would he think that?"

"Because apparently someone's trying to steal it. You *are* a con man, Jeff, the best, and an antiquities specialist. And here you are in town, hanging around the exhibition. If this guy is with an intelligence organization"—he jabbed the photographs with a pudgy forefinger—"you'd better watch your back."

"He's not with any intelligence organization," said Jeff, looking at the photos intently, one after another. "He's a thief. I can feel it in my bones. He's working for this Sharif Rahbar. Possibly with Daniel Cooper's help."

Jeff's contact said, "I think so too. So what now?"

Jeff thought about it. "If he has Rahbar's money and Cooper's expertise behind him, he's dangerous. They might actually do this thing. They might actually steal and destroy the Shroud."

Jeff pulled out a wad of cash and handed it to the other man, who swiftly slipped it into his jacket pocket. "Thanks for this. You've been a great help."

"What are you going to do?" the man asked.

"I think I'm going to break the habit of a lifetime. I'm going to call the police."

Comisario Alessandro Dmitri was in his office at the new Sevillan police headquarters on Avenida Emilio Lemos when his telephone rang. Known as "the Greek" on account of his last name and unusually long nose, Comisario Dmitri was a short, arrogant peacock of a man with the sort of ego a rap star could be proud of.

"*Sí?*" he barked into the receiver.

"There's going to be a robbery. Someone's going to steal the Sábana Santa."

Comisario Dmitri laughed. "Really?"

"Yes. Really. It's going to happen in the next few days unless you act now to prevent it."

The voice on the end of the line was male, American and supremely confident. Comisario Alessandro Dmitri disliked its owner instantly.

"Who is this?"

"My name isn't important. You need to take notes. One of the men involved is short, around five foot seven, with dark curly hair and a hooked nose."

"No one is going to steal the Shroud."

"He often wears a green parka and is known to the exhibition staff as a police officer."

Alessandro Dmitri was starting to lose his temper. "I don't have time for this. Unless you tell me your name, I—"

"You should also try to trace a Mr. Daniel Cooper. He's a similar height with brown eyes and a small mouth and looks kind of effeminate. Cooper is dangerous and brilliant. You *must* increase your security, *comisario.*"

"Who the hell put you through to my office?" Dmitri fumed. "I'm a busy man. I don't have time for conspiracy theories. The security at the Sábana Santa exhibition is excellent."

"No, it's not. It's okay, but nothing Cooper can't get around. Hell, *I* could get around it."

"I sincerely advise you not to try," Dmitri said icily. "Anyone foolish enough to attempt to steal the Shroud will be apprehended immediately. You'd be looking at twenty years in a Spanish jail, Mr.—?"

"Please. Just listen to me . . ."

Dmitri had hung up.

"Señora Prieto?"

"Yes?"

Magdalena Prieto answered in English. A long career as a museum curator had given her a good ear for accents. She could hear at once that the caller was American, and switched from Spanish without even thinking.

"Someone is planning to steal the Sábana Santa."

Great. A crank call. That's all I need.

The curator of Seville's most prestigious exhibition had already had a long and trying day. The fine-art-and-antiquities world in Spain was still almost exclusively run by men, and Señora Prieto battled sexism and bigotry on a daily basis. A lot of noses had been put out of joint when Magdalena had landed the plum job of curating the Sábana Santa's first exhibition outside of Italy. Every day was a struggle.

"A man posing as a police officer may be involved," the caller went on. "He's using the name Luís Colomar and is already known to your staff. Another man, Daniel Cooper, may be working with him. Cooper's an ex–insurance investigator. He's incredibly sharp and—"

"Señor. If you seriously suspect anybody of attempting to steal the Sábana, I suggest you call the police."

"I already have. They didn't take me seriously."

"I can't imagine why," Magdalena Prieto observed drily. "I can assure you that our security here is state-of-the-art."

"I know your security systems," the caller said, somewhat disconcertingly. "They're good. But Daniel Cooper's better. Please, tell your staff to be hypervigilant."

"My staff is always hypervigilant. Do you have any evidence of this supposed plot?"

The caller hesitated. "Nothing concrete."

"Then I suggest you stop wasting my time, señor."

For the second time in an hour, Jeff Stevens heard the click of a phone line going dead.

Damn it!

"IT'S HARDLY SURPRISING."

Professor Domingo Muñoz sat opposite Jeff over dinner at the Alfonso.

"You don't give your name, you call up with these wild accusations, and you offer no proof. Why *should* they listen to you?"

"Dmitri's a buffoon," grumbled Jeff. "The classic big fish in a little pond. I shouldn't think he's listened to anyone about anything since 1976. Arrogant prick."

"Señora Prieto's supposed to be very good. Thorough and tough. You have to be to make it to her position as a woman, especially in Spain."

"Well, she's not thorough enough. I don't know about this other guy, but Cooper's a machine. You don't know what thorough is until you've seen him operate."

"*You* outsmarted him, though, didn't you? You and Tracy? For years. He can't be *that* good."

Jeff sat back in his chair. A contemplative look came over his face. Professor Domingo Muñoz could practically see his mind working.

"What?" he asked nervously. "What are you thinking, Jeff?"

"If the police and the museum authorities won't save the Shroud from Daniel Cooper, then maybe we need a plan B. Like you say, I've outsmarted Cooper before."

Domingo frowned. "You're not going to try to steal it yourself?"

Jeff looked up at him and grinned.

"SEÑORA PRIETO. THANK GOD you're here. You need to see this."

Magdalena Prieto had just arrived at work. Her half-drunk coffee was still in her hand and her dark hair was

290 / SIDNEY SHELDON

still wet from the light spring rain that had been falling all morning. The look on her deputy's face told her at once that what she "needed to see" wasn't good.

"What is it, Miguel?"

"The Sábana Santa. There's been a security breach."

Magdalena Prieto's blood ran cold. She thought immediately of the mysterious phone call she'd received two days earlier. *"Someone is planning to steal the Sábana Santa."*

Why didn't I take it seriously?

If anything had happened to the Shroud on Magdalena Prieto's watch, her career would be over and her reputation shredded. Following her deputy at a run toward the central room where the Shroud was housed, the American caller's voice drifted back to her, taunting her.

"I know your security systems . . .

"They're good, but Daniel Cooper's better."

Magdalena felt physically sick. As she turned the corner, her knees practically gave way with relief. *It's still there. Thank God!*

The Shroud was housed in a case of reinforced, bullet-proof glass, laid flat on an aluminum support stand, mimicking the conditions in which it had been kept in Turin. Infrared alarms protected it, both inside and outside the case, which could only be opened after entering an elaborate series of codes. Within the glass, the temperature was carefully controlled in order to protect the delicate and priceless fabric. Magdalena checked the dials on the control panel. Everything seemed normal. No alarm had been triggered. The temperature and humidity remained at the correct levels, as did the argon and oxygen levels (at 99.5 and 0.5 percent, respectively). If anyone had broken into the case, the readings would have gone haywire.

Magdalena Prieto turned to her deputy. "I don't get it. What's the problem?"

He pointed. There, at the base of the aluminum stand, propped up casually like a hand-delivered Christmas card, was a white envelope. It was addressed simply: *Señora Prieto*.

Magdalena's voice was a whisper. "Call the police."

"THIS IS A DISASTER."

Felipe Agosto, the mayor of Seville, paced the room melodramatically. "If Seville were to lose the Shroud, or allow it to be damaged in any way, it would bring shame on our entire city. On the whole of Spain!"

"Yes, but the Shroud hasn't been lost, or damaged." Magdalena Prieto spoke with a calmness she did not feel. Along with Mayor Agosto and Comisario Dmitri, she had gathered in Dmitri's office to discuss the security breach at the Sábana Santa exhibition. "This letter was a warning. A friendly warning. I'm not saying we shouldn't take it seriously but—"

"There's nothing 'friendly' about breaking and entering and endangering a priceless relic, señora." Comisario Dmitri interrupted her rudely. "Whoever did this is a criminal, pure and simple. He must be caught and punished severely."

Dmitri talked tough to hide his own nerves. Señora Prieto had admitted receiving a warning phone call about the shroud two days earlier, but Dmitri had denied all knowledge of the mystery American.

"That's odd," Prieto commented. "He told me he'd already called the police, but no one had listened to him."

"There's nothing odd about criminals lying, señora."

Mayor Agosto said, "Let me see that note again."

Inside the envelope was a single sheet of white paper, folded twice. It read simply: *If I can do it, so can Daniel Cooper.*

"Do we think this Daniel Cooper even exists?"

"Probably not." Dmitri was dismissive. "I'm more concerned about an actual break-in than an imaginary super-thief supposedly hiding out in the city. This man probably made him up to throw us off the scent."

Magdalena Prieto said, "I doubt it. The other man he mentioned, the man posing as a cop, was definitely seen by my staff. We should at least check out this Cooper guy. Have you contacted Interpol, *comisario*?"

Alessandro Dmitri looked at the museum director with withering contempt. The last thing he wanted were a bunch of international busybodies on his turf. *Bloody woman. How did she land the directorship of the Antiquarium anyway? She should be at home making soup, not stirring up trouble, telling professional men like me how to do our jobs.*

"I have no need of Interpol's help, señora. If Mr. Cooper exists, and if he is in Seville, my men and I will find him. Have *you* contacted the authorities in Turin, to let them know what happened at your museum, on your watch?"

Magdalena blanched. "No. As I said, nothing's been damaged or stolen. There's nothing to tell."

"Well, I expect both of you to keep it that way." The mayor jabbed a finger accusingly at the police chief and museum director in turn. "For now, this stays within these four walls. But I want the police presence doubled at the museum and surrounding areas and I want staff on duty at the exhibition *around the clock*. Are we clear?"

"Clear," said Magdalena Prieto.

"Clear," said Comisario Dmitri. "Just as long as city hall's prepared to pay for it."

DAYS PASSED. NOTHING HAPPENED.

Jeff Stevens began to grow anxious.

Perhaps Daniel Cooper wasn't in Seville after all? None

of Jeff's contacts had managed to track him down, and neither, it seemed, had the police. Perhaps the Roman-looking fellow posing as a cop wasn't Cooper's accomplice but was acting alone, on behalf of the shady Iranian sheikh? Since Jeff's little stunt with the letter (a simple matter of tripping the main fuse had disabled all the alarms, while leaving the temperature controls intact), police had been crawling over the Plaza de la Encarnación like flies on shit. Maybe the Roman had thought better of it and left town? Jeff hoped so, but he wasn't convinced.

It was too dangerous to go back to the exhibition himself. He might be recognized as the electrician who'd arrived to do some "maintenance" the day of the security breach. He really ought to leave Seville, but until he was certain that the Shroud was safe, he couldn't tear himself away. Instead he hunkered down in his luxury suite at the Alfonso, sightseeing and shopping and trying—without success—to relax.

It was a full six days after Jeff's letter stunt that he received a letter himself. It was delivered to him by a waiter over at breakfast at the Alfonso. Opening it, he almost choked on his croissant.

"Where did you get this? Who gave this to you?"

The elderly waiter was shocked by the panic in Jeff's voice. "A gentleman left it at reception, sir."

"When?"

"A few minutes ago. He didn't give any indication that it was urgent, although . . ."

Jeff was already running. Erupting out of the hotel's grand front door, he sprinted down the steps and out of the cobbled driveway into the Calle San Fernando. The streets were relatively empty, but there was no sign of Daniel Cooper.

Five minutes later, Jeff was back at his breakfast table, out of breath, his heart pounding as he read the letter again.

Dear Mr. Stevens,

I was impressed by your efforts at the Antiquarium last week. I see that you are aware of some of my plans regarding a certain object, although I fear you have been gravely misinformed as to my intentions. It would be my pleasure to enlighten you, and possibly even to work with you in this endeavor. The money involved in a successful acquisition of this object would be substantial. I would be prepared to split any fee equally, should you do me the honor of becoming my partner.

Jeff thought, *So he thinks I'm greedy. He thinks I'd steal the Shroud for money. I guess he isn't such a shrewd judge of character after all.*

But it was the final paragraph of the letter that really aroused Jeff's excitement.

I suggest we meet. There's a little church across the river, San Buenaventura. I trust you not to alert the police but to meet me privately and hear me out. You will not regret it. I will be there on Wednesday night at eleven P.M. Naturally, if you do attempt to contact the authorities, I will not be at the rendezvous and you will not hear from me again.

Respectfully, D.C.

Jeff's mind raced. He was intrigued by Cooper's claim that he had misunderstood his intentions. Was the Iranian not involved? Was Cooper double-crossing him perhaps, or in competition with him somehow? Either way, it was hard to imagine any good reason someone might have for wanting to steal the Shroud of Turin. Stealing it for money was better than burning it, but it was still outrageous and flat-out wrong.

Talking to the police was out of the question. Jeff had no doubt that Cooper would find out if he tried anything. He knew him too well to imagine otherwise. Besides which, involving the moronic Dmitri, or the smart but complacent Señora Prieto, had done him precious little good so far.

Perhaps if I meet Cooper, I can talk him out of it? Or string him along, pretend to be interested in the money for long enough to sabotage his plan in some way?

To go or not to go.

That was the only real choice Jeff had to make.

CHAPTER 22

*J*EAN RIZZO PULLED HIS bag off the carousel and looked around wearily for a cab.

He ought to be feeling elated, or at least excited. The call from Magdalena Prieto at the Antiquarium museum in Seville was the first break he'd had in his search for Daniel Cooper in months. Elizabeth Kennedy's arrest in New York had felt like a coup at the time. But Elizabeth had promised much and delivered little. Like everyone else who'd worked with Daniel Cooper, she knew shockingly little about the man. Cooper's motivations, impulses and private life were all closed books. After Lori Hansen's murder in New York, the trail had gone completely cold. Not even Tracy Whitney could help Jean Rizzo now.

It had been a tough few months for Jean Rizzo in other ways too. His ex-wife, Sylvie, whom he still loved deeply, had met someone. Evidently it was serious.

"Claude's a good man, Jean."

"I'm sure he is."

They were going for a walk in the park *en famille* the week after Christmas. Jean had missed the day itself, unable to tear himself away from New York in the wake of Lori Hansen's murder, and was trying to make up for it now. Clémence and Luc had forgiven him on sight, as young children do. For Sylvie, it was harder. Making excuses for Jean's broken promises had been bad enough when they were married, but was even more of an imposition now.

"He's a teacher," Sylvie went on. "He's thoughtful and reliable."

Jean frowned. Was this last word a dig at him?

"The kids adore him."

"That's great." Jean tried to be gracious and hide the fact that every word Sylvie said felt like a thorn in his eyeball. "I hope I get to meet him someday."

"How about Thursday? I thought we could all have dinner."

Dinner was even worse than Jean imagined. Claude, the bastard, turned out to be one of the nicest people he had ever met: cultured, unassuming, kind and obviously besotted with Sylvie. As well he might be.

And I opened the door, Jean thought miserably. *I let him in. If I hadn't neglected her, if I hadn't been so obsessed with work, we'd still be together.*

Perhaps if he had something to show for his work obsession, he'd have felt better. If Lori Hansen were still alive. Or Alissa Armand, or Sandra Whitmore, or any of Daniel Cooper's victims. But they weren't. And Cooper was still out there. Jean was failing at his job, just like he'd failed at his marriage.

He longed to unburden himself to Tracy Whitney. He couldn't put his finger on it, but he felt Tracy Whitney would have understood. She too had made sacrifices in the name of her profession. She had lost in love, seen her family disintegrate around her not once but twice. But unlike Jean, Tracy kept moving, kept looking forward, not back.

Unfortunately, Tracy had stopped returning his calls the day she left New York. Her silence wasn't hostile but its message was clear: *I've done all I can, told you all I know. I kept my side of the bargain. Now keep yours and leave me be.*

As much as it frustrated him, Jean admired Tracy for returning to her new life in the mountains, and for clinging to her new identity as Tracy Schmidt, philanthropist and mother, quiet private citizen. Was she bored? Probably, sometimes. But boredom was a small price to pay for peace of mind.

Slinging his bag over his shoulder, Jean walked out of the airport and hopped into a cab.

"*Avenida Emilio Lemos, por favor.*"

"*¿Comisaría?*"

"*Sí.*"

Jean didn't even have time to go to his hotel and change before today's meeting, but that was okay. If he wound up finding Daniel Cooper here—if Señora Prieto was right—it would all have been worth it.

"You will not find Daniel Cooper in Seville, Inspector."

Comisario Alessandro Dmitri was angry. Jean Rizzo recognized the expression on the Spanish policeman's face all too well. It was a combination of anger, resentment and arrogance. Interpol agents got it a lot, especially from disgruntled regional police chiefs.

"Señora Prieto seemed convinced that—"

"Señora Prieto is misinformed. She had no business contacting your agency directly. I'm afraid she has brought you here on a . . . what is the English expression? You are chasing wild geese."

Jean Rizzo walked over to the window. Seville's new police headquarters boasted spectacular views of the city, but today everything was dreary and gray. Traffic crawled sluggishly around the roundabout immediately below them. *Like me*, thought Jean. *Going in circles.*

"Señora Prieto mentioned the letter she found inside the case protecting the Holy Shroud. You knew about that?"

Dmitri bristled. "Of course."

"She said she received a phone call two days prior—"

"Yes, yes, yes," Dmitri interrupted rudely, waving Jean away like a pesky fly. "I got a call myself, as it happens, from the same man. American, spouting all sorts of wild theories about the Sábana Santa being stolen."

"You never reported this call?"

"Reported it to whom?" Dmitri grew even angrier. "*I* am the chief of police in Seville. I dismissed the call as nonsense and I was proven right. No attempt has been made to steal the Shroud. I'm afraid Señora Prieto has rather a feminine sensibility, prone to drama and conspiracy theories. I prefer to stick to facts."

"So do I," said Jean. "Let me tell you a few facts about Daniel Cooper."

He filled Dmitri in on the bare bones. Cooper's history as an insurance investigator, his obsession with the con artists Tracy Whitney and Jeff Stevens and his subsequent involvement in a string of art and jewelry thefts worldwide. Finally Jean told Dmitri about the Bible Killer murders. "Daniel Cooper is our prime suspect. At this point he's our only suspect. I can't stress strongly enough how important it is that we find him. Cooper is brilliant, deeply disturbed and dangerous."

Comisario Dmitri yawned. "I daresay, Inspector, and I wish you luck. However, the fact remains, he is not in Seville."

"How do you know?"

Dmitri smiled smugly. "Because if he were here, my men would have found him."

JEAN'S MEETING AT THE Antiquarium was more productive. He found Magdalena Prieto to be reasonable, intelligent and polite, a welcome change from the obnoxious Dmitri.

"Is he always that much of a jerk?" Jean asked. He was seated in Magdalena's office, sipping a much-needed double espresso that her secretary had kindly brought him.

"Always." Magdalena Prieto sighed. "He's furious with me for calling Interpol. Thinks it undermines his authority, which I suppose it does in a way. But I felt it was my duty to do everything I could to protect the Shroud. I can't tell you how shaken I was, finding that letter."

"I'm sure."

"Whoever was in that case could have damaged the Sábana, or even destroyed it. It doesn't bear thinking about."

"But they didn't," Jean observed.

"No."

"They didn't try to steal it either. Or to extort money."

"Exactly. I truly believe that the person who left the letter and telephoned me was trying to warn me. I think he was sincere. More than that, he was well informed. My staff confirmed that they'd seen the other man he told me about, the one posing as a policeman. You've seen the CCTV footage?"

Jean nodded. The hunched, dark-haired man in the parka was not familiar to him. If this was Daniel Cooper's new accomplice, he was certainly very far removed from Elizabeth Kennedy, his former partner in crime.

"The way this guy broke in . . ." Señora Prieto continued admiringly. "It wasn't just that he bypassed our alarms and cameras. That glass is bulletproof and the key codes supposedly impenetrable. He knew *exactly* what he was doing. He even ensured that the atmospheric balance of argon and oxygen was left intact. Who does that?"

"So he understood about the need to preserve the Shroud?"

"Yes. And *how* to preserve it. If I didn't know better, I'd say he must be a curator himself. Or an archaeologist."

Jean Rizzo smiled. *An American expert on antiquities who can crack codes and bypass alarms, with a flair for the dramatic . . .*

Magdalena Prieto looked at him curiously. "Am I missing something?"

"The man who left you that note is called Jeff Stevens. And no, Ms. Prieto, you're not missing something. Although I think I might be. And Comisario Dmitri certainly is."

Magdalena waited for him to elaborate.

"If Jeff Stevens thinks Daniel Cooper's in Seville to steal the Shroud, then Daniel Cooper is in Seville to steal the Shroud. Under no circumstances should you reduce your security."

Magdalena blanched. "All right. We won't."

"And e-mail me the footage of the second man."

"I'll do it this afternoon. Do you think you'll find him, Inspector? Because in all honesty, I don't think Comisario Dmitri's even trying."

"I'll find him," Jean Rizzo said grimly. "I have to. Your Sábana Santa's not the only thing at stake."

JEAN RIZZO WALKED BACK to his hotel through Maria Luisa Park. The shrubbery glowed lush and green after the rain.

Vivid pink laurel blossoms dazzled in the spring sunshine, in contrast to Jean's gray, dour mood.

He thought about Jeff Stevens. About the showmanship and panache of his latest stunt, followed by the letter to Magdalena Prieto. A man would have to have serious glamour and charisma to attract a woman like Tracy Whitney, and clearly Jeff Stevens had it in spades. Equally clearly, behind the one-liners and the suave, James Bond exterior lurked an almost palpable loneliness. Like Jean, Jeff had loved deeply once and had lost the only woman he'd ever truly loved. Jeff blocked out the pain with hookers. Jean had never had it in him to do that. In a way, he wished he did. But both men had thrown themselves into work, into their respective passions, as a way to survive loss.

Jean wondered if the strategy was working better for Jeff Stevens than it was for him. *At least I have my children.* Without Clémence and Luc, Jean truly didn't know how he would survive. *Stevens has a son, a beautiful son, and he doesn't even know it.* The thought made Jean Rizzo profoundly sad.

After his meeting with Magdalena Prieto, he'd gone to see the Shroud for himself, listening to the same audio guide to the tour that Daniel Cooper's mysterious accomplice had apparently taken some four times. It was fascinating, but gruesome. The idea that someone would torture to death an innocent man in order to fake Jesus' burial cloth . . . that someone would go out and find an individual, abduct, beat and crucify him . . . it beggared the imagination. Even by medieval standards, that was some serious depravity. The fact that it had likely been done for money only made it worse.

Jean Rizzo thought, *Am I wasting my time? Let's say Daniel Cooper really is the Bible Killer, and I find him and stop him and punish him. Does it really matter in the long run? Won't there be another serial killer after him, and an-*

other, and another? Isn't mankind intrinsically, irredeemably cruel?

But then he answered his own question.

No. The world is full of goodness. It's the freaks, the anomalies like Cooper, who go out there raping and slaughtering women. The fact that there were freaks back in the Dark Ages who liked to torture and kill to mimic some scene from the Bible doesn't mean . . .

He stopped walking. A thought, a theory, something began to form in his head.

Daniel Cooper.

Torture and murder.

The Bible.

The Shroud of Turin wasn't just a holy relic. It was evidence of a crime. Of a murder. A murder surrounded in mystery.

Jean Rizzo ran back to his hotel. Bounding up the stairs two at a time, he opened his laptop, tapping his feet impatiently until his in-box appeared.

Come on. Be there. Be there be there be there.

And it was. His most recent e-mail. Magdalena Prieto must have sent it as soon as he left the museum. Jean clicked open the attachment, zooming in closely on the image of the man's face. The prominent forehead. The hooked Roman nose. The dark, springy curls of hair erupting out of the scalp like springs bursting out of an old mattress.

He zoomed in again.

And again.

Only on the third time were the seams of the wig visible. Or the tiny bumps in the latex where the prosthetic nose had been molded to the cheeks. Even with a trained eye and a state-of-the-art computer, Jean had to look so closely he felt like his eyes might cross. But once he saw, he knew.

That's no accomplice.

THE MAN IN THE green jacket was back at his hotel. The Casas de la Judería was a strange mishmash of rooms and courtyards linked by subterranean tunnels in the old Jewish quarter of Seville. Wedged between two churches and set back from a pretty but dark cobblestone street lined with cafés and precariously leaning medieval houses, it was a throwback to an old, largely lost Spain. The interiors were gloomy and musty, with a preponderance of dark brown fabric, permanently drawn curtains and heavy mahogany furniture. A smell of beeswax polish mingled with wood smoke and incense from the church next door. The decor was simple, the rooms small. There were no televisions or other signs of the modern world beyond the beautifully carved, heavy wooden gates at the hotel's entrance. In the courtyards, old men smoked pipes and sipped coffee and read novels by Ignacio Aldecoa. A widow in a black-fringed head scarf, frozen in time, said the rosary by an unlit fire in the salon.

Returning to his room, the man in the green parka locked the door. Then he removed his coat, socks and shoes and sat down on the end of the bed. He tried not to think about the countless generations of Jews who had slept in this room before him. The man did not like Jews. It was the Jews who had crucified Our Lord.

He had chosen this hotel because it was central and private and reasonably priced. But the irony of sleeping in a former Jewish ghetto did not escape him. Feeling dirty and full of sin, he stripped fully and ran himself a boiling-hot bath. Removing his false nose and the latex that made his forehead more prominent was time-consuming and painful, but he carried out the process without complaint. He deserved the pain. Relished it, even.

He stepped into the cramped bathtub. The water burned

his skin, scalding his scrotum as he sat down, immersing his legs fully.

Daniel Cooper sighed with pleasure.

DANIEL JAMES COOPER HAD committed his first murder at the age of twelve.

The victim was his own mother.

Daniel had stabbed Eleanor Cooper to death in a fit of rage over her affair with a neighbor, Fred Zimmer. Zimmer was convicted of the crime and ultimately executed, largely thanks to young Daniel's poignant testimony, which reduced more than one juror to tears. Daniel was placed in the care of an aunt, who often heard the boy scream himself to sleep at night. Daniel Cooper had loved his mother.

But Daniel Cooper's mother was a whore.

Daniel believed in hell. He knew that his only hope of salvation was to atone for his past sins, for his mother's death and Zimmer's. Atonement was what he had spent most of his adult life trying to achieve, in one way or another.

Now, here in Seville, at last everything was falling into place.

Tracy would come to him now. With Jeff Stevens as bait, she'd be drawn like a moth to a flame. Inspired by the Holy Shroud, as so many pilgrims had been before him, Daniel Cooper would finally be able to complete his life's work, the penance that the Lord had prescribed for him. With this one, final sacrifice, he would atone for his mother's death. Then he would save Tracy Whitney's soul, and his own, through the sanctity of marriage.

Daniel Cooper's beloved mother had died in a bathtub.

Reaching under the water, Daniel started to masturbate.

Soon it would be time to go.

EL IGLESIA DE SAN Buenaventura was a hidden treasure. Tucked away in an obscure alleyway, Calle Carlos Cañal, its simple, understated wooden doors belied the utterly sumptuous splendor within.

It was late at night and both the church and the alley were deserted, but a dim light burned constantly above the altar, a gleaming slab of gold that would not have been out of place in a Roman emperor's palace. Jeff Stevens gasped. There must be millions of dollars' worth of art in this tiny church alone, one of scores scattered throughout the city. Ornate carvings in ivory and marble competed with burnished gold statuary and stunning medieval frescoes to capture worshippers' attention—although their true purpose was, of course, to glorify God.

Jeff thought, *I could be a believer in a place like this.* Inhaling the lingering scents of incense, candle wax and wood polish, he remembered the dour, Presbyterian chapels of his upbringing in Marion, Ohio, all whitewashed walls and simple crosses and foul, orange 1970s carpeting. *No wonder I'm an atheist.*

"Hello?"

His voice echoed around the empty church. The air was so cold he could see his breath.

"Cooper?" he called again. "I'm alone."

No answer. Jeff checked his watch. It was a few minutes after eleven. The Daniel Cooper Jeff remembered was a stickler for punctuality. *He wouldn't have left already, would he?* No. That made no sense. It was Cooper who'd requested the meeting. Cooper who felt he had something to say, who wanted to make some sort of deal.

Jeff knelt down in one of the back pews and gazed up at the ceiling, drinking in the beauty and majesty of the place. He'd been nervous on his way over, apprehensive about seeing Daniel Cooper face-to-face after all these years.

But now that he was here, alone, he felt a profound sense of peace.

He was turning to admire a statue of Saint Peter when the blow came. It was so sudden, so utterly unexpected, Jeff didn't even register it as pain. The cold metal smashed into the back of his skull with an audible crack, like a breaking egg. Jeff slumped forward, momentarily aware of something warm and sticky running down his neck.

And then there was nothing.

WHEN JEAN RIZZO WAS trying to track down Tracy Whitney, back in L.A. after the Brookstein job, he'd physically gone from hotel to hotel. There was no time for that now. Instead, the moment Jean recognized the man in the museum's photographs as Daniel Cooper, he began e-mailing and faxing Cooper's disguised image all over Seville.

There were over a hundred hotels in the city and countless guesthouses and B&Bs. Jean knew from Elizabeth Kennedy that Cooper was both practical and cheap. That meant he'd probably chosen to stay somewhere close to the museum, but nowhere too expensive or flashy. The Alfonso was out, as were the real dives on the outskirts of the city. Using Google and the tourist map of the city center that his own hotel had provided, Jean narrowed his "hit list" to ten establishments.

I'll try them first. Then I'll move farther out, street by street, mile by mile.

I'll find him.

I have to.

Not even Jean expected to hit the jackpot so soon, however. On only his third follow-up call, to a small hotel in the Jewish quarter, the girl at the desk answered obligingly,

"Oh, yes! Of course I recognize him. That's Señor Hernández. He's been with us for almost a month now."

A month!

"Is he still checked in?"

"I believe so. Let me check the computer."

The wait was agonizing. Jean Rizzo could hardly stand the tension.

At last the girl came back on the line. "Yes, he's still here. Would you like me to check his room, see if he's in the hotel at the moment?"

"NO!" Jean almost shouted. "I mean no, thank you, there's no need for that."

The Casas de la Judería was only a short walk away, back across the park.

"It's rather a delicate matter. I'll come over myself. I can be there in five minutes."

WALKING BRISKLY THROUGH THE underground passage that led to room 66, Jean Rizzo felt an eerie sense of calm. The comforting solidity of his gun pressing against his rib cage beneath his blue windbreaker was certainly a factor. As was the fact that, win or lose, live or die, this saga was about to be over.

Thirteen women.

Eleven cities.

Nine years.

And it ended here, tonight.

The occupant of room 66—Juan Hernández, aka Detective Luís Colomar, aka Daniel Cooper—had nowhere to run. In a few short moments, he would either be captured or killed. Rizzo had called Comisario Dmitri as he arrived at the Casas de la Judería, announcing his imminent strike on Cooper and then hanging up. If Cooper somehow managed to shoot Jean and escape, Dmitri and his men would be waiting. It would be irritating to have to let the obnoxious Spanish policeman take the credit for apprehending the Bible Killer, Jean thought as he drew nearer to room 66, traversing a courtyard enclosed by high stone walls. On the plus side, though, for that scenario to happen Jean would have to be dead, and ergo oblivious. Every cloud had a silver lining.

At the far side of the courtyard four stone steps led to another passageway that stopped almost as soon as it had begun. Jean found himself at a dead end, the wooden door of room 66 directly in front of him.

Drawing his gun, he knocked twice, hard.

"Señor Hernández?"

No answer.

"Señor Hernández, are you in there? I have an important message for you."

Nothing.

Taking out the key that the girl at the reception desk had given him, Jean started to push it into the lock. The door creaked open by itself. Jean stormed into the room, gun drawn.

"Daniel Cooper, this is Interpol. You're under arrest!"

Damn it.

The bed was made. There were no suitcases. Everything was spotless, clean and sparkling to within an inch of its life. By the side of the bed, a Bible lay open to John, chapter 19, verse 1.

The highlighted quote read, *"They took Jesus, therefore, to the place of the skull. And there they crucified him."*

Jean Rizzo felt his stomach lurch. So he'd been right! Daniel Cooper *was* the Bible Killer. There could be no doubt now. Room 66 was like all the other crime scenes, with one crucial exception.

There was no body.

Yet.

Only then did Jean Rizzo notice the envelope, crisp and white like the one Señora Prieto had found at the foot of the Shroud. It was propped up against the pillows, and addressed in a clear, cursive hand:

To Tracy Whitney, c/o Inspector Jean Rizzo.

Ripping it open, Jean started to read . . .

CHAPTER 23

*J*EFF WAS IN THE house in Eaton Square. He was naked in bed, with Tracy lying next to him. Only, when he leaned over to kiss her, it wasn't Tracy. It was another woman, a stranger.

Tracy was standing in the doorway shouting at him.

"How could you?"

Jeff felt sick. He ran to the door, but when he got there Tracy had gone. Now it was Jeff's mother, Linda, who was talking. She used the same words Tracy had: *How could you?* But she was in another house, in another time, and she was shouting at Jeff's father. Linda Stevens had caught her husband out in another affair.

All her inheritance money was gone, squandered on Dave Stevens's latest get-rich-quick scheme.

"Get off me, you bitch!"

Cowering outside their bedroom, Jeff heard the crack of bone on bone as his father's fist smashed into his mother's cheek.

Linda screamed, "Stop it, Dave! Please!"

But the beating went on: *thwack, thwack, thwack*.

THWACK, THWACK, THWACK.

Something hard and cold slammed again and again into Jeff's back.

He was lying on the floor, a metal floor, being thrown around like a potato in a sack.

I'm moving. Where am I?

He heard a sound like roaring engines and felt the shaking intensify.

A plane? A cargo plane?

Then he slammed down hard on the floor. The blackness returned.

THE BED WAS WARM and soft but Jeff had to get out of it. His stepmother wouldn't leave him alone.

"Hold me, Jeffie! Your dad won't be back for hours."

Her breasts were like pillows, soft and enormous, suffocating him. Rolls of smooth, feminine flesh pressed down on him like dough. He couldn't move! Panic rose up within him.

Jeff ran to the window and jumped out, naked, into the snow.

He started to shiver. It was so cold. So deathly cold.

Some instinct told him, *Don't fall asleep. If you sleep you'll die.*

Wake up, Jeff. Wake up!

"WAKE UP!"

The voice was real. The cold too. Jeff wasn't moving anymore, but he was still on his back. The stone beneath him was like a block of ice.

"I said 'wake up!'" A sharp kick to the ribs made Jeff scream and writhe in agony.

The voice was distinctive, masculine yet oddly high-pitched, and with a distinct note of hysteria. Jeff recognized it at once, and a flood of memories came back to him.

Seville.

The church.

Going to meet Daniel Cooper.

Cooper was quoting from the Bible. He sounded utterly deranged.

"'Are you still sleeping?' said the Lord. 'The hour has come. I am to be delivered into the hands of sinners. Wake up!'"

Jeff groaned. "I'm awake."

His ribs hurt from Cooper's jackboot, but that was nothing compared to the pain in his head, a constant throb, as if his brain had swollen to such catastrophic proportions that it was about to shatter his skull from within. Instinctively he moved to touch the wound, then realized that his hands were bound.

Hands, arms, legs, feet.

He was dressed, but not in his own clothes. What he had on was flimsy and insubstantial, like a hospital gown. A blindfold of something thicker and coarser had been tied around his head. Could it be a bandage?

"I need a doctor," Jeff croaked. "Where are we?"

Another kick, this time to the collarbone. The pain was excruciating. Jeff couldn't understand why he hadn't passed out.

"*I* ask the questions," Cooper squealed. He sounded like a stuck pig, or an angry child who'd just inhaled the helium out of a party balloon. "The Lord will heal your pain. Only the Lord can help you now."

Unless "the Lord" had a flair for emergency cranial surgery, and/or an ability to convince deranged psychopaths to release their hapless prisoners and walk into the nearest mental hospital, Jeff couldn't bring himself to share Cooper's confidence in His present usefulness.

He remembered another quote from the Bible, something Uncle Willie used to say: *"The Lord helps those who help themselves."* Jeff's survival instincts began to kick in.

Step one was to figure out where he was. From the echoing quality of Cooper's voice, he could tell they were in a very large building of some sort, something high-ceilinged and drafty. *A church?* No. All churches had a certain smell to them that this place lacked. *A barn?* That seemed more likely. When Cooper wasn't spouting off about the Lord or kicking him like a dog, the silence was total. There was no sound of traffic, no ambient noise, no birdsong even. Just an enveloping blanket of soundless peace.

We're in a barn, somewhere remote.

The cool temperatures suggested that it was nighttime. Also that they were probably no longer in the south of Spain. The plane ride came back to him . . . if it was a plane ride. And something else. *A car?*

He wondered how long he'd been unconscious. Hours? Days?

They could be anywhere by now.

Jeff tried to work back logically. What was the last thing he could remember? The pain in his head and body made it hard to focus for more than a few seconds. Thoughts and images came back to him piecemeal. He remembered the church in Seville. The smell of incense, the beautiful altar.

Then what?

The plane. The cold metal. Tracy. His mother.

It was so hard to untangle what was real from what was imagined.

Jeff's mother had been dead for twenty-five years, but her voice, her screams, had felt so *real*. He felt himself on the brink of tears.

"Do you know why you're here, Stevens?"

Cooper's voice stung like a cattle prod.

"No." Talking seemed to require an inordinate amount of strength. Each word was exhausting. "Why?"

"Because you are the lamb. The third and final covenant."

Great. Well, thanks for clearing that up.

A weak smile played at the corners of Jeff's bruised lips.

"Do you think this is funny?" Cooper seethed.

Jeff braced himself for another blow, but none came. *What's he waiting for?*

He tried to put himself in Cooper's shoes, to get inside his mind-set—not easy given that the man was clearly a card-carrying fruit loop.

He's talking to you. That means he wants to engage in a dialogue.

He could easily have killed you by now, but he hasn't.

Why not?

What does he want?

What does he need that you have?

Jeff's mind was a blank. But he knew he had to do something, say something. He had to keep Cooper engaged. On instinct he said, "I'll tell you what I think. I think this has nothing to do with the Lord, and everything to do with Tracy."

Cooper erupted. "DON'T SAY HER NAME!"

Jeff thought, *Jackpot.*

"Why shouldn't I say her name? She is my wife, after all."

Cooper made an awful, howling noise like a dying animal.

"No. No no no. She is *not* your wife!"

"Sure she is. We never actually divorced."

"It doesn't matter. You defiled her. You took what was mine. You took something beautiful, something perfect, and you made it filthy. Like YOU."

Jeff heard the little man scrabbling around on the floor. Then he felt himself being rolled over onto his stomach and the thin garment he was wearing being ripped off his back.

"You will atone." Cooper let out a wild shriek, then struck Jeff hard on the back with some sort of crude whip. It felt as if it were made from electrical wire, with sharp metal tips that ripped into Jeff's flesh like razors.

Jeff screamed.

"You WILL atone."

The whip came down again.

And again.

And again.

The pain was beyond words, beyond anything Jeff had ever experienced.

He was still screaming, but the sound seemed to be coming from outside him now. Inside, he had shut down, waiting for oblivion, knowing that it must surely come soon.

The last thing Jeff remembered was the sound of Daniel Cooper's labored breathing, the little man gasping with exertion as the blows kept raining down. Then, like a lover, the silence rushed up to greet him.

"DO YOU PLAY CHESS?"

Jeff opened his eyes. He could see nothing but blackness. For a second he panicked. *I'm blind! The bastard's blinded me!*

But then he remembered the cloth bandage over his eyes and took a breath. He waited for the pain to shoot through his rib cage as air entered his lungs. Or for his headache to return or his raw, flayed back to start screaming. But all the agony he'd felt before was gone. It was miraculous. Wonderful.

It wasn't long before the obvious thought struck him:

Cooper must have drugged me.

But he didn't care. Jeff's whole body felt warm, as if a glow of contentment and well-being were heating him from within. He had no idea how much time had passed since he was last awake—since the beating—but whatever Cooper had given him felt great. The strange thing was that Jeff felt none of the mental fog usually associated with morphine or other opiate-based painkillers. His body might have been lulled into a false sense of security, but his mind was clear. Perhaps, he wondered, adrenaline was keeping him focused? Very obviously he was still in danger. Other than his hunch about Tracy, Jeff still had no idea why he was here or what Daniel Cooper wanted with him.

"Chess?" Cooper repeated. "Do you play? Oh, never mind, it's a rhetorical question. I know you do." His earlier anger seemed to have dissipated to the point where he sounded positively cheerful. "Let's play. I'm white, so I'll go first."

Jeff heard the sounds of a board being set up, of wooden pieces being set down gently in their respective battle lines. He barely knew how to play chess, hadn't played since his teens, in fact. But he sensed this would be a bad time to admit as much. Something told him Cooper wasn't likely to go for a hand of poker instead, or to whip out the Monopoly board.

"Haven't you forgotten something?" Jeff asked.

"Of course not," said Cooper. "I never forget things."

Jeff said, "I can't see. Or move my hands. How am I supposed to play chess if I can't see the board or touch the pieces?"

Cooper seemed amused by the question. "With your mind, Mr. Stevens. I'll tell you my moves and you tell me yours. Then I'll move your pieces for you. It'll be just like on the *QE2*. The game you rigged between Melnikov and Negulesco. Remember?"

Jeff would never forget it. It was the first scam he and Tracy had pulled off together and it had worked like a charm. The two grand masters had sat in separate rooms and unwittingly copied each other's moves. Jeff had run a book on the match for fellow passengers and cleaned up. The question was, how did Daniel Cooper know about it?

"How much did you make on that fraud, out of interest?"

Jeff's voice was hoarse. "Around a hundred thousand dollars, I believe."

"Between you?"

"Each."

"Your idea or Tracy's?"

"Mine. But I couldn't have done it without her. She was magnificent. Tracy was always magnificent."

Cooper said nothing, but Jeff could feel his jealousy in the air between them like a living, malevolent thing, a hovering falcon poised to strike. On the one hand, it seemed crazy to keep provoking a man who was obviously totally crazy and who already wished him dead. On the other, Tracy was Cooper's one weakness. If Jeff could get him to reveal more about himself and his obsession with Tracy, maybe he could use that information to figure out a way out of here . . .

It was worth a shot.

"C4 to C5." Cooper scraped his piece across the board. "Your move."

Jeff hesitated. How did it work again? The horizontal rows had numbers and the vertical ones had letters? Or was it the other way around.

"I said YOUR MOVE!" Cooper shouted.

"Okay, okay. I wanna move my knight. That's *N*, isn't it? . . . er . . . Nd5."

"Hmm." Cooper seemed unimpressed. "Predictable."

"Sorry to disappoint," said Jeff.

"Don't be sorry. Be better. This might be your last game. You want to leave a good impression, don't you?"

Jeff ignored the threat. Instead he focused on keeping his captor engaged.

"I guess no one could accuse *you* of being predictable, could they, Daniel?"

"Don't call me by my first name."

"Why not?"

"Because I said so, that's why not."

"You don't like your name?"

Cooper muttered under his breath. "*He* used to call me that. *Zimmer.*"

Jeff registered the loathing in his voice.

"Zimmer?"

"Fred Zimmer. He was disgusting. A lech, like you. Bxd5. Say good-bye to your knight."

More clattering on the chessboard. Jeff tried to picture the pieces but it was so hard to focus.

"G5 to E5." He tried to draw Cooper back into the conversation. "How did you know him?"

"He was our neighbor," said Cooper. "He used to come over to our house and defile my mother."

Defile. He likes that word.

"Fred Zimmer and your mother were lovers?"

"It was disgusting. Afterward he would pass me in the hall as if nothing had happened. 'Hey, *Daniel,* how are you?' 'You wanna go to a game, *Daniel*?' Zimmer turned my mother into a whore. But I brought down the Lord's vengeance on him. On both of them."

"What did you do?"

"I did the Lord's will. I spilled the blood of the lamb. That was the first covenant. Ra5."

"You killed Fred Zimmer? How?"

"Are you deaf? I said 'the lamb.' *The lamb!* Zimmer wasn't the lamb. He was a wolf. Your move."

Jeff tried to wade through Cooper's deranged logic. It was like trying to swim through molasses with your arms tied behind your back. If the neighbor was the wolf . . .

"Your mother. She was the lamb?"

"I loved her so much." Cooper started to cry. "But just as Abraham had to sacrifice his beloved son, Isaac, so I too was called by God to bring the lamb to the altar."

"God had nothing to do with it," Jeff said bluntly. "You murdered your own mother, Daniel. No wonder you're so screwed up."

"DON'T CALL ME DANIEL! I told you already."

"You were jealous of her boyfriend, so you killed *her,* and then, what? Got got rid of him too, I suppose?"

Cooper was crying softly to himself.

"Jesus," Jeff exhaled. He didn't know what he'd expected exactly, but certainly not this. Not only was Daniel Cooper insane, but he'd been insane for a very, very long time.

"I am the instrument of the Lord."

"Like hell you are. You're a psychopath."

"I am a vessel!" Cooper was growing hysterical. "The blood of the lamb will be shed for you, and for all men, so that sins may be forgiven. That's what the Lord said. So that sins may be forgiven. *'Do this in memory of me.'*"

"Do what? Murder your own mother?"

"You don't understand! My mother had to atone. To sacrifice. Just as I have had to sacrifice, to earn Tracy's love. If Tracy had come to me in the beginning, like she should have, all of this could have been avoided."

"Oh, so now you're blaming Tracy? That's not very gallant of you, Daniel."

The chess game was apparently over. But Jeff had a strong feeling he was playing for his life. Provoking Cooper was a risky strategy, but right now it was all he had.

"Just now you said it was your mother and Zimmer who turned you into a killer. So which is it? Who's to blame?"

"NO! STOP TALKING! My mother was perfect!"

"I thought you said she was a whore?"

"*Tracy's* the whore," Cooper muttered darkly. "Tracy tempted me, like Eve in the garden. Because of *her* sins, and mine, many lambs have been sacrificed. But now the price has been paid. Well, almost paid. It's time for the new covenant. One last sacrifice . . ."

Many lambs? Did that mean many murders? If Cooper really had killed his mother—if it wasn't one of his sick, fantasy projections—what else could he be capable of?

He continued rambling.

"I did the Lord's will. I obeyed, but it was awful. Awful. So much blood! Just like with my mother. You don't know what I went through. But then, you see, there was so much sin with these women."

"What women?" Jeff asked quietly.

Cooper didn't seem to hear the question.

"So much sin. So much recompense to be made. I thought it would go on forever. But the Lord in His mercy had other plans. He brought Tracy back to me, you see." He paused then, and after a few seconds seemed to regain his composure. When he spoke again, he sounded totally calm. "That's why we're here, Mr. Stevens, you and me. Playing our last game. The time has come. The Lord has demanded a new covenant. A new lamb must suffer death, death on a cross. Only then can Eden be restored."

A new lamb? A new covenant? Death on a cross? For a moment there Jeff had felt as if he had Cooper on the ropes, emotionally. But now he was losing him.

"Once the new covenant has been made, Tracy and I can at last be married. Our sins will be forgiven. We will walk hand in hand, pure and clean in the light of the Lord."

"You want to marry Tracy?"

"Naturally. After the sacrifice."

The sacrifice.

Death on a cross . . .

Jeff held his breath. Slowly, very slowly, the shoe was beginning to drop.

"After the sacrifice, Tracy will come to the tomb, like Mary Magdalen." Cooper sounded positively cheerful now. "But like Mary, she will find it empty, but for a shroud. She will press the new shroud to her face and she will weep. Then, at last, she will believe. She will see her Messiah face-to-face and she will understand." Jeff felt the hairs on his arms stand up and the bile rise in his throat.

The new shroud . . .

Daniel Cooper had never been planning to steal the Shroud of Turin.

He was planning to make a new shroud all his own.

He came to Seville to learn how to do it.

What had he said a few minutes ago?

"Do you know why you're here, Stevens?

"Because you are the lamb."

Jeff had shrugged off the words as lunatic ramblings. But now he knew what they meant. Panic gripped him like a frozen fist clenched around his heart.

"Your move."

Jeff couldn't breathe.

Jesus Christ.

Daniel Cooper's going to crucify me!

CHAPTER 24

$\mathcal{T}$RACY WAS AT HOME, reading, when the telephone rang.

"How are you with riddles?"

Jean Rizzo's voice shattered her peace of mind in an instant, like a bullet through a windowpane.

"Terrible. I hate riddles."

"You might want to improve your skills. Real quickly."

"Yeah? Well, *you* might want to get lost. I've told you, Jean. Leave me alone."

Tracy hung up.

Twenty seconds later the phone rang again. Tracy would have left it, but Nick was downstairs in the kitchen and might pick up if she didn't.

"What?" she barked into the receiver.

"I need your help."

"No. No more. You *had* my help and it *didn't* help, remember? Please, Jean."

"Daniel Cooper's got Jeff Stevens."

The silence on the other end of the line was deafening.

"Tracy? Are you still there?"

"What do you mean he's 'got' Jeff?"

"Kidnapped. Abducted. Maybe worse, I don't know. Cooper left a letter. It's addressed to you."

"It can't be!" Tracy suppressed a sob. "Why?"

"I don't know why. But I opened it and it's a riddle, and I'm pretty sure that if you can't help me solve it, Jeff Stevens is a dead man."

More silence.

"I'm sorry, Tracy."

After what felt like an age, Tracy's voice crackled back onto the line.

"Read it to me."

Jean exhaled. "Okay. This is it. *'My dearest Tracy . . .'*"

"He wrote 'my dearest'?"

"Yeah."

"Okay. Go on."

"*'My dearest Tracy. I have taken Mr. Stevens hostage. I hope, for Mr. Stevens's sake and for your own, that you will act on the instructions contained in this note. What I write below will make sense to you and you alone. Do what I ask and neither you nor Stevens will be hurt. And come alone. Yours ever, D.C.'*"

"Has he sent you messages like this before?" Jean asked.

"No. No messages. Never. I'd have told you if he had. What else did he write?"

"Nothing. Just the riddle. You ready?"

Tracy closed her eyes. "Go ahead."

"Okay, so it's sort of like a poem. It's in four stanzas."

Four stanzas? Jesus. "Okay."

Jean cleared his throat and began to read Cooper's words aloud in his soft, Canadian accent:

" *'Twenty Knights at three times three*
Waiting for the Queen will be.
Her lover, husband, destiny
Beneath the stars, where God can see.'

"That's the first stanza. Mean anything to you?"

Tracy sighed. "No. Nothing. Knights and queens, maybe something to do with a card game?" She realized she was clutching at straws. "Go ahead and read to the end. Maybe it'll make more sense as a whole."

"Okay." Rizzo went on: "So then he writes:

" *'Thirteen lambs at altar slain,*
Fourteen suffers daily pain,
Soon to end, his sins erased,
The shroud of old will be replaced.'

"Then:

" *'Dance the dance in black and white,*
Where masters meet, the time is right.
Six hills, one was lost,
Here shall sinners learn the cost.'

"And the last verse:

" *'Twenty Knights at three times three,*
Upon the stage of history,
At last, my love will come to me,
And what the Lord demands will be.'

"That's it."

"That's it?" Tracy sounded bereft. "Nothing else?"

"Nothing else."

Silence descended again. Jean broke it first.

"Do you know what it means?"

"No," said Tracy.

"Not any of it? You have no ideas at all?"

"I need time, Jean! You can't just call me up out of the blue and read me some crazy poem and expect me to solve your case for you like that." She snapped her fingers angrily. "Daniel Cooper's insane. How am I supposed to know how his warped mind works?"

"Fair enough. I'm sorry. It's just that we don't have much—"

"Time. I know."

Tracy could hear the disappointment in Jean Rizzo's voice. The truth was, she *did* have an idea. But it was half formed and not yet clear and not a solution as such. She wasn't ready to share it with Rizzo.

Jean said, "I'll e-mail the poem to you now so you have it in writing. I have to leave Seville and fly back to France in the morning, but you know how to reach me. You will let me know if anything comes to you? Any idea or clue or thought, however unlikely."

"Of course I will."

"You're the key to this, Tracy. I knew it before but now Cooper's confirmed it directly. He's trying to tell *you* something. This is personal."

"Are you sure he has Jeff?" Tracy asked. "How do you know he's not bluffing about that? Using Jeff as a ploy to lure me in?"

"I don't," Jean Rizzo said truthfully. "But do you really want to call that bluff, Tracy? If you're wrong . . ."

He didn't need to finish the sentence.

I know. If I'm wrong, Jeff dies.

Tracy sat back in her chair and rubbed her eyes. Her

palms were sweating and her mouth felt dry, as if she were chewing a ball of cotton.

She thought, *I'm afraid. I'm afraid for Jeff and I'm afraid for myself.*

Jeff had saved Tracy's life once. Now it was her turn to return the favor. Except that what she'd said to Jean Rizzo before was true. She hated riddles. She was terrible at puzzles of any kind, always had been. And this one had been concocted by a madman.

"Give me twenty-four hours," she told Jean. "I need to think."

"We don't *have* twenty-four . . ." Jean began.

But the line was already dead.

TRACY DROPPED NICHOLAS OFF at school the next day. Instead of heading home, she turned onto Route 40 and headed toward the tiny town of Granby.

The Granby chess club met four days a week, in a small room above the general store. Its members were mostly retired men, some local, some from as far afield as Boulder or even Denver. For a tiny local club, Granby had a big reputation.

"I need to know about chess moves."

Tracy sat at a Formica table, opposite a man in his late sixties named Bob. Bob had a wrinked face like a pickled walnut. He was short and bald, and had tiny, wide-set brown eyes that glinted with intelligence and interest as he listened to Tracy talk.

"That's a big subject. Can you be a bit more specific?"

Tracy handed Bob a piece of paper with Cooper's poem written on it.

"It's a riddle," she explained. "The answer should be a

place, a very specific geographic location. It may also specify a time. At first I thought the writer was alluding to a card game, with the knights and the queens. But then I looked at that third stanza, and the phrases 'dance the dance in black and white' and 'where masters meet.' And I realized it wasn't cards. It was chess."

The old man nodded. "I can see the dance might be an allusion to chess. But there are no references to moves here."

"Twenty knights at three times three, waiting for the queen?" Tracy asked hopefully.

Bob smiled. "A chessboard has four knights, my dear, as I'm sure you are aware. Two white, two black. There are no moves with twenty knights. Unless, of course, you had five boards. Five games, playing simultaneously."

Tracy wrote *Five games?* on the pad in front of her.

"Let's forget the numbers," she told Bob. "Can you tell me about moves where a player uses knights to trap his opponent's queen?"

The old man's face lit up. Now Tracy was talking his language.

"I can do better than that, my dear. I can show you."

Two hours later, driving back to Steamboat Springs, Tracy knew a lot more about chess moves. But she still had no idea what Daniel Cooper was trying to tell her.

She tried to think sequentially.

Chess.

Jeff and I did a scam together on the QE2 where we hoodwinked two grand masters, Pietr Negulesco and Boris Melnikov. Does Cooper know about that? Is the QE2 "where masters meet"?

Presumably I'm the queen in this "dance of black and white."

But who are the "twenty knights" waiting for me?

Five boards. Twenty knights . . . Shadows of answers danced before her eyes, but there was nothing she could grasp, nothing that was real.

THE STEAMBOAT LIBRARY WAS practically empty. A few young mothers sat in a circle in the children's section, listening to "story time" with their toddlers, but that was it. Tracy remembered coming here with Nick when he was little and felt a momentary pang of nostalgia.

"Can I help you?" The librarian smiled at Tracy. "Mrs. Schmidt, isn't it?"

"Do you have a history section?" Tracy asked.

"Of course. I'll show you."

"Thank you. Also, do I need a code to log on to the computers here?"

The librarian nodded. "I can give you a temporary library card so you can log on."

THAT NIGHT, AFTER NICHOLAS was asleep, Tracy read through the notes she'd made until her eyes began to cross. Numbers swam in her head like pieces of an elaborate jigsaw puzzle.

Twenty knights. Five chessboards. Thirteen lambs. Six hills. One lost.

At the library earlier, she had searched both the books and online for references to "six hills" and "places with six hills."

The results were not encouraging. There were six hills in Alpharetta, Georgia. The Russian city of Tomsk was integrating its universities into a "six hills" campus. Then there were the *tepeta,* six syenite hills in Plovdiv, Bulgaria.

A famous string of Roman long barrows—ancient burial grounds—in Hertfordshire, England, was known as the six hills. Jerusalem famously had seven hills—seven was six, after "one lost"?

It was hopeless. Jeff could be anywhere from Jerusalem to Georgia. She tried not to think about what might be happening to him, what torture a man like Daniel Cooper might have devised. But panic crept into her body with each passing minute and hour. Jeff needed her! She was his only hope. If Cooper was playing chess with Tracy, he was winning. Hands down.

She read the poem again. The only verse that made no sense at all to her was the third, the one about the shroud and the lambs. *Fourteen suffers daily pain.* What significance did the number fourteen have? None. All that Tracy could think of was "unlucky thirteen," and that wasn't going to get them very far. She'd been sure that chess was the key to this, but her trip to Granby had made her more confused, not less.

Someone would be *waiting for the queen*—was she the queen?—*beneath the stars.* Did that mean Cooper's meeting place was outside, in the open air?

A thought suddenly occurred to her. The line in the last verse: *upon the stage of history.* A stage could be outside in the open air. Something of historical importance.

Racing into the study, she switched on her computer. Her first idea was London and the Globe Theatre. The meticulously restored stage where Shakespeare's plays had first been performed was in the open air, *beneath the stars.* But how did it link to six hills? Or chess?

What about other outdoor theaters? Greek or Roman amphitheaters?

Cooper knew about Jeff's interest in archaeology. Was that a clue? What about the six hills in England, the Roman long barrows? Was there an amphitheater nearby?

Tracy could feel herself getting closer. But as the hours ticked by—eleven, twelve, one in the morning—the answer still eluded her. She went to bed and had terrible nightmares of torture and death, of Jeff Stevens being ripped from her arms out into a cold, black, endless sea.

TRACY AWOKE WITH A start. The clock beside her bed read 5:06 A.M.

Five chessboards.

Six hills.

And suddenly it was there. Not the answer. But the question.

I know the question Cooper wants me to ask.

I know where I'm going to find Jeff.

JEAN RIZZO PACED HIS Lyon apartment, depressed. He'd picked up his children from school today and taken them to a pizza place for lunch. They'd all talked politely. Jean felt like a stranger.

Sylvie told him, "There are no shortcuts. You need to see them more."

Jean had snapped at her out of guilt, because he knew she was right. Then he'd gone home feeling even worse. Checking his phone and e-mails, he found no message from Tracy, but two from his boss summoning him to a meeting in his office first thing tomorrow morning.

That could only mean one thing. Henri Marceau was assigning him to another case.

Jean couldn't blame his boss. Henri had already cut him far more slack than he would have with any other detective, out of respect for their friendship. But Henri had bosses too, and budget cuts to deliver. The Bible Killer case was as cold as ever. Jean's investigation had been an expensive failure.

Pouring himself a large glass of whiskey, Jean dialed Tracy's number.

"Any progress?"

"Not really." Tracy told him about her conversation with the chess player and her research into "six hills" and Roman ruins. Jean couldn't put his finger on it, but something in her tone made him suspicious. Perhaps it was the fact that she sounded so relaxed. Jeff Stevens, a man she had married and clearly still loved, was in all likelihood being held captive by a known killer. And yet Tracy was talking to Jean about dead ends and false leads as if this were nothing but a game they were playing.

He asked her bluntly, "What aren't you telling me?"

"Nothing! Why are you so suspicious?"

"I'm a detective. And you're a con artist."

"Retired," Tracy reminded him.

"Semiretired," Jean reminded her back. "You know where they are, don't you?"

"Absolutely not."

"Why aren't you telling me? Do you want to go alone, is that it? Because he asked you to? I hope you know that's out of the question."

"I don't know where they are, okay? I don't know and that's the truth."

"But you suspect?"

Her split-second hesitation confirmed it.

Jean's voice became urgent, anxious. "For Christ's sake, Tracy. Do *not* go to find them alone. It's madness. If you know something, anything, you *must* tell me. Cooper will kill you, whatever he wrote in that note. He will kill you both without blinking."

Tracy said, "I don't think he'll kill me." Jean could hear Nick's voice in the background. "I have to go."

"Tracy!"

"If I find out anything concrete, I'll tell you, I promise."

"Tracy! Listen to me!"

For the second time in a week, Tracy hung up on him.

"Goddamn it!" Jean said aloud. Tracy Whitney was without a doubt the most infuriating woman he had ever met.

If anything happened to her, he would never forgive himself.

CHAPTER 25

BLAKE CARTER WATCHED TRACY and Nicholas as they rode up the hill toward him. Tracy's hair had grown out a little and was now almost at her shoulders. It sailed behind her like the tail of a kite as she galloped into the breeze, racing against her boy, her slender figure perfectly meshed with the horse's rhythm and movements as if they were one creature, not two. Tracy was a natural horsewoman. You couldn't teach that kind of skill, just as you couldn't fake the natural beauty that shone out of her like light from the sun.

Blake thought, *I've loved her for so long, I hardly even notice it anymore.*

Then he thought, *I don't want her to go.*

Out of nowhere Tracy had announced yesterday that she was flying to Europe tomorrow for a week. Supposedly she was attending some fancy cooking course in Italy. But Blake Carter wasn't stupid. He could smell something fishy, and it wasn't bouillabaisse.

Nick wasn't happy about it either.

"I win!" he panted, pulling his pony up short beneath the oak tree where Blake was waiting for them and grinning at his mother. "That means I get to give you a forfeit. And I say you can't go to Italy."

"Sorry." Tracy laughed. She was panting too. The fast ride in the June sun had exhausted both of them. "Doesn't work like that. Besides, it's only for a week."

Tracy smiled at Blake, but he looked back at her sternly.

Nick said, "They have cooking courses in Denver. Why can't you take one of those?"

"Exactly," Blake Carter muttered darkly.

"I could," said Tracy. "But Denver's hardly the culinary capital of the world. Besides, I *want* to go to Italy. All this fuss over a little vacation! You two are quite capable of taking care of yourselves for a week."

Nick rode off toward the lower fields, where Blake had set up some jumps for him to practice on. Left alone with Blake, Tracy shifted uncomfortably beneath his disapproving gaze.

"What? Why are you looking at me like that?"

"Because I'm not a fool. I don't know what you're playing at, Tracy, but I know this trip is dangerous."

Tracy opened her mouth to speak but Blake waved her down angrily. "Don't you dare repeat that cooking school nonsense to me one more time. Don't you dare!"

Tracy looked at him openmouthed. She didn't think she'd ever heard Blake raise his voice before, and certainly not to her. Ridiculously, she felt her eyes well up with tears.

"You've lied to me for a long time," Blake went on. "About who you are. About your past. And I let it go because the bottom line is, I don't care who you are, Tracy. I don't. I only care *that* you are. I love you and I love Nick. And I don't want you to go."

Tracy leaned out of her saddle and touched his arm. It was as solid and unyielding as the branch of a tree. *Like its owner,* thought Tracy. *I've spent my life bending and twisting and compromising. But Blake lives in a world of black and white, right and wrong. Nothing moves for him.*

"I have to go," she said quietly. "Someone once saved my life. Someone I loved dearly. Now I may have a chance to save theirs. I would tell you more if I could, but I can't."

"That Canadian Rizzo's involved in this, isn't he?" Blake spat out Jean's name like a mouthful of rotten fruit.

"No. Jean knows nothing about it," said Tracy, semitruth-fully.

"What if something happens to you?" Now it was Blake who was holding back tears. "Is this person you're flying across the world for more important to you than Nicholas?"

"Of course not. No one's more important than Nick."

"Then don't go. Because if you die, Tracy, that boy has no one."

"Nonsense. He has you," Tracy said fiercely, turning her mare around to head back down to the ranch. "And I'm not going to die, Blake. I'll be back in a week, just like I told you. If you stop being so horrible to me, I may even bring you back a piece of pie. Just as soon as I've learned how to make one."

That was Blake's cue to smile, to break the tension between them, but he just couldn't bring himself to do it. Instead he watched, stony-faced, as Tracy rode back down the hill and out of sight.

DANIEL COOPER PRESSED HIS hands to his temples.

He had a terrible headache.

Jeff Stevens's screams were starting to get to him.

The path to righteousness is lined with suffering, he reminded himself as he turned up the voltage on the machine that was delivering electric shocks to Stevens's wrists and ankles. *Think of our Lord in Gethsemane. Even He felt abandoned.*

Tracy should have been here by now.

Where is she? Didn't she get my message?

It was hard to keep faith. But Daniel Cooper trusted in the Lord.

BLAKE CARTER HAD JUST put Nick to bed and was about to make himself some supper when the phone rang. Tracy had left for Europe that morning and Blake was home alone.

"Schmidt residence."

"Blake. How are you?" Jean Rizzo's voice was the last sound on earth Blake wanted to hear. "It's Jean Rizzo here. Tracy's friend."

"I know who you are."

"I'm sorry to call so late but I need to speak to Tracy. I'm afraid it's rather urgent."

"Well, you can't speak to her."

"I'm sorry?"

The old cowboy's anger crackled down the line. "Why don't you just crawl on back to wherever it is you came from and leave Tracy the hell alone?"

"You don't understand . . ."

"No, mister. YOU don't understand. She's not here. She flew to Europe this morning. Now, why don't *you* tell *me* what business that lady has in Europe? With her son and her life back here? *You* put her up to this, Rizzo! If anything happens to that woman I swear to God—"

Jean interrupted him. "Where did she fly to, Blake?"

Carter didn't answer.

With an effort, Jean controlled his temper. "It's vitally important that you tell me what you know."

Blake recognized the note of panic in Jean's voice. He was doing his best to sound calm, but he was worried. *So I was right. Tracy really is in danger. If she hasn't even confided in Rizzo, it could be serious.* "Italy. That's what she told me. Rome. But I don't know if she was telling the truth. She's been lying a lot lately. All I know for sure is that she got in a cab to Denver Airport this morning."

"Did she say anything else? Anything at all?"

"She said she was trying to help a friend. Someone who'd saved her life once. She said she'd be back in a week. That's it. Now, are you going to tell me what's happening?"

"I wish I could," said Jean, and hung up.

Jean stood in his apartment with the phone in his hand, frozen, for almost a minute. Blake Carter's words had hit him like a glass of acid in the face. He'd been afraid that Tracy might do this. That she might be crazy enough to try to confront Daniel Cooper on her own, if she believed Jeff Stevens's life might depend on it. Had something in Cooper's letter, in the riddle, convinced her that it did? Jean had hoped that some sense of self-preservation, and concern for her son, would kick in at the last minute and pull Tracy back from the brink.

No such luck. Tracy Whitney always had been impulsive. Apparently the leopard hadn't changed its spots.

Jean had to find her before she found Cooper.

If anything happened to Tracy, Jean thought, *Blake Carter wouldn't need to kill me.* Jean Rizzo would never be able to live with the guilt. He'd already failed his sister, and his wife, and his children and all those poor, dead, murdered women. If he lost Tracy too . . .

Think, Jean. Think! Where is she?

He picked up the phone and started to dial.

JEFF DRIFTED IN AND out of consciousness.

It couldn't be long now. His body would shut down. The pain would end.

It had to. The alternative was unthinkable.

He felt something damp and soft being pressed against his lips.

A sponge?

He sucked weakly, desperate for water, but the liquid wasn't water. It was bitter. Narcotic. He drank anyway, pushing the horrors of what he knew was to come from his mind.

The lamb.

Death on a cross.

The pain had stopped for now. Idly Jeff wondered whether anyone would come to his rescue. Was anybody even looking for him? The police? Interpol? The FBI? Cooper was obsessed with Tracy. But Tracy wouldn't come. How could she? Tracy knew nothing about any of this.

Besides, Tracy didn't love him anymore.

Tracy hadn't loved him for a long time.

The bitter liquid worked its magic.

Jeff slept.

JEAN RIZZO WAS READY to cry with frustration.

"There must be something. Have we checked passenger lists for every airline?"

His colleague sighed. "Out of Denver yesterday? Yeah. We have. No Tracy Schmidt. No Tracy Whitney."

"How about domestic flights? Maybe she had a stopover in another city."

"If she did, she used a different ID. She's a con artist, right?"

Retired, thought Jean.

"She probably has a lot of passports. You released her picture?"

Jean grunted. He *had* given the photograph of Tracy that Interpol had on file to the staff at Denver Airport and had it mass–e-mailed to law enforcement agencies across the United States and in a string of major European cities, along with Jeff Stevens's image. The problem, in both cases, was that the pictures were about fifteen years old. *Why the hell didn't I take Tracy's picture when we were together in New York? I had all that time.* He could have asked Blake Carter for a more up-to-date image, but he knew such a request would only cause the old man to panic. The last thing Jean needed was for Tracy's disappearance to go public.

"Call me as soon as you hear anything."

While he waited in vain for the telephone to ring, Jean turned his attention back to Daniel Cooper's riddle. He suspected strongly that Jeff Stevens was already dead. With the other victims, the women, Cooper had never hung around but had dispatched them swiftly and mercilessly. But Tracy was a different story. Wherever Tracy had gone, she'd been following the clues Cooper laid out for her. Jean Rizzo had no doubt that Tracy would be walking right into Cooper's trap. But if she could decode Cooper's message, so could he. And *if* Stevens was alive, the trail would lead to him too.

Jean's first stop was at his friend Thomas Barrow's apartment. Barrow was a foreign transplant in Lyon, just like Jean. A Londoner by birth, Thomas Barrow taught international relations at the university. He and Jean Rizzo had become friends years ago, when Thomas consulted on a case Jean was working on. He'd done a lot of work with Interpol since and the two men remained close.

"I don't see how I can help." Thomas poured Jean a cup of coffee so thick it was technically a solid, and he turned down the Wagner that was playing on his sound system. Jean had given Thomas a brief history of the Bible killings and Daniel Cooper. He explained that Cooper was holding a man hostage and that the man's life, among others, depended on his, Jean's, deciphering Cooper's letter to Tracy.

"You're a crossword nut," said Jean.

"This isn't a crossword."

"It's a puzzle. Crosswords are puzzles."

"Well, yesss . . ." Thomas answered hesitantly.

"Just read it as if it were a crossword and tell me if anything comes to mind. I need a time and a place."

Jean watched as his friend read in silence. After about a minute Thomas announced cheerfully, "I've got a few ideas."

"Great!"

"They're just ideas. I'm not a psychiatrist. I don't know how your average mass murderer thinks."

"Understood. Go on."

"All right. So starting at the beginning. *If* this were a crossword—which let's not forget, it isn't—then 'twenty knights' might really mean 'twenty nights.' Puzzle writers use that sort of 'homophonic' wordplay a lot. 'Three times three' is nine. So your bloke might be waiting for somebody, the queen, for twenty nights, at nine o'clock."

Jean's eyes widened in astonishment. "That's amazing!"

"It might be total bollocks, remember. It's just a thought," Thomas reminded him.

Jean calculated how long it had been since Cooper wrote the letter. Assuming the twenty nights had begun the day after he wrote it, that meant they had . . . eight days left.

A week in which to save Jeff Stevens's life. If he was still alive.

"Moving on then, line by line." Thomas was clearly warming to the task. "'Beneath the stars' probably means what it says: outside. The meeting place is outside. But references to altars and such suggest a place of worship. So it may also be a church with stars painted on the ceiling, for example? Lots of possibilities."

Jean scribbled feverishly on a notepad.

"'Thirteen lambs slain' has to be your thirteen murder victims. I imagine 'fourteen' is the hostage."

Of course! It sounded so obvious when Thomas said it.

"If he's 'suffering daily pain, soon to end . . .'" Thomas paused. "That sounds like a death threat to me. Torture and death. Especially followed by references to a shroud. Shrouds go with bodies, don't they? You need a corpse to make a shroud."

Jean shivered.

"The next two verses are the most important," said Thomas. "The 'dance in black and white' has to be a reference to chess, especially with all your knights and queens."

"I thought so too," said Jean.

"In which case 'where masters meet' is a place reference. Somewhere where chess masters play. Perhaps outside? I know in Russia they play in the parks, don't they? Or a chess championship of some kind. 'Six hills, one was lost' is another place reference, his most specific. But don't ask me what it means because I haven't a clue. I suspect 'on the stage of history' is place specific too. All your geographical information is in that stanza. You just need to untangle it."

"Okay," said Jean. "Is that everything?"

"That's it."

Jean finished writing. And stood up to leave. "Thank you."

"It's not much, I'm afraid," Thomas Barrow said, handing Jean his jacket. "But if I were you, I'd look into six hills, and chess games in outdoor venues. Or weirdos hanging

around the same spot at nine o'clock at night for three weeks
in a row."

JEAN RACED INTO HIS office, made himself another coffee
from the machine in the lobby and had just sat down at his
desk to start following up on Thomas Barrow's ideas when
his colleague burst in.

"Progress. Tracy Whitney took the two fifteen P.M. Delta
flight from Denver to London Heathrow. Someone at a fast-
food restaurant in the airport recognized her picture!"

Antoine Cléry was young and ambitious, with a wiry
frame, pale, pockmarked skin and a permanently eager expression. He delivered this news to his boss like an enthusiastic puppy dropping a ball at its master's feet. *If he had
a tail,* Jean thought, *he'd be wagging it.* On this occasion,
however, Jean shared Cléry's excitement.

"Did she take a connecting flight out of London?"

"No. Not that day. She cleared customs."

"Under what name?"

Antoine looked at the paper in his hand. "Sarah Grainger.
She used a British passport."

"Terrific work," said Jean. "I want the British police on
high alert."

"I've already spoken to our office in London."

"Not just at Heathrow. I want her picture at all the airports,
and the Eurostar and the ferry ports. Dover, Folkestone, all of
them. I don't believe Cooper's in London. Chances are she's
already left England and I want to know where she went next
and when."

"Sir."

Antoine Cléry left the room. Jean Rizzo felt elated. It was
the first piece of good news he'd had in days.

I'm going to find you, Tracy.

I'm going to find you, and Jeff Stevens and Daniel Cooper.

And then I'm going to end this thing, once and for all.

THREE DAYS PASSED.

Nothing happened.

Elation gave way to anxiety and finally to despair. Tracy had come to London and evaporated. No trace of her had surfaced, as Sarah Grainger or any of her other alter egos.

The staff members at Interpol's London office defended themselves to Jean Rizzo.

"Do you know how many passengers pass through Heathrow every day? Almost two hundred *thousand*. And you expect people to remember one woman's face? She could be flying under any number of identities. Eighty-two airlines use Heathrow, Jean, flying to a hundred and eighty destinations. And that's assuming she flew out of Heathrow. Forget needle in a haystack. She's a speck of dust in the Royal Albert Hall."

While he waited, increasingly desperately, for a positive sighting of Tracy, Jean redoubled his efforts to solve Daniel Cooper's riddle. Tracy had done it by herself, after all. Then again, maybe Tracy knew something he didn't. Some secret that only she and Cooper, and possibly Jeff Stevens, shared?

The chess angle was taking him nowhere fast. He spoke to players and chess clubs and to the editor of *New In Chess* magazine, the most widely read and respected publication in the game.

"There are as many outdoor venues for chess matches as there are stars in the sky, or grains of sand on a beach," the editor told him. "All you need is a board. As for official championships, those always take place in indoor venues. The WCC—World Chess Championship—is the most prestigious, of course. But 'where masters meet' could be a reference to any number of matches or competitions."

Jean refocused his attention on the "six hills" clue. He contacted the local police in Hertfordshire, England, and had staff at the long barrows site shown Daniel Cooper's picture as well as Tracy's. No one had seen them, or reported anything suspicious. Nor had any significant chess matches been held in the area in the past ten years.

The police in Six Hills, Georgia, clearly considered the whole thing a joke. "A riddle? Sounds like somethin' out of *Batman*. We don't get too many hostage situations down here, but if we see your fella, we'll be sure and let you know. You want us to look out for the Penguin too?"

Jean was irritated, but didn't dwell on it. Cooper was almost certainly still in Europe. Although it was technically possible to enter the United States with a hostage in tow, there was no need for him to make his life that difficult.

Sylvie called him. "It's Clémence's birthday tomorrow. She'll be seven."

Jean winced. "I'm sorry. I totally forgot."

"I know. That's why I'm calling you. I bought a present from you and wrapped it. It's a camera."

"Thanks. I'm sorry."

"You're taking her and Luc to the movies tomorrow afternoon at four."

Jean balked. He had less than four days to find Daniel Cooper and the trail was almost cold. "Sylvie, I can't. I have to work. I—"

"I booked the tickets already. It's her birthday, Jean. She wants to see you. Be there."

CLÉMENCE AND LUC WERE in a state of high excitement.

"Can we have ICEEs?"

"Can we have Pick 'n' Mix?"

"As it's Clem's birthday, can we have popcorn *and* Pick 'n' Mix?"

"Can we see it in 3-D?"

Jean experienced a familiar feeling of happiness combined with the guilt that he always felt in his children's company. *They're so sweet. I should see them more.*

Against their mother's express wishes, he bought both of them an enormous bag of candy and settled down between them in the dark theater. The movie was formulaic, a lazily written cartoon complete with a wisecracking sidekick and an improbably proportioned if feisty heroine.

Tracy would make a great heroine, he thought. *Bull-headed and brave. Intelligent but impulsive.*

His mind drifted back to the case. He'd spent the morning watching CCTV footage provided by London's Transport Police, showing Tracy clearing customs and emerging into the arrivals terminal at Heathrow four days ago. She was wearing a head scarf and glasses, which did a good job of concealing most of her face. Her demeanor was casual and relaxed. She neither hurried nor dawdled and she never looked over her shoulder or behind her as she walked toward the tube.

Jean had played and replayed the clip for hours, searching for a clue, for anything that might jog his memory or stir up a new lead.

Was Cooper in London? In England, at any rate?

Some instinct told Jean he wasn't, but he told himself that perhaps his instincts were wrong. Just before he drove to pick up the kids, he'd learned that there was a painting in the National Gallery in Trafalgar Square entitled *Six Hills*. He'd dropped a quick e-mail to Interpol's London field office to contact the authorities at the gallery, but he was itching to get on the phone to them himself.

Pulling his cell phone out of his pocket, he switched it on, ignoring the disapproving glances of the other parents. He set it to vibrate. Immediately it began to jump and buzz in his lap, like an angry bee.

Nine missed calls.

Nine! Something must have happened.

He opened his text messages and began to read.

SYLVIE RIZZO WAS CURLED up on the couch at home, reading a novel and enjoying some well-earned peace, when the front door opened and two crying children burst in. Their father trailed behind them, looking stressed.

"I'm sorry," Jean mumbled. "I have to go. I have to catch a plane."

"What, right now?"

"The film wasn't even halfway through!" Clémence moaned.

"Dad wouldn't let us stay. I didn't even get to finish my ICEE!" Luc sobbed.

"You bought them ICEEs?" Sylvie's frown deepened. "I told you they make Luc sick."

"I have to go."

"For God's *sake*, Jean!" Sylvie snapped. "I'll have to go to court if this goes on. You can't keep letting them down like this. It's Clémence's birthday!"

At that moment Luc vomited violently, spraying blue sugary puke all over the living room carpet.

Jean ran to his car and didn't look back.

Tracy had been spotted at Heathrow. The footage was two days old, but it was clear. With a new alias, and dark brown hair extensions, she had boarded a Britannia flight to Sofia, Bulgaria.

This year's World Chess Championships were being held in Bulgaria.

Jean had Antoine Cléry look up the date and venue.

"The competition began yesterday. It's in Plovdiv, a provincial city, in a conference center attached to a hotel."

Jean Googled "Plovdiv" as he left Sylvie's house.

"Plovdiv is often referred to in Bulgaria as 'the City of the Seven Hills . . . Inside the city proper are six syenite hills, called *tepeta* . . .'"

Jean Rizzo slammed his foot on the accelerator.

CHAPTER 26

$\mathscr{P}$LOVDIV, BULGARIA'S SECOND LARGEST city and the
venue for the latest World Chess Championships, is set on
the banks of the Maritsa River, about a hundred miles southeast of the capital, Sofia. With over six thousand years of
history, the city is a treasure trove of archaeological wonders, with sites from antiquity, including two ancient amphitheaters, set beside Ottoman baths and mosques and the
remainders of medieval towers.

Tracy booked a hotel in the old quarter, a pretty maze
of narrow, paved streets lined with old churches and homes
from what was known as the National Revival period. The
Britannia Hotel was really little more than a guesthouse,
with a few rooms, a grubby reception area and a salon that
served fruit, bread and coffee for breakfast but nothing else.
It suited Tracy perfectly. From her bedroom window she
could see the heights of Sredna Gora rise to the northwest,

above the alluvial plain on which Plovdiv had proudly stood since four thousand years before Christ was born. It had been a decade since she'd set foot in Europe. In other circumstances she would have drunk in the culture and beauty of her surroundings like a wanderer stumbling upon a water hole after years in the desert. As it was, the pealing church bells and sights and smells of the Old World barely registered.

Tracy wasn't here to sightsee. It had taken her a long time, too long, to figure out the first line of Daniel Cooper's riddle. By the time she arrived at the Britannia Hotel, she was hot, exhausted and nauseous with stress . . . What if this was all a sick joke? What if Jeff wasn't here after all, but already dead, and Cooper had lured her here so he could kill her too? What if Blake Carter was right and she was making a terrible, deadly mistake? . . . Her "twenty nights" were almost up.

She had to meet Cooper tonight. Tracy knew from bitter experience that Daniel Cooper would not tolerate lateness, or extend a deadline once set, not even for her. The problem was she still wasn't certain *which* open-air theater he was referring to in his "beneath the stars" line. The Antichen Teatar, built by the Emperor Trajan in the second century was the most famous. It was also situated between two of Plovdiv's six hills, making it an obvious choice. But the Ancient Stadium, built a hundred years later by the Emperor Hadrian had as much claim to be a "stage of history," as well as the advantage of being closed to the public for restoration work.

With nothing else to go on, Tracy decided that Cooper would choose the abandoned theater for their rendezvous. *He'll want to meet me alone.* Dropping her suitcase on the bed, she showered, changed and walked across the street to a tiny café where she forced herself to eat a Pritnsessi sandwich, a traditional Bulgarian snack of feta cheese and egg, and drink a cup of strong coffee. Feeling slightly better, physically at least, she checked her watch.

Six P.M.

Three hours to go, assuming she was right about "three times three" meaning nine P.M. From the tourist map she'd picked up at the reception desk, Tracy knew that the stadium was situated in the north of the city, no more than a twenty-minute cab ride away. She decided to get there early. When going into battle, it always made sense to check out the terrain first. Especially when the battlefield had been handpicked by the enemy. Daniel Cooper had chosen this spot for a reason.

I should find out what it is.

Reaching into her purse for her wallet, Tracy fingered first her cell phone and then the gun she'd brought with her, a tiny, custom-made Kahr PM9 micro 9mm that could be disassembled into pieces that looked like lipstick tubes and other "permissible items" when passing through airport scanners. Jeff would have laughed and called it a "woman's gun." But its bullets could kill, just like any others.

In all her years as a con artist, Tracy had never gone armed to a job. Not since that fateful night at Joe Romano's house in New Orleans, the night that had seen her wind up in jail and that had changed her life utterly and forever. Tracy didn't like guns. She wasn't in the business of hurting people. But this was different.

Daniel Cooper was a psychotic killer.

And he had Jeff.

Tracy paid her bill and walked out into the street.

THE MAIN BUS STATION in Sofia is right next to the railway station. Jean Rizzo arrived just as the bus to Plovdiv was leaving and was told he would have to wait another half an hour for the next one.

"Goddamn it!" Jean shouted aloud.

It was already five o'clock. As ridiculous as it sounded, numerous people had told Jean that the fastest and most reliable way to get to Plovdiv from Sofia was by bus. Taxi drivers invariably took unnecessary detours to jack up their prices, the trains were frequently canceled, and renting a car was complicated and involved navigation, never Jean's strong suit. In other circumstances he'd have asked the local police to drive him the ninety miles, but by the time he'd explained about Daniel Cooper and Tracy Whitney and the Bible killings and deciphering riddles, more valuable hours would have been lost.

At last, another bus arrived and Jean climbed onboard, paying the eleven levs fare. It was crowded and almost unbearably humid, and the suspension of the vehicle was atrocious, as was the cell-phone reception. Not that it mattered much. After three barely audible, then dropped calls to his office, Jean learned that they still knew precisely nothing about where Tracy might be staying. Nor had there been any sightings or leads on either Cooper or Jeff Stevens. Local police had been dispatched to the chess championships—"where masters meet"—as well as to a variety of possible open-air meeting places. Tonight's tense match between the Russian Alexandr Makarov and his Ukranian rival Leonid Savchuk at the Plovdiv Royal Hotel was a highlight of the competition. There was at least a chance that Cooper might choose to meet Tracy there, or leave some further clue to his whereabouts, thinking himself safe in the anonymity of the crowd.

As for Jeff Stevens, Jean Rizzo privately believed that he was probably already dead. Holding a hostage for long periods is a complicated business, fraught with risk. Transporting one across international borders is even more dangerous. In Jean's experience, killers like Daniel Cooper tended to stick to what they knew. Thirteen murdered women bore witness to the success of the Bible Killer's MO. Although if anyone could push Cooper to step outside his comfort zone, it would be Tracy Whitney.

Jeff Stevens was right about Daniel Cooper. He's in love with Tracy. In his own, sick mind, he always has been.

The bus rattled on.

JEFF STEVENS WAS CALLING for his mother again.

Daniel Cooper had heard many others do the same. It was a very common thing to do at the point of death. That primitive bond to the womb that bore us existed in all cultures. It was the love that endured to the end.

I loved my mother too. But she betrayed me.

Blood. That was what Daniel remembered from his mother's death. Blood pouring from her wrists and neck, blood filling the bathtub and spilling onto the floor, staining the linoleum livid red.

Jeff had bled profusely too, especially when Daniel nailed his hands to the wood.

Infuriatingly, blood had spattered onto Daniel's clean white shirt. He wanted to look his best when Tracy finally came to him. Tonight was the last night. He could feel her presence already. Her closeness. Like the scent of jasmine on the air.

Tonight.

JEAN RIZZO STEPPED OFF the bus in Plovdiv outside the Intercontinental Hotel.

His watch said five after seven.

Less than two hours. If Tracy's here, I have less than two hours to find her. Luckily, the team is already in Europe.

He stood in the pretty cobblestone square still busy with tourists, wondering where to go next. Before he'd made a decision, his phone rang.

"Where are you?"

Milton Buck's voice was as demanding and charmless as ever. It had been months since Jean Rizzo heard from the FBI. They sure knew how to pick their moments.

"I don't have time for this now," Jean said brusquely.

"I know you're in Bulgaria. Have you already reached Plovdiv?"

This gave Jean pause. *How the hell does Buck know where I am?*

"As a matter of fact, I have. Not that it—"

"Do not interrogate Cooper without me. Do you understand? My team and I will be in the city by nightfall."

"By nightfall it'll be too late," Jean said bluntly.

"Now you listen to me, Rizzo." Milton Buck's voice took on a threatening edge. "We've been tracking Cooper for months. We now have concrete physical evidence implicating him in the New York and Chicago jobs. It is imperative that you do not alert him to your presence, or scare him off before we have a chance to interrogate him. Is that clear?"

"Kiss my ass, Buck," said Jean, and hung up.

He called his own team next. "Any news?"

"No, sir. Nothing yet."

Jean thought, *I'm on my own. I have less than two hours to work out where Tracy and Cooper are meeting. Think, Rizzo. Think!*

TRACY ARRIVED AT THE stadium just as dusk was beginning to fall. The air was still warm and humid and she could feel sweat running down her spine underneath her white T-shirt. She'd dressed casually for tonight's encounter, in jeans, sneakers and a light jacket. The latter meant she could conceal her gun, but it also meant that she was uncomfortably hot. Hopefully by nine the temperature would have dropped considerably.

The area around the stadium was all but deserted. Tracy saw a number of boarded-up kiosks, the kind that sell tourist crap at every "attraction" in Europe. Evidently the restoration work was expected to go on for some time, months or even years. A few people crossed the square adjacent to the main entrance, but everybody was passing through, hurrying home after work. Nobody paid either Tracy or the stadium any attention. There was no one taking photographs and no one who looked like a tourist, other than Tracy herself.

Good.

"Closed" signs had been erected around the ancient structure, and here and there some lines of yellow tape had been haphazardly stretched between dilapidated wooden poles. But no significant effort had been made to keep out any would-be intruders.

How different from the States, Tracy thought. *A place like this would be padlocked and alarmed to within an inch of its life.* She strolled the perimeter, looking for CCTV cameras, but there was nothing. As meeting places went, this one was both spectacular and private. Tracy grew increasingly confident that it was the place where Cooper would be waiting.

"Confident"? Was that the right word?

The truth was, Tracy felt sick with nerves. And not the sort of preheist stage fright she'd grown used to experiencing over the years. That was a blessing, a necessary adrenaline rush that hardened one's determination and honed one's reactions. This was different, debilitating.

Jeff's life could depend on what happened tonight, on how

she handled Cooper. And she didn't know what to expect. Through Jean Rizzo, she'd come to know Daniel Cooper as a sadistic and remorseless killer. But she couldn't totally shake her own perceptions of him as a weak, rather pathetic figure. She would never forget the day Cooper had come to visit her in the Louisiana State Penitentiary. His receding chin, twitching nose and wide-set, shifty eyes gave him the look of a vole, or some other small rodent. She remembered his small, effeminate hands and struggled to imagine them strangling a grown woman, let alone overpowering a man like Jeff.

And yet, she now knew, Cooper had done both of those things. Her fear returned.

Tracy had underestimated him that day in prison. She had misread both his intentions and the enormous power he wielded over her life and future. She would not make the same mistake again tonight.

By eight thirty, the square was totally empty. What streetlamps there were were widely spaced and dim, and the stadium floodlights had been disconnected. Treading carefully in the dark, Tracy glanced briefly around her before slipping under the construction tape and walking up to the main entrance.

It was quite beautiful. Masonry pillars on either side of the entrance were decorated with intricate marble reliefs. Two busts of Hermes on the pilasters were topped with vases and palm sprays, and something that looked to Tracy to be a bit like a mace, or in any event a thoroughly unpleasant-looking weapon with spikes. Everything looked as if it had been carved yesterday. She couldn't imagine how it had remained so well preserved, with no protection and in the middle of a busy city.

Inside, the ground immediately seemed to fall away beneath her feet and Tracy felt herself to be inside an immeasurably vast structure. The space! You got no sense of it at all from walking around the perimeter. Seats made of solid marble, some decorated with lion's claws, were arranged in fourteen rows, with steep, stepped aisles between them leading down to a circular track. Walking down through the empty, white rows, Tracy had an eerie sense of having stumbled into a ghostly and supernatural place. Inside the stadium one felt completely cut off from the world outside. It was as if she had crossed over into a different dimension, a place frozen in time and space.

Standing in the center of the arena, Tracy spun around, allowing her eyes to become fully accustomed to the gloom. Cooper wasn't here. No one was here.

It's still early, she told herself. She could not entertain the thought that he'd gone to Plovdiv's other amphitheater. That Jeff might be there too, waiting for her, hoping against hope, praying for rescue . . .

She thought about calling out into the darkness but dismissed the idea. *Daniel Cooper wants to meet me. He asked me to come. If he's here, he'll find me.*

Just then she caught sight of an opening directly in front of her. Hidden as it was in the shadows, she hadn't noticed it before. But now it gaped at her like the ugly mouth of a monster, lurking in wait. Some sort of tunnel or cave ran beneath the tiered seats. *A vault? Or a passage, leading somewhere? Leading out? Leading in?*

Feeling her palms start to sweat and her mouth go dry, she reached into her jacket and coiled her fingers around her gun. Then she walked into the tunnel.

It was pitch-black, and narrower than it looked from a distance. With her arms outstretched, Tracy found she could touch the walls on either side. Slowly, like a blind woman, she began to move forward, her feet alert to any bumps or potholes in the uneven ground.

If it branches off, which way should I go?

The thought of getting lost, trapped here in the darkness, filled her with profound fear. And then she remembered. *My phone! How could I have been so stupid?* She stopped, pulled out her cell phone and turned it on. The moment the screen came to life, the light was blinding, dazzling. Tracy saw at once that the tunnel was in fact very short, running only a few more feet. After that it forked both left and right into a long, curved corridor. Looking right, she saw abandoned machinery, including a small cement mixer and a pair of pneumatic drills. *This must be the part they're restoring,* she thought. *Astonishing that they don't lock those up, or take them home at night. Anyone could wander in here and steal them.*

She looked left.

"Hello, my love."

Daniel Cooper, his pale face lit up by a revolting smile, stood just inches away from her. Panicked, Tracy opened her mouth to scream but Cooper was too quick for her. Clamping one hand over her mouth, he forced her back against the wall. Tracy reached for her gun. With terrifying ease, Cooper twisted it out of her hand, pressing the barrel against her temple.

"Don't struggle, my darling." Cooper's breath was on her neck, in her ear. Pinning her back against the wall, he slid one hand down to her left breast and squeezed hard, pinching her nipple beneath the fabric of her T-shirt. "You've waited for this as long as I have."

Tracy's phone clattered to the ground.

All the lights went out.

JEAN RIZZO CHECKED IN to a guesthouse in the center of town with a view out over the city walls. He jumped on his phone at the first ring.

"Any word on Tracy?"

"No, sir. Not yet. The local police had reports of some sort of disturbance outside of town. A small farming hamlet. It's probably not worth mentioning but—"

"What sort of disturbance?"

"Screams, apparently. They sent two men out there."

"And?"

"They didn't find anything. Probably just a wild animal being killed. Someone got spooked."

Probably. Jean was tempted to go and see for himself. He had no other leads, and would at least feel like he was doing something. But if Tracy *was* meeting Daniel Cooper in Plovdiv and he was stuck out in the sticks on a wild-goose chase . . .

"Okay. Let me know if anything else comes up."

He hung up, but the phone rang again immediately. Antoine Cléry sounded breathless.

"I think we've found her!"

"Here? In Plovdiv?"

"Yes, sir. She checked into the Hotel Britannia two nights ago." Cléry blurted out the address.

"I'm on my way."

Jean Rizzo started running.

TRACY HIT AND KICKED for all she was worth, lashing out with her nails and teeth, fear and rage both driving her on. But for such a small man, Cooper was astonishingly strong. In just seconds he had pinned her down on the ground. Unable to move her arms or legs, Tracy was utterly powerless, like a butterfly with its wings pinned to a board. The darkness was total, like death. She felt Cooper reach down and undo the button and zipper of her jeans, shoving them roughly to her knees. Within seconds, his clammy hand was inside her underwear, touching her.

"My wife." He sighed. "My angel."

Vomit rose up in Tracy's throat. Cooper's fingers prodded and invaded while his foul breath assailed her nostrils. He was slow, delighting in what he was doing. Every few seconds he let out a little squeal of excitement.

No! This couldn't be happening. Not again.

Tracy flashed back.

She was in Joe Romano's house in New Orleans. She was twenty-two years old, pregnant with Charles Stanhope's baby, and she'd come to avenge her mother's death, to force Romano to admit the truth: that he and his Mafia buddies had killed Doris Whitney, killed her with their lies and greed and arrogance. But it had all gone wrong. Joe Romano overpowered Tracy easily, laughing as he pushed her down, ripping her blouse away and pinching her nipples.

"Fight me, baby! I love it! I'll bet you've never been fucked by a real man."

Tracy had reached for her gun and shot Romano, leaving him for dead. But her gun was gone now. She was powerless. Daniel Cooper was on top of her, grunting like a pig. Tracy heard him unzip his fly. Terror overcame her. *I can't do it! I can't fight him off!*

She forced herself to focus. There had to be something else, another way to stop him.

What did she know about him?

What were his weak spots? His fears?

He's the Bible Killer. He hates prostitutes.

His breath was coming faster now.

He hates immoral women. He believes he's on a mission from God.

Cooper pushed up her T-shirt. His wet lips were on Tracy's breasts, sucking at her like a baby at its mother's teat. Tracy sobbed, squirming away from him, aware that her struggling only heightened his excitement. Ripping off her jeans and panties completely, Cooper straddled her, forcing her thighs farther apart. His erection, tiny but rock hard, pressed against Tracy's stomach.

For God's sake, Tracy! Think of something! Make him stop.

And then it came to her.

"We have to stop." She spoke firmly, like a schoolteacher admonishing a child. "Daniel! We have to stop NOW."

Her tone made Cooper hesitate for a split second.

"We're not married yet."

Cooper froze on top of her like a statue.

"What?"

"I said we're not married. This is against God's law and you know it. We're not married and we *can't* marry. Not while Jeff Stevens is still alive."

Reluctantly, Cooper slid off Tracy onto his knees. She was still pinned underneath him and the gun, her gun, was still pressed against her skull.

"What makes you think Jeff Stevens is still alive?" Cooper sounded petulant.

"Well, isn't he?" Tracy masked her fear as best she could. She kept her voice steady but her legs had begun shaking uncontrollably. *Please let him be alive. Please don't let all this have been for nothing.*

"I don't know."

This wasn't the answer Tracy had expected. She knew she had to think quickly.

"You know where he is, though, don't you, Daniel?"

"Of course I do." Cooper laughed, a high-pitched, oddly feminine giggle. Tracy remembered it well.

"The lamb is at Golgotha, my dear. The sacrifice has been made. There's nothing for you to worry about."

Golgotha. Place of the skull. Tracy's mind raced. Wasn't Golgotha on a hill? Or perhaps Cooper was speaking purely metaphorically.

"I asked the Lord to spare him until you came. I wanted you to see. But you took so *long,* Tracy. He may be dead by now."

"Take me to him, then," Tracy blurted.

"I don't think so."

"But you have to!" She could hear the desperation creeping back into her voice. "Let me see before it's too late. Isn't that what you wanted? What the Lord wanted?"

"No. Not anymore."

"He's my husband, Daniel. The Bible says we can't—"

"I SAID NO!"

The hard metal of the gun slammed into Tracy's cheek. The blow was so sudden, she felt it more as shock than pain.

"I'm your husband! *I'm* the one God chose to save you. It was your lust for Stevens that blinded you all these years. But that's all past now."

He began again, and this time there was no stopping him. Tracy knew what would happen, and the knowing took away the fear. Hands were on her, hurting her, but they weren't his hands. This time the hands belonged to Lola and Paulita and Ernestine Littlechap. Tracy was on the concrete floor of her cell in the Louisiana State Penitentiary, and the women were beating and violating her while she wept and pleaded. She heard their voices. "Carajo! *Give it to the bitch.*"

Then came the voice of the prison doctor.

"She's lost the baby."

That was Charles's baby. Tracy had changed forever that day. *If Tomorrow Comes,* she'd told herself, *I'll get my revenge.*

Later there had been another baby, with Jeff. She'd lost that one too. And then came Nicholas. *My Nicholas. My dar-*

ling. My life. Nicholas had saved her. Did she love him so much because she'd lost the others?

✓   Suddenly Tracy felt overwhelmed with rage. The fear was gone, but a wild, primitive fury took its place. Daniel Cooper was not going to rob her of her son! He was not going to rob her darling Nicholas his mother, or enact his sick fantasies on Jeff, the love of Tracy's life. She was not going to let it happen, not while she still had breath in her body.

With a scream of fury, Tracy flung both arms behind her head. She could feel Cooper's penis pressing against her, his hips bearing down on her like a lead weight. Scrabbling around in the dust, her fingers brushed against a loose rock. It wasn't particularly large or heavy but it would have to do. With a strength she didn't know she possessed, Tracy grabbed the stone and slammed it down with all her force into the back of Daniel Cooper's skull.

Tracy heard a shriek of pain and felt his weight slide off her. But he wasn't unconscious.

"You bitch!" he hissed. One hand shot out and grabbed her neck as she scrambled to her feet. He squeezed hard, crushing Tracy's windpipe. She kicked out wildly in the darkness, barely able to breathe, completely disoriented. He seemed to have dropped the gun, but she knew if he got his other hand around her throat he would strangle her easily, just as he had strangled those other poor women. A stray kick caught him in the groin, provoking another animal screech. For a second he was knocked off balance and his fingers uncoiled from around Tracy's neck.

She seized her chance, knowing it would be her last. Charging head down into the blackness, like a bull, she slammed into him with all her body weight. Everything slowed down then. She was aware of fingers grasping, a slipping of feet in the dust. Then a crack, like an egg breaking on the side of a mixing bowl.

Tracy waited, frozen in the dark, breathless silence.

There was a muffled thud as Cooper's body crumpled to the ground.

Then nothing.

THE RECEPTIONIST AT THE Hotel Britannia was skinny and pale. She had twiglike arms, covered in tattoos, and long, lank hair dyed an unforgiving shade of black. Jean Rizzo wondered how long she'd been doing drugs, but only for a moment.

"Do you speak English?"

She nodded. "Leetle."

"I'm looking for this woman. Tracy Schmidt." He pushed a crumpled head shot of Tracy across the desk, along with his Interpol ID card. At the sight of the latter, the girl's eyes narrowed. "What room is she in?"

"You wait. Please."

The girl disappeared into a small back office and did not return. Instead a vastly fat man in an ill-fitting jacket waddled out to meet Jean.

"I am the manager. There is a problem?"

"No problem. I need to locate one of your guests, urgently."

"Ms. Schmidt. Yes, Rita told me."

"I need her room number and key."

"Certainly." The manager smiled nervously. Jean wondered what exactly it was he was trying to hide. "However, Ms. Schmidt is not in the hotel at present. She left this afternoon at around five and has not yet returned."

Jean Rizzo experienced a sharp pain in his chest. *I'm too late.*

"Did she say where she was going?"

"I'm afraid not. But she has been interested in the chess

championships we're hosting here in Plovdiv. She attended a game yesterday. It's the final tonight. Viktor Grinski is playing Vasily Karmonov. It wouldn't surprise me if she'd gone over to watch."

Seven nights at three times three. Nine o'clock. Jean looked at his watch. It was already ten after nine. The meeting with Daniel Cooper would be happening now. If Tracy had found him. There was a chance she was still scrambling around in the dark, trying to solve the last piece of the riddle, just as he was doing.

Jean grabbed a piece of paper and scrawled down some numbers. "This is my phone. I'll be at the championships. If she returns, the moment she returns, I want you to call me at once. Do not let her leave under any circumstances. Do you understand?"

"Of course. May I tell her that the police—"

"No," Jean shouted over his shoulder. He was already halfway out the door. "Don't tell her anything. Just keep her here."

TRACY DRAGGED DANIEL COOPER'S limp body out of the tunnel back into the amphitheater. It was only a few yards back to the light of the outside world, but it felt like miles. Cooper weighed a ton. He was a slight man, but his limbs seemed to have been filled with lead. By the time she got him outside, she was soaked with sweat.

He was breathing, but barely. Blood poured hot and red from the gash on his head, like magma spilling out of a fissure in the earth's crust. The whole left side of his skull had folded in, like a child's soccer ball that had been stamped on.

"Where's Jeff? Where is he!"

Cooper groaned. A hideous gurgling sound started somewhere in his throat.

"Tell me where he is!" Tracy demanded. She was becoming hysterical. "What did you do to him?"

Cooper was slipping in and out of consciousness. It was clear he didn't have much time left. That it was now or never.

Tracy forced herself to calm down. She tried a different tack.

"You're dying, Daniel. You need to confess. Make your last act of contrition before the Lord. Do you want the Lord's mercy, Daniel?"

Cooper grunted. His lips were moving, but no sound came out.

"Jeff Stevens . . . ," Tracy prompted, bending low so her ear was right next to his mouth.

"Golgotha." Cooper's voice was a whisper. "The lamb. Sacrificed, like the others."

"What others? Do you mean the women you killed? The prostitutes."

A smile played around the corners of Daniel Cooper's lips. "I killed them for *you,* Tracy." The gurgling started again. "You were my salvation. My reward . . ."

Tracy couldn't allow the horror of what Cooper was saying to sink in. Those women were dead. There was a chance Jeff might still be alive. She had to save him, had to try.

"*Where* is Golgotha, Daniel? Where is Jeff?"

"Place of the skull . . . death on the cross . . ."

"Is it here? In Plovdiv?"

"Plovdiv . . . on the hill."

This was hopeless. Cooper was rambling. His voice grew fainter. He began calling for his mother, and moaning. He kept talking about blood. Before long Tracy had lost him again.

She ran back into the tunnel. Her cell phone was on the ground close by the entrance, where Cooper had first attacked her. The screen was cracked but the phone still worked. Switching it on, she punched out the familiar number.

Jean Rizzo sounded frantic. "Tracy? Tracy, is that you? Are you all right?"

"I'm fine. I'm sorry I disappeared on you. I'm in Bulgaria."

"I know. In Plovdiv."

This brought Tracy up short.

"I'm here too."

"You are? Thank God! Have you found Jeff?" For the first time, her voice started to crack.

"No. Not yet. Where are you, Tracy?"

"At the amphitheater."

The amphitheater! "The stage of history." Of course.

"Are you alone?"

"I am now."

"But Daniel Cooper was there?"

"Yes. He was. He tried to . . ." Despite herself, Tracy started to cry. "I fought him off. I think he's dead, Jean."

"Christ. Okay, stay where you are, Tracy. I'm on my way."

"NO!" The vehemence in her voice took Jean by surprise. "Forget me! I'm fine. We have to find Jeff. There may not be much time."

"Okay, okay. Calm down."

"No, Jean. You don't understand. Cooper's done something to him. Hurt him. I tried to get him to tell me where he was, but I . . . I couldn't. Jeff's out there somewhere, alone, maybe dying. We *have* to find him."

Jean Rizzo took a breath. "What did Cooper say? Exactly?"

"Nothing that meant anything. It was just . . . religious rambling. He was semiconscious."

"But he said something?"

"He said Golgotha. Golgotha, Golgotha . . . Place of the skull . . ." Tracy closed her eyes, trying desperately to remember. "It was all about the crucifixion. He said Jeff was being sacrificed for my sins, just like the women he killed. He said he killed them all for me. That it was my fault."

"It wasn't your fault, Tracy."

"Death on the cross, death on the hill . . . something about a lamb . . ."

"Wait." Jean Rizzo interrupted her. "I remembered something. There was an incident today. A farming hamlet, up in the hills outside the city. Someone reported hearing screams. The local police checked it out but said there was nothing but sheep up there."

Tracy's mind whirred into life.

Sheep.

Lambs.

The hill.

"What's the name of the hamlet, Jean?"

"I can't remember. Oreshak or Oreshenk or something like that. I'll find it. You just stay there, Tracy, okay? I'm sending someone to get you. An ambulance."

"Are you out of your mind? I'm not staying here! And I don't need an ambulance. How far is the place, Jean? Jean?"

But Jean Rizzo had already hung up.

CHAPTER 27

$\mathcal{J}$EFF STEVENS LOOKED AROUND him. The tiny chapel was beautiful. Its walls were covered with frescoes and the sun streamed in through the stained glass windows, throwing rainbows onto the altar like confetti.

Jeff thought, *How appropriate. Confetti for my wedding day.*

Tracy walked in then, the sunlight blazing behind her like a halo. She'd outwitted Pierpont and she was about to become his wife. Her chestnut hair fell to her shoulders in loose waves and her green eyes danced with happiness as she glided up the aisle toward him. Jeff felt a wave of happiness wash over him.

I love you, Tracy. I love you so much.

THE VIDEO WAS PLAYING. Tracy was leaving the hotel after her assignation with Dr. Alan McBride. McBride had white-blond hair and was always smiling. He made Tracy smile too.

Jeff hated him.

The hatred settled in his chest, making his heart feel tight. The pain grew acute, then unbearable. Jeff's hatred was killing him. It was if someone were tearing him in two right down the middle, like a piece of paper, ripping effortlessly through his organs.

Jeff screamed.

He heard a woman laughing. *Elizabeth Kennedy? Or perhaps it was his first wife, Louise?* It was all so confusing. But it didn't matter now because soon the pain would end and he would be dead.

HIS MOTHER WAS DEAD.

So was the baby.

Which made it rather odd that his mother and the baby were playing chess together.

"Your move." Jeff's mother smiled at the baby and waited.

The baby was a girl. She was much too young to play chess. Jeff reached out to pick her up but she slipped through his fingers, like a ghost. She picked up a piece, a black knight, and banged it down on the board, again and again and again. Jeff's head started to ache.

"Why did you die?" Jeff asked her. "Tracy wanted you so badly. We both did. Why didn't you live?"

The baby ignored him and continued banging. *Bang, bang, bang.*

Jeff's mother started to cry.

Bang, bang, bang.

Jeff was crying too. The noise was awful.

Stop! Please stop!

"STOP!"

Jean Rizzo grabbed Tracy by both shoulders as she tried to force her way into the barn. He'd watched the squad car arrive, looked on in horror as Tracy jumped out of the back-seat and tried to run across the moonlit field toward him. She was limping, dragging her left leg behind her, but sheer determination drove her on.

"You shouldn't be here, Tracy. You need a doctor."

"Let go of me!" Tracy kicked him hard in the shin.

Jean grimaced but held on to her. "I mean it. You can't go in there."

Bang, bang, bang. Tracy heard sledgehammers pounding away behind Jean, inside the barn. It sounded as if his men were trying to smash down a wall.

"Is he in there? Have you found Jeff?"

"We don't know. There are signs that he *was* here but . . ." Jean's voice trailed off. "It looks like Cooper may have built a false wall. Perhaps to conceal a body."

Tracy let out a wail of anguish. She went limp in Jean's arms.

"What happened?" Jean hissed at the Bulgarian police-man who'd driven the squad car. "I told you to take her straight to the hospital."

The man shrugged. "She wouldn't go. The ambulance take the suspect, but this lady refuse."

"The suspect? You mean Cooper's alive?"

"He was. I don't know. Maybe not now. He looked pretty bad."

Rizzo tried to process this. If Cooper really was alive, it was good news. There might be a trial, a confession even. Some sort of closure for the families . . . Milton Buck might even recover some of his precious stolen jewelry and art-work. Not that Jean Rizzo gave a damn about the FBI.

"Inspector Rizzo!" The voice came from inside the barn. The banging had stopped. "You'd better get in here, sir."

Reluctantly releasing Tracy, Jean ran back inside. Tracy followed.

The barn was an old stone building, originally built to house cattle or sheep. It was dark inside, but Jean's men had set up a few battery-powered lamps. In one corner a few ancient farm implements lay rusting in a heap, like broken bones. But it was the wall next to them that caught Tracy's eye. It was covered in blood, like a child's splatter painting. Chains had been nailed into the masonry, and various instruments of torture, including electrical wires, a whip and a hacksaw had been propped neatly against a wooden chair. Tracy put a hand to her mouth to stop herself from vomiting.

"Sir!"

The young officer was standing on top of a pile of rubble. He looked like he might be about to vomit himself. A stone wall had been erected at the back of the barn, just a few feet from the original, creating a sort of false back to the building. Rizzo's men had hammered a four-foot hole in it, large enough for a person to squeeze through.

The officer threw Jean a flashlight.

Jean turned to talk to Tracy but he was too late. She'd already darted past him into the cavity.

The cross was enormous, at least ten feet tall. The first thing Tracy saw was a huge, iron nail impaling both of Jeff's feet.

"Oh my God." She burst into sobs. "Jeff! Jeff! Can you hear me? JEFF!"

There was a groan, then another.

"Jesus Christ. He's alive." Jean Rizzo looked at his men. "Don't just stand there, for Christ's sake. Get him down! And call an ambulance."

It took twenty-five minutes to get Jeff onto a stretcher.

22

His nervous system appeared to have shut down. There were no screams as the nails were pulled out of his hands and feet. A number of his ribs were broken and his torso was badly burned, but he showed no sign of pain.

Tracy talked to him constantly. "It's okay. You're okay, Jeff. I'm here. It's all okay. You're going to a hospital. You're going to be fine."

At one point he opened his eyes very wide and said, "Tracy?"

"Yes, darling!" Tracy bent down and kissed him. "It's me! Oh, Jeff, I love you. I love you so much. Please hold on."

Jeff smiled and closed his eyes. He looked profoundly at peace.

Tracy rode with him in the ambulance. The paramedics had him wired up to all sorts of machines. There were needles in his arms and electrodes on his chest and a screen with green lines that beeped intermittently. Tracy had a million questions but she was too afraid to ask any of them. She scanned the doctors' faces, looking for any sign of hope or despair, but saw nothing to hold on to. She started to pray.

Please, God, let him live. Please give me a chance to make things right. To tell him I love him. Please . . .

A loud, long beep startled her.

"Jeff?" She looked at the paramedics in panic. "What's happening?"

Strong hands pushed her aside. She could no longer see Jeff, only a wall of backs in green scrubs bent over him. Someone put paddles onto his chest. Tracy watched in dumb horror as Jeff's thin frame leaped up off the gurney, then fell back again, limp and lifeless.

"Again!"

Another charge to the chest.

"Again!"

And another.

The long, loud beep continued.

After that, everything became blurry. Someone was shining a light into Jeff's eyes. Tracy saw the man look up and shake his head.

Don't shake your head! Don't give up. Try again.

Someone else looked at his watch. "Should we call it?"

Call it? Call what? Tracy tried to move closer. *She* could help Jeff. *She* could save him. If he knew how much she loved him . . . if he knew what he had to live for . . . he'd fight. But when she tried to move her legs, or stretch her arms out to him, she found she was frozen. A black mist was descending. She was losing her balance, slipping, falling.

"Time of death . . ."

No! NO!

Strong arms grabbed her under the shoulders. But they weren't the arms Tracy needed. They weren't Jeff's arms. This was all a horrible nightmare and she was going to wake up any minute. Any minute.

The voice in her head was calm and insistent. It sounded like Blake Carter's voice. Darling Blake! Was he here? He was repeating the same words, over and over.

Let go, Tracy. Let go.

Tracy trusted Blake. She did as he asked.

She closed her eyes and tumbled backward into the mist.

CHAPTER 28

COLORADO
THREE MONTHS LATER . . .

*T*RACY STOOD AT HER kitchen window, chopping carrots for the soup. Outside, the ranch looked more beautiful than ever. Fall had bathed Colorado in a warm amber glow. The leaves on the trees shimmered in every shade of brown and gold and ocher, contrasting beautifully with the vivid green pastures and white wooden fences, which Blake had lovingly repainted.

Since Tracy had come home from Bulgaria, emotionally exhausted and physically weak—she'd barely noticed, but she'd lost fifteen pounds during those grueling two weeks and was badly bruised after her encounter with Daniel Cooper—Blake Carter had taken care of everything. He drove Nicholas to school while Tracy slept. He cooked meals and made sure Tracy ate them. He'd done laundry and booked doctors' appointments and kept the rhythms of life on the ranch going when Tracy could not. He'd held Tracy when she wept, racked with sobs that confused him deeply. Blake could see that her tears were only part sadness. There was also some sort of deep release going on, a necessary reaction to post-traumatic stress of some kind, like a soldier returning from battle. Most important of all, from Tracy's perspective, Blake Carter hadn't asked her a single question about what had happened on her "cooking trip" to Europe. He simply assumed that she would tell him when she was ready. Or perhaps, he thought, she might never be ready. Blake could accept either scenario, as long as she was home safe and staying home.

"You won't leave again, will you, Mom?" Nicholas asked on Tracy's first night back.

His tone was light but Tracy could hear the anxiety underlying it. She'd explained away her injuries as the result of a minor car crash, but her appearance when she'd first walked through the door had clearly frightened him.

"No, my darling. I won't leave again."

"Good. You're so thin. Was the food in Europe really disgusting?"

Tracy grinned. "Yeah. It was pretty gross."

"We should go to McDonald's tomorrow."

"We should."

That was three months ago. Today, Tracy felt like a different person. Not her old self exactly, but a new self. Content. At peace. Reborn. It was Nicholas, more so even than Blake's kindness, that had brought her back to life. She watched him now, horsing around in the yard with Blake on their way in for lunch. The two had become inseparable recently, and Tracy noticed that Nick was starting to take after Blake more and more. The thought made her happy.

"Something smells good."

Strong male arms snaked around Tracy's waist from behind. She turned around, unable to stop a broad smile from lighting up her face.

Jeff Stevens smiled back. "When's lunch? I'm starving."

CHAPTER 29

*Y*OU KNOW IT'S NOT often a man dies on the cross and then miraculously comes back to life."

Jeff's surgeon, Dr. Elena Dragova, an attractive woman in her late forties, beamed down at her patient. As well she might. The case of "the man on the cross" had made headlines all across Bulgaria. Jeff's recovery was being hailed as a modern miracle and Dr. Dragova was about to become a household name, along with the rest of the staff at UMBAL Sveti Georgi, Plovdiv's largest and most prestigious hospital.

"So I hear," Jeff quipped. "Every couple of thousand years or so, isn't it? If I start my own religion, will you join?"

"I don't believe in God."

"Nor do I. Only in beautiful women."

Dr. Elena Dragova laughed. She didn't know what to make of Jeff Stevens, or of the strange, hauntingly beautiful woman who'd brought him to Sveti Georgi, insisting that she'd seen renewed vital signs in the ambulance and demanding that the emergency room staff make another attempt at resuscitation. Jeff Stevens's heart *had* started again, against all the odds. But he'd needed surgery afterward, for eight grueling hours. His condition was so severe he'd been placed in a medically induced coma. Through it all, for three straight nights, the woman had sat by his bedside, barely eating or sleeping, just watching him breathe. She'd refused to leave him, for anything. Even getting her to allow the nurses to dress her own wounds, or put her in clean clothes, had been a battle. She'd told them her name was Tracy, but beyond that, nothing.

Policemen came and went. As well as Mr. Stevens, the hospital was housing another gravely injured American, Daniel Cooper, believed to be the madman who had tried to crucify Stevens up in the hills. Cooper had been found in the amphitheater with his skull smashed in the same night that Stevens was rescued. Rumors swirled that he was in fact a serial killer and rapist, that the woman at Jeff Stevens's bedside had narrowly escaped becoming his next victim. But no one knew the truth and "Tracy" wasn't talking.

Then one day, without warning or any words to the nurses, Tracy suddenly left. It was a day Dr. Dragova would never forget, for many reasons.

At around seven in the morning, another group of Americans had arrived—this time it was the FBI—and the scene at UMBAL Sveti Georgi's main reception area had rapidly descended into farce.

A very rude and obnoxious agent by the name of Milton Buck burst in as if he owned the place, demanding loudly and repeatedly to be allowed to interview Daniel Cooper.

"We have an international arrest warrant," Agent Buck hissed. "This man is wanted in connection with a string of jewelry and art thefts. He is sitting on stolen property worth hundreds of millions of dollars and I *will* speak to him!"

Having first taken his frustration out on Cooper's surgical team, who point-blank refused to allow him anywhere near their patient, Buck turned his ire on Jean Rizzo.

Aside from one brief trip back to his hotel to shower and change, Rizzo had been at the hospital constantly since the night Jeff Stevens was brought in. He'd come to formally charge Daniel Cooper, monitor Jeff's progress and to check on Tracy, whom he no longer trusted to be let out of his sight.

"*You* spoke to Cooper!" Milton Buck glared at him accusingly.

"Early yesterday, yes. There was a brief window when he was still lucid. He was quite forthcoming about the Bible killings." Jean smiled. "Of course, that was before the second stroke."

"Why wasn't I informed! I heard about Cooper's arrest on the goddamn Bulgarian radio news! My case—"

"—is not important," said Rizzo. "Not compared to what's gone on here. Not compared to thirteen lives lost. Besides, you've got Elizabeth Kennedy, haven't you?"

"Elizabeth only took half the money. Daniel Cooper had the other half. If we don't recover those assets—"

"What? You won't get your promotion?" Jean gave Milton a conciliatory pat on the shoulders. "That's too bad, man."

"The case isn't closed!" Milton Buck said furiously. "If Daniel Cooper can't help me trace the missing McMenemy Pissarro, or the Neil Lane jewels he stole from the Chicago store, then your little girlfriend Tracy Whitney's going to have to fill in the gaps."

Rizzo's eyes narrowed. "Leave Tracy out of this. She knows nothing."

"She knows how these scumbags think."

"You made a deal," said Jean, "when Tracy delivered Elizabeth Kennedy to you on a platter. She had immunity. Remember?"

" 'Had' is the operative word, I'm afraid. You didn't seriously think the federal government was going to wave goodbye to hundreds of millions of dollars' worth of stolen goods just to stay in the good graces of a wanted con artist, did you?"

Jean Rizzo glared at Milton Buck but said nothing.

"Speaking of Tracy, where is she?" Buck asked, smiling. "Perhaps you'd like to go and tell your little girlfriend that I'd like a word? Right now, if it's not too much trouble."

"She's gone."

The smile died on Buck's lips.

"What do you mean, gone?"

"I mean she left the hospital last night and switched off her phone. I haven't heard from her since. I went to her hotel this morning but they told me she'd checked out."

"I don't believe you. Not even you would be so incompetent as to let a key asset like Whitney slip through your fingers."

Jean Rizzo shrugged. "I really don't care what you believe, Agent Buck. And for the record, Tracy isn't an asset. She's a friend. If it hadn't been for her, Jeff Stevens would be dead and Daniel Cooper would still be out there killing women. Check her hotel yourself if you don't believe me. It's the Britannia, on—"

"I know where she's staying, you moron! I've had her under surveillance for months."

"Pity you didn't pick her up earlier, then, isn't it?"

Jean walked away, leaving the FBI agent spluttering in his wake.

A FEW MINUTES LATER Jean knocked on the door of Jeff Stevens's room. When there was no answer, he went inside.

Stevens was heavily tranquilized and sleeping like a

baby. He was out of the woods now, according to the doctors, and was expected to make a full recovery. But he hadn't been fully conscious for more than a few seconds since he was brought in.

Tracy was asleep in a chair next to his bed. She looked so peaceful, Jean felt bad waking her up. But he knew he had to. Shaking her gently by the shoulders, he told her about his exchange with Agent Buck.

"You need to leave here. As soon as possible. Get a flight out of Bulgaria today."

Tracy looked stricken. "What about Jeff? He hasn't woken up yet, not truly. He doesn't even know I was here."

"I'll tell him," Jean said kindly. "When he comes to I'll need to question him. I'll tell him everything."

Tracy hesitated. There were things *she* needed to tell Jeff. Many, many things. Although she still had no real idea where she should begin.

"If I write a note, will you give it to him?" she asked Jean.

"Of course. But you need to hurry, Tracy. Buck's not kidding around. If he finds you here, he'll arrest you."

Tracy nodded. She had already started to write.

"Where will you go?" asked Jean.

Tracy seemed surprised by the question. "Home, of course. To Nicholas."

"You can't stay there, you know," said Jean. "Buck will find you. He'll force you to work for him. You need to grab your son and get out. Start again somewhere new, somewhere far away."

Tracy shook her head. "I can't do that. Colorado is Nick's home. I can't raise my son on the run."

"But, Tracy . . ."

She smiled, kissing Jean Rizzo on the cheek. "I'll take my chances. You worry too much, Jean, you know that?"

Three hours later, Tracy was on a plane.

Three days later, Jeff Stevens woke up and read Tracy's letter.

Three months later, Jeff watched as Dr. Elena Dragova signed his release papers.

"We'll miss you," Dr. Dragova told him.

"I'll miss you too. Especially Sister Katia. You will give her my love?"

The surgeon laughed. "You're incorrigible. Where will you go? I hope you have someone prepared to take care of you. Or at least to put up with you."

"I'm going to stay with a friend," said Jeff. "It turns out we have some unfinished business."

CHAPTER 30

$\mathscr{W}$E NEED TO TALK, TRACY."

Jeff gently removed the chopping board from Tracy's hands and put it to one side.

Tracy sighed. "There's nothing to say."

"Oh yes there is. There's everything to say. We've both been too scared to say it, that's all."

He was right. Jeff had been staying at the ranch for five days now. Five incredible, precious, magical days. Tracy had introduced him to Nick as an "old friend" from college days and promised dear, patient Blake that she would explain later. It had been wonderful to have Jeff here, and even more wonderful to see how well he got along with Nick. Nick admired and respected Blake Carter. More than that, he loved him. But he shared a sense of humor with Jeff, not to mention a pronounced rebellious streak. The two of them had bonded instantly, giggling away at risqué cartoons like *Family Guy* like a pair of naughty kids.

The problem was that having "Uncle Jeff" as a house-guest had almost been *too* easy. It felt so natural and comfortable that neither Tracy nor Jeff had dared to talk about the past, or their feelings. Or, worst of all, the future. Instead they had immersed themselves in the joy of the present, neither one able to let it go and break the spell.

Jeff followed Tracy's gaze through the window. Nicholas was jumping up onto Blake Carter's back, trying to knock his Stetson off his head. His blond hair was blowing in the wind and his eyes had crinkled up into tiny slits thanks to the huge smile he was wearing.

Jeff said quietly, "He's mine, isn't he?"

Tracy nodded. "Of course he's yours. There's never been anyone else."

"What about Blake?"

She shook her head.

"He obviously loves you, Tracy."

"I love him too. Just not enough."

Jeff took her face in his hands, forcing her to look at him. "Tracy, I love you. I always have and I always will. Can't we try again?"

"Please, Jeff. Don't." She started to cry.

"But why not? I know you still love me too."

"Of course I do!"

"So why . . . ?"

"You know why." Tracy broke away from him. "Because love isn't enough. Look at him." She pointed outside at Nicholas. "Look how happy he is. How stable and secure. *I* did that. I made that happen. I built a life for him here, Jeff, a life for us, away from all the madness, all the chaos."

"Yes, you did. And you did an amazing job. But at what

cost, Tracy?" Reaching out, Jeff stroked her cheek. Tracy closed her eyes, inhaling the scent of his skin, the agony and the ecstasy. "What about *you*? Who *you* are, what *you* want? You can't be a housewife, for God's sake. You tried it with me and you hated it. You were bored out of your mind, dying a slow death. Can you really tell me you aren't dying inside, living up here?"

"Sometimes I am," Tracy was surprised to find herself saying. "Part of me does miss the thrill of our old life, I admit it. But Nicholas comes first. He's the one totally good thing in my life, Jeff. The one thing I haven't failed at, I *can't* fail at. My mom sacrificed everything for me. She was a wonderful woman."

"She must have been," said Jeff. "To have such a perfect daughter."

Tracy laughed. "Oh no. Not perfect. *Very* far from perfect."

"Perfect," said Jeff. Pulling Tracy close, he kissed her, slowly and with infinite tenderness. It was a kiss they would both remember for the rest of their lives. Neither of them wanted it to end.

"What if I said I'd give it all up for you?" Jeff pleaded, once Tracy finally pulled away. "For us? What if I swore to give up the scams and the capers for good. I did it once. I could do it again."

Tracy shook her head sadly. "Maybe you could. But then a part of *you* would die. And I won't be responsible for that, Jeff. I won't be the reason."

"But, Tracy. My darling, you *are* the reason. You're the reason for everything. I—"

Tracy put a finger to his lips. "I love you, Jeff. I'll always love you. But we had our chance at happiness. We had it a long time ago. Now our son has a chance. He has a chance of living a normal, happy life. Don't deny him that."

Jeff fell silent. Was she right? Had their time simply passed?

He didn't know. All he knew was that he felt immensely sad.

Eventually he asked Tracy, "Are you going to tell him the truth? About me?"

Tracy inhaled deeply. "No. I can't stop you telling him, if you feel you have to. But Blake's been a wonderful dad to him since the day he was born."

"I can see that," said Jeff.

"I don't want him to lose that."

"No." Jeff swallowed hard. "Nor do I."

At that moment the back door flew open and Nicholas sailed in.

"I'm starving. What's for lunch? Oh, hi, Uncle Jeff. Do you want to play Super Smash Bros. with me after lunch? Blake hates the Wii."

"Sure do," said Blake, hanging up his battered hat. "Rots your brain."

"And Mom's useless."

"Hey!" said Tracy, forcing a smile. "I resent that."

"I don't mind beating you at Smash Bros. after lunch," said Jeff. "As long as you don't cry about it."

"Ha!" Nicholas scoffed. "You'll be the one crying. Beat me, as if!"

"But it'll have to be our last game for a while, sport. I'm leaving in the morning."

Tracy, Blake and Nicholas all froze. Nicholas looked stricken.

"Leaving? Why? I thought you were staying till Halloween at least?"

"Something came up," said Jeff, as casually as he could. "Couldn't be helped, I'm afraid."

"What came up?"

"Work. It's been a great vacation, buddy, but all vacations have to come to an end."

"Hmm." Nicholas sounded distinctly unimpressed by this logic. "What *is* your work anyway, Uncle Jeff?" he asked. "What do you do?"

"Er . . ." Flustered, Jeff looked at Tracy. "I . . . well, I, er . . ."

"Uncle Jeff's in the antiques business," Tracy said firmly, not missing a beat. "Now go wash up for lunch."

THE NEXT MORNING TRACY woke early, long before dawn. She'd had terrible dreams.

She was drowning, sinking, gasping for breath as huge waves crashed over her and powerful currents pulled her deeper and deeper into the black icy depths. She could hear Jeff screaming. *"I'm here, Tracy! I'm here! Take my hand!"* But when she reached out for him he was gone.

She made herself some coffee and sat downstairs alone, waiting for the sun to rise. She'd felt so peaceful here once, so contented. In this kitchen, this house, this little town in the mountains. Just her and her son and Blake. She'd buried the past. Not just Jeff Stevens, but herself too, the person who she used to be. She'd laid them to rest and mourned them and she'd moved on. At least that's what she'd told herself all these years.

What a fool I was! Tracy knew now that the past could never be buried. It was a part of her, the same way that her eyes and skin and heartbeat were a part of her. Jeff was a part of her, and not only because of Nick.

She wondered if she would ever feel contented again. Or was she destined always to live a half-life? To choose one version of herself and sacrifice the others, forever?

Jeff left after breakfast. He came down packed and smiling, making light of his departure, for Nicholas's sake. There were no lingering good-byes. He and Tracy had agreed on that last night. Instead they kissed each other on the cheek and hugged, like the old friends they were.

"Take care of him," Jeff said gruffly. "Take care of yourself."

Then he climbed into his rented station wagon and drove away.

Nicholas stood on the porch, hand in hand with his mother, watching Jeff's car until it disappeared out of sight.

"I love Uncle Jeff." He sighed. "He's so fun. We will see him again, won't we, Mom?"

Tracy squeezed her son's hand tightly.

"I expect so, my darling. You never really know what tomorrow might bring."

ACKNOWLEDGMENTS

My thanks once again to the Sheldon family, and particularly to Alexandra and Mary, for entrusting me not only with these books but with Tracy Whitney. Your help and encouragement mean a great deal, and your advice at the editing stage of this book has been invaluable. Thanks also to my editors, May Chen in New York and Kimberley Young in London, for putting up with me; and to the whole talented and committed team at HarperCollins. To Luke and Mort Janklow, my wonderful agents, also Hellie Ogden in London, and everyone at Janklow and Nesbit. And to my family, especially my husband, Robin, and our darling children, Sefi, Zac, Theo and Summer. I love and adore you.

Chasing Tomorrow is dedicated to my dear friend Katrina Mayson (née Blandy), who should have had a book dedicated to her long ago! KB, you are completely irreplaceable in my life. Thank you for everything and I hope you like the book.